The Generosity of Women

Books by Courtney Eldridge

Unkempt

The Generosity of Women

The Generosity of Women

Courtney Eldridge

Houghton Mifflin Harcourt

BOSTON · NEW YORK · 2009

For information about permission to reproduce selections from this
book, write to Permissions, Houghton Mifflin Harcourt Publishing
Company, 6277 Sea Harbor Drive, Orlando, Florida 32887-6777.

www.hmhbooks.com

Library of Congress Cataloging-in-Publication Data
Eldridge, Courtney.
  The generosity of women / Courtney Eldridge. — 1st ed.
    p. cm.
  ISBN 978-0-15-101101-8
  1. Women — Fiction. 2. Domestic fiction. 3. Psychological fiction.
I. Title.
  PS3605.L37G46 2009
  813'.6 — dc22   2008051112

Book design by Melissa Lotfy

Printed in the United States of America

DOC 10 9 8 7 6 5 4 3 2 1

Lines from "Mercedes Benz" written by Janis Joplin, Michael McClure,
Robert Neuwirth. Published by Strong Arm Music (ASCAP). Used by
permission. All rights reserved. Lines from "Sentimental Lady" written
by Robert Welch. Published by Crosstown Songs (ASCAP). Administered
by Kobalt Music Publishing America, Inc. Used by permission. All rights
reserved.

FOR CATHY

November 2006

1

Joyce

HERE'S THE QUESTION — here's what you got to ask yourself, okay. The question is, do you want the truth, the whole truth, and nothing but the truth, or . . . *or* do you just want me to blow sunshine up your ass? Wait, he said, I have to choose? Yes, I said. But just one? he said, and I said, See, this is the part men never seem to understand: given two options and told to choose one, one means one, sweetheart. Just one, he said. *Just,* I said.

Well, that's tough, he said, taking a drink and clenching his jaw, exhaling through his teeth. Because the sunshine . . . I have to say, the sunshine's tempting, *very* tempting. But in that case, he said, scratching his cheek, I think I'll take — honesty. And I said, You're brave, Paul. I like that in a brave man. Joyce, do me a favor: leave me some eyebrows, huh? They've just grown back from the last time I asked you for an honest answer, he said, stroking his right brow with two fingers. All right, then, I said.

My first impression, honestly? I hated that bitch from the word gofuckyourself, I said. And not a twitch — I mean, the man doesn't bat an eye — then he says, You know what I like about you, Joyce? And before I could answer — because I had an answer, trust me, I had

1

a very good answer—he said, You don't mince words. Yeah, well, in whiskey veritas, I said, throwing out my arm, offering him my empty glass.

Would you like another? he asked, standing from his chair. Paul, I said, so long as we're being honest with each other, have you ever known me to say no? Actually, Joyce, he said, turning around, so long as we're being honest, has any man ever known you to say no? You're funny, Paul. I like that in a funny man. Now off you go, I said, running my fingers in a scurry.

And could you make it a little stronger this time? I said, sitting up, hearing him drop a couple of ice cubes into a glass, then he stopped. You want it a little stronger? he asked, and he walked back, carrying my glass in one hand and the whiskey in the other. How's that? he said, handing me the bottle, keeping the clean glass for himself. I smiled, taking the bottle; he's a cool customer, all right. I'll give him that.

So, go on, he said, holding out his glass, and I had to bite my tongue, reeling him in. I knew it—I knew that would get him. I mean, really, what's more seductive than the promise of a heavyweight catfight? What do you want to know? I asked, pouring him another drink. For starters, he said, what didn't you like about her?

Oh. I don't know, really, I said, taking a swig. I mean, aside from the fact that she was beautiful, she had an incredible body, and the real killer, she was smart. We're talking four years—*four years* on a full ride, okay. But what's really infuriating is that she wasn't the one who told me she was on scholarship. To this day—*to this day*—Bobbie's never mentioned it, not once. And modest, to boot; I love that in a brilliant, beautiful woman, he said, getting up to stoke the fire.

I said, Oh, so now you're interested? I've been trying to get you to meet her for months, and *now*? Joyce, come on—can you hear yourself? Honestly, do you ever hear yourself, talking? he said. What do you mean? I said, adding: Cut to the chase, will ya? What I mean is that you sound like an old Jewish mother sometimes, you know that? And I said, Paul, I *am* an old Jewish mother. Anyhow, he said, returning to his chair.

Anyhow, I said. She walks into our little dorm room, right, and

2

first thing — I mean, not even a hello or nice to meet you, oh no. She walks in, all la-di-da, perky nose in the air, then she proceeds to kick — I mean, the girl has the nerve to *kick* — my suitcase out of her way, and then she goes: Excuse me.

So I take one look at her, and it's like — I mean, I'm on the phone with my folks, who've managed to get lost somewhere between the second floor of the residence hall and the car, don't ask me how. Wait, he said, you had a phone in your dorm room? Of course, I said. This is the Ivy League — we're talking girls of the Ivy League here, Paul.

Anyhow, all I know is one minute I'm giving my dad directions, and the next minute I hear my brand-new Samsonite suitcase sliding across the linoleum floor like a shuffleboard. So I look up, and I'm telling you, one look — *one look* — and, looking her up and down, I thought, *I hate you. As a matter of fact, I hate absolutely every fucking thing about you.*

But of course, seeing as her dad's there and her little sister's standing in the doorway like the church mouse, I put my hand over the phone and I said, Oh, hi — you must be Roberta? And then — then, just to add insult to injury, she goes, It's Bobbie, actually. No one calls me Roberta, she says. So I said, O-kay. Well, *Bobbie,* I'm Joyce, and everyone calls me Joyce, but you can call me whatever you please. And then I smile at her, just as big as I can, thinking, *You want to rumble, princess? Because I'll take you out.*

So I wait until her dad and sister leave to get another load of her small-town crap out of the station wagon, and then I go, So, *Bobbie,* what's your major? And she goes, Premed. And I go, Oh, really? Like dermatology, or —, and she goes, Gynecology, actually. Have you heard of it? So I smile, like I'm just joking around — it's all fun and games until someone gets her eyes scratched out — and I go, Oh, well, dermatology, gynecology, same difference. So you've always been this way, he said, rubbing his index finger across his forehead. I said, Witty, you mean? There's that, too, he said, raising his brow. Anyhow, I said, taking another drink.

Then she goes — get this — she goes, And you, Joyce? What's your major, stand-up? And I'm thinking, *Well, well . . . looks like Goldilocks's got herself a right hook, huh?* I said, Art history, actually. Heard of it? And without missing a beat, she goes, Oh, well, art history, stand-up, same difference, right? Then she cocks her bubbly head to the side, giving me this shit-eating grin, and just then . . . *just* as I'm about to lunge across the room and choke her to death, who walks in the door but Irving and Sonja, my long-lost parents.

And of course, being that it's Barnard and there are Negroes lurking around every corner, Sonja walks in, huffing, holding hand to chest, like they've narrowly escaped with their lives, running from the natives. Forty minutes they've been gone, okay. Swear to god, how many Jews does it take to find a better parking space, you know?

So I go, Mom, Dad: this is my new roommate, Roberta Myers. *Roberta,* I said, these are my parents, Irving and Sonja. Nice, Paul says, very nice. Of course, I said, I mean, what a name, Roberta. I like the name Roberta, he said, and I said, Excuse me, who's telling this story here, you or me? You, he said, it's all yours. Thank you, I said.

As I was saying, I said, lying back, stuffing a pillow beneath my head and propping my feet on the arm of the couch. The way I figured it, not only would *Bobbie* have to correct me in front of my parents and repeat the fact that no one called her by her full name or . . . *or* she'd have to deal with my parents calling her by a name she obviously hated. Which, in the business, is what we like to call a win-win, or better yet, a fuck-you–fuck-you situation.

Besides which, I knew once my mother heard that this girl had a boy's nickname, she'd be sure to give one of those famous Sonja looks, like she just walked out of a truck-stop toilet on Interstate 90. And best of all, when I finally got around to telling them that the girl wanted to be a gynecologist — a female gynecologist? — Sonja was sure to take her for a lesbian. I mean, keep in mind, this is nineteen seventy, oh . . . let's say —. Nine, ten? Paul offered. Exactly, I said: Keep in mind, this is nineteen seventy-ten, or thereabouts. So, he said, did your mother give you the truck-stop-toilet look and assume your new roommate was a lesbian?

No! That was the real shocker, I said. Bobbie corrects me, right away — like she's not going to take any shit, right? She looks at me and goes, It's Bobbie: please, call me Bobbie, she says, smiling, and then turns to offer her hand to my mother. Then my mother says, Bobbie? Well. How *adorable,* she drawls. Bobbie, she says, speaking to my dad as though he hasn't been standing there, listening the whole time. Oh, I love that! Sonja says. And would you look at her? she says. What a face — Irving, would you take a look at this face. Bobbie, she says, you could be a model.

May I say something? Paul said, interrupting, and I said, Make it quick, and he said, You know, the way you describe her sometimes, your mother sounds right out of central casting, and I said, Paul, please, my mother *invented* central casting, okay? That's where she made the family fortune. But, as I was saying.

So I'm about to puke, and Sonja says, Bobbie, sweetheart, you aren't alone, are you? And Bobbie says, Oh, no. My dad and sister will be right back — they drove me down. Then, of course, being the nosy-body she is, but playing it off as common courtesy, Sonja smiles and says, And your mother? And then Bobbie says, My mother died when I was young. And Sonja . . . I swear to god, I'll never forget this — hearing those words, Sonja *gasps,* okay. I mean the woman literally *gasps* and covers her mouth with both hands — not one, but two — a two-hander. Because one hand just wouldn't be enough, he says. Exactly, I said, quietly snapping and pointing at him.

So a good minute passes in this state of animated Jewess horror, and then, finally, Sonja drops her hands and says, Oh, you poor angel. Paul finally cracked a smile. But wait, I said, it gets better. Then Sonja repeats herself for good measure: Oh, you *poor, poor angel,* she says, all but reaching out her arms. Now, I said, sighing, now keep in mind, it's nineteen seventy-something, and we've been watching years of Vietnam casualties, assassinations, potbellied children starving in Cambodia or Bangladesh or wherever the hell they were all starving in those days, and not once, *not once* have I ever heard the woman say, You poor angel.

There you have it, I said. Eighteen years in the making, but at long last, Sonja Kessler had finally found the daughter of her dreams: my new roommate. So that was it, he said. Yes, I sighed, it was official: Roberta-it's-Bobbie-actually Myers was perfect in every possible way,

I said, counting on my fingers: Smart. Gorgeous. Great bod. And, last but not least, motherless. I mean, despite myself, despite my worst intentions, I just looked at her, thinking, *Ohmygod, you're . . . you're everything I ever wanted to be.* So basically, you wanted her dead, he said. And I said, In so many words: yes.

So when do I get to meet this amazing woman? he said, slouching farther down in the chair as he crossed his ankles. I said, Well, Paul, here's the real question, okay. The question is, what's in it for me? He started to speak, then stopped himself, shaking his head no, don't. He scratched behind his ear, then said, Well, what do you want, Joyce? For now, I said, taking a sip, for now, let's just say you owe me one. Deal, he said, swinging out his glass for me to pour him another.

By the way, I said, topping off his drink, nice fireplace you got here. Thank you, he said. Be sure to mention that as one of my selling points, won't you? One of many, Paul — but one of many, I said, kicking out my feet, letting my shoes drop to the ground. Yes, I said, sighing and resting the bottle on my stomach, a hot fire and a warm penis. What more could a woman want? he said, and I just had to laugh. Oh, Paul, I said. Paul, Paul, Paul . . . you have so much to learn, my friend.

Bobbie

WELL, OBVIOUSLY SHE had lost her mind. First of all, she didn't call me back. I called her at least five times, starting immediately after I hung up with Adela, Saturday night: I called her cell, I tried her at home, I even tried the gallery on Sunday. She wouldn't take my call. I've known the woman half my life, and no matter how angry she's been, Joyce has never once passed up an opportunity to speak her mind. Then, when she finally called me back Monday, all she said was, Can you meet?

Tell me when and where, I said, and she said, How about the dog run at Washington Square Park at four? I was stunned, but of course I said yes, asking one of my partners to cover for me. Then, when I got to the park, I was so nervous I was sweating — and there she was,

6

sitting on the bench, smiling at the dogs, sweet as could be. Imagine: I'm sweating, and Joyce is the very picture of composure. What was the world coming to?

Sorry I'm late, I said, and she shook her head, not to worry. Have you been waiting long? I said. No, she said, still staring at the dogs. Not long. Just since I called. I said, You called me three hours ago, and she nodded yes. Joyce, what have you been doing in Washington Square Park for three hours? I asked. Oh, she said, you know — people watching, dog watching . . . I just looked at her.

Then she finally looked up and said, What? What's wrong with that? Nothing, I said, nothing's wrong with that — aside from the fact that you hate dogs, you hate parks, and you hate people. That is not true: I love dogs, she said. Oh, really? I said. Oh, really, she said. Since when? I said. Since always — I *always* wanted a dog, growing up, she said. I begged and begged my dad to let me get a dog, and then, one day, he finally had to sit me down and explain the sad truth. Which was that Sonja has an aversion to living beings — he and I were on thin ice, as it was.

Well, you're still funny, I said. And you're still tall, she said. Mind taking a seat? Did you get my messages? I asked, sitting down beside her on the bench. Yes, she said, but I didn't know what to say. Joyce, I swear I didn't know anything about it; I would never lie to you. I know, she said, I know you didn't. You have no idea how awful I feel, I said. What can I do? Nothing, really, she said, sighing and shaking her head.

Well, I brought you something, I said. You didn't, she said. I did, just a little something, I said, removing a white paper bag from my purse. Part of the reason I was late, I said, handing it to her, then she took the bag and tore it open, peeking inside. Oh, Bob . . . Vicodin? It's perfect, thank you, she said, squeezing my thigh.

Don't mention it, I said. I won't, she said, I promise. Where have I heard that before? I said. Anyhow, are you sleeping at least? Yes, she said, as a matter of fact, I slept twelve hours yesterday. That's not sleep, that's mild hibernation, I said, reaching to take the bag away from her. But Saturday, she said, turning, shielding the bag from me, Saturday, it got so bad, guess who I called? Who? I said. You'll never guess, she said. Not Michael? Worse, she said. Worse than Michael? I don't know who that could be, I said. Yes, you do, she said. Who? Tell me, already. Sonja, she said, grinning. No, I said. Yes, she said. *No.*

You called your mother? I said. Scout's honor, she said, holding up three fingers. What did you say? I said, at a complete loss. Oh, that's the best part, she said, starting to laugh. I'm sure, I said. What did you tell her? Then she doubled over, shaking with laughter, and I said, Joyce, you didn't tell her, did you? No, she said, waving me off. Relax, Bobbie, will you? All I said, she said, starting to laugh again, all I said was . . . I love you. I said, I love you, Mom.

You actually said I love you? Yep, she said, my exact words. You must have been out of your mind, I said. And you must have scared the poor woman half to death. Yes, I did, she said. And had I known the effect it would have, I would've called her years ago, believe me. So now I'm thinking I'll just have to try her again, first thing tomorrow: *once more into the breach.*

You're evil, you know that? I said, You are truly evil. Then she finally turned her attention away from the dogs to look at me, and said, Oh, *please* — don't kid yourself, sweetheart . . . because without me, you'd be nothing.

Lisa

SHE'S CHANGED? I mean, he actually had the audacity to tell me she's changed. That's what he said, he goes, She's changed, Leese, and I just looked at him, like, you gotta be fucking kidding me. Let me tell you about Joyce Kessler, all right. In a word, in a single word: totalfuckingcunt. Or, as Joyce would say, We're talking cunt with a capital *cunt,* okay. I didn't say that, of course, but he knew what I was thinking.

What, you don't believe people can change? he said, and it was all I could do to keep from laughing in his face. Well, obviously some people do, I said. Take you, for example. You've certainly changed your tune. Who was it — I'm sorry, I said, what was it — how did that go, Greg? *Joyce Kessler wouldn't know a work of art if it . . ?* Or maybe

8

you don't remember that part, either, I said, then he looked away, ashamed. I mean, assuming he has any conscience whatsoever.

Joyce

HONESTLY, I DON'T KNOW what I expected, really. All I know is that when I dialed her number, I was so desperate I would've told her everything — every last gruesome detail, starting, what, Wednesday? Thursday? Christ, I can't even remember now. No, Thursday, it was Thursday. Anyhow.

Thursday, I've got conference calls up the ass — we're talking eight, nine, ten, eleven, and noon, okay. So when I finally had two seconds to pee, my assistant comes in and says there's some sort of emergency and my new cleaning lady needs me to call her right away. And I'm like, Alana, what sort of emergency? And she says, I don't know, and I said, *Well.* Did you try asking her, maybe? Then she holds up her hand: Joyce, she's called four times, and she says it's private. So I look at her, and seeing that she's even more frustrated than I am, I reached for the phone, Jesus H. Christ . . .

So I call Rita, and before I have a chance to say anything, she starts in saying she's so sorry, she broke the machine, dusting in the bathroom, but it was an accident, nobody told her. And I'm just like, Hold on, back up, Rita. I said, You called me at work to tell me you broke the vacuum, dusting? No, no, she says, not the vacuum, the muh-cheen on top of the peek-churs. And I'm thinking, *What machine on top of the pictures is she talking about?*

I had a lunch, so after lunch, I swung by the apartment. And sure enough, I found the thing on the dining table, alongside a note from Rita: *Deer Mrs. Kessler, you tell me what I ow you and I pay you bak . . .* And let's be honest, I took one look, and I knew what it was, but I couldn't admit the truth. I mean, really, I have people I pay to do that for me. Which is why I sent the driver back to the gallery, then called Alana and told her to reschedule my three thirty and send Steve, our IT guy, back in the car.

Well, turns out, I was right: it's a camera. The muh-cheen is actually a mini spy cam, and, as Steve put it, ever so tactfully, *it would*

9

appear that someone has been spying on me in my bathroom. And in my bedroom. And in my walk-in closet. Three: there were three cameras, total. And seeing as I didn't put them there — because god knows I can barely stand to look at my naked ass in real time — I just looked at Steve, dumbfounded.

Who? Who could have done this? I said. Well, who has keys? he said, and then I just shook my head. No one, I said, no one else has keys. Then it hit me. No one except Benjamin, my son. My one and only child. At least until I get my hands on that squawk box of a pubescent throat and snuff the living daylight out of him, you . . . *You deviant little turd, you.*

I mean, call me old-fashioned, but am I wrong in thinking that a kid three months shy of his fifteenth birthday should not be videotaping his mother in the shower or sitting on the toilet? I mean, what the hell would possess him to *do* such a thing? And more importantly, what about me? How worried should I be, here? Seriously, forget drugs and alcohol and unprotected sex, what I want to know is how do you recognize perfectly normal teenage-boy behavior from that of a future sex offender? Because right now, from where I'm standing, I can't tell the difference.

So yeah — and this will attest to just how upset I was, okay. Thursday afternoon, I found myself dialing Sonja. As if she could offer some sort of advice, or support, or god knows what, but anyhow. All I could think was: Is there some history of mental illness and/or sexual deviance in our family that no one's ever told me about, or am I right to blame his father for this, too? Really, I just needed someone I could trust, family — and Sonja's it. Then again, I called assuming I'd get her machine and I could just vent a bit, so when she answered, it completely threw me. So I told her I had another call, and I'd call her back.

It wasn't true, of course, but her voice worked like smelling salts. Besides which, the first person I had to talk to was Michael, Benjamin's father, better known as my ex-husband-to-be. Because the one thing we agree on — the one and *only* thing we agree on — is that we always discipline Ben as a united front. Because we don't need him playing us off each other — we do that just fine without his help, thank you very much.

10

Lisa

I MEAN, THE EGO, the *fucking ego* of the guy, you know? First, he tells me Joyce has changed, then he goes: So did you see the show? That was his attempt at changing the subject, okay. So I said, What show? He just smiled, pursing his lips, and I said, Oh, *your* show, you mean? No, and believe it or not, I have no intention of stepping foot in that godforsaken place ever again.

I understand, he said. But that only made it worse. You understand? I said, *Really?* Go on, then, tell me. What do you understand, Greg? I just meant I understand why you wouldn't want to go back to the gallery, he said. I'm sorry, Leese, I didn't —. I said, No, Greg, answer the question, please. What do you understand, exactly?

I could barely breathe by the time I got out of the store. Then, of course, as soon as I caught my breath, I was seething, arguing with ghosts on the street. How . . . *how* could you possibly understand? You weren't there, remember? You bailed on me; you lied to me; you stole money from me; and *now* you understand? I asked Joyce for four hours off work — that's all I asked of her. I asked once; I asked again; and then, when I reminded her I'd be out . . . No, Greg, you don't understand: you aren't capable. So why don't you just go back to your precious little paintings, you fucking coward. I swear I almost wanted to turn around and track him down just to say it to his face, you know.

Well. Being the masochist I am, I went home and I finally read the *New York* article. I looked it up online and I read every last word. Then I had to lie down. It was just too much — seeing him, then the article — I shouldn't have read it. No, I knew I shouldn't have read it, so that's exactly what I did. Classic.

Just as I was falling asleep, my phone rang. And for some reason, don't ask me why, but for some reason, I thought it was Greg, calling to apologize or I don't know what. Hello? I said, sitting up, and then a woman's voice said, Is this Lisa Soutar? And I said, Yes. Who's calling, please? This is Donna from Dr. Myers's office. I said, I'm sorry, who is this? Donna, from Dr. Myers's office, she said, and I said, Yes? Do you have a sister named Lynne Yaeger? she said. And I said, Yes — well, technically.

Bobbie

LAST SUMMER, I was supposed to visit July Fourth weekend, but there was an emergency and I couldn't leave. I wasn't on call, but she was my patient — anyhow. Joyce had been trying to get me up to see her new house for months; she kept insisting, so I took the train the following weekend.

Joyce met me at the station, and on the way to her place she told me she had to go to some barbecue to meet her neighbors. She said that since she's only there a couple of weekends a month, she wanted to meet some people, hoping they'd keep an eye on her house. Then she said, Hey, why don't you get cleaned up and come with me? Which should've tipped me off, obviously, but she hasn't tried setting me up in years.

I said: J, I came up here to get away from people, not to be surrounded by a bunch of people I don't know and have no interest in getting to know. I can do that in the city any day. Come on, we'll just go for an hour, she said, and to be honest, I could not imagine what had possessed her. All I could think was, *Oh, no . . . has it come to this? Really, is she actually becoming* community-oriented? *Are we really that old?* Please? she said. Oh, all right, I said, one hour.

When we got to her house, she gave me the tour, and then I showered and put on a sundress I'd brought. I admit, I was pleased I got to wear my new dress, at least. We walk over, and the place is — it's absolutely gorgeous. The backyard, alone, is twice the size of a football field, and it's impeccably groomed, with all these trees and lilac bushes in bloom. And it was one of those delicious summer nights when your skin floats, buoyant in the air.

Joyce went off to meet and greet, while I watched some people play croquet — I almost said kids, but they must've been in their thirties. But there was quite a mix of people, really, all ages. There was this incredible spread of food that covered two picnic tables, and then a third table with liquor. Just as I was about to make a move for a drink, I stopped and looked around, sniffing, because someone was smoking a joint, and all I could think was, *Joyce Kessler, I swear, I can't take you anywhere.*

Well, I'm standing there, when this man comes up and says hello. My name's Paul, he says, offering me his hand, and I say, Nice to meet you, Paul, I'm Bobbie, and we shake hands, and then I feel my tongue become so engorged, I can barely speak; he's so handsome. Late forties, early fifties, maybe, I don't know: because, apparently, I can't think, breathe, and look at him at the same time. Naturally, I stare at my feet, wiggling my toes in the plush grass, thinking, *Can't talk, but at least I got a fresh pedicure* . . .

So you're visiting? he said, smiling, trying to make conversation. I said, Yes, I'm up for the weekend — my friend has a place nearby. Otherwise, I don't know anyone here, I said, smiling and nodding like an idiot. And you? I said. No, I don't know anyone here, either, he said, nodding at my nodding.

Where do you live? I asked, and then he pointed and said, Just over there, and I said, Down the road? No, that house, right there, he said, cocking his chin. It was his house: his party. You don't know anyone at your own party? I laughed. Well, I know Joyce. And now I know you, Bobbie, he said, making a point of saying my name. Then I just smiled and nodded some more, hoping I'd think of something terribly clever to say next round, because that one was a forfeit.

As a matter of fact, Joyce has told me a lot about you, he said, and I couldn't help smiling. Oh, really? What did she tell you? I asked. Well, he said, uncertain. Let's have it, I said, knowing I'd regret asking, but still. She said you were *beautiful,* he said in a good-news-first tone of voice. And? I said. Desperate. She said you were beautiful and desperate. It was just a joke, he quickly added, looking at me. No kidding, I said.

But as soon as he said it, I could hear her. I could hear that nasally Power-Jewess voice of hers: She's beautiful *and* she's desperate: you'll love her, she'd say, waving with that, *ach* wrist action. No, I knew Paul was quoting her verbatim. Whether it was necessary for him to repeat the comment was another matter, but still. You have to know her to understand: he wasn't talking about me as much as he was simply imitating Joyce.

I started laughing. What else are you going to do when your best friend is going around telling strange men that you're desperate? But then I suddenly felt like a complete idiot because obviously they'd been laughing at me. Nice to meet you, Paul, I said, starting to walk away, and he said, I'm sorry, that didn't come out right — she talks about you all the time. So I hear, I said. She says she can't understand why you haven't met a nice man, and I can't imagine why, either, he said, and then I stopped. I couldn't look at him, though. I felt exposed, undressed, really.

Can I get you a drink, at least? he offered. Please, I said, still not able to look up from the grass. What are you drinking? he said. Beer's fine, I said. You sure? he said. Vodka tonic, I said, changing my order. Vodka tonic? he said. Just vodka, actually, I said. Coming right up, he said. With a twist, I called, and he looked back: Least I can do.

A minute later he returned with our drinks — in glasses, even — and I thanked him, and we toasted cheers. Bobbie, he said, would you like to go out for coffee sometime? Seeing as I'm desperate? I said. Now, now, he said, beautiful *and* desperate. Thank you, but no, I said. I hope it's not my lack of social skills, he said. There's that, too, I said. I have a nice yard, though, don't I? he said, appraising the yard, speaking in a tone as though he almost didn't believe his good fortune. Unreal, I agreed. Well, that's got to be worth something, he said. Yes, so far, it's your best feature, I said, taking a drink. Ouch, he said, wincing. Look who's talking, I said. Fair enough, he said.

Can I at least call you? In case you change your mind and decide you'd like to have a drink with me? he said. I thought you said coffee. I did, he said. But now I think I'll need a drink first, so why don't you join me? Thanks, I said, trying not to laugh, but I don't think I'll change my mind.

Then I'll just call to say hello, he said. And why would you do that? I said. Because you're a beautiful woman, and I don't know many beautiful women, he said. Oh, bullshit, I said, pshawing. I couldn't help laughing out loud, shaking my head in flirtatious disgust, looking at the half-dozen leggy nymphets chasing badminton birdies around his yard. No, I swear, he said. I swear on my mother's grave: I don't know any beautiful women who'll take my calls these days. *Ha, ha,* I thought, biting my lower lip. I can't imagine why, I said, looking at him, and he nodded yes.

14

Your mother passed away? I said, trying to recover, and he said, No — oh, no. My mother's very much alive. But I've got just the spot in mind for her eternal resting place. I walk over there and swear all the time — it's no trouble, really. Besides, you don't even have to give me your number, he said. Because Joyce already gave it to you/me, we said, speaking in unison. Jinx, he said. How thoughtful of her, I said, nodding. Yes, she's a very thoughtful woman, he said, and I had to laugh. So we'll be in touch, he said, as though I'd consented. We'll see about that, I said, as he started walking away. Then he turned back. Yes, we will, he said, and I looked at him, thinking, *Oh, aren't you suave.*

I know I'm going on like a schoolgirl, but the truth is, I couldn't remember the last time a man put so much effort into asking me out. I'd forgotten how much fun it could be: how your heart pounds and your cheeks flush and your labia flutter — the sheer thrill, the rush. The second I was alone at Joyce's, I dialed Adela, then I ended the call. I couldn't decide if it was appropriate to tell my daughter about some man less than one hour after meeting him, so I turned off my phone. It was a month before I finally told her about him.

Lynne

WELL, IT SERVES me right. No, it does — it really does. Because first thing, the very first thing I did that day we got home after Jordan went to her room, was call Lisa. I called Don and told him he had to come home right away, and then I called Lisa. I didn't expect her to answer, but when she did, I simply told her I had a friend who needed a referral, and Lisa said, Oh, Dr. Myers — Roberta Myers, she's the best in New York. So I wrote the number down, and then we hung up a minute later because we had nothing more to say to each other.

But it's not the lying I'm ashamed of, really. It's the fact that I didn't lie to protect Jordan: I lied to protect myself. Simply because I didn't want Lisa to know I've failed, because I couldn't stand the thought of her gloating. So of course the first person I saw, when the nurse helped me into the hall, was Lisa.

Lisa

WELL, BASICALLY, WE had two separate families. I mean, we have the same parents, but still. There's such a gap in our ages that it was like we didn't grow up together, really. I mean, I was always close with my dad, and Lynne wasn't. Lynne remembers my mom, and what I remember most was my mom being sick all the time. Lynne wasn't a sister, she was more like — I don't know — an aunt, I guess. It's true, she was like this busybody aunt who knitted me sweaters, and who my mom sent pictures of me in the school play.

We're just . . . we're just very different people. Lynne was happy to stay in a small town, where she's a big fish in a small pond. I don't think she ever really wanted anything more than she has. And frankly, I don't understand that. Not wanting more, not wanting to be someone and do something with your life — for me, it's like breathing. I just feel bad for Jordan, because Lynne's got such a stranglehold on her.

Anyhow, I got there as soon as I could, and leaning over to speak to the nurse seated behind the front desk, I said, Hi, I'm Lisa Soutar. I'm here to pick up my sister, Lynne. I got a call that she was sick? And I still have no idea what's going on, when another nurse comes over and says, Are you picking them both up? I said, Both? And she said, Are you picking up your sister and your niece? My niece? I said.

Then, out of the corner of my eye, I see Jordan sitting in the waiting room, alone. She's just sitting there, biting her thumbnail, staring at the carpet. Jojo? I said, even more confused. Then I turned back again. Yes, I said. I'm picking them both up. Your sister will be right out, the nurse said. Thank you, I said, walking over to Jordan.

I sat down in the chair beside her, and I said, Baby, what's going on? And she was so spaced out, I almost waved my hand before her eyes, then she finally said, *I tried.* I told her I couldn't drive, but she wouldn't listen to me, she whined, tearing up. I said, Jordan, what happened? And she says, I scratched the car and my dad's gonna kill me . . .

Shhh, I said, whispering in her ear, shuh-shuh-shuh. Listen to me, your dad loves you, and he would never kill you. That's what they all say, she said, and I had to laugh. I couldn't help it: she's funny.

16

She gets it from my side of the family. Then she started sobbing, and I said, Okay, okay, let's not do this here. I looked around the waiting room at the women becoming agitated by our display. Come on — upsy-daisy, I said, helping her stand, and she was so limp. I should have known. I should have felt it, but I didn't.

You want to tell me what's going on? I asked, once we got down the hall, and she shook her head no, and I said, Good, because I was just making conversation, really — you know how I hate small talk. I thought it was big talk, she said, and I smiled, grabbing her chin. That, too, I said, and I almost — almost — got a smile.

I'd grabbed a couple of Valium, leaving the house, and that was before I knew anything about Jordan being there, too. So I slipped them to her before we all got in the car, and she was out cold before we even hit the parkway. You know, one day you wake up, and the whole world's gone mad. But what I don't know is what day that was, exactly.

Joyce

SO I CALLED Michael. I called his office. I called his car phone. I call his cell phone. And finally, I called him at home. No answer, so I left another message. I said, Michael — Joyce. I've called you a total of *four times* now, and if you can see fit to spare a minute, I'm sure your son would appreciate your time. Asshole, I said, hanging up. And I have to say it's not nearly as satisfying hanging up with a cell phone; you don't get that resounding click or that good old-fashioned slam of the rotary phones anymore.

Anyhow. I waited Thursday afternoon, Thursday night, Friday morning . . . no call. So I had to take matters into my own hands. I borrowed my assistant's cell phone and tricked Michael into answering because he didn't recognize the number — he was so polite. Oh, hello, Joyce! Sorry I didn't have a chance to call you back, he says, and starts telling me that he just got into Palm Springs. I literally held out the phone, in disgust, because I was thinking, *Michael: I don't give a dead rat's ass where you are, when I call you four times in forty-eight hours, you call me back, you fuckhead.*

Yes, well, I said, not half as sorry as I am to have to keep calling because you don't return my calls. But when you're through doing whomever it is you're doing there, you think we could discuss our son's funeral arrangements before I murder him? And I admit, I was almost shouting by that point, but then, in that clenched-jaw voice, he goes, Joyce, I'll get back to you as soon as I can, how's that? *How's that?* I said, laughing. What — you're giving me a choice? Then he hung up on me.

Which was neither here nor there, except that the son of a bitch never called me back, and that's just plain rude. Then, sitting at my desk, thinking, *God, this is all so wrong* . . . It was only then that I realized, *Wait a minute. Isn't it supposed to be the other way around? I mean, aren't I supposed to be the one spying on my teenage son?* And for a moment, I had to wonder: Is Michael behind this? Is he trying to blackmail me, somehow? Ridiculous, I know, but what can I say? The whole thing just made me a little paranoid. I am many things, but paranoid is not one of them, okay.

Lisa

TEN MINUTES LATER they finally bring Lynne out, and I had the two of them wait downstairs while I went to get their car. Then I called Will to tell him there was a family emergency, and I called Rosalee to tell her Will — my husband, Mr. Will, as she calls him — would be home as soon as possible, and it's, it's nuts. The entire situation is just . . . nuts. I mean, let's call a spade a spade: Lynne was out of her fucking mind, okay.

I'm telling you, she was tripping off her ass. Not only that, but by the time we get in the car, she's on the downward spiral, sobbing and weeping, going on and on about how sorry she is she was never there for me, begging for my forgiveness . . . Lynne — this is *Lynne* we're talking about.

Jordan

WHEN LISA ASKED me what happened, I was just like, I don't know, you know? I mean, seriously, I don't know *what* her problem is, but it's like she's just been acting totally crazy, you know. Like Thursday — Thursday, we get in the car, right, and Mom goes — she pushes the garage door opener, and she goes, Well, don't ever say I didn't try. And I was just like, don't even, you know, like don't *even* give me that. So I go, Oh, yeah, Mom, like you *really* tried, and then she just lost it. I'm not even kidding, like she starts pounding the steering wheel, screaming, *Goddamnit, Jordan!*

I mean, she's just wailing on the wheel, screaming, *Goddamnit! Goddamnit!* And I'm like, ohmygod, you know? And the whole time, it keeps getting brighter and brighter, so I had to cover my eyes for a second because of the glare in the rearview, or whatever, and then . . . I don't know, it's like she just snapped back or something. I mean, the garage door jerked to a stop and she stopped screaming, just like that. Seriously, two seconds later, she tucks her hair behind her ear, adjusts the rearview, and backs out, like . . . like nothing happened.

So we didn't say anything the whole way, and when we got to school, I was just like, Bye, and I started walking in, and then she called me back to the car. So I walk back, and I'm just like, What?, and then she goes, I'm going to see Grandpa tonight, so go ahead and warm up the chicken I made for you and Dad . . . And I was like, 'Kay, whatever, and then I walked away, because I was just like, fuck you, you know.

So I got to my locker and I started taking out my books, and . . . I mean, everyone's heading to class, and it's just like every other day — but that's the problem, that's *exactly* the problem. I mean, it's like nothing changes, you know? Nothing ever changes here. And I thought I could get through one more day, I really did, but when first bell rang, I just started bawling, like right in the hall. But it's not even — I mean it wasn't because of my mom or school. It was Rusty. I started crying because of my stupid dog, because I was so mean to him, you know, and he still loves me. I mean, no matter what I do, he'll still love me, and it's just so *wrong.*

Lynne

OF COURSE JORDAN idolizes her. No, really, Jordan thinks Lisa walks on water. Oh, Jordan wants to be just like her when she grows up, and what can I say? Really, what can I possibly say? Nothing. I can't say a word because that would only encourage her. Of course Jordan's heard all about Lisa's exploits, but not from me. No, I simply have to accept the fact that my daughter idolizes the person who least resembles me in this world.

I mean, it's quite simple, really. I was the good girl. Yes, I was the good girl, and Lisa . . . well, Lisa was not a good girl. In fact, half the time, Lisa didn't even want to *be* a girl. No, Lisa was the one who shaved her head and smoked cigarettes and got picked up for drinking and doing drugs, barely fourteen years old, and then . . . and then she just waltzed through the front door at seven o'clock, the next morning — regularly. And my parents weren't young by that point, either. They didn't know what to do with her, how to discipline her, so they let her go.

But what's crazy — I mean, the crazy thing is that Lisa was born with something I wasn't: Lisa never cared what people thought. She doesn't listen, and she doesn't care, and I . . . I admit, I criticize her for that. No, I do, all the time. But the truth is, I've always envied that about her — I mean, really, can you imagine how much easier the world is when you don't care what anyone thinks of you? In fact, there are times when even I'm in awe of her . . . but then, a moment later, I'll come to my senses and think, *Yes, how wonderful to be deaf and unconscionable. Just like Daddy.*

Jordan

LOOK, I'M SORRY, but I wasn't the one who wanted to get into it, okay. I mean, seriously, it's like eight in the morning — I didn't sleep all night, my face was all puffy from crying — so I was like, let's just leave it alone, you know? So I go downstairs, and I wanted to give Rusty a special treat, but I knew — I *knew* she was waiting for me in the kitchen, so I just opened the garage door. Then she goes, Jordan, come here, please, and I was just like, *Oh, here we go . . .*

So I walk into the kitchen, and she gives me this look, like she's all concerned, right. And for a moment, I was just like, wow, maybe she's going to tell me she loves me and we'll get through this together

20

or whatever — I don't know, just something, you know? And then she goes, Jordan, tell me: what do you *see* in this person?

That's exactly what she said, too: *this person.* So I was just like, Whatever, Mom. I mean, seriously, if she can't even say his name, how much does she really want to know about him, you know? And the thing is, I was so ready to go off on her, too, but then I was just like, no, you know, like I'm not getting into it right now. So I go, Can we talk about this later? And she started to say something, but then my dad walked in, so of course she dropped it.

So we get in the car, and I put on my seat belt, and I wasn't going to say a word, right, but then she goes, Well, don't ever say I didn't try. And I was like, *Excuse me?* I mean, I almost had to laugh, and then she goes, Honestly, Jordan, every time I try to talk to you, you shut me out. When? I go, *When* did you try to talk to me? And she goes, Not two minutes ago, I asked you —, and I go, No, Mom: you didn't *ask me* anything, you said, Jordan, what do you see in *this person*? And she goes, At least I'm trying, and I was just like, Oh, *please,* and I looked away, because it was such bullshit.

Then she goes, This is *exactly* what I'm talking about. Really, Jordan, are you even capable of having a civil conversation? So I said, I go, You know what, Mom? You're right, it's me, I'm the problem. Because all you ever do is try and try. I mean, every day, there you are, trying *so hard* to understand where I'm coming from, and how *I* feel —. And that was it: *Goddamnit! Goddamnit!* I mean, crazy, right?

Lynne

I JUST WANTED to talk to her. Honestly, I was awake all night Wednesday night, and I must've heard her phone turned on and off ten times, easily. And at one point — at one point, I got up. Yes, I actually got out of bed and tiptoed, standing outside her door, listening to her crying, and I came *so close* to knocking. Honestly, I raised my hand to knock, so I could tell her. So I could say, Jordan, stop checking your phone, sweetheart, because he's not going to call. I'm sorry, but he's never going to call you again . . . But I didn't tell her. No, I lowered my hand, and I walked downstairs and made coffee.

Then I sat at the kitchen table the rest of the night. I sat there watching the sunrise, and I decided that I was going to tell her the truth. I even — I mean, I actually had this idea that she would sit down at the table with me, and I would say, Jordan, sweetheart. What do you say we forget about school today? Let's stay home today, just you and me, and talk, all right? You think we could remember how to do that?

Finally, when she came downstairs at 7:45, I took a deep breath, listening as she grabbed her coat from the closet, and then I said, Jordan? And she said, What? She said it in that voice that just makes the hair on the back of my neck stand on end, I swear, but I'd made up my mind. So I said, Come here, please, and she came into the kitchen, but the way she looked at me. Honestly, she can't even stand to *look* at me anymore, and it hurt so badly, I couldn't say his name. I'm sorry, but I just — couldn't. I just couldn't.

Really, I never meant to scream like that — that was my last intention, believe me. But every time I try to speak to her, she shuts me out. I'm sorry, but it's gotten to where I can barely say five words, looking her in the eye. No, I felt terrible that I lost my temper with her, but I've had it up to here with her snide comments, and her attitude, and her . . . her hatred. But when we got to school, I watched her walk away, thinking, *You know what? You can hate me all you want, but I'm still your mother, so get used to it.*

Joyce

A FEW MONTHS AGO, I heard this ad on the radio: *Ever wish your child came with an owner's manual? Is your child sullen, hostile, uncommunicative, belligerent, or just plain out of control? If so —* I loved that — *if so, there's help. The Total Transformation Program offers real-world solutions for the most challenging problems parents face, such as defiant, disrespectful attitudes, lying and cursing, lazy, unmotivated behavior, and more!*

Instantly, I knew a man wrote that. And you know how I knew? Think about it. Seriously, what woman wants to read a manual, ever? What woman would ever *think* of suggesting such a thing?

Well, anyhow. I left work early Thursday, and I went home and waited on the couch in the living room, but I had no idea what to do. I mean, my first thought was to fire Steve and burn the evidence, in no particular order. Then, for a moment, I actually considered showing the tapes at the gallery, every last uncensored, hideously naked minute of my private life, or however many of them my son had captured. But then I realized that would just turn the kid into some cause célèbre, and probably even land him a spot at the Whitney Biennial . . . no. No, I'd think of something, some just punishment.

When I finally heard the front door open, I listened for a moment as Benjamin dropped his bag in the hallway. Benjamin? I said. Yeah? he grunted. Would you come here, please? I said. What? he snapped. I said would you *come here,* please, I said. What? he says, and that was enough of that. In other words, get your snotty little fuckface in here *now,* I said.

So he saunters in, begrudgingly, and I turn to look at him. Come over here, I said, nodding toward the center of the room, and he starts walking around the couch, then he stops cold, looking at the coffee table. Take a seat, I said, and he just stared. Busted . . . oh, he was *so busted.* Sit down, please, we need to have a little chat, I said. But he just stood there in shock. Well, that made two of us, all right. Park it — right there, I said, nodding at the far end of the couch, directly in front of three dismantled spy cams.

Jordan

I KNOW WHAT she thinks, too. I do. She thinks Misha's just like this pervert or this pedophile or whatever, and I'm just like, oh, please. And we weren't sleeping together, either — it wasn't like that at all. I mean, seriously, I was *so* not interested in him when we first started working together, we didn't speak two words to each other until that night he gave me a ride home. And the only reason he gave me a ride was because I got stood up, okay — I didn't tell my mom that, but it's true, I swear.

Like, about two weeks before school started, I was working the express lane on Friday night, and by eight o'clock the place was so dead, it was like you could hear crickets over the PA system. So anyhow, I'm just standing there, staring out the window, completely spaced out, you know, when I notice these two guys walking in and that one of them is waving his hand . . . at me. I mean, he's waving at me, right, like, *Earth to Jordan!* So I wake up and then I realize . . . I'm just like, oh-mygod, because they are so hot. I swear: two of the hottest guys I have ever seen just walked through the doors of Price Chopper's on a Friday night. And I don't know who they were, but they definitely weren't from around here. And they definitely weren't in high school, either.

So like five minutes later, the guy who waved at me walks over with his two bags of Tostitos or whatever, and of course I'm trying to be all cool — I mean, I wasn't rude, I was just like, hey, whatever, you know — and I start swiping his stuff. Then he asks me where's the nearest gas station, and it was so obvious, you know? I mean, it was such a dumb question, I was just like, Dude, you drove right past it turning into the parking lot, and then he goes, Oh . . . guess I missed it. And I'm just like, Yeah, good guess. Then he goes, So, you got plans tonight?, or What are you doing later?, something like that. Anyhow, I look up, and don't ask me *what* I was thinking, but I go, What's it to you? I mean, I sounded like *such* a bitch, right, but then he just started laughing.

Well, *Jordan*, he says — like right in front of me, he reads my boob, okay — and I felt like *such* a dork. Seriously, I was just like, ohmygod, I'm in hell . . . and you have to wear name tags in hell. Then he goes, Well, we're having a party later, and I thought maybe you'd like to come, bring some friends. And I was just like, Your total's $5.37. And he takes out his wallet, and he goes, I can give you directions, if you're interested. And I was just like, Thanks, but I don't have a car, taking the twenty he handed me. And he goes, Well, I could give you a ride, if you want to come, and then I just looked at him, like, *Dude, did you honestly just say you could give me a ride if I want to come?* I mean, I didn't say it, you know, but he knew, right away, so he goes, I'll pick you up, how's that? So I just looked at him, nodding, like, oh, yeah, that's so much better — you're really quick on your feet, huh, college boy?

And I tried not to laugh, handing him his change, and then I go, I don't even know your name, and he goes, Zach. Then he holds out his hand and he goes, Sorry, my name's Zach — or you can just call me Dude. And then I started blushing, just as we shook hands. So I just stepped back and go, I'll think about it. And he said, Good. You think about it, and I'll pick you up around ten, how's that? And I was like, Maybe, and I shrugged like, we'll see . . . but he knew — oh, he *totally* knew. He's like, See you at ten, Jordan, and then he smiles, taking his bag and heading out the door, where his friend was waiting outside.

So like two minutes later, I called my mom to tell her I was spending the night at Alex's, right. And my mom was so thrilled to hear I was hanging with my friends again, she didn't even ask what we were doing. She was just like, Oh, honey, I'm so glad to hear that, have fun — and no drinking and driving, Jordan, and I was just like, We won't . . .

So I'm standing out front at ten o'clock on the dot, and I just wait there until like ten fifteen, ten twenty. I mean, I'm just staring at the empty parking lot, waiting, but it was only like sixty degrees that night, so I went back inside to warm up for a minute. A few minutes later, I saw a car, so I walked back outside, but it was just someone turning around. And then, by like ten thirty . . . I mean, I knew he wasn't coming, but I just wasn't ready to let it go, you know? I mean, it's like one minute I'm as high as a bird, and the next minute, I'm about to hit the ground from the top of a twenty-story building.

That's when Misha walked out and sat down on one of the benches in front of the store and takes out a cigarette, not really paying me any attention. Which is fine: I don't want to talk to him, he doesn't want to talk to me, *fine.* Then, like a minute later, he looks over and goes, You waiting for someone, Jordan? And I was just like, Not really, and I looked away.

So he takes a drag and exhales, then he goes, Not really, you aren't waiting? Or not really, they aren't coming? And I was like . . . I was just like, please, this is coming from a guy who wears clip-on ties with short-sleeved dress shirts? Then he goes, Jordan, you need a ride home or not? And when he said that . . . I mean, hearing those words, I was so relieved not to have to call my parents, I just looked at him, and I go, Would you mind? He didn't say anything at first, then he flicked his butt in the air, and he goes, Let's go.

25

Lynne

HONESTLY, FOR THE PAST MONTH, I haven't slept more than two . . . at most, three hours a night. But I didn't take anything — I won't take anything. No aspirin, Tylenol PM, doesn't matter what. Which is probably because, deep down, I see taking a pill as some sort of moral deficiency. I mean, I'm not a Christian Scientist, and we don't have any drug addicts in the family, really — well, unless you count Lisa, of course. That might have something to do with it, I suppose, but otherwise, no, that's just how I am.

Then again, I absolutely had to get some sleep because Friday was going to be a very long, very difficult day because we had to drive to the city. I'd been averaging twelve hours of sleep per week for the past month, so by that point, by Thursday night, I wasn't sure I was fit to drive, to be honest. So at eleven, before I crawled into bed, I finally got off my high horse and I took a Lunestra, Lunesta, whatever they're called, anyhow. I was hoping they'd knock me out for eight hours, but no. One o'clock rolled around, two o'clock, and I was lying there, wide awake, listening to Don snore.

Of course I could have simply slept in the guest bedroom, but I didn't because I can take the guest bedroom about as well as I can take pills. No, I truly hate that room: it's at the back of the house, it doesn't get proper light, and it always feels . . . it just feels cold, somehow, no matter what the temperature is. But most of all, sleeping down there feels like I'm openly admitting what a failure our marriage has become. Which would not be wrong, but still, I think that's obvious enough when I sleep in our bed.

Lisa

DON HELPED ME put Jordan and Lynne to bed, then he ordered dinner and sent Lance to town to pick it up. So there I was, Friday night, sitting at the dinner table in my sister's cozy-chic, shabby-chic — whatever the fuck it's called — dining room, eating this gooey disgusting pizza with her husband and son, trying to make conversation with two people I have nothing in common with. Well, aside from a sister I have nothing in common with.

I said, How's work, Don? Busy, he said, nodding, trying to smile. Very busy. Lots of people buying second homes up here, renovating, he said, and I said, So I hear. Then there was an awkward silence, while Lance reached for another slice. And you, how's not working? Don says, and then he catches himself. No offense, he said, looking up apologetically. None taken, I said, smiling.

And Lance . . . what could I say? So, Lance, how's the Air Force Academy? Still planning on dropping bombs on innocent civilians the world over? I just don't understand what happened, Lance says, finally speaking up. You make it sound like she was on drugs or something, like she was tripping — *my mother,* he says, looking at me like it was my fault. I didn't answer, and Don just nodded his head, not knowing what to say anymore than I did.

Come on, that's *bullshit,* Lance said, daring Don to reprimand him for his language. And I'm looking at the kid with his crew cut and his jockey aggressive posture, thinking, *Look, you Hitler Youth, your mother was tripping off her fucking ass, okay. Trust me, I've done a few drugs in my day. And if I knew where she hid her stash, I'd do a few more right about now.*

Lisa, did you notice anything? Don said, and I just looked at my plate, collecting my thoughts. I knew what he was saying, and I never would've believed it, myself, but yes, I noticed something the second she saw me sitting with Jordan, and she got these crocodile tears in her eyes, and then she started blubbering, *I'm so, so sorry.* Because that's about the craziest thing I've ever heard, Lance said, refusing to listen. I don't know what happened, but something's not right, he said, and I said, Then you'll have to ask her, yourself. Ask me what? Lynne said, stepping into dining room, and we all looked up.

Lynne

ASK ME WHAT? I said, staring at her, thinking, *Honestly, Lisa have you no shame? You would actually talk about me that way in my own house, at my own table?* No, she thinks it's all a joke — my house, my family, my life. No, Lisa has no respect for anyone, and she never did. So I looked at her, thinking, *Oh, you're just so much better than the rest of us, aren't you, Lisa? That's right: it's all just one big joke, ha, ha, ha . . .*

What are you doing up? Don asked, and I said, I wanted to change the bedding in the guest room. You didn't need to do that, he said. It's done, I said. What did you want to ask me? How are you feeling? Don asked, and I said, Tired. Very tired. You should eat something, he said, and I took a seat across from Lisa. Then I said, Lisa, if you took the ten-forty train that would give us enough time to visit Daddy. Because I know he'd love to see you again, I said, staring at her. *You don't believe me? We'll see. We'll see who's laughing, Lisa.*

Lisa

I WISH — I JUST WISH I'd known, that's all. I kept thinking, *Jordan . . . Jordan, Jordan, Jordan, why didn't you call me?* So I went in to check on her after dinner, and I said, Jordan, believe me, I know: high school is a living hell. Yeah, well, I live your living hell, she said, and I had to laugh, because Jordan's so earnest. She's so like her mother sometimes. I'm serious, she said. I know you are, I said.

Leese, can I ask you something? she asked, turning on her side and curling up beside me. Anything, I said, and she said, Did you really have a Mohawk? Yes, I said, laughing. What can I say? It was a bad-hair year —. Or a no-hair year, she said, lips pursed. Oh, aren't we funny, I said, about to poke her ribs, but stopping short. I didn't want to hurt her.

And did you really get into fistfights with boys? she said, and I said, Girls, too. And did you really run away five times? No, I drawled, looking at her like *that's crazy.* It was closer to ten — your mother missed a few on her honeymoon. And did you really —, she said, then she stopped. What? I said. Did I really do a lot of drugs and sleep with a lot of anything that moved when I was younger than you are now? I said. And she nodded, with that gleam in her eyes. Yes. Why, yes, I did. And those were some good times, too, let me tell you, I said.

28

Jordan just wanted a little dirt, that's all. She wanted to know how it looked and felt and tasted and what I saw and was it everything or even anything like she imagined. She wanted to hear the war stories of my wanton youth, same as a boy yearns to hear the sailor's tale. And that's fine by me — I have nothing to hide. Not from her, at least.

I said, You want shameful? She lit up. All right, beat this: I blew the founding member — forgive the pun — of the first Poison cover band of the greater Hudson Valley. And they're *still together,* I said, almost shrieking. Believe me, I said, you don't know shame until you've blown the lead singer of a hair cover band — not even an original hair band, mind you — a hair cover band. And that managed to get a smile.

How you feeling? I asked, rubbing her back. Okay, she shrugged. Don't forget to call Dr. Myers in the morning, I said, and she nodded yes. I love Dr. Myers, she said, rolling over, hugging her pillow. Me, too, I said. I wish Dr. Myers were my mom, she said, smiling. Me, too, I said.

Adela

SHE KICKED ME OUT. Before we hung up Saturday night she promised, she promised she'd call. So I waited all morning Sunday, but she didn't — she didn't call. And of course I didn't sleep all night. So finally, Sunday afternoon, I went over to speak to her face-to-face, knowing — I knew she wouldn't understand, but I had to try. It was unbearable — I mean, I waited *four hours* for her to get home, and when I heard the door open, I thought, *This is it. This is the last time she's ever going to speak to me.*

So of course we got into it, and the whole thing was so out of control. She said, How could you? And I said, He loves me. He loves me, Mom. And she said, He loves you? That's your justification, he loves you? Yes, I said. Did he say that? Did he actually say he loves you? she asked, disgusted, and I said, Yes, he did. Many times. Which only proves he's as desperate as you are, she said, and I said, And you'd know all about that, wouldn't you? Then she said, Leave, pointing her finger at the door, like I was a dog. I just stood there, thinking, *This isn't really happening.*

Please, she said, waiting for me to do as I'd been told. Adela, I said I'll call you when I am able to discuss this, she said. You're kicking me out of my own house? I said, but she wouldn't even look at me. Fine, fine, you got it, I said, grabbing my bag and walking out, thinking, *I hate you. I fucking hate you.* Walking to the elevator my whole body was tingling, numb, but the elevator didn't come, so I had to take the stairs.

I made it half a flight before I started crying and had to sit down, trying to breathe. So I'm sitting in the stairwell, when along comes this woman with her Yorkie, and she's got it all dressed up in this rhinestone collar and fur — I'm serious, the thing was wearing a chinchilla coat, whatever. When I hear them coming up the stairs, I try to pull it together, pretending I'm looking for something in my purse.

Then, when they reach me, the woman goes, Excuse me, even though there was plenty of room for them to get by. In this completely bitchy tone, too — I mean, I was so taken aback, I automatically said, I'm sorry, and pressed myself against the wall, trying to make room for her fat ass to squeeze by, but she didn't say thank you, nothing. It's ridiculous, I know, but at that moment I thought it was so rude, I almost started crying again — because of this stupid woman and her dog.

And it was so juvenile, but at that point, I was just like, You bitch — I actually called her a bitch out loud, hearing her open the door. Which was completely unnecessary, but all the more reason. Then, just before the stairwell door closed behind them, I yelled it, *I said I'm sorry, you fat bitch!* And I felt better for a minute, then I puked on the stairs.

Lisa

AFTER I SAID GOOD NIGHT, I grabbed my coat and went outside to call Will. Of course he was annoyed that he'd had to go home to relieve the nanny instead of taking a client out for drinks. And I was just like, tough shit, you know?

I said, Will, she was sick: what was I supposed to do, leave her there? I just don't understand, he said. Will, she's my sister, I said, knowing he was about to ask why I spent two hours driving her home instead of taking her back to our place. I'll be back in the morning, I said, and he said, When? As soon as possible, believe me. I hate it here, I said, looking at the sky, then we hung up.

I didn't want to talk, really; I just wanted to ask about the baby. Which is funny, considering that all I've dreamed about for the past six months was having a night to myself—no baby, no husband. But then, standing there alone, all I wanted was to be home with my son. I don't know how it happened, but he's the only thing that makes sense to me anymore. Besides which, I'd never left him alone with Will overnight before, and it scared me. Just not as much as the baby being left alone with me, I guess.

Then there was a moment, just before we hung up—there was a second when I almost said, Will, I fucked up today. I really fucked up. But then I thought, *No, don't.* I mean, would he ever trust me again? Would he believe that it will never happen again and promise not to take my son from me? I don't know if I can believe that myself, but I wasn't taking any chances. There was one thing I wanted to say, though: I wanted to say, Babe, I wish you could see the stars up here. But all I said was, I'll be home as soon as I can, all right?

I stayed outside for a while, happy to breathe clean air. You know after I got home from the store, I wanted to get as far away from the baby as I could . . . I just never thought that place would be here.

Jordan

YOU KNOW WHY I got a job there? I got a job there because it was the lamest place I could think of, like it was my little way of telling everyone, I don't care what you think about me, you know? I mean, it's like Lisa had a Mohawk, and I had Price Chopper's. Okay, so maybe her fuck-you was a little more fucked than mine, but whatever.

But you know what he said? I go, Leese, you know what he told me? He said I was a cool chick—a *cool chick*, okay? And I was just like, please, you've got a pinecone air freshener in your Tercel, what do you know about cool, you know? And she goes, I'm so sorry, babe, she said, squeezing my thigh. I just nodded my head, and I'm like, Yeah, and to think that I actually defended him to my mom, that I called him my *friend*. What friend? I go, I don't have any friends — nobody calls me, nobody texts me, nobody e-mails me —. And that's a bad thing? I mean, Lisa's just like, And that's a bad thing? And I go, It's not a *joke*, okay? And she's like, I know it's not, I'm sorry.

I go, Seriously, when did I become such a loser? I mean, I used to be pretty; I used to be popular —. Then she snatched my hand, like she'd just caught a fly, and she goes, First of all, you're *gorgeous*. And second of all, let me tell you a little secret about the popular girls in high school: they'll all be married within ten years, and ready to kill themselves or their husbands within another ten. And I was like, But not you, right? And she goes, No, I wanted to kill my husband within two years: I was on the fast track. And I was just like, Yeah, but seriously, Leese, Lance was popular, *my mom* was popular —. And Lisa goes, I rest my case.

Lynne

I SAID GOOD NIGHT to Don sometime around ten, and then, as I was heading back upstairs, I heard . . . I stopped, then I heard it again: *laughter* — it was Jordan, laughing. I thought, *She's home — Jordan's home!* I swear I practically *ran* up the stairs, hoping to catch her before she disappeared again, and when I got to the door — I literally had my hand on the doorknob — I heard Lisa's voice. So I stood there, and I listened, yes. I listened to their conversation, because they were talking about me, laughing at me.

I hate to say it, really, but she has a six-month-old baby, and she thinks she knows what it is to be a mother? My god, the vanity of every new parent, pointing their lightning rod at the sky, thinking they'll be the one to get it right — they're the one, the exception to the rule. Honestly, I listened to the two of them, thinking, *Oh, Lisa, you have no idea what you're in for* . . . and I almost laughed. But instead, I knocked and opened the door.

Bobbie

THE PLAN WAS to have dinner with Paul and Adela on Thursday; meet Joyce and Del for brunch on Saturday; drive to Paul's on Saturday afternoon; and take the train back first thing Monday morning. But when I met Adela for lunch, Thursday, I could barely eat, I was so nervous for her to meet Paul.

After lunch we did some shopping, and then, while we were standing on the street, she got so angry; she kept saying, You know, Ixnomy. Ixnomy, Mom, *Ixnomy!* Gibberish; I couldn't understand her. Then, practically shouting at me, she said, Mom, seriously — when are you going to get a fucking life? I said, Dela, I'm trying, believe me — now calm down. She was so furious; I thought, *Where is this coming from?* I sat there — I sat right across from her at lunch, then all night Thursday — and I didn't see it. My own daughter, and I just didn't see it.

Adela

ADELA? SHE SAID, calling me from the cab, and I turned back. Yes? Don't be late, she said, and I just nodded my head, like, okay, Mom . . . I was going to be an hour late, but now that you remind me not to. I'm sorry, but it was funny; I'd never seen her so stressed out like that before. I knew she'd dated a few guys, but she hadn't introduced me to anyone in years. I said, *Ixnay, Ommymay,* then she kissed her hand and threw me the kiss. I turned and walked east on Fourteenth because I'd told her I was staying at Ana's, which was a lie. I mean, I'd already seen her on Wednesday, when we hung out at her apartment before we went to the park.

We took Lulu for a walk, and Ana said, I know it's been over a year, but I can't get it through my head. I mean, it's just so weird that you live in Boston. You're telling *me*, I said, as we passed a mural on Avenue C, and I said, What is this? It was a mural of a little girl with some banner that said, YOU ARE AN ANGEL, some crap like that. You didn't hear about that? Ana said. No, I said, standing there, and she said, Wow, it was front page for like an entire week. Seriously, Del, how do you survive without the *Post*? Babe, we've got to get you back to civilization. I'll be back soon, I said, and then I almost told her everything, right there, on the corner of Sixth and C.

By the way, she said, did I ever tell you about that guy who molested Lulu? I started laughing. No, it's *true*, she said, and it was so awful, I got her steak for dinner. Sorry you got molested, Lulu, have some steak? I said. Look, she said, it's not funny. We were traumatized . . .

Lisa

SHE USED TO WORK at a clinic, downtown. That's where I met her. I'll never forget the moment when she walked in, I was just like, *you . . . you're my doctor?* No way, you look way too cool to be a doctor. And when she went into private practice, I followed her. Because I love her. I'm serious, I love Dr. Myers. Every time I go in and she gives me a hug, I think, *God, I wish you'd been my mom.* I mean, she's not old enough, but still.

I've been seeing Dr. Myers for so long, I've watched her little girl grow up. I remember sticking my foot in my mouth the first time I saw a picture of her daughter. I don't remember why we were in her office, I think I had an irregular Pap or something, I don't remember. But I sat down in front of her desk, and I saw this picture and said, Who is that?, looking at a photo on her desk of this beautiful little girl, topless on a beach, somewhere lush and exotic. Why, that's my daughter. Can't you see the resemblance? she said, beaming, and I said, Ohmygod, she's so beautiful. Excuse me, she said, and what am I? Why, you're Dr. Gorgeous, of course, I said, trying to work my way out of the hole, turning the picture back.

I envied her, that little girl, with her big eyes and dark skin and perfect mother. I could feel how rich and warm and safe her life was going to be. All the beautiful things she would have, all the right schools, the perfectly stylish clothes, the way she would always know how to dress, what to say. All the things I never had. The person I would never be, no matter how rich and famous I became, and it made me sad. Then it sickened me, it — it angered me, and for a moment, I actually wanted to destroy that picture, burn it. Which is terrible, I know, I do. But still.

Joyce

YOU KNOW I ALWAYS wanted a girl. For the simple reason that girls are smarter. But God gave me Benjamin. Oh, I mean, I was perfectly happy to have a boy — aside from the fact that I was afraid of him. I just didn't know what to do with a boy, you know. And the first few days, when I'd look at him, all I could think was, *What do I do with you?* Of course you soon realize you have no idea what to do with a baby, period, but still.

When Benj was old enough to start toilet training, one of the mothers at his preschool told me the Cheerios trick. She said the easiest way to get them to use the toilet was to toss a few Cheerios in the bowl, because they're visual creatures, males. And if there's no target, if there's nothing to piss on, what's the point, right? So I gave it a try, and sure enough, it worked. Then, one day, Benjamin offered to teach his best friend, taking sweet little Ruben into the bathroom with him.

Walking through the hall a few minutes later, I heard the boys talking in the toilet, trash talking to each other about, *My dad can this!* Oh, yeah? *Well, my dad can that.* I tiptoed to the kitchen and waved to Michael. *Come, come,* I gestured, holding my finger to my lips, quiet. Oh, yeah? Benjamin said, Well, my dad's twinkler is a thousand million times bigger than your dad's twinkler! Of course, me, I'm thinking, *Twinkler? Where the hell did that come from? We don't use baby talk in this house.*

Michael, on the other hand — Michael doubles over, before standing, placing his right hand on his chest, overcome with pride. He had his little moment, deeply inhaling through his nose, and then, tiptoeing backward, far enough so that the boys wouldn't hear, as he snapped, repeatedly pointing his index finger at the bathroom door: *My son! That's my boy!* I just stood there, rolling my eyes, *Oh, puh-lease.*

Every family has its silent movies; that was one of ours. Not the first to star Michael's penis, but still. An hour later, I noticed the Cheerios box was missing, and the boys were long gone, playing in Benjamin's room. Course I knew right where to look for the box, but when I opened the bathroom door, I gasped, covering my mouth in horror.

It was only a half bath, but there was . . . there was piss *everywhere* — clusters of soggy Cheerios sticking to the new wallpaper, oozing down the walls, just Cheerios spooge everywhere. I swear they'd been skeet shooting in the guest bathroom. After I could breathe again, I lost it: Benjamin, Ruben . . . you get in here *right now*. Michael, you, too! All of you, get your asses down here *now!* You think I was put on this earth to clean up your mess, you got another thing coming, and it's called motherfucking Pine-Sol!

I called Ruben's mother, Carla, right away to apologize for my language. Carla said, Tell them I'm on my way, and I practically giggled, hanging up the phone. *Carla, I like your style,* I thought, because two mothers are ten times worse than one, and sure enough, there they were, two little boys, barely four years old, sitting on the couch, staring at the ground, miserable. If there's original sin, well, that was the original bust all right.

And in all fairness, I could see how it would happen. I mean, it starts out with an innocent toss of toasted oat into the bowl, quickly progresses to a spirited little aim-and-shoot, and next thing you know, it's an all-out piss orgy . . . I get that, okay. But what I cannot understand is how they could just leave the scene, that they could just walk away, like . . . like no one would notice the bucket of Cheerios and urine slopped all over the bathroom walls. That they just picked up and walked away, that's the part I can't get my mind around. Except to say the attention span of the male brain . . . truly baffling.

When Carla buzzed, Michael let her in. I have come to collect my little Honduran Jew boy, she announced, loud enough for the whole house to hear. But I had a soft spot for fat little Ruben — he always said *please* and *thank you* and *may I have another cookie, Mrs. Joyce?* I mean, Carla was tough: she'd already raised five younger brothers while her parents worked multiple minimum-wage jobs to keep a roof over their heads. Poor Ruben never had a prayer, and it showed, too, in his good manners, sound fear, and deep respect for the female sex. So I told her, walking down the hall, I said, Let me just say one thing, which is that I'm certain — I am *absolutely certain* — that Benjamin was the instigator. Carla just stopped and looked at me: Why, because my son is such a putz, he'd never think of pissing on your walls all on his own?

When we arrived at the end of the hall, I told her to prepare herself, and then I opened the door. *Ach!* she gasped. *Dios mío!* she said. Oh. My. *God.* Ruben! Carla yelled. Then she stormed into the living room, walked straight to the couch — the kid was already whimpering — took him by the collar, and dragged him to the bathroom. Look at that, you little pig, she said, bending over and violently snorting in her son's ear. I had to turn my back to keep from laughing out loud.

Don't give me that, Carla said, scolding his whimpering. Don't you piss all over this house and cry to me, young man — *I won't have it,* she said, in such a screech that it made the hair on the back of my neck stand on end. But of course it makes you feel better to hear another mother berating her own child — I felt a hundred times better, before we'd even sat down. So I sent Michael out for Windex and Bounty, and we put the boys to work while we had a cup of tea.

Then I told Carla about Benjamin's boast that his father's penis was a hundred million times larger than Ruben's father's penis, and Carla took a bite of her cookie. Mmm, she moaned, inspecting the chocolate-macadamia cookie. Yeah, well, you can file that one under Sad but probably true, she said, sighing. Shit, that reminds me, she said in her droll Queens tone, I'm pregnant. You're what? I said. Fucked. I'm what you might call fucked, she said, with a little what-can-you-do shrug. *Mijo!* she called, throwing her head back and shouting toward the bathroom: Hey, boys, too bad you won't be getting any cookies, because they're *really* good, she said, taking another bite. Which was just so, so heartless and cruel. I loved it. Yep, Carla was my idol, all right.

So we made plans to have them over for dinner a week later, but then my dad got sick. By the time we returned from the funeral, I didn't have the energy to speak or eat or see anyone, least of all the mothers of my son's friends. But I liked her, I really did. And she sent a birth announcement; she had another boy and they named him

Isaac. Ruben and Isaac Gonzales-Goldberg. Kills me, just kills me . . . only in New York.

Bobbie

I WAS THIRTY when I took my daughter home. Which seemed so old at the time, what was I thinking? Well, anyhow, when Dela was a little girl, I used to tell her the story about Josephine Baker.

Josephine Baker had a brood of both adopted and biological children, and when the natural-born children would taunt the adopted ones, telling them they weren't her real children, she'd sit them all down. Then, one by one, she'd point her finger, informing each of them: You, I had to have . . . You, I had to have . . . Then, when she came to one of her adopted children, she'd say: And *you* I chose. That's what I used to tell her, too: You I chose. But it wasn't exactly true, I'm afraid. What I mean is there are times when things choose us first, for better or worse.

The first time I laid eyes on my daughter was in 1986, back when I was working at a clinic on the Lower East Side. One day, I was in the office, when Yolanda poked her head in the door — Yolanda was our full-time Spanish-speaking nurse — and said in this singsong voice, Dr. Myers, there's someone who wants to meet you . . . To be honest, I hadn't slept in two days, I had a stack of work, and all I could think was, *Not now,* when Yolanda stepped forward with this cherub pinned to her hip. She was just this little thing, with these fat cheeks and these Betty Boop lips and these big black eyes. She had her hair parted on the side, with a white plastic butterfly barrette holding back a few curls.

But her little butterfly was falling out and I had to fix it for her: I don't know why, I just had to. I got up, and of course she had these zirconium studs in her ears, and I thought, *Why do they do that?* Then I started laughing, because by the time I reached her, I wanted to bite her cheek — just this . . . this overwhelming urge to bite and tear out a chunk with a snap of my jaw. It was that carnal, yes. And that wasn't me. That wasn't me at all.

This is Adela, Yolanda said, swinging the child around to face me. Whose is she? I said, taking her without even asking. The foster parents brought her in, Yolanda said, handing her over. What's her name? I asked again, kissing the baby above the ear, needing to smell her cheek, and Yolanda said, Adela. Adela Hernandez. And I said, Hello, Adela Hernandez, I'm Bobbie Myers.

I'll never know if Yolanda had any idea the effect that the child would have on me. All I know is that when I looked at that baby, all I could think was: *Mine. You're mine.* People talk about love at first sight, and I don't believe in such things, even though Adela is my living proof. She's the best thing that ever happened to me.

Lisa

WHEN WE GOT BACK in the car, Saturday morning, Lynne asked if I believed her, and I said, No, completely disgusted. My father is a good and decent man. Maybe we're talking about two different people, she said. Obviously, I said, checking my watch.

We got to the station a few minutes before my train arrived, and then I told her, straight out. Lynne, I said, Jordan needs to get out of this town —. She's not you, Lisa, and just because it was right for you, doesn't mean it's right for her. No, it doesn't, but that doesn't mean she shouldn't have the right to choose for herself for once, I said, twisting the knife. Lynne didn't say anything for a minute, and then, finally, she said, Thank you for coming to get us —. Wouldn't have missed it for the world, I said. Safe trip, she said, nodding. You, too, I said, opening the door.

I walked through the station to the platform, and then I bummed a cigarette from a guy waiting for the train. I wanted a cigarette so badly — *ugh.* It smelled divine. But just as I'm about to light up, I hear my name, and there's Lynne, holding this box in her hands. I was so confused; I just stared at her. It's for you — open it, she said, so I did.

It was a bowl, a ceramic bowl. I said, It's beautiful, Lynne, and then, with a perfectly straight face, she goes, You can use it for potpourri, to stash drugs . . . Thank you, I said. You're welcome, she said, smiling shyly. I mean, twenty minutes ago, I slapped her face, and not only does she turn the other cheek, she gives me a potpourri bowl?

Bobbie

MY SERVICE CALLED Saturday, just as we sat down for brunch. Jordan Yaeger had left a message, and I needed to call her back to make sure she was all right. I have to make a quick call, I said, and Dela rolled her eyes. She's always hated the fact that I can't leave my work at the office. Sorry, I'll just be a minute, I said, heading for the door.

Dr. Myers? she said, answering. Hello, Jordan, I said. How are you feeling? Okay, she said. Cramps? I asked. It's okay, she said. Bleeding? Yeah, she said, but it's fine, normal. But the nausea's gone — I mean, it just stopped — just like *that,* she said, snapping her fingers on the other end. It's so weird, you know? she said, and I smiled. It was good to hear her voice — I knew it wasn't over, but at the very least her voice sounded better. It's a start.

And your heart? I said. Same, she sighed: cramps and bleeding. That'll get better, too, I said. Promise? she said, and I said, I promise, Jordan. Dr. Myers, she said, can I ask you something? And I said, Shoot . . .

Adela

I TRIED TO GET OUT of brunch, Saturday — I swear I tried everything I could think of to get out of brunch, every possible excuse, because I knew I was going to get the third degree. And sure enough, the second Mom stepped away, Joyce asked what I thought of Paul, and I told her. I said I liked him, and I did. But I said I thought they'd had a fight when I left the table Thursday night, and Joyce waved me off. Paul's just what she needs . . . I mean, look at her: Doesn't she look *fabulous*? she said, looking up as Mom returned to the table.

Then she said, What about you, Señorita Thang? You must have a hundred guys on the line. And I'm thinking, *God, get me out of here, just get me out.* Hardly, I said, nodding at the table; I couldn't even look her in the eye. But of course Joyce wouldn't drop it. Oh, don't give me that, she said. What you need . . . what *you* need is an older man, Del. Twice plus seven, I always say —. No wonder you're still single, they're all dead, Mom said, taking a sip of coffee. Joyce

40

shot Mom a look, then she said, Trust me, Del, I'll introduce you to some *amazing* men, okay. Granted, they don't have the stamina of guys your age, she said, winking, then I had to push my plate away.

You feeling all right, baby? Joyce said, reaching for my face, and I said, I'm fine, pulling away so she couldn't touch me — honestly, it was so shameful, I couldn't stand her touching me. Then I told them I had to go; I said I needed to meet Ana, which wasn't true, but I couldn't take it anymore. But I walked downtown because I wanted to see that mural again. I don't know why, I just needed to see it before I went back to the hotel.

Joyce

DELA GOT ANGRY with me for mothering her at brunch, so I quickly changed the subject, telling them about Benjamin's little surveillance scheme. Christ, I said, whatever happened to good old-fashioned porn — I mean, with someone else's mom, you know? I said, What, he needs my password? All he had to do was ask.

Where is he now? Bobbie said: In shackles? Close enough, I said. He left this morning for a school trip to Boston. Model UN or some bullshit, I said, quickly nodding, bowing my head to Del, apologizing. He'll be back tomorrow night. I told him to enjoy himself — might be his last two days on this planet.

Oh, but you know what that little half-breed called me? A Nazi, I said. That's right. He goes, You're a Nazi! Benjamin, I said, doing my best to sound hurt, that's *horrible*. I'm sorry, honey, did your father show you those pictures? He swore he would never show them to anyone. And Benjamin's face went from twisted rage to utter disgust in a blink, I said, snapping. I mean, he couldn't even speak. All his mental energy had to be directed at blocking the thought of me and his father in any sexual, never mind sadomasochistic role-play scenarios, above and beyond our eight-year divorce proceedings, I said. Then Benjamin goes, I said, laughing, he goes, You're *disgusting*.

I said, Me? *I'm* disgusting? You videotape your own mother naked and *I'm* disgusting? Benjamin, if that isn't a case of the pot calling the kettle nigger, I don't know what is. Joyce, honestly, Del said, turning up that dainty nose of hers. That word is vile, she said. And I said, Yes. Yes, it is. In fact, I couldn't agree with you more. Which is why it's the mot juste, I said, and Dela just rolled her eyes, clenching her jaw.

Bobbie

ON OUR FIRST DATE, I went up to Paul's house and he made me dinner. Then he built a fire, and we sat in the living room, drinking wine. Did you always want a child? he said. No, never, I said, I never wanted children. Really? he said, surprised. Really, I said.

It was true. I felt no maternal instincts whatsoever; my patients were as close as I came. No, long before friends started handing me their babies, I knew it wasn't for me. Simply watching an infant regurgitate a mouthful of peas, before shoving its chewed mush into his mother's mouth, fist and all . . . ugh. People cringe at the sight of blood: I cringe at the sight of that.

You? I said. Did I ever want kids? he said. Yes . . . yes, I did, but only after my wife left me. For a while, I became convinced that a child would've been the solution to all our problems. Which were? I said, realizing I'd thought out loud. I'm sorry, I said. Me, he said, shrugging, I was our problem. Thank god we didn't have a child — I can't imagine what we would've done to the poor kid.

Well, it's not unlike sex, I said, thinking out loud again — too much wine. Sorry? he said, confused and intrigued. I said, What I mean is, when you're young, and you realize how crude the sexual act is, you say, Not me . . . oh, no, I'll never do *that!* That's how I felt when I saw people with their kids, I said, laughing, shaking my head. But you did eventually want to have sex, right? he said.

Paul, I said, let's be honest. So soon? he asked, and I said, You won't be offended if I don't have sex with you tonight, will you? Because I like to take my time with a man —. That's not what Joyce said, he said, raising his eyebrow. You know what? I said: No offense, but fuck you both. No offense taken, he said. And frankly, I think Joyce could be persuaded without much effort, he said, and I laughed, covering my mouth.

This should be good, he said. And I said, No, I just remembered something Michael once said. He once described sex with Joyce as bullfighting naked, I said, remembering that night at their apartment. Joyce had just put the baby down, and we'd finished a few bottles of wine, and Michael said, Now . . . now imagine you've got this, this masterpiece of an erection —. Oh, I do, Joyce snorted, I imagine it every day, baby.

Imagine you're standing there, he said, speaking to me as though Joyce wasn't there, and you're ready, right — you're ready, willing, and able . . . When, out of nowhere, someone shoves you from behind and you find yourself naked — we're talking buck fucking naked, standing in the middle of a *corrida* with your masterpiece of an erection hanging out. Then, just as you begin to wonder what the hell you're doing there, the crowd goes wild, chanting, he said, raising his arms in glory: You're the man! *Eres el hombre! Eres el hombre!* This is what you think about when we're having sex? Joyce said. Well, he shrugged, variations on a theme. No wonder, she said.

So you hold up your arms, you turn in a circle, acknowledging your stadium of adoring fans, and just then they release the bull on the opposite side of the ring . . . And there you are, he said, counting: No clothes. No cape. No sword. Just you and your —. Defenseless masterpiece, Joyce said, reaching for the bottle. Exactly, Michael said. Which is deflating with a sharp squeal, seeing this huge motherfuckin' bull scrape his hooves in the dirt, preparing to charge your bare ass. Well, he concluded with a sigh, that, in a nutshell, is lovemaking with my wife.

Oh, babe . . . that's about the sweetest thing you ever said to me, Joyce said. Here, hit me: give me some lip, Joyce said, leaning over the coffee table, and Michael got up and kissed her. Well, I should probably be going, I said. I have to get home and relieve my sitter. Or better yet, Michael said, why don't you bring her here, so that she can relieve us? *Oh,* Joyce moaned, in mock agony, falling back on the couch, before sitting up again and raising both hands, as they gave each other a congratulatory high-five for having successfully doubleteamed me. Joyce said, I was going to say, Is she cute?, but that —. Skills, Michael said, fanning himself with his hand: skills . . .

I didn't tell Paul all that, but I remembered. In a moment, I remembered everything.

What was he like, her ex? Paul asked, taking a drink, and I said, He's not her ex yet — not until he gives her the house. But he was smart, very smart. Hilarious. Sexy. And no bullshit. Then again, for a no-bullshit guy, what a lying son of a bitch that man can be. What can I say? Michael was her great love, and he broke her heart. Joyce is a very different person than she was ten years ago, I said. Aren't we all? he said, and I smiled. It must've sounded trite, I know, but I knew the difference; I watched it happen.

The thing about Joyce, I said, sighing, well, frankly, that body has seen more action than a Saigon brothel in 1971 — *the year* 1971 — but her heart . . . her heart is completely monogamous.

Joyce

MY FATHER DIED of melanoma within six weeks of being diagnosed. He died in a hospital room. No matter how many times I pleaded with him to let us take him home, so he could be in his own bed — and not in some sterile private room with that stupid fucking Craftmatic bed that scared him half to death every time the nurse adjusted him — he said no. He said, No, Joycie, we have to think of your mother, and I said, Why?, and he said, Now, Joyce, you know she's going to live in that house until the day she dies. Exactly, I said, exactly, Dad. So what's it matter if you die there first?

Listen to me, he said. I'm listening, I said. No, you aren't listening. I am —. Joycie, I keep trying to explain this to you, but you can't talk and listen at the same time, he said. Now listen, will you? I don't want that because it's always been such a happy home for us, and I don't want her to have any bad memories, you hear? That's what hospitals are for, he said, sighing. And I was just like, *Such a happy home? Us? For us, who?* Now, Joyce . . .

The last thing my father asked was that I take care of my mother. I said I would, and then he asked me to promise him, and I couldn't at first, but the man could be very persuasive when he put his mind to it.

Joyce, he said, taking my hand, she's my life. And my eyes started tearing, but all I could think was, *Damn . . . damn you, man*. All right, already, I said, and then I said the words: Yes, Dad, I promise you.

I wasn't the only one — he even got Sonja to promise she wouldn't sit shivah. He told her he'd never been religious, so he didn't want any religious ceremony. I only knew this because I was eavesdropping, standing on the stairs, where I'd learned half of what little I know about my parents. Sonja was in the kitchen talking to my uncle Lenny and aunt Doris, asking them what she should do, because it was his dying wish, and that he'd told her if God had a problem with that, they could discuss it soon enough.

But of course that didn't fly, so he played his trump card: he said he wasn't asking for himself, he was asking for his grandson, his only grandchild. Because that's what Benjamin would remember most about him, seven days in a house, silently mourning. That's not how he wanted his grandson to remember him, he said, so finally she agreed. Of course, always keeping up appearances, Sonja felt it necessary to repeat the story to everyone all week long, but at least she did as he asked. So we had a simple funeral, people came to the house afterward, and then we all went to bed.

When I woke the next morning, I prepared for battle. Because naturally I'd assumed Sonja would blow through the house with gale force, removing every trace of my father, but it was just the opposite. She left everything exactly the way it was the day he had collapsed and they'd rushed him to the hospital. Everything, right down to the placement of his marbled fountain pen on the desk in his study. Pen and cap left separated, as though he was sure to return in a minute and get back to work.

She never cried — at least I never saw the woman shed a single tear. But after he died, Sonja embalmed the house, stopping time as best she could. I went into his study a few months later to look for some paperwork and the loose cap was still there, lying on its side, waiting to be reunited with its pen. For a moment, I expected him to return, too, because I could still smell him in the air of that hermetically sealed room, that sandalwood aftershave and Ivory soap I'd always smelled when kissing his cheek good night. I found myself turning, looking behind me . . . I could still feel him, then it was just too much, and I got up and quickly closed the door.

Bobbie

THE NEXT MORNING, Paul served breakfast on the terrace, as he calls it. He has a sunroom at the back of the house, and we ate in there. It's so beautiful up here, I said, smiling at the plate he'd placed in front of me. Thank you, I said. Bon appétit, he said, taking a seat before removing and snapping the napkin, placing it across his lap. Dig in, he said, watching me take my first bite. So, is that about the best fucking thing you've ever tasted or not? Ohmygod, I said, melting as I bit my fork. No, I said, you were good; this is fucking *amazing*, I laughed, pointing at the plate before cutting another bite.

Were you always a morning person? he asked, taking a sip of juice, and I nodded, reaching for my coffee: Occupational hazard, I'm afraid. What time do you usually get up, Bob? Five, I said. *Five*, he said, shuddering. I get up, go to the gym, and if I'm lucky, I make it to the office by seven, at the latest, I said. That's obscene. We really have to work on that, he said, and I was so thrilled to hear him speaking in a future tense, but of course I did my best to disguise the fact. I said, Work on my not working, you mean?

For starters, he said, popping the last bite of toast in his mouth. Think of me as your personal trainer. We'll start — or rather we'll *not* start first thing Monday morning, he said. Now, my daughter, I said, laughing, changing the subject, Adela is not what you would call a morning person. No? he asked, and I shook my head no. Never was, never will be. And the way I saw it, if I could get my butt out of bed, she could, too.

But every once in a while, when she'd wake in a particularly foul mood, furiously sulking, glaring at the breakfast table, I'd say, Well, I see you haven't greeted the day, have you, Miss Adela? Greeted the day? he asked, smiling, and I said, That's right. Of course she'd just ignore me, or she might even go so far as to snarl at me — literally snarl. Then I'd have no choice but to get up and walk around the table, reaching for her hand: Come on, I'd tell her, let's go say hello to the day, so you can have your breakfast.

If she still resisted, which she always did, I'd have to take her by the arm and walk her out to this little princess balcony we had at the old apartment — we lived on Fifth and Fifteenth for a while. Then I'd say, Good morning, day, and I'd wait for her to say it, too. But sometimes, she was so stubborn and so angry with me; she'd start sobbing, refusing to speak the words, but I said, No. I told her we would not go inside until she'd said, Good morning, day, and that was that.

So, one morning, we were standing sixteen floors above Fifth Avenue in the cold, and Dela still had her nightgown on — her princess nightgown, which Joyce gave her, of course. Joyce spoiled the child rotten, I swear — all our problems stem from Joyce. Anyhow, we're standing there, and then Dela finally turns to the street and snarls, Good morning, day. So I put my hand to my ear, and I said, What? What's that? I didn't hear you, and then she shouted, *Good morning, day!* And then, out of nowhere, a man's voice shouts back, *Yo! Shut the fuck up!*

Well, of course my mouth fell open, hearing this asshole yelling at my child, but before I could respond, Adela lunged for the rail and leaned over, yelling right back at him: *Hey! Was I talking to you?* Then she proceeded to answer her own question: *No! So be quiet!* At which point, I started laughing — I couldn't help it, and that was the last straw. Poor Dela . . . she just couldn't take it from both sides, so she broke down sobbing, and I had to pick her up and carry her inside, my little girl. It's like she went from four to forty and then back to four years old again, all in the blink of an eye. A real New York City girl, huh? he said, smiling, and I nodded, Through and through.

Adela

TRAUMATIZED? I SAID, laughing at her, as we passed a little old white-haired lady with her cane, hobbling like Yoda. Then the lady stops right in front of us, and says, Bless you, you beautiful girls. Bless you and your little doggy, too, she says, and Ana said, Thank you, completely blowing her off, and the woman says, What's your little doggy's name? Ana gives her this bitchy smile and says, Lulu, and without missing a beat, the lady says, Do you have any change, sweetheart?

Not today, Ana said. I do, I said, opening my purse, giving the woman a few quarters. But once we'd walked a few steps, I was just like, I can't believe you. You don't have any change for the old lady? Look, I pass her every day, and she blesses me and asks Lulu's name every day, and she *never* remembers, okay. So maybe if she'd remember my little doggy's name for once, I'd pay her, she said, and I just looked at her. No, I don't have any change, she said. And I'm not giving her a twenty, okay.

We passed two gay guys with a Boston terrier, and Ana pulled Lulu away, and then she waited until we were out of earshot: You know what I miss most about New York — the old New York? And I said, What's that? A cat whistle, she said. I can get a dog blessing, but I can't get a cat whistle to save my life. It's true: I can't get a fucking cat whistle, but my dog gets molested in the park —. You aren't serious, I said. Del, I didn't tell you about that? I must've been too upset, she said, sighing.

So what happened? I asked. Well, you know that big black dude who walks around with his tan leather vest open, showing his bare chest, wearing that Indian-bead choke necklace? No, I said. Well, anyhow, she said, I'm walking Lulu one day, and we're heading for the dog run, and there he is, and just as we're about to pass him, he stops — right in front of us, okay. So I stop, and then he leans over, and he starts petting Lulu, right?

So I'm like, okay . . . we'll just let scary dude pet her a second, and then we'll get the hell out of here. But then, then he starts *fondling* her —. Fondling? I said, laughing. Fondling! Like this, she said, making this obscene cupping gesture, rocking her right hand back and forth. *Eww*, I said. What could I do — he's like six foot four, two-forty, and obviously on crack, and one minute he's petting my dog, and the next minute he's assaulting her. And the worst part is that he looks up — I mean, he's bent over with his hand between her little hind legs, then he looks at me and says, And is she fixed? Gross, I said, genuinely repulsed. Would you have felt better if he'd whistled at you? I said, and she cocked her head: A little, maybe, yeah.

48

Anyhow, I said, so what was that mural all about? What mural? she said. You know the one on C, the little angel thing? I said. Oh, terrible story, she said. She was this little girl who was killed by her stepfather—awful story . . . Of course the *Post* didn't stop creaming themselves for an entire week, she said. See what you're missing?

Bobbie

A FEW MONTHS before I met Paul, I was on my way to see a friend in the West Village. I walked out of this deli, conveniently tucked between a sex shop and Burger King, in that divey stretch on Sixth right across from the basketball courts, and I was looking down, twisting the cap off my water bottle, when these two guys almost ran into me. They were in their late twenties, maybe, and they both had pocked skin and all these runny tattoos; one was wearing an oversized Knicks jersey, and the other wasn't wearing a shirt, just his scrawny bare white chest—they looked like Appalachian homeboys, or I don't know what.

In any case, the only reason I avoided running into them was because I heard the basketball one of them was bouncing, while the other's saying: And I'm just banging this chick, right? I mean, I'm just banging her, like *bang! bang! bang!*, says the shirtless guy, repeatedly pounding his fist into his left palm, as if his friend wouldn't have understood without a demonstration. No sooner said, the same guy bumps into my shoulder, and my first thought was, *Ex-cuse me . . .* But he didn't notice me, didn't apologize: nothing.

What's strange is—I mean, they were repugnant, and I would never want them to notice me, really. But then I couldn't help thinking, *You know, there was a time they would've apologized.* As a matter of fact, there was a time I would have stopped them in their tracks. I got used to all those insidious disclaimers years ago—oh, you know, you're still beautiful, or, you look great for your age. But then, one day, it hits you: literally. You're no longer sexually viable—to anyone, apparently.

Of course my next thought was, *Well, they sure as hell would've noticed Adela, I'll tell you that.* Sometimes I wonder if she knows how

49

beautiful she is. Then again, she's twenty-three years old, how could she possibly know that yet?

Adela

I LIKED HIM, honestly. Paul's handsome, he's smart, he's funny, he's obviously crazy about my mother, and that's all I ask, really. When we were at dinner, he said, Your mother tells me you want to work for the UN. I do, I said, but I want to work in the field. Which field would that be? he said. The Sudan, I said, I want to work with the refugees.

Then he asked me if I'd always wanted to go into relief work, and I said, No, actually, I wanted to apply to the curatorial program in Chicago and become a fabulous, hotshot gallerist like Joyce, I said, laughing. What changed? he asked. And I said, My junior year of high school, I went to Europe for the summer as an exchange student. I chose Italy, because I wanted to see all the great Renaissance painters. I wanted to see Florence and Venice . . . But honestly, I just wanted to see myself on the back of Vespas, breaking the hearts of all those hot Italian boys, going out to clubs, just one big party, right, I said, nodding at myself. What a moron . . .

Then, when I got there, they stuck me in this little town south of Trieste, which is not exactly a cultural hub, you know. So I get there, and my little brother, one of the sons of the family, took me around to see the village, which took about five minutes. Then he takes me to the top of this hill where you can see the entire valley, and it was beautiful, but I was just like, ohmygod, where's the action, you know? Like, this is nice and all, but this is not what I signed on for, I said, laughing.

So I said to Raphael or whatever his name was, I said, Tell me, what do people *do* here? He was this little nine-year-old kid, and he looked at me like I was the village idiot. I mean, if you could've seen the look on his little face . . . it was a cross between pity and disgust. Then he said, *Viviamo . . . viviamo e basta.* Live, he said. We live, that's it.

Honestly, I've never felt so stupid in my entire life. It was the first time I realized how small my world was, how small my thinking was.

And suddenly art wasn't something precious on a wall, it was all the people outside the walls, I said, shrugging. From then on, I wanted to meet people, see how they lived their lives — how to live, I guess. I know that's corny, I laughed. No, it's a wonderful story, he said, smiling at me.

Of course Joyce was crushed, I said. She was grooming me to be her protégé. Ah, my mom said, waving me off, she'll have other protégés. Acolytes, I said. Slaves, Paul said, and we all laughed.

Bobbie

I KNOW SHE can be a bit much, but still. Few people know this about her, I said, but if you get Joyce Kessler really, really drunk — or, if Joyce Kessler gets Joyce Kessler really, really drunk — she will karaoke Joplin's "Ball and Chain." Really? he said, taking a drink. True story, I said, doing my best impersonation of Joyce, taking the mike in hand and introducing herself: *Ladies and gentleman . . . Janis* Fucking *Joplin!* I said, lowering my hands.

Though I've never seen anyone do peyote, I have dragged Joyce into a mildewed shower in a motel in Mazatlan, so fucked up on mescaline that she was hallucinating little people — a troupe of sombreroed Mexican wood elves. Trust me, I said, crossing my legs, facing him, until you've stood in a shower with all your clothes on, trying to peel Joyce out of all her clothes, getting soaked to the bone, listening to Joyce converge with the Latino sprite kingdom, well, you haven't seen her other side.

Joplin, huh? he said, and I said, Oh, Joplin's her idol. Except Joyce's version is a bit more layered — more like Joyce imitating Bette Midler covering Joplin, where she does that bobble-headed move as she cha-chas around, circling her arms like a locomotive, before exaggeratedly pointing her finger at the audience. You do know that Joyce invented karaoke, I said. Is that so? he said. According to Joyce, I said, giving my best impersonation of her: Oh, please, if Al Gore can invent the Internet, I sure as hell can invent karaoke.

Honestly, how can you not love Joyce Kessler? Well, unless you're Michael, I said, answering my own question. They don't speak, do they? Paul said, and I had to smile. Speak? No, I said, although they find ways of communicating. Yes, Joyce mentioned something about carrier pigeons, he said. To carry messages? I asked. No, she said they're always looking for new and interesting ways to shit on each other, he said, and I had to laugh.

How did they meet? he asked. Joyce and Michael? I asked. Yes, he said, taking a sip of his drink. I don't remember, actually, I said, through a mutual drug dealer, maybe?

Joyce

OH, THAT'S FUNNY. Ha ha. No. It was at an opening, thank you very much. We met at a group show, so to speak. I mean, the work made me want to slash my wrists, so I headed straight for the bar. Then, across the room, I saw this tall, skinny, pierced guy with spiky hair and a leather jacket and his jeans were peg-legged, safety-pinned together, and I thought, *Oh man, oh man . . . wouldn't Sonja just shit her panty hose if I brought that guy home?*

So he sees me, and you can see his head puffing up, thinking, *Hey, I'm getting checked out,* and he walks over. So I'm laughing before he even reaches me, right, which he obviously finds charming, because he's getting his shoulders into the act, he's walking the walk. So he comes up to me and says, Hey, and I said, Not interested.

Then he says, That's funny, because I couldn't help notice you were looking at me, and I said, I wasn't looking at you, I was staring —. Even better, he says. Well, thanks for saving me the trip. I just have one question, I said. Just one? he said, raising a brow. Just one, I said, looking him up and down: How much? And he laughed: By the hour or the night? Yeah, yeah, yeah, I said, give me the group rate. And he raises his eyebrows, all hey-hey . . . like maybe I had some hot-little-number girlfriend waiting in the wings. Really, how the male imagination can be so exaggerated yet so limited at the same time never ceases to amaze me. Yeah, think again, I said, my mother goes first.

What can I say? I took him home twenty minutes later and fucked his brains out. Next morning, I woke to the sound of my toilet flushing, and when I sat up, there he was, standing naked, in all his morning glory. Hello, sailor, I said, rolling over. Morning, he said, crawling back into bed. I have to tell you, I said, yawning, I'm so relieved none of that shit was yours. You mean at the show? he said, yawning at my yawn.

Yes, I said, shivering with disgust, pulling the sheet over my shoulder. So what, you wouldn't have had sex with me if any of those paintings had been mine? he said, laughing, turning me on my back. And I said, Oh, please . . . of course I would've had sex with you. I just wouldn't have swallowed. Well, he said, pulling the sheet back, how fortunate for us both.

Lisa

THE ONLY GOOD thing about the *New York* article was that it mentioned Joyce's ex. That must've infuriated her, reading Michael's name in her story . . . I just had to laugh. But I remember Michael — he came by a few times right after I started, when they were still speaking. Oh, I remember him, all right.

I mean, he wasn't . . . he wasn't what I'd call handsome, no, but man, did he have sex appeal. And charming — extremely charming. Michael could charm the knickers off a nun, as my dad used to say. Needless to say, I was always very nice to Michael, very pleased to see him stop by. Then, soon as Joyce walked in, I'd be banished from the room like some maidservant — I'm serious. Yeah, they had an interesting marriage, all right.

Joyce

MICHAEL WAS MARRIED once before. We didn't talk about it much, because it was annulled after two months, so there wasn't much to talk about, really. But I once found a picture of them while unpacking a random box of stuff, aptly marked ODD MICHAEL STUFF, right after we bought our first apartment. Ohmygod, is that her? I asked, pulling the photograph out of an old accordion file that had nothing in it but the five-by-seven photo.

They got married in Vegas, naturally. Michael was obviously in some sort of altered state, and his wife . . . ? Well, for starters, his first wife had her head shaved — the left side, that is. Yep, half-shaved head and the rest was teased and hair-sprayed so that it resembled this insane platinum . . . it was just like a funnel cloud of tumbleweed shooting out of her skull. But she was cute, I suppose. In a fat Deborah Harry sort of way.

I said, Ohmygod, Michael, look at you — you two look like a couple of glue sniffers coming down after a rampage at Salvation Army. Ohmygod . . . I just kept saying it over and over, looking at him, this tall skinny guy with a head of black hair that looked like a startled porcupine, standing next to his insane girlfriend, wife, whatever, in front of the Chapel of Love. Give me that, he said, walking toward me. Wait — wait a second, I said, inspecting the image. Michael, this isn't — this isn't even the Chapel of Love! Too pricey, he said, so we decided to give the Chapel of Lust a try — it was perfectly fine, he said, swiping the photo of himself and Spiral Betty from my hand. That's what I coined her, then and there.

So a few weeks later, he stops and he says to me, he goes, Just out of curiosity, why do you call her that? What, Spiral Betty? It's a pun, see: it's a pun on *Spiral Jetty,* the Robert Smithson sculpture, I said, and he just looked at me. Michael, the sculpture with the rocks in the form of a spiral, I said, twirling my finger. Yeah? he said, waiting. *Spiral Jetty,* Spiral *Betty* — you get it? I said. Joyce, I get that part, yes, he said.

Then what? I said. Betty. Why do you call her Betty? he asked, shaking his head at me. Uh . . . because that's her *name,* I said, shaking my head back at him, and then — honestly, only then did it occur to me that I had her name wrong. Oops . . . unless that isn't her name, I said, trying to laugh it off, oh, silly me. No, that isn't her name: her name is Bonnie, he said. Bonnie? Are you sure? I said, thinking, *Did you look at that picture — you could've gotten her name wrong, you know.* Yes, I'm sure, he said.

Well, anyhow, I said, why anyone would think to name their child Bonnie is beyond me, but for some reason, I can't seem to remember her name. Here, let me help you: Bonnie, as in, what a Bonnie Lass she was, he said. Ugh, I winced, moaning out loud. There: now you'll remember, won't you? he said, getting up to leave the room.

It took a second to see if I could get out of it somehow, then I just had to knock my head against the air. Damn. Damn him. It was true; I would remember. I still do. It was a relief that she was so unattractive, but I have to say, I saw something in Michael that day I'd never seen, that he could marry such a homely girl, that . . . that showed real soul, that he genuinely cared about the person, not just the package. And that he'd obviously learned from his mistake, marrying me — two points in his favor. Which is about as high as any man can score, really.

I have to say Michael loves women, he really does. All sizes, shapes, colors; small tits, big tits, big ass, flat ass, six foot two, four foot six . . . I think that's why he has such a gift for making women shine. Some men just have the Midas touch that way. Granted, I've met maybe two men like that in my whole life, but he was one of them. Michael is one of those rare breeds of men who like women almost as much as he likes fucking them.

Adela

OHMYGOD, ARE YOU KIDDING? I had *such a crush* on him when I was a kid . . . I mean, Michael was never around much, but Joyce used to have all these pictures of him, and I always thought he was so handsome. But then, whenever he was home, he scared me. He'd ask me questions, and I'd just sort of stand behind my mom's chair, using her as a shield. What can I say? Men are scary when you're little — they're big and they have hair on their hands.

I just remember staring at my feet a lot, and then, after he'd gone, I'd concoct these wild fantasies that mostly entailed me being able to answer simple questions with the greatest of ease and sharpest of wit. *Oh, yes, Michael. Ha, ha, ha.* And of course my brilliant repartee would leave him thinking, *That Adela, now isn't she something?* And of course he'd mention me to people, saying, *Oh, I know this incredibly beautiful girl Adela, who is the maturest eleven-year-old you've ever met.* Colorful, but limited, yeah. I'd even take it as far as the possibility of a kiss, but then it just got too disgusting, really.

I hadn't spoken to him in years, when one day last June he called out of the blue. He left me a voice mail, saying that Benjamin was up for the week, visiting him on the set of a movie they were shooting in Boston, and Benjamin asked him to invite me to join them for dinner sometime that week. Then Benjamin e-mailed me, too, and I wanted to see him, but I had too much going on that week, and I just never called Michael back.

Then he called again a few weeks later, saying he'd love to see me, if I wanted to stop by the set for a cup of coffee, or maybe he could treat me to a nice lunch sometime. I didn't call him back then, either, but I thought about it. I mean, everyone knew about the film; every other day there were pictures in the paper of streets they'd shut down for filming. One morning, I was reading the paper, when I noticed a shot of Jack Nicholson talking to some tall guy, turned in profile, and I bent forward, staring. Ohmygod, I said, that's Michael.

I admit, the picture might've gotten to me a bit, because I thought about calling him that morning, but I didn't. I mean, it was nice of him to invite me to the set, and there was a part of me that really wanted to stop by and check it out. Then again, it was kind of weird that he called; the whole thing just seemed so awkward, and I didn't know what we'd have to talk about without Benjamin there, so I didn't call him back.

No, I never called him back, but I kept saving his voice mails for some reason . . . well, flattery, I suppose. I liked the attention, yes — and vanity trumps sanity, as Joyce would say. I guess there was a part of me that still liked the idea of him telling everyone, including Jack Nicholson, Oh, I know this incredibly beautiful girl named Adela, who is the most . . .

Lisa

ONE YEAR, IN SIXTH GRADE, I came up with the best Halloween costume ever. I got a pair of pointy black boots and black stretch jeans and I found a tight sleeveless black muscle shirt, and I pinned up my hair so you couldn't see a single strand. Then I got these big nerdy Coke-bottle glasses, and I washed out one of my mom's plastic orange flowerpots for a hat. I took one last look at myself in the mirror, and then I licked my finger, putting it out on my ass: *pssss* . . . hot stuff.

I was so pleased, too, because I never had any good ideas for costumes. I mean, I never knew what to be, and for once in my life, I knew who I was — me, myself, and I — *we are DEVA!* D-E-V-A! It was an awakening, all right. But knowing I'd have to spell it out for the rest of the world, I wrote DEVA across my chest in white masking tape.

So I get to the Halloween dance, I walk into the gymnasium, and it's like the record scratches. I mean, everyone stopped and stared, and then, one by one, every sixth, seventh, and eighth grader in school started smirking at me. I was crushed: no one got my costume, no one knew who I was . . . All I could do was turn and walk out so no one would see me crying. Twenty-some years later, I realize they had no choice but to make fun of me because they were a bunch of fucking losers, that's why. Small consolation, really, but the fact is that by the age of eleven, I was already ahead of my time — we're talking a galaxy light-years ahead of that town. And that's a pretty fucking lonely place to be, let me tell you.

To this day, every September when I see a school bus I wince, thinking, *I'm sorry.* Seriously, it's like watching lambs sent off to slaughter. I don't want that for my son, I said. What do you want for him? she said, and I tried to put it into words, but all I could say was, The chance to be his own person, his own man. You don't think he'll be his own man if you stay in New York? she said, and I said, Not as much of one, no. What does Will think? she asked, and I almost said, Will thinks therapy is for assholes, but I always tell him it takes one to know one. I didn't, though, because I was just avoiding the question. I said, What does Will think about the sort of person we're raising our son to be? Yes, she said, and I shrugged, Dunno. Have you ever asked him? she said, and I said, No. It never crossed my mind.

Adela

THE THING IS, we never had any men around when I was growing up. No, I mean, Mom had boyfriends, just no one . . . no one special. No one who seemed to make her truly happy. So the only man in my life, really — aside from my grandfather — was Lionel. I've known Lionel since I was eight years old, when we moved into the building. Lionel opened the door for us that first day and tipped his hat, saying, Ladies. I loved him from that moment; no one had ever called me a lady before. Lionel's the face of this building, really. All the other doormen, they emulate him — they all want to have that sort of dignity and style, to command that sort of respect.

My grandfather used to say that there are some men who will read every word of the Bible and be none the wiser for it, and there are some men who are born knowing every word, never having read a page. Special men: men of faith. Lionel's special that way. He's got more class than anyone in that building, and we all know it — nothing to do with his station, that's just who he is.

I used to think men like that — men like my grandfather, Lionel — I used to think they were a thing of the past. Now I realize that those sorts of men are rare in every generation, and they always will be. But when I was little, I used to think, *Oh, I wish Lionel were my dad.* And for a second, I'd think, *Well, he could be — hey, maybe Lionel is my dad!* And I'd feel so happy to think he was right in front of me all this time. Then I'd look at his big kind eyes, and I'd realize, *No, Lionel could never be my dad: because he's too good.*

Jordan

I MEAN, WE didn't say anything the whole way because it was just like what did we have to talk about, you know? So when we got to my house, he peered over the steering wheel, and he goes, Nice place, and I was just like, Yeah, thanks. Then he was just like, Well, guess I'll see you tomorrow, or whatever, and then for some reason, I go, Misha, can I ask you something? And he just shrugged, like, sure, shoot, and I go, I'm sorry, but why . . . I mean, why would a guy do that?

So he looks out his window for a moment before he turns back and he goes, Straight up? And I'm like, Of course I want you to be straight —. Get over yourself. That's what he said — he goes, Get over yourself. And I just looked at him, like, *Excuse me?* He goes, Come on, you know why — you know what's up, and I was like, Oh, right: I know why a guy would ask me out and two hours later just stand me up. I mean, I was just sitting there, like a complete idiot—. Stop, he goes, just stop, okay?

Then he goes, Listen, you seem like a smart girl, so why are you doing this? And I was just like, Doing what? And he goes, Look, I know who you're talking about; I saw him walk in. So you talk to this guy for, what, thirty seconds? It was longer than thirty seconds, okay? I mean, I was just like, It wasn't thirty seconds, and he goes, Fine, thirty minutes, then. How's that? You talk to this guy for a whole half hour, and now you're all worked up, worrying why he did or didn't do x, y, z, whatever. And you want me to tell you why you're so worked up? And I was just like, Oh, since you know everything. And he goes, No, I don't know everything. But I know you're sweating this guy because he's not from here, and because you think he might be your ticket out.

I didn't say anything; I just stared straight ahead. Come on, Jordan, everybody's waiting for the winning ticket. So here it is, straight up: you're upset because you were hoping he saw something in you that no one else sees, right? Well, maybe he did, maybe he didn't. And I was just like, Excuse me, but you don't even know the guy—. Neither do you, Jordan: that's what I'm saying. I don't know this guy, and you don't know this guy, and now you're defending him? Jordan, be real. What did you think was going to happen? What, he was gonna drive you home, give you a kiss good night, and ask if you'd like to go out next Friday?

I couldn't swallow for a minute, thinking about what I'd imagined, but it was none of his business, so I was just like, I don't know, Misha. What's it to you? Nothing, he goes, he was just like, Nothing. All I know is you were standing outside for an hour waiting for some stranger to pick you up, and now you look like you're about to start crying or something. And when he said that—I mean, I was so pissed at him for saying that to me, but all I could do was clench my jaw because I didn't know what to say.

So finally I go, Are you through? And he goes, I don't know, is there anything else you want to ask me? And I go, No. And he goes, Well, then I'll see you tomorrow, and I'm like, No, because I don't work tomorrow, but thanks for the ride, and I started opening the door. And then he goes, What, so now you're angry with me? And I was — I mean, I wasn't angry at Misha because I got stood up, or maybe I was, I don't know what my problem was, but anyhow.

I was just like, No, I'm not angry with you, and he's like, Good, because I'd have to fire you, if you were, and I go, Misha, you can't fire me: you're only the assistant manager. Besides which, I'm joining the union, and then you'll never be able to fire me. And he goes, That's great, so why don't you ask the union guy your guy question next time? And I was just like, Good night, and I started getting out of the car, and then he peers over the steering wheel while I closed the door, and he goes, Good night. Of course I didn't look back because I didn't want him to see me smiling about his stupid little union joke, and because the whole thing was just so stupid, you know, but I remember that he waited until I'd closed the front door before he drove away. I just thought that was really nice, you know?

But the thing is . . . I mean, honestly, I don't think I knew how lonely I was until that night, walking upstairs to my room. Because I felt so stupid — I mean, I just felt so completely humiliated, that that was like the first time I could stop pretending everything was okay. It was like the first time I didn't have any pretend left, you know? So when I got to my room, I closed my door and then I just sat on my bed for a minute, thinking about what Misha said. And at first, I was so angry at him, because . . . I don't know, for seeing the truth about me, I guess. Like he had no right to do that, you know? And then I just felt like sobbing.

I mean, I didn't cry, but it's like . . . like have you ever been so grateful to someone for being honest and seeing you for who you really are that your eyes just start welling, even though you feel totally ashamed, too, because they *know* you're full of shit? And for once maybe being honestly fucked up is better than pretending you're somebody else all the time, you know what I mean? I mean, he likes me for who I am, and he's my friend, okay, that's what I see in this person. And he's the only real friend I've had in so long, I don't care — I really don't care what my mom says about him, no. Because I know he's going to call, and I know he cares about me, I do. I know.

60

Bobbie

ADELA WENT THROUGH a Joyce phase when she was about nine or ten. I don't think it was conscious, really, but suddenly she started going to the Met and MoMA every weekend, and we signed her up for special art history classes after school. One day, one of the nurses asked her if she wanted to be a doctor when she grew up, and then Dela wrinkled her nose and said, No way. The nurse said, What do you want to be? Then, perfectly matter-of-fact, Adela said, I want to be the most important art gallerist in New York.

She even invited Joyce to speak at show-and-tell and give a slide show on different artists she represented. I was a little hurt, I admit, but I understood. Besides, I couldn't exactly show slides of my patients. Anyhow, girls go through phases where they become infatuated with an idol of their own creation — I didn't, but I know many girls do.

Adela

NO, I KNOW it wasn't the right time to talk to her, but when is? I mean, I waited six weeks for the right time — trust me, it never came. Besides the fact that I had to fly back to Boston on Monday morning, and I had to see her before I left. I had no idea what I was going to say, but I thought if she could at least look at me, she would see how sorry I am.

Then, when I told her he was just some guy, she went off. Some guy? You're throwing your life away for *some guy*? I said, No, Mom, it's not for some guy — he has nothing to do with my decision. And I don't think I'm throwing my life away: you do. But she wouldn't listen — she won't.

And she'd never believe me, but the truth is I have the worst luck with men. Stick me with a hundred guys, I'll find the biggest asshole; the most callous, inconsiderate, self-centered bastard in the room, I'll find him. And once I do, I'll put him on a pedestal, like he's God's gift. I mean, Marshall didn't want me, he didn't want anything to do with me. He didn't give a flying fuck what happened to me, and that was the most desirable thing about him. I couldn't let it go. And my mom . . . my mom would never understand that sort of behavior. Never.

I know — I lived with her for eighteen years, and I know what she thinks. My mother despises weakness, especially in women. And that's how she would see me, yes, as weak. Even worse, she'd lose respect. Really, how can you love someone you don't respect? So how could I tell her that? How could I explain that I wanted some guy to make everything better, when I don't even know what's wrong to begin with? Me: I'm wrong. I don't know why — I just am. No, she would never understand. So it's not worth it, really.

Bobbie

WELL. SEEING AS I couldn't talk Del or Joyce into shopping, I walked to Union Square and sat down on a bench, and then this beautiful girl walked by, talking on her cell phone. Which made me think of Adela talking to Paul at dinner on Thursday night.

Dela double majored in linguistics and political science, I told him, openly bragging, even though I'd told him at least once before that she'd attended my alma mater and was now in her second year of grad school at Cambridge. Then I smiled, grabbing Dela's hand, seeing that I'd mortified her — honestly, she was white as a sheet. How many languages do you speak, Adela? Paul asked, and she considered the question. Oh . . . four or five, she said, shrugging. Four or five? he said, laughing. Depending on how much I've been drinking, she said smiling, even though she'd been nursing her wine all night.

I got up from the bench, deciding to pick up some wine myself. When I got home Saturday afternoon, I took off my coat, set down the bottles, and then, in a moment of weakness, I checked my messages again: You have no new messages. You have no new messages. You have eight saved messages. Well, fine. That's just fine, I said, opening the more expensive of the two bottles, and then I made up my mind.

What I decided was that I was never going to call Paul again. No, I told myself, I'm not calling him tonight; I'm not calling him tomorrow . . . And you know what? This is the best decision I've ever made. As a matter of fact, I'm fucking ecstatic, I said, raising my glass, toasting thin air.

Joyce

FRIDAY NIGHT, my old friends Joe and Betsy flew in for the weekend, so I had Alana book them a suite at the Gansevoort, and I'd planned to take them out to dinner on Saturday. When we spoke on Saturday morning, I told them I'd pick them up at eight thirty, and I'm thinking, *This is good. This is exactly what I need — I need to get out. I need a little R & R with friends — a few drinks, a few laughs, a few more drinks . . .*

So I walk into the lobby, making a mental note to talk to them about their artwork, and just as I'm pulling a pen out of my purse, I look up, and standing at the front desk, I see this . . . this woman who stops me dead in my tracks. My god, was she hot . . . I mean, I couldn't see anything but her legs and that ass, but still. She was gorgeous.

Jordan

WHEN LANCE KNOCKED, Saturday night, I was just like, What? I mean, seriously, Lance has been *such* a dick to me for so long, I was just like, yeah, thanks for coming home for the weekend, but where've you been, you know? I mean, for the past three years, it's like he wouldn't talk to me at school; he made fun of me in front of his friends; he wouldn't even give me a ride home, okay. And if I showed up at a party, he'd go — right in front of everyone, too — he'd look at me and he'd go, Who invited *you*?

This one time, my freshman year, he ruined all my new jeans and he didn't even say he was sorry, you know? And the thing is, because I'm so tall, it's really hard to find pants long enough, so I can't dry them — I mean, Mom never dries my pants. So Lance came home one night and he threw all my stuff in the dryer on high, because he wanted to wash a shirt — like one shirt, okay. So when I realized what he'd done, I pulled out four pairs of brand-new jeans, and one was like a pair of two-hundred-dollar jeans, and all the legs had shrunk like two inches. I mean, I was just like, *I am going to* kill *you. . .*

I heard him in the kitchen, so I walk in and I'm like, Lance, you dried my jeans! And he just looked at me — like he's hunched over, reading the sports page, eating cereal, and he's like, What's your problem? And I was like, My problem is you ruined all my jeans! I go, Seriously, why did you put my clothes in the dryer? And he goes — I mean, he gets up and takes his bowl to the sink, like he couldn't care less — and he goes, I wanted to wear my air force shirt to work out. And I was like, Lance, you have like fifty shirts! And he goes, Yeah, but I want that one, and he just shrugs, like, get over it, and I was so angry — ohmygod, I was so pissed — I mean, it's like he enjoys treating me like a total asshole, you know? So I took the juice pitcher and threw it at his head. I mean, there wasn't any juice in it, but like two seconds later, he had me in a headlock, so I started kicking his shins with the back of my heel, and then Mom came in, all, What is going on here? Stop it, you two, stop it!

Oh, so now he flies home like he wants to be there for me, like he's really got my back, right. Mom, too. I mean, Mom, Dad, Lance, they're all there for me, right? But you know what? You know what's gonna happen? It's like, sure, they're all going to feel bad and kiss my ass all weekend, but Monday morning everything will go back to exactly the way it was. Just watch.

Joyce

Saturday afternoon and still no word from Michael, but Benjamin was away, so I had some time to prepare. It's hard to remember now that his hair's always in his face, and he mutters, if he deigns to speak, and does nothing but sit at his computer, but still. He was such a sweet little boy, and such a happy baby, too. But fat — ohmygod, Benjamin looked like a miniature Michelin man with a patch of wispy black hair on top of his head.

God, I loved the way he smelled after I bathed him — he smelled so good, I could've eaten him up. His little ears, and his little toes, and little pinkie penis, and his little . . . his little cream puff of testicles. Who's delicious? I'd coo. My baby's delicious. Then my voice would get shrill, as I'd start to squeal, Oh, Michael, doesn't he have the most scrumptious little scrotum you've ever seen? Michael would be sitting there, trying to read a script, pressing his thumbnail against his lips, then his eyes would dart, looking at me for a moment before returning to the page.

You know, there were times I'd have an orgasm that made me want to shove Michael into my vagina — penis, trunk, limbs, head, everything — just shove him in and keep him there, you know. There were times I felt the same about my son, but all I could do was press my head to his stomach and breathe him in until I couldn't inhale any further. There are things you can never say, and that was one of them.

Then again, sooner or later you realize you are who you are, and they are who they are, and none of it makes any sense, really. Because the truth is that children, like so much in this life, are a complete crapshoot. Take Sonja and me — there: perfect example.

Bobbie

HER MOTHER NAMED her — her biological mother, yes. What little I know about the woman is that she was a twenty-year-old crack whore who left her infant alone in order to score, and ended up OD'ing in a stairwell in the Bronx. It was a day or two before a neighbor heard crying and finally called the police. They aren't even sure how long the baby had been alone, but she was fine. Dehydrated, but perfectly healthy otherwise.

It's horrible, but I've always tried to say that with the same candor I had when I taught Dela the names of male and female anatomy. I wanted her to know the truth, but mostly — mostly, I just couldn't stand the thought of her being teased, sheer cruelty. Are you kidding, the way people throw around *ho* these days? Ho this, ho that . . . no. I thought if she heard me say it first, the words might not be so scary. Which is naïve, but still.

I told my share of fairy tales. Until she was six or seven, Dela's favorite bedtime story was one I made up about the day I went to pick her up at the foster home. Which is true, I did pick her up. But my version was more like the story of Madeleine, the French orphan raised in a convent school, telling her how I walked into this pristine nursery, lined with rows and rows of cribs, and then it came time for me to choose my baby. Which is pretty twisted, now that I think about it, but anyhow.

Every time I told the story, I'd pretend that she wasn't sitting right beside me, as though she didn't exist. Then Dela'd get so excited, she could barely contain herself, rattling both fists: Me, me! I swear, she'd become frantic each time I'd say, Here's a nice baby boy. No, not that one! she'd shout, pulling my arm, leading me to the next imaginary crib. Then I'd continue: Hmm, not that baby, I'd say, patting my pursed lips with my index finger, before continuing. Oh, but who is this pretty little girl? I'd say, pretending to stop and look at baby Adela for a second. Me, me! It's me!

I used to get her so worked up that she'd blow the occasional snot bubble and drool, and then, when she just couldn't take it any more, she'd wrap herself around my torso and twist my shirt in her hands, beseeching me: Me, Mommy, me! Take me, take me! Oh, yes, I'd say, suddenly seeing her, before cradling her like a baby, I want this one, little Adela! I'd coo. And once again, she was safe. And you could feel her entire body relax, because once again everything was exactly as it was supposed to be.

It never ceased to amaze me that she believed it every time. That she could believe with such a pure heart — that she truly believed her mother could do anything, including turning back time, changing the entire course of our lives five minutes before bedtime.

Adela

I REMEMBER THIS one time when I was about fourteen, fifteen, maybe, and I was in my bedroom, talking on the phone with the TV on. I think I'd been watching *Oprah* or something, talking to my friend Stella, but when I hung up, the local news was on. It was toward the end of the program, when they always throw on those dippy human-interest stories, and they had this segment about these socials for children in foster care. They were like orphan socials, meet and greets, but specifically for older kids, who are always hard to place because everyone wants a puppy, right.

So this organization came up with the idea to throw these events where older kids, hoping to be adopted, strutted down a runway in front of an audience of prospective parents. They even set up this cheap little catwalk with all these metallic streamers hanging down, and while the children were taking their turn on the runway, an emcee would tell the audience a little about them, reading from their cards: *Timmy likes playing baseball and soccer. He knows lots of jokes and would love to have some brothers and sisters to tell them to, but he says he'd be happy just having a mom and a dad* . . . Then Timmy would turn at the end of the runway and walk back, and the next orphan model would come on.

Then, of course, they edited in these dopey little one-on-ones with several of the kids, asking them, basically, if the kids didn't feel whorish strutting down the runway, and the kids would say, No! I love all the attention. Then they'd ask what sort of parents the kids were hoping to meet, what sort of family they dreamed of, and, last but not least, why they should be adopted. I'm not kidding. The reporter actually asked this kid Timmy, or whatever his name was, why he should be adopted.

I was speechless, but I remember thinking, *How could you?* I mean, really, how could you possibly look a child in the eye and say, Tell us, kid: Why do *you* deserve a family? Why should *you* be loved? I mean, if that little boy should have to answer the question, shouldn't we all?

I was lying on top of my bed with a magazine when they showed a clip of this one girl who was nine or ten, maybe. She had orange hair, and these huge splotches of freckles, and this really bad Prince Valiant haircut . . . she was just so dumpy-looking, you know? But the worst part was that she was trying to show real personality on that stage, because she knew that otherwise she was too old and way too homely to appeal to anyone.

I mean, she was trying so hard to look like a happy, deserving child, too; putting on this ridiculous act, strutting down the catwalk . . . god, it was so pathetic. And it wasn't just that she was fat, but

67

she had on this white polo shirt that was too small, so it kept pulling up at the waist. And it was too tight in the chest, so it drew all your attention to her fat buttercup nipples, and this huge belly—and of course the camera was positioned right beneath the stage, worst possible angle.

I swear it was the saddest thing I'd ever seen. I mean, it was fucking speed dating for orphans. And at that moment, watching that little girl walk up and down the runway, that was worse than any war coverage I'd ever seen. I had to bite my lower lip to keep from crying, and then—and then I just had this overwhelming urge to slap her. It was so violent, I changed the channel, and then I got up and walked over to my full-length mirror in sheer defiance.

This is terrible, I know, but I was just like, fuck off, all of you . . . I just stood there, checking myself out in the mirror, and I remember being especially pleased with how my ass looked in my new underwear. And I knew exactly how lucky I was, lounging in bed in my beautiful room in our beautiful apartment, but I felt completely entitled to that life. I don't know how long I stood there, posing this way and that, but to this day . . . to this day, I don't know if I did that for show, if it was just an act or if it was real.

Either way, I had to get in a few more kicks, just to be sure I was free of her. So I returned to my magazine, flipping through *Vogue,* reading about the Miller sisters or whoever the young socialites of the moment were, taunting her, pretending to be that fat little girl. Talking out loud, *And I should be adopted because I'm nice, and I like people, and I'd like to be a good helper to my family, and I'll* . . . Face it: you're ugly, I said. U-G-L-Y, you ain't got no alibi . . . *you's ugly!* I don't remember what I said, exactly, but I fell over in bed, cracking myself up.

I know how awful it is, I do. Because I know what became of that little girl; I knew, then, what would become of her: she never got her family. No, she got shuffled around for another eight years of her sad, lonely life. More than likely abused physically, emotionally, and/or sexually, before and after, heading into a long life of low-paying jobs. She was smiling on that catwalk. She believed someone would want her, she hoped—and you knew she had no chance. One look, and you knew she was one of those quiet tragedies just waiting to happen.

I bet most people would look at that girl and imagine me thinking to myself, *That could have been me.* But I don't, ever. Because that was never going to be me: it wasn't in my cards. I'm sorry, but I have no more in common with that girl than anyone else does.

Joyce

I KNEW WHAT I would name her, too, if I had a little girl: Roni. Like Roni Horn — without the sexual politics or the bad haircut, you know. Still, sometimes — even now, almost ten years later — I'll see a school bus pass by, and just out of the corner of my eye, I'll catch a little girl's face, and I'll turn, thinking, *There she is — there's my Roni!* And I'll just stand there, frozen, watching her go.

It passes — the moment, the bus: the light changes, someone honks a horn. Time snaps back and the moment passes. Then I'll remind myself how far I've come, and I think, *Good. Now get those little fuckers back in school.*

It killed me; it really did. I wanted — I wanted a beautiful, precious little girl like Adela, you know. I mean, they have the most amazing relationship, those two — not perfect, but amazing. Honestly, Adela calls Bobbie almost every day — they adore each other, you know? I wanted to feel that bond. And yes, of course I have Benjamin, but that's not what I'm talking about. No, I'm talking about what I never had with my mother: god, just *once*, you know? So it goes.

It was October 1998, and I was pregnant. I left New York to visit Michael in L.A., having already decided that if, in two weeks, I never found the right time to tell him, there would never be a right time. I returned to New York four, five days later, and I was such a mess, I stayed in bed all weekend, and then, first thing Monday morning, I quit the Manning Gallery. Decided it was time I went on my own, so I did.

Lisa

DON'T GET ME WRONG — I was shaking and shitting in my boots the first time I met her, the original downtown high-art priestess and notorious JAP, Joyce Kessler. Seriously, as long as I live, I will never forget the day I interviewed, when Joyce sat back in her chair, legs crossed, hands folded in her lap, and she asked me a question that would change the course of my entire life. She said, So tell me, Lisa . . . why should I hire *you*?

Not only did I get the job; I was her first hire. So I was there at the first opening at the Joyce Kessler Gallery. It was the biggest event of the year, too: Lou Reed, Patti Smith, Deborah Harry, Joey and Dee Dee Ramone were all in the same room at the same time. I'd just been hired, and it was . . . it was a punk-rock girl's wet dream come true — I mean, I was *sopping*. Greg said I almost broke his finger, squeezing his hand as I gawked, pretending not to gawk, because I was much too cool to be impressed, I said.

But still, when I saw Patti Smith talking to Laurie Anderson, and then when I saw this blond head walk through the door, I practically had a seizure. Ohmygod, ohmygod . . . it's *Kim Gordon,* I said, whispering through clenched teeth. Of course I'd seen her around like a thousand times, but I'd never actually stood next to her. Kim Gordon's here, I said, I, I can't breathe. Breathe, Greg said. I said, Don't tell me to breathe when I can't breathe!

For the first time in my life, I felt like I'd finally made it — I'd died and gone to heaven. Which just goes to show, careful what you wish for. Because here's what you'll always remember about the day you finally met your idol: you'll remember feeling like an utter and complete asshole. You'll remember the thousands of times you fantasized about meeting them, how witty and intelligent and memorable you'd be when the moment came . . . no. No: you weren't witty; you weren't clever; you weren't memorable; all you managed to say was, Hi, nice to meet you. Then you watched them walk away . . .

Sunday morning, I went to the storage unit to grab the shoes, and I was tempted to take a peek, seeing the canvases stacked exactly where I had left them five years ago. You know I've always wondered about those stories of masterworks discovered in old attics, basements . . . how could it happen? Now I know. *This,* this is how.

There must be a good seventy, eighty paintings, total. Not counting all of the drawings that Greg nearly burned or destroyed while in some black mood. Standing there, staring into the storage cage, I realized, *Wow, I could sell them now. I could sell them, decide if I want to stay in this marriage or not. Maybe even open my own gallery; put that evil bitch out of business. Or not. Or, I could just leave them where they are, hidden in a storage unit on Avenue D . . . and no one would* ever *know.*

But I had to look — after five years, I had to see them again. I didn't have much time, but I couldn't resist unwrapping a few of the canvases, just to see. The work was actually better than I remembered, but young. So young it brought tears to my eyes. It's hard to remember those people now.

I mean, even Lynne — even *Lynne* noticed how much I've changed. Driving back, Friday, she said, I know you look down on me, my life —. That's not true, I said. Lisa, you know it. You think I'm crafty, don't you? Lynne, you *are* crafty: you're amazing with your hands. But that's not art to you, is it? she said. I'll never have the sort of talent you admire! Lynne, *I* don't have the talent I admire —. Lisa, she said, what do you see when you look at me? Honestly, what do you see? I couldn't answer, and Lynne goes, What happened to you, Lisa?

I kept thinking about that all weekend, because it really bothered me, I said. Why? she asked, crossing her legs. Why did it bother you? Because she's right, I said.

Joyce

WELL, WELL, WELL . . . Michael finally called me back on Sunday — three times, even. Funny, that. Anyhow, Sunday night we had a little talk, Benjamin and me. And we made a deal. I told him, I said, You hold up your end, I swear on Poppy's grave you can buy anything you want; price is no object. It's his choice, really.

And Bobbie, yes, I got her messages. All six of them, starting Saturday night. And I could hear how much she was hurting, even before Dela dropped her bomb. Bobbie's in love and it pains her. And whatever happened Thursday night, I knew she wouldn't call him because she doesn't know how. Which was why I decided to teach her a lesson, show her how it's done — just not if I could get Paul to do it for me.

So I picked up the phone and invited Paul to lunch on Monday. We ordered a few drinks, or at least I ordered a few drinks, before I gave him the lowdown, and you know what he says? You know what the man says to me? He says, And you wonder why men don't understand women?

2

Bobbie

I THOUGHT I was in luck, Monday, when I managed to hail a cab at 3:45, and I said, Washington Square Park, please. And cut across Sixth, will you? I don't want to get stuck in traffic. And there we were, stuck in rush-hour traffic on Sixth Avenue because the man didn't listen. I started losing patience, and then, when my phone rang, I practically jumped, thinking, *It's him! He's finally called!* But it wasn't Paul. It was Adela.

I was so disappointed that I clenched my jaw, as I replayed the entire argument in the back of the cab. I'd said, Adela, what do you expect me to say? I love you, she'd said, but I couldn't look at her. Finally I said, I told you I'm not prepared to have this conversation —. Not prepared? She said, Jesus Christ, Mom, I'm not some fucking patient — I'm your *daughter*. I said, Let's stop before we both say something —. What? She said, If you can't be in control, forget it, right? Isn't that how it works, Mom? I said, Adela, I think you should go now. And where do you expect me to go? she said, and I said, You mean you aren't staying with Ana? Fine, she said, glaring at me, having caught her in her lie. I knew she wasn't staying with Ana, as she'd told me.

But you asked what I expected you to say, and I told you. So say it — say you love me no matter what, she said. But I couldn't. You know, I feel sorry for you, she said. All your education — for what, Mom? *For what?* Then the cab jerked, as the driver tried to get in better position, and I silenced the ringer, angrily shaking my head at the phone, no. The answer is still no, Adela: I'm not speaking to you right now . . .

Then I tapped on the window, telling the guy I was getting out, because I was already ten minutes late, and I was still six blocks from the park. But I was in such a foul mood and wearing the worst possible shoes, I swore out loud the whole way there. By the time I reached the park, I was shaking — shaking, sweating, and swearing — and there's Joyce, looking so ladylike, sitting on the bench. And I'm thinking, *What has become of us . . . ?*

Hey, I said, walking over and standing in front of Joyce. Hey, she said, and I sat down, handing her the white bag. I waited a few minutes before I found the courage to tell her: We need to talk. And Joyce said, I know — why do you think I've been avoiding you for two days? Do me a favor, she said, popping a couple of pills and pulling out an Evian bottle from her purse. Anything, I said. Just give me a few minutes to achieve altitude, okay? she asked, smiling, watching a pug nip at the ankles of a cowering Great Dane. Of course, I said, even though I wanted to have it out. I couldn't take much more.

Have you talked to Adela? she said. No, I said. Paul? No, I said. Do you want to talk about it? No, I said. All right, she said, and then we sat silent for a minute. So, she said, is there anything else you don't want to talk about, Bob? No, I said, that's it, really. Feeling better? I asked, patting her thigh.

I'll let you know, she said, slouching deeper into the bench. But the thing is, she said, skipping thoughts like stones, I don't think she tries to be cruel, really . . . Honestly, I don't think it even occurs to her that she's *being* cruel — because that's just who she is. That's just Sonja, she said, shrugging.

Joyce

I'M TELLING YOU, I tried calling the woman at least, *at least* six or seven times — but she just kept answering. I could just see her, too, standing there, all five feet and ninety pounds of her, impeccably dressed for dinner, wearing her signature oversized paisley-shaped amber-with-rhinestone brooch and her two-tone polished patent heels, even though it was only two o'clock in the afternoon. Then, hearing the phone, she'd walk to the doorway, where her new cordless phone is mounted in the same spot where the old rotary phone was mounted all my life.

Because I can't get her to understand that the whole concept of a cordless phone is mobility, see, you don't need to stand there, holding it to your mouth with both hands like you're listening to the sound of the ocean coming out of a conch shell. And I've told her — god knows, I've told her a thousand times if I've told her once — Mom, you can walk all around the room — all around the house, even. It's this amazing thing called *technology*. Benjamin can tell you all about it. No, she'll never change.

I mean, she had to have a hip replacement two years ago, and the doctor told her that she has got to stop wearing high heels, but she waves him off every time, deigning orthopedic shoes *uncivilized*. So he looks at me, and I just hold up my hands. Doc, I said, she was Chinese in a former life: this is progress, trust me.

What's that? Sonja said, pretending she hadn't heard a word. So I leaned over and looked her in the eye. He said we have to amputate both legs, I said, enunciating each syllable so clearly that a blind man could've read my lips. So she gives me this dull blank stare, trying to hide the fact that she understood every word, then she looks away, primly tucking her toes beneath the chair and daintily crossing her hands on her lap.

Now I realize the woman is partially deaf, but she's working it, okay — please, she knows exactly what she's doing. Honestly, half the time she can't hear, she pretends she can; and half the time she can hear, she pretends she can't. She's got it all sewn up, see?

Finally, Friday night, before I went home, I finally said to her, I said, Mom, listen. Do me a favor and hang up the phone, will ya? Really, I was just calling to leave a message, so hang up and I'll call you right back, okay? So she thinks about it for a minute, and then, finally, she goes — she goes, But Joyce, I don't understand, and I go, Mom, there's nothing to understand. Just hang up the phone, and in two seconds, when the phone rings, don't answer, because it's me, calling you right back. So just let your machine pick up, and I'll leave you a message, okay. *But Joyce,* she says, in that nasally singsong, why can't you just tell me *now*? At which point, I was just like, Jesus Christ, Sonja, just hang up the phone, already! Seriously, I wait fifty-three years to make the call; the least she can do is listen for once.

But what really drives me crazy is that she's started getting this quivering in her voice whenever she doesn't understand something you're saying, or, *or* when she simply doesn't want to listen to something you're telling her — hard to tell which is which, right? And granted, the woman is eighty-five years old, but I still find it hard to believe that she's actually become frail. Because the thing is, I've never heard the woman sound confused or hurt or — scared, so . . . So I don't know how to deal with that, really. But to be perfectly honest, it's fucking infuriating.

Seriously, I waited my entire life for the woman to show any softness or kindness, any real emotion — just *anything*, you know? I stood there beside her at my father's grave, and the woman didn't shed a single tear, okay. So then, when she started in on me with that feeble tone, I was just like, not now — don't you *dare* show me how fragile you are now, because it's my turn, goddamnit. I am the child here, okay — *I'm the child!*

Well. Fortunately or unfortunately, I managed to pull it together, and I said, You know what? Never mind, Sonja, forget it. But, but what is it, Joycie? Oh, but that did it. That did it, all right. I said, *Don't* . . . don't *ever* call me Joycie, I said, and I knew I was being petty, but I didn't care. That's what my dad called me, that was his name for me, it wasn't for her to use as she pleased, ever.

Well, all right, she said, but I just don't understand. I'm not supposed to answer my phone when you call. I'm not supposed to call you by your name when we speak —. She was right, of course, but that was beside the point. So I said, Okay, listen. I'm going to hang up now, and this time I'm not calling you back. Not today. Not tomorrow. As a matter of fact, I could get through the rest of my life, perfectly happy, if we never spoke again. In fact, Sonja, that might be the answer to all our problems, what do you think?

When she didn't answer, I realized I'd scared her—for the first time in my life, I'd actually scared the woman. But then, hearing her so quiet for once, I almost felt sorry for her, I really did. And for a moment there, I could hear myself snapping at her like some rabid teenager, and I thought, *What am I, fucking thirteen?* Seriously, I felt like I was fifty-three going on thirteen. And really, I mean, I'm the one who called her, and it was rude—it was just plain rude. I'd never let my son get away with that sort of behavior.

So just as I was about to apologize, she has to go and open her big mouth: Joyce, are you feeling all right? You sound upset, she says, and before I can say, well, actually, I am upset, as a matter of fact, that's what I was calling to talk to you about, she says, Where are you, anyhow? I said, I'm at the gallery, Mom, and she says, Well, then maybe you should go splash a little cold water on your face—you don't want anyone to see you like this, do you? And at that moment . . . at that moment, I thought, *Swear to god, lady, if I was in the same room with you right now, I'd smack you one. I would, too.*

I even had this vision of myself slapping her across the face—actually striking my eighty-five-year-old mother . . . It was so shameful, to think that I have that in me, I put my hand over my mouth; I was so repulsed. *My god*, I thought, *I'm really losing it, aren't I?* So of course I had no choice but to make a joke out of the whole thing, about how that's worse than people who abuse animals. Because the elderly can't fight back, they can't scratch or bite—Christ, they can't even chew solid food, you know? And I got to say, I thought that was pretty good, the solid food bit. So I started laughing, then . . . I don't know what happened, but the whole thing turned on me, and I broke down crying.

It must have *horrified* old Sonja, too, not knowing how to respond, or rather, not knowing what to do or say to make me stop. Because there is nothing more obscene to my mother than excesses of emotion, and I was sobbing by that point—I mean, just *sobbing* . . . So then, finally, she says, Joycie, tell me what's wrong. Mom, I said, are you deaf? I said, don't call me that! All right, she said, I'm sorry. I just don't —. Sonja, I just wanted to leave a message and tell you a few things, okay? Because I . . . I had this crazy idea you might want to know something about me, and the life I've been living, and who I am, you know? Me, Joyce, your daughter, your only child, let me tell you a little about myself before we go our separate ways for the rest of fucking eternity, all right?

And just so you know, I said, just so you know, this wasn't easy for me, but I did it. I picked up the phone, I decided it was time to reach out to you, and then . . . and then you answer? I mean, goddamnit, Mom! Ah, shit . . . can you hold on a second? I said, putting her on hold before she had a chance to answer, and coughing to clear my throat, because I had another call coming in. You know what? I said, switching lines again, I'm sorry, Sonja, but I have to take this call. I'll call you back, okay? I really did have to take the call, too — the other six times I said I'd have to call her back, no, but that time, yes.

All right, then, but can I just ask you one thing? she said, and I felt so badly about the whole conversation, I said, Sure. What is it? So I answer next time you call, is that right? she says, and I said, That's right. If you're home and the phone rings, answer the phone. And then she goes, But . . . ? But what, Mom? No, never mind — don't let me keep you, she says, I know you're very busy. No, I said, it's fine. But what?

What if I'm not home when you call, Joyce, then what do I do? she said. And then I just had to take a deep, deep breath, looking down at my ten-thousand-dollar-custom-made-of-American-black-walnut desk, imagining the hundreds of oblong dent marks that would cover its flawless surface as soon as I finished pounding my forehead from one end to the other . . . All right, gotta go, Mom, talk soon, I said. Click.

Lisa

ONCE WE GOT in the cab, Friday afternoon, I smiled and said, Can you say totalfuckingcunt? Then the cabbie looked at me in the rearview, and I just stared back, like, *Excuse me, was I talking to you?* Then I looked out the window, locking my jaw into place.

78

I thought about calling Kate, but there was nothing to say that I hadn't been said before. There are limits, even with your best friend. Besides, I didn't want anyone to know I'd seen Greg again. Because maybe then I could pretend it didn't happen and return to my life, as it had been one hour ago. I swear, every time I see the guy, he fucks up my life, and then he just goes skipping on his way . . . Fuck you, I said, no longer caring if the cabbie heard, before covering my face with one hand: Why? Why me, why now?

Bobbie

AN HOUR LATER, walking back to her house, Joyce stops in the middle of the road, and, practically shouting, says, What, so you aren't speaking to me? As though I'm the one who was out of line, so I kept walking. Then she said, Christ, Bobbie: lighten up, will you? At which point I turned around and said, Cut the bullshit, Joyce: you told the man I was *desperate*?

Well, it worked, didn't it? she said, and then I turned away again, nodding. Oh, come on, it was a joke, she said, and I said, No, a joke is funny, and that's not funny, that's mean. That's just plain mean, Joyce, and sadly, you've never learned the difference. Well, maybe not, she said, but since when are the two mutually exclusive?

I knew she was drunk and I should let it go, but she was so pleased with herself that for the first time in our lives, I turned to her and I said, You know what? *Fuck you.* I think I was more surprised than she was, but still. No, really, J, I said, you want funny? How's this? How about I tell him a few things about you and your miserable life, and we'll see who's laughing then, how's that sound?

Wow . . . you really liked him, didn't you? she said in all serious-ness, and all I could do was nod my head. I said, You are truly unbe-lievable —. Look, Bob, she said, if you want to tell him I'm desperate, be my guest. But it's not exactly breaking news, you know.

I turned and started walking away, because I knew I was about to say something that I would regret and that Joyce was too high to re-member. Bobbie, she said, wait — don't go. But I left her there, think-ing, *You can stand there all night, for all I care.* Look, she said, I know I

79

promised not to try and set you up —. Yes! I said, turning back again. Yes, you did. You *did* promise, Joyce. That's what I said, Bobbie, I know I promised, but —. But you lied to me, I said. No, I didn't —. Yes, you did. No —. Yes, Joyce. Yes, you did!

All right, she said, so I broke my word, but I would never lie to you. Then I turned to look at her like, *you can't be serious.* I didn't lie, I just didn't stick to the letter of our agreement, she said. The letter of our agreement? Joyce, our *agreement* is what's known as a promise, and when you give me your word, I expect you to keep it, I said, feeling my cheeks flush. Besides which, if you were half as cute as you think you are, *you'd* be going out with the guy, not me. Ouch, she said, genuinely stunned.

I shouldn't have said that. I knew I shouldn't have said that, which is why I know better than to speak in anger. It's dangerous, and she knows that — she knows I have a temper, and the best thing to do is leave me alone. She looked so stunned, and then, finally, she said, Oh. So *you are* going out with him? Joyce, I said, are you stoned? I mean, obviously she was, but I was so angry, it hadn't occurred to me until that moment. What, you think I could spend two hours at a barbecue with a bunch of strangers without a big fat fatty? she said, lips flapping as she burst out laughing again. I said, Joyce, this isn't funny, and she said, No, actually, Bob, it's very funny, you just aren't laughing yet — keep up, will you?

I started walking again, leaving her right where she stood. So as I was saying, she said, yelling after me, my thinking went something like this: One . . . Bob, are you listening? I said, Joyce, even if I weren't listening, I couldn't help hearing you, all right? All right, then, she said. One, I think Paul seems like a great guy. Two, I think even if he's not a great guy, he's still got a great body, in case you didn't notice. And three, she said, practically shouting for all the neighbors and neighboring counties to hear, I don't think you've had sex with a man *this millennium.*

I turned around. That's low, I said. And, last but not least, she said, walking toward me, then kicking out her right leg and shaking her foot, freeing a pebble from her sandal, look on the bright side: if things don't work out between you two, he lives two hours upstate, so you'll never have to see or speak to the guy ever again. In other words, she said, continuing to walk, you're perfect for each other.

You don't stop, do you? I said. Beautiful night, isn't it? she said. I mean, don't you . . . don't you just love all the trees up here, seeing everything in bloom, she says, leaning over and removing her shoes, before looking up. Seriously, everything's just so, so lush and green and . . . *green*, she said, and I couldn't help laughing. I turned around to find her standing in the middle of the road, framed by an amphitheater of trees, both sandals dangling from one finger, like the catch of the day.

Then she looked up to the heavens and she belted it out, *Oh Lord, won't you buy me a Mercedes-Benz? My friends all drive Porsches, I must make amends. Worked hard all my lifetime, no help from my friends. So Lord, won't you buy me a Mercedes-Benz?*

I was actually moved. I don't know why, really, maybe just the earnestness of her voice, but still. It took me a moment to recover, then I realized . . . Wait a minute, Joyce? You do, I said, but you do own a Mercedes, then she stopped and smiled: Why, yes, I do, she said as she carefully walked toward me, barefoot in the dirt. And I hate to be the one to tell you, Bob . . . but there is a God.

Lisa

IT'S FUNNY, YOU KNOW. I mean, Friday morning, I woke up, and . . . and I got up. I went to yoga. I took Lee to meet Kate for lunch; we went for a manicure-pedicure, and then I just had to press my luck, stopping by Whole Foods. So I walk in, grab a basket, and then I hear this voice: Lisa Barrett, is that you?

I knew who it was, immediately — it was Greg. And the truth is I'd always hoped he'd just disappear, drop off the face of the planet. Take his genius with him, and never be seen or heard from ever again. I heard he was in and out of rehab for a few years, but I never called, never wrote, because I didn't owe him anything, as far as I was concerned, certainly not compassion. Besides which, I'd met Will. And he wanted me. And I wanted — I just wanted.

Seriously, I said, looking up at her: people disappear every day, why not Greg? Who disappeared? she said. I did, I said. I disappeared. When I married Will, I said, answering her next question before she had a chance to ask. So why did I marry him? I said. Because . . . I mean, I'm hardly the first woman to meet the wrong man at the right time. And when we met, everything I had, everything I'd worked for had just burned to the ground — Greg, my job, everything. And Will offered me a ticket out — first class, even. Then I realized something about myself I'd long suspected and denied, hidden in my Mohawks and my piercings, which was that I like first class. I do. Some punk, huh?

So when I heard a voice calling my name, when I heard his voice say, Lisa Barrett, is that you?, the first thing I could think to say was no. No: not anymore.

Joyce

COME ON, it was a joke — I was just joking, Christ. The fact that she happens to be desperate is sheer coincidence. What matters is that I knew Paul was right for her the first time I laid eyes on the guy. Look: I just want to see her happy. Honestly, that's all I want. Oh, all right . . . so I wanted to see her squirm a bit, too. But it's for her own good, trust me.

So I told her to lighten up. I said, Sing! Come on, Bobbie, sing! But she just kept walking in a huff. So I sat down and I said, Hey, Bob? Hey, Bobbie — yo! *What?* she shouted. Don't . . . don't you just love the leaves? I said. Don't you just love how they make like a . . . a — what would you call that? Joyce, she snapped, why don't we talk about this when you're sober? But what fun would that be? I said.

Seriously, Bob, what would you call that, a screen? A scrim, what? You know — that thing they do when you look up, and it's all these leaves . . . everywhere? *Joyce,* she screamed, turning around. You're high! No, I'm not, I said, waving her off: I am so fucking high, Bob, you have no idea — come! Join me, my friend, and we shall dance and sing our merry songs. Then I fell over, laughing, in the middle of the road.

Hey! Hey, Bobbie . . . you know what we should do? We should start a band — with Paul. We'll be just like Peter, Paul, and Mary, ex-cept we'll be Bobbie, Paul, and Joyce — we'll call ourselves the Mary Pranksters, you get it? I said, trying to stand, but I was laughing so hard, I had to sit down again, watching as Bobbie turned to look at me.

J, why can't you ever be this nice when you're sober? she said. No, really, I said, come on . . . let's sing, Bobbie! *Sing! Sing through the mouth of your wounds* . . . You know who said that, Bob? Bob, know who? Guess, I said, but she kept walking. No?

Then I'll give you a hint, okay? Think of the most famous, the *most famous* French artist I've ever slept with, I said, but still no answer. Oh, *all right* . . . Jean Cocteau, that's who! I mean, seriously, who the hell but a Frenchman would have a wound with a mouth on it, you know? Joyce, you did not sleep with Jean Cocteau, she hissed. Tech-nically, no . . . but — *but,* I said, holding up my finger, I did sleep with someone who slept with someone who slept with Cocteau, okay? Thus, by the transitive property of Allen Ginsberg, I did sleep with Jean Cocteau, ha! Honestly, Bob, why let a little thing like death stop you from fucking someone famous, know what I mean? And let me tell you something else — let me tell you . . . Jean Cocteau was the best lay I *ever* had.

New York Magazine

JOYCE KESSLER HAS *a burning question. "Tell me something," says one of New York's most successful and controversial art dealers, meet-ing me at the front door of her sleek Chelsea gallery, wearing a black Prada satin dress and five-inch rhinestone-studded Louboutin heels. "Tell me," she repeats, lightly tugging at the J. Mendel leopard fur coat draped over her shoulders, her money-green eyes coolly looking me up and down: "You ever had sex in a public toilet?"*

Finding myself at a loss for words and more than a little excited, which would be to my wife's chagrin, Kessler, in her habitual cut-to-the-chase-already-chop-chop impatience, responds, "Well, then. Let me show you what you've been missing," she says, handing me a battered orange hard hat. "Welcome to the Toilet Gallery," she says, opening the door, before turning back and adding, with a sexily sharp tone: "Watch your step."

So begins our tour of the work site that will become the next installation in an ongoing series of commissions at the Joyce Kessler Gallery, called, simply, Public Urinals. It's hardly your usual tour. Three times a year, Kessler commissions a different artist to remodel the bathrooms of her gallery, giving the artist carte blanche and complete artistic freedom.

Asked where she got the idea for the commission, Kessler warns, "I said watch it," nodding at an I-beam on the floor. "First of all, let me just say it kills me — I mean, it just kills me — when I hear people say they don't know about art, not to mention the number of people in the art world who encourage this view. Because everyone knows about art," Kessler says, her icy eyes boring holes in my soul, "and I do mean everyone.

"But first," she continues, "first, you have to forget what you're told — light, form, perspective, composition — forget everything you were ever taught in Art History 101, because it's bullshit, okay. Here's all the art history you need: pissing, shitting, and fucking. That's life and death and art in a nutshell, right there." As we're leaving the site, a workman steps out of a Porta Potti, startled to find Kessler standing there, then she turns. "I'm sorry, what terrible manners I have. Coffee?" she asks, as we return to the main gallery, heading to her office. I'm transfixed, hardly able to walk straight.

"It's true," she says, removing her hard hat, fluffing her Sally Hershberger bob, taking a seat at her desk. "Whether you admit it or not, we're all obsessed with pissing, shitting, and fucking, in no particular order. Duchamp knew this; John Waters knows this — all the great artists of the twentieth century." As it happens, Waters, another close personal friend of Kessler's, was the first artist to accept her commission. Entitled The Fourth Type of Sex, *the project was a phenomenal success.*

While fans cheered, "Joie de vile!," others charged: repugnant, nauseating, grotesque, an abomination. "And? Since when are vulgarity and art mutually exclusive? I mean, personally, I've always found death an incredible aphrodisiac," Kessler shrugs. Needless to say, countless con-

84

servative organizations called for a boycott of Waters's installation.
Which, of course, only increased the exhibition's profile, both nation-
ally and internationally. "Say it," Kessler says, "go on, say it: the word is
salesman. I am a salesman. And a damn good one, if I do say so myself.
Ask my buyers if you don't believe me. Or, better yet, ask my artists. I
like to think I've done as well by them as they've done by me."

Of course, Kessler's populist views have ruffled more than a few
feathers in the art world. Renown and reviled, alternately described as
outrageous, outspoken, and/or simply offensive, in the past few years
Kessler, in those aforementioned Louboutin heels (she has more than
400 pairs), has taken some rather unorthodox approaches to increas-
ing the foot traffic in her gallery. Her critics claim Kessler is more inter-
ested in showmanship than in the artistic merit of the work she exhib-
its. "Oh, yeah? Two questions: First and foremost, who the fuck do they
think they are, these so-called critics? Secondly, where, exactly, do these
all-knowing cultural arbiters draw the line? And lastly, like I could give
a flying fuck what they say — or what anyone thinks.

"Then again, truth be told, I love hearing what people have to say
about me — the good, the bad, and the ugly. I do. I enjoy the criticism,
the envy, the bile, and, at this very moment, I love the thought of cer-
tain people seething when they read this article. It's all grist for the mill,"
Kessler says. "I mean, you never know when or where inspiration will
come from, right?"

Right.

Lisa

A FEW MONTHS AGO, we were lying in bed one Saturday morning and I started flipping through the *Times*, when the Arts section
caught my eye, and I suddenly felt this chill, before I even registered
the image on the top fold. The headline read, THE PAINTING IS
DEAD! LONG LIVE THE PAINTING! And then I knew — I knew
in my gut, then I looked at the picture and dropped the paper, like
pulling my hand from a flame. It was Greg. He'd gotten the cover of
New York magazine the week before, but I'd managed to avoid it because I don't subscribe. But the *Times* . . . I didn't see that coming,

and between his picture and the headline, I couldn't help remembering day I walked out on him.

The last thing I did before closing the door behind me was to walk up to that chipped marble mantel for the last time, and then I held a knife to the Queen's throat and said, I could kill you, you know? Then I pressed the switchblade to her neck, placing my ear to her lips, listening to her beg, as the taut silk began to screech — faintly, but still screeching under the pressure of my body weight. Then I debated, long and hard, because it would feel so good to tear her to pieces . . . Even now, what I wouldn't give to have seen Greg's face, walking through that door.

Art? Honestly, it makes me sick to my stomach to hear her talk about art. Until I came along, Joyce Kessler was well on her way to being just another big-time has-been — I gave her Gavin, I gave her Tomiko, Mila, *Greg* . . . I'm sorry, but I saved her fat fucking ass. So I'm sitting there, in bed, legs crossed, having an all-out psychic brawl, but of course the whole time, Will's completely oblivious to my vengeful apoplectic trance. Oh, he's just reading Sports or Real Estate or whatever, and then he says, So what do you want to do today, babe? And I said, *Kill.*

Not really, but I should have. Would've been honest, at least. Two minutes later, when my phone rang, I knew it was Kate. Hold on, I said, getting out of bed and walking into the other room. You want some more coffee? I asked Will, nonchalantly holding my hand over the receiver. I'm fine, thanks, he said, nodding.

Hey, I said, reaching the kitchen. Don't read it, she said. I know, I said. No, you don't know, she said. You want to take a walk? Sure, I said, meet you in an hour? See you then, she said, hanging up. Naturally, it took me closer to an hour and a half to get the baby and myself ready, but anyhow. I saw her from the distance, and she stood there, wincing sympathetically. Oh, babe, she said. I know, I said, maneuvering the stroller and taking a seat beside her. But did you see the pictures? I whined, agonizingly. I saw, she said, sighing.

Ugh, and the way they posed him, with his arms crossed, wearing his paint-speckled short-sleeved shirt, looking all machismo, Malone Pictured in His Upstate Studio, I said, drawing the blade and *hfpht,* falling on my sword. Oh, please, I said. Just because the guy pisses in a socialite's fireplace doesn't make him Jackson fucking Pollock, you know? Christ, what's next? A GAP ad? Kate made a face. What? I said.

Should I break it to you now? she said. *He's in a GAP ad?* I gasped. Worse, she said. Let's have it, I said. He's engaged, she said. Oh, I said, feeling my heart ripped out—but why? Why? I left him—I left his sorry ass. Well, I said, that's not surprising. To a model, she said. Oh, I said, trying to get a foothold before being knocked over by a wave of anger. Jesus, I said, since when did he become such a famous-painter cliché? Why are you making that face? I said, and Kate said, She's a Victoria's Secret model. No, I said. Yes, she said. *No.* I'm sorry, she said. Don't be sorry for me, I said, be sorry for him. I mean, what a fucking loser, I said, shell-shocked.

After everything I did for him, I still can't believe he got into bed with that woman—. You don't think they slept together, do you? Kate said. I wouldn't put it past either one of them, I said. Well, if it's true, that would be the Mother Teresa of charity fucks, she said, laughing, and I said, For Greg or for Joyce, you mean? Ouch, she said, laughing. I still got it, I said. Five months without sleep, and I still got it, baby. That's right, she said, you do. Now let it go. I'll tell you what it says, but don't read the *Times,* okay? And whatever you do, do not read that *New York* story; trust me, it'll just upset you, she said.

Why? Does it mention me? I asked, equally fearful and hopeful. No . . . no, not really, she said. Kate, no, or not really? No, she said. You don't sound so sure, I said, even though she did. One comment, she said. Well, not really a comment, more like a mention—. What, I don't even rate a full comment? Never mind, I said, let's have it. He mentions a girlfriend, she said. It says he went on a bender after he broke up with a girlfriend and then he just checked out, basically. A girlfriend, I repeated. That's what he called me, a girlfriend? Yes, she said, wincing sympathetically.

Okay, I said. First of all . . . first, I'm not *a,* I'm *the.* I am *THE* girlfriend. Secondly, Greg checked out long, long before I left him, which is why I left him—get the order there? Furthermore, we didn't break up: I dumped his ass. And lastly, *fuck that, man.* I mean, how insulting is that, a girlfriend? Try, the-love-of-his-life-who-finally-bailed-after-years-of-his-fucking-bullshit girlfriend. Ugh, I said, doubling over. Well, who knows, maybe it's not even you, she said, trying not to grin. Oh, piss off — all of you can just piss and fuck off, already. Look, she said, taking my arm, all I'm saying is don't vivisect the messenger, here, okay. But I just sat there.

Did it say I was the one who gave him his first break? Did it say I was the one who spent two and a half years begging Joyce to look at his work? Did it say I supported him while he spent his days shooting up? Maybe that part got cut, she said. Oh, but the fact that his adolescent girlfriend is a Victoria's Secret model found its way in? Look on the bright side, she said. Which is what? I said, crawling in my skin, so annoyed I got short with Kate. You still have a lot of his work, right? He's famous now, and you could always sell it, you know, she said. Or burn it, I said, cheered, envisioning a Technicolor pyre.

By the way, Leese, you're leaking, she said, looking at my chest. Ah, shit, I said. When it rains, it leaks, Kate said, laughing. I shifted Lee, lying him back. Lunch is served, I said, unsnapping my bra. Listen, she said, just don't read it, ever. Kate, I'm a new mother; I'm not deaf, okay? I said, irritated. Then let it go, already, she said. But I couldn't — I can't — because the truth is that it's all I have left of him: my rage.

Sure enough, two months later, I went home, Friday, dropped the groceries on the counter, handed the baby off, and I looked up the *New York* story online. Read every last word, too, and then I had to lie down because I thought I was going to retch. You know . . . I never imagined I'd feel so jealous the day the rest of the world finally recognized the talent I'd always seen. Or so alone.

It was the first time in my life I had something like a narcoleptic fit. But just as I was falling asleep, my phone rang. Hello? I said, sitting up in bed, ready to forgive him for everything. I was sure it was Greg: I was so certain it was him, calling to say . . . to say he still loves me. That he'd always loved me, and now he knew we had to be together . . . I don't know what — anything. Even just to hear him say my name again.

But it was a woman's voice. Lisa Soutar? she said. Yes? I said. This is Donna from Dr. Myers's office. Yes, I said, worrying that my tests had been mixed up and maybe there was a problem, maybe I had—. She said, Your sister is here, and she gave us your number, and I said, Okay . . .

Do you think you could come and pick her up? she said. What —what's wrong? I said, and she said, Seems something has upset her stomach. Her stomach? I said, thinking out loud. If you can't make it, we'll call her husband. No—no—but it's going to take me at least half an hour to get there, I said. Is that all right, or . . . ? Yes, she said, that's fine, so long as we know someone's coming.

All right, I said. I'll get there as soon as possible. You have our address? she said. Yes, Warren Street, I said, I'm a regular patient. No, the Lexington office, she said, and I shook my head, thinking, *Lexington? What's she doing at Dr. Myers's Lexington office? Is that why she called me to get a referral for her friend?* I said, I'm sorry, can you—can you hold on a second, sorry . . .

Bobbie

I'M SO SORE today for some reason, I said, sitting back down at the table, Saturday, and Joyce said, Careful: sex is dangerous at your age. And I shot her a look. Believe it or not, Doc, heart attack is the number-one killer of women in the United States today, she said. Which I can easily explain: after years of searching for a man who can make you come, once you find him, it's so shocking, an orgasm's liable to kill you, she said.

The waiter came to take our order: What can I get you ladies? And Joyce said, Bob, you know what you're having? No, I said, I need a minute, go ahead. All right, she said, pointing back and forth between Dela and herself: We're going to share an order of cornmeal pancakes and the huevos rancheros—. None for me, Del said, and Joyce looked at her. I'm hungover, Dela said, and Joyce said, Then eggs are exactly what you need. Huevos and the pancakes, Joyce said, handing the waiter her menu.

Lisa

WILL MADE DINNER on our first date. Do you have any brothers or sisters? he asked, pulling a roast out of the oven. Whoa, I said, surprised. Not bad, huh? he said. So, siblings — yes, no? You know, honestly, I said, leaning against the counter in a kitchen the size of my entire apartment, with glass in hand, I've got to get up early tomorrow, so let's just cut to the chase. If you want to have sex, let's have sex. But I really hate small talk, all right?

So you aren't going to ask if I have any siblings? he said, and I just looked at him. I have a sister, I said. What's her name? he said. Lynne, I said. Older or younger? Much older, I said. How much? Ten years, I said. Are you two close? he asked, removing his mitts. Not if we can help it, I said. And what does your sister do? he asked, cutting a slice of roast and offering it to me. She makes pillows, I said, taking the meat in my fingers. Last question, I said, chewing. And, last question: describe her, he said. Describe her? I said, and I had it, but then I hesitated. Go on: let's hear, he said.

I said, You know the newsstand on St. Mark's, across from Cooper Union? Yeah? he said. I spent years there, just reading magazines, I said. And when I was about sixteen, seventeen, one month, Morrissey was on the cover of *SPIN* — you've heard of *SPIN*, right? Listen, he said, just because I work on Wall Street doesn't necessarily mean I'm culturally illiterate, and I said, Yeah, you keep telling yourself that, sweetheart.

Anyhow, I used to read that magazine cover to cover, every month — right before I thumbed my nose at it, of course. The month after Morrissey's cover story, a reader wrote a letter to the editor that said, and I quote: *What Morrissey needs is a cheeseburger and a good fuck — and not necessarily in that order.* I read that, standing at the newsstand at three in the morning, and then I busted out laughing, thinking, *Ohmygod, that's Lynne!* That's Lynne to a T — just hold the cheeseburger, I said, finishing my wine. Now, I said, setting the glass on the counter. It's getting kinda late, don't you think?

He looked at me — he really looked at me — then he said, Lisa, why

90

are you so mean? I wasn't expecting that, I wasn't expecting that at all. I mean, I was hoping to get nailed, but that wasn't quite what I had in mind. I have to say, it was a nice surprise, but in my usual fashion, I didn't answer. All I said was, Since when do I need a reason?

Lynne

I SUPPOSE IT was about two, by then, Friday morning, and at first, I thought maybe I should've tried drinking them with a beer or something alcoholic, because I didn't feel anything for the longest time, really . . . Just sort of warm and tingly in my legs, like a . . . it was like a . . . a what do you call it? A whirlpool — that's it — it was like a whirlpool in my veins. So I sat up and I took a good look around, and then I finally realized, *Well, here's the problem, right here: I'm dying, you see. No, really, I'm dying here. And it's not just — it's not just the guest bedroom, either; it's everything — it's this house, and my marriage, and my, my kids . . .*

But there I am, day after day, strolling the aisles of ShopRite, acting as though everything's just peachy, and I'm great, and we're great, oh, we're doing *just great,* I say, smiling and nodding my head like some, some — I don't know what, really. Like some queen of the parade or something. No, really, I run into someone every day at the grocery store or in town, if it's not the wife of one of the guys from work, or the mother of one of Lance's old school friends — I mean, *whoever,* you know? And that's what I say, every time: Oh, we're *just great,* thanks. And you, Linda? And you, Barb? How are you?

Well, Tuesday night, who do I run into but Delphine Schroeder, my old boss's wife, whom I haven't seen in ages, now that she and Raymond spend half their year in Florida. Anyhow, Delphine hasn't seen Jordan in six years, at least, so she remembers her as standing about waist-high, you know. Well, naturally, the first thing Delphine says is, How is that beautiful girl of yours? How's Jordan? she said, squeezing my forearm. Oh, she's doing great, I said. For a teenager, I added, winking. And at that moment, I heard something so phony and shrill, it sent a chill down my back . . . My mother.

91

Adela

CALM, COOL, and collected, that's my mom all right, until you really get to know her. Because when she gets angry, she won't speak to you, she won't look at you. If you get anywhere close to her, she walks to the opposite side of the room — like she can't even stand to be in the same room with you, to breathe the same air — like you're a piece of shit. And you will never believe that more about yourself than at the moment when you reach to touch her and she flinches in disgust.

No, I told him she could quit speaking to me — just like that: *snap.* I'm not sure it's even conscious, but still, my mom gets so angry, she shuts off. I said, Cross a line, and she'll never speak to you again. I'll be here, he said, and I looked at him: thanks.

So when she told me to leave — when she kicked me out — I bit my lip, thinking, *Unfuckingbelievable.* I mean, she always said, be brave, because you're my daughter, and you can do anything. I just didn't realized until now that there was a catch: you're my daughter, and you can do anything — so long as I agree.

Jordan

I LOVE HOW everyone thinks she's like so perfect, you know? I mean, I love how everyone's always like, *Oh, Jordan, your mom's so pretty. Oh, Jordan, your mom's so sweet, your mom's so . . .* And I just want to say, Full of shit? Seriously, anyone who tries to be as perfect as my mother tries to be, it's just a sign of how fucked up they really are, okay.

I mean, it's like all the girls at school who say, Oh, I'm going to be a psychology major and become a child psychologist, and I'm just like, ohmygod. Because they're like the most fucked-up girls in the entire school, it scares me — I mean, it *truly scares me* to think of them counseling anyone. Seriously, I wouldn't trust them with my dog, okay?

Anyhow, it's like this one time, I was trying to tell her something in the car, on the way home, and I was like, So like Tracy's mother's sister comes over to me —, and Mom goes, Tracy's aunt, you mean. The word is *aunt,* honey. Words: use your words. Then she looks both ways, and she's just like, Remember, Jordan, God gave us words so we wouldn't have to sound like rednecks, and I just looked at her, like, how do you do that? After she turned onto the highway, she looked at me, waiting, and she's like, Go on. Tracy's aunt came over . . . ? But I just turned and looked out the window, because I was just like, yeah, and God gave us cities so we wouldn't have to live in the fucking sticks with our mothers all our lives, either. I mean, seriously, why can't she just *listen* to me?

Bobbie

HE DID CALL. As a matter of fact, Paul called seven times before I finally agreed to meet him for a drink, figuring I'd get it over with because it's the same old story. What I mean is, no matter how old you get, it's the same damn thing, every time. You meet someone. You go out for a drink. You ask them about themselves, make small talk; if you're interested, you try to sound funny and clever and sexy . . . That much doesn't change, whether you're twenty-five or fifty. The only difference is that instead of asking if their parents are still married, you ask if they're still alive.

In any case, we were sitting at the end of the bar when Paul turned and said, Can I ask you something? May I, I said. Pardon me, he said. May I ask you something? Of course you may, I said, smiling sweetly. What would you like to ask me? Why wouldn't you go out with me? he said, and I started laughing. Classic: let's just put our ego on the table right now: How could I possibly turn you down? Honestly? I said. I don't like the sound of that, he said, but yes, honestly.

Well, then. Honestly, I'm not attracted to you, I said. Physically? he said, taken aback. And he almost fell off his stool before regaining enough composure to say, Oh, bullshit . . . you didn't find me physically attractive — that's good, and I grinned, staring straight ahead. You're funny, he said, I like that in a funny woman. You've been hanging out with Joyce too much, I said. I guess you know all her lines, huh? he said. A few, I said, but that's not her line; it's Michael's old line, actually. Oh, he said, raising his eyebrows.

I said, You're quite a fan, I see, and he said, I love Joyce. Oh, do you? I said, laughing. Truly, he said, she's got a foul mouth, a dirty mind, and she always says what she thinks — what's not to love? The one thing she doesn't talk about, he said, is her marriage. No, I said, but no one knows what goes on in someone else's marriage. Ain't that the truth, he said. What was she like, your ex-wife? I asked, then I immediately regretted asking: I'm sorry, it's none of my business.

No, it's fine, it's . . . it's like you said. No one knows what goes on in someone else's marriage. I'd venture to say most people don't know what's going on in their own — at least I didn't, he said, shrugging. How's that for a start? he asked, and I looked at him. What's that look? he asked, and I shook my head. You surprise me, that's all, I said, and he said, More than just a pretty face, huh? Anyhow, I said, ignoring him, Joyce was my cool, arty, rocker-chick girlfriend, and I was her nerdy, straight-A friend. We made each other look good, in other words, I said, laughing. What are friends for, he said.

Jordan

SO THE NEXT TIME we worked together after he gave me a ride home, Misha kept saying hi every time he walked by, but I kept giving him the cold shoulder because I was just like . . . I don't know, I was just annoyed. I mean, I was just like, you don't know me, you don't know anything about me, you know? So finally he walks up to me and he goes, Jordan, can I talk to you a second? So I'm like, Sure, and then he walks me over to the exit, and at first, I thought he was going to take me outside and yell at me about my bad attitude.

Then he goes, I want you to take a look at something, and he stares at that picture that's hung by the exit, over by the manager's office. I'd never asked about it, but someone had blow up this picture of our manager, Richard, and this tall middle-aged woman with this gray horse face standing in front of this Doritos display. I mean, Richard's smiling, looking all, like, fat and tickled pink that we had a winner in our store, and the woman's holding up a bag of Doritos like it's some trophy, right, except she's not smiling.

94

I mean, I don't know what the story is, but I always ignored it when I was walking out because it's just so sad. Like it reminds me of those half-finished paint-by-numbers you see at Goodwill, except it's like somebody's half-finished paint-by-numbers life, and you *know* no one's ever going to buy it, either, and that's why she's not smiling—I think she knew that, standing there. Of course if my mom saw it, all she'd say is like, Would you look at that frame? *Really.*

Anyhow, we're just staring at the picture, right, and then Misha goes, Jordan, I'm sorry if I was harsh the other night. It was a long day, and sometimes I get a little short when I'm tired. And I was just like, Thanks, hoping he'd drop it, but then he goes, I just hate to see people being stupid about these things, you know? And I know he meant well, but then again, it's like I didn't appreciate being called stupid, you know. So I was like, Yeah, Misha, and look where your brains got you. Oh, he said, smiling and nodding, putting one hand across his gut. Then he goes, So that's how it's going to be, huh? But I didn't say anything, so finally, he's like, Well, all right, and then he just turned and walked away.

That was it: he went back to his office, and I walked back to the register. But it was different after that; it was just . . . different. And then, a couple of days later, when I was leaving work, Misha goes, he calls after me and he goes, Hey, Jordan? So I was just like, Yeah? And he goes, It's his loss . . . I mean, right in front of everybody, he said that to me—it's his loss. So I just stood there—I couldn't even look at him because that's all I wanted—god, I just wanted someone to think I was worth coming back for, you know?

After that, I started working until close on Fridays so I could ask Misha for a ride home. I mean, it wasn't a big deal—all we'd do was sit in Misha's car, at the end of our road, eating Wendy's or whatever, talking about the people at work. Misha had some hilarious stories about our manager—like the time Richard asked Misha if he could rap . . . I couldn't stop laughing when he told me that. But seriously, that's all we did, really. I mean, it was just nice to have someone to talk to, you know?

Joyce

SO I WAITED, and waited, and waited. And every hour that Michael didn't call me back, I got angrier and angrier. So I kept trying Sonja, but every time she answered, I just wanted to go off on Michael and tell her what an utter and complete bastard he was to leave me hanging like that, but of course we don't discuss Michael. The reason being that she thinks I gave up — my own mother thinks I gave up on my marriage. Not just that I quit, but that I quit because my career was more important to me than my marriage.

Also: keep in mind, this is coming from the woman who told me my whole life, Work hard, Joyce: you've got your father's body. So I did; I worked my ass off to get where I am. I mean, I worked, Michael worked — our careers were extremely important to us, no apologies necessary. Seriously, two years before we split, when he finally moved out to L.A., we both knew the score. I knew he needed to be there — he knew I needed to be here — there was no argument. In fact, it was the only thing we didn't argue about, really.

Still, no matter what Sonja thinks, I did care about my family, and there was nothing more important to me than our son — even if that meant staying married to his father. Finally, in a last-ditch effort, I took two weeks off work — which, at the time, was practically my entire year's vacation, but anyhow. I took two weeks off in order to fly out to try and save my marriage, and four days later, I'm sitting on a plane, headed back to New York, knocked up, with a cast on my right ankle. Which is a long story — well, not the knocked-up part, that was a very short story, I'm afraid — the broken ankle, I mean.

But basically, I shipped Benjamin off to Camp Nana for a few days so the two of us could be alone, and I spent the whole day preparing this romantic surprise dinner, and then Michael didn't come home until after midnight. Didn't even bother to call, either. And I'm nobody's fool; I knew something was going on; I'd known for months. But my attitude was like, Look: you can fool around, or you can not call, but you can't fool around *and* not call — no fucking way.

So when he finally walked into the dining room, I threw my shoe at him — five-inch wooden platform sandals, and I just hurled the fucker at his head. Then I tripped, landing. Next thing I know, it's two a.m. and I'm in the emergency room, getting my ankle put in a cast.

Next morning, all of four hours later, I hopped into the bathroom, lifted the lid, and took a seat on the toilet. Michael was standing in front of the mirror, having just stepped out of the shower and dried his hair, so it was all mussed on his head — well, what hair he had left. He didn't say anything, either, he was just leaning forward, cocking his chin at the mirror, pursing his lips one way and the other, debating whether or not to shave, then I came out with it. I mean, I knew — I *knew* the answer, but I just had to say the words: Michael, is there someone else?

Then he looked at me, caught completely off guard — looked just like Benjamin, too, I'll never forget that. He looked exactly like Benjamin, whenever I'd bust him for something; you could see it in his eyes — you could see the kid considering every angle, every possible lie he could tell and what the odds were of escape, before realizing there was none. And then Michael said, I'm sorry, in a tone that was so sincere, that said he knew he was wrong, but despite everything, he'd never meant to hurt me — truly.

I'm sorry, he said, and I just shook my head no, no . . . like, don't be, you know? I mean I knew; I asked; he had the decency to tell me the truth; and aside from being wrong, what more did I want? But what I don't understand is why we have to ask the question, why must we say the words when we already know the answer? More important, when are they going to come up with the drugs to fix that problem? *Fuck.*

So I reached for the toilet paper — I couldn't believe how calm I was. In fact, I felt so calm, I didn't stop peeing the whole time. It was just like, please, I'm Joyce Kessler: when my husband tells me he's having an affair, I don't even break a stream. Seriously, at that moment, all I could think was, *Well, at least he's an honest cheat, right?*

So I sat there, looking at us, Michael looming so prominently, with that thick white terry-cloth towel wrapped around his tan neck, and me, sitting fifteen feet behind him, with my chin propped in my right hand. Just this sad little figure hunched over the john in the corner of

97

the mirror, wearing this absurd silk nightie I'd actually worn to bed. Purely out of spite, of course, but for whom, I don't know.

I mean, knowing it might be one of our last nights together, I'd actually spent yet another day of my vacation shopping for this sexy little slip, thinking: *If this is it, then this* — this *is how I want to be remembered.* I'd actually imagined myself splayed across satin sheets like some Jewish Jean Harlow, and there I was, parked on the pot, coon-eyed, wearing this . . . this turquoise silk and black-lace number, too dazed to bother pulling the left strap back over my shoulder. God, the whole scene was so absurd.

You want some help? he asked, rousing me from my pathetic reverie, and seeing that he wasn't sure whether or not he was allowed to touch me, I said, Yes. Which is how I came to find myself carried like an injured bride by my naked, adulterous husband, a man whom I suddenly missed so much, I almost wept in his arms.

I mean, I was so tired, and it had been ugly for so long — every day had become such a battle, I'd forgotten how much I loved him once, and probably still did, deep down. Honestly, for a few years there, we were just sickening, we were so in love. And the thing is, I didn't feel bad for me, and I didn't feel bad for Michael, I felt bad for *those* people, the people we once were. Because they deserved so much better than we gave them. And for our son, of course . . . poor Benjamin.

So Michael got me all set up with the remote controls and the landline and my cell phone, then he brought me a tray with coffee and juice and toast and a fresh bottle of Percocet, and made sure I was comfortable and that I had enough pillows . . . Anything else? he asked, placing his hand on the back of my head, and I shook my head no. I'm fine, I said, smiling, looking up at him. Then he kissed me very tenderly — at least that's what I thought, when he leaned over to kiss my neck, I thought, *How tender.* But that was it.

And when it stopped there — when he concluded the tender kiss with a gentle but firm squeeze of my shoulder — I realized it wasn't tenderness; it was pity. And it came as such a surprise that he'd already opened the garage door by the time I realized what was really going on, and I thought, *Wait a second — wait one fucking minute . . . that's it?*

So I sat up, as it finally dawns on me: he's not having an affair. What I mean is this isn't one of those things that we'll just have to get through together, no. We aren't getting through this — we aren't anything — because there is no more *we*. I'm sitting there, looking at a tray of buttered walnut-raisin bread, listening to Katie Couric, thinking, *Ohmygod, he's . . . he's in love with this woman.* And the real kicker is that he's not leaving me for her, no, because he's already left — he's gone.

It was such a one-two punch that for the first time in a decade, I couldn't even insult my own husband. Even worse, for the first time in my life, I was speechless. Which quickly passed, but still. A moment later, hearing his engine turn over, I got up, hopped over to the window, opened the sliding-glass door, and managed to hop up on the balcony. Then, just as he pulled out, right beneath the balcony, I let him have it. *Michael!* I shouted, right on top of his head.

So he looked up, startled, and I said, What was that? What the hell was that, a pity peck? That's all I get — eleven years together and you can't even do me the kindness of a proper pity fuck? You, you —. And then, right on cue, he revved the engine, censoring the worst of it, before turning his head, looking behind him, and backing down the long drive. I swear, if I could've hopped fast enough, I would've grabbed the other platform heel out of the closet and hurled it like a brick at the hood of his shiny fucking Maserati. But there was no way — hop? Christ, I couldn't move.

Watching him back down the drive, I ran the numbers. Because I was nine weeks pregnant, give or take, which would've been his last trip to New York. The trip he cut short the morning after he arrived, claiming there was some sort of emergency and he had to fly back, jumping like my bed was on fire. You know what else? I screamed at him. That was the most pitiful pity fuck I ever had! And then, the coup de grace: having pulled into the street, he corrected the wheel before honking once and throwing me a wave of the hand, then disappeared from sight.

There I was, in my ridiculous negligee, leaning over the balcony rail, with my saggy tits sagging and my ass hanging out for all of Greater Los Angeles to see, while the neighbor's silver-haired Mexican gardener continued pruning the shrubs, pretending he hadn't seen a thing. I remember it was freezing, too — fifty degrees, maybe, but I couldn't go inside yet. I kept thinking: *Come back, Michael . . . tell me this isn't really happening — tell me this isn't how you want to end it, at least.* It was so pitiful, too, because I knew he wasn't coming back — I knew it in my bones, and I pleaded anyway.

I don't know how long I stood there, really. I mean, it was your typically stupid, sunshiny fall day in Los Angeles, but I could feel it behind me, like there was this black hole in the bedroom waiting for me, getting larger and larger by the second, feeding on my fear. Because all I could think was, *How do I do this? I don't know how to do this . . . Don't do this, Michael. Please don't leave me.* Too late.

Well. Seeing as I'd already taken the time off, when I got back to New York, Bobbie and I stayed in bed watching movies all weekend. And as luck would have it, there was a *Godfather* marathon on AMC. Just before every commercial break, they'd cut to the violins and that still of young Michael Corleone that makes me weak in the knees. Ugh, I'm telling you, Bob, every time I see that face, I just want him to throw me on the ground and fuck me like a — like a rabid dog, I said, practically growling, clenching my teeth at the TV. Bob looked up from the paper, looking at my cast, propped on the pillow at the end of the bed, and I said, Not *now* — in general, I mean, and then she calmly returned to the paper, shaking it out and turning the page. Wait, wait — here's the best part, I said, elbowing her, because it was that shot of Diane Keaton, standing in the doorway, about to stab her negligent husband with her deep, dark secret . . .

Lisa

AS FAR BACK as I can remember, all I ever wanted was to be somebody. But not just somebody, *Somebody.* I wanted people to know my name; I wanted people to see my picture and want to be me, envy me. It was this insatiable need to prove something, or to right something — both, I think. Why, I don't know, and I didn't care, so long as I made it big.

The only problem was that I never had any talent — well, not unless raw ambition is a talent. And then, one day, standing in the corner at the newsstand on St. Mark's, I came across an article on Mary Boone. It was eighty-six, eighty-seven, maybe, and I remember the article said Boone's mother died when she was young. Or maybe it was her father, I don't remember, just the part about her graduating high school by fifteen and college by eighteen. She looked so glamorous, too, with her raven hair, I decided, then and there, what I was going to do with my life: I was going to be Mary Boone.

It was such a comforting thought, I returned every day, sometimes twice a day for a month, grabbing another copy of *Vanity Fair* and holing up at the back of the newsstand. I even told people that about myself sometimes, plagiarizing her story for my own. At least the part about the dead mother, and graduating high school at fifteen, becoming an art history major. The best part was that some of it was true.

Lynne

A WEEK AFTER I spoke to Lisa, I called the school to tell them Jordan would be out sick for the day, and we drove down to the city. We both met with Dr. Myers, and then she asked me to wait in the waiting room while she examined Jordan. So I sat there, leafing through house-and-home magazines. Two weeks earlier, I would have devoured the magazine whole, but sitting there, looking at pages of pillows and chairs . . . Honestly, reading the words *window treatment* made me so sick to my stomach, I had to put the magazine down.

When Jordan returned, I stood up as the doctor spoke to the nurse. I'll see you in two weeks, Dr. Myers said, handing me a card. Thank you, I said, and then we walked out. She was a little cold, don't you think? I said, once we got into the elevator. Sorry you didn't like her, Mom, she said. I said, Jordan, I didn't say I didn't like her, I'm just saying that we could talk to someone else —. Because there's so much to talk about, she said, resting her head against the side of the elevator, and then I couldn't say anything more. Anyhow, I liked her, she said, standing up, as the elevator door opened again. I liked her a lot — and she really cares, Jordan said, as though I might not catch her insinuation. But I didn't say another word.

That night, I told Don exactly what I thought. I don't like her, I said, speaking to him from the bathroom, putting cream on my face. Why not? he said, changing channels, tiring of the news. She's just a type, I said. What type? he said. She's one of those New York women — successful, sophisticated, well-educated — but she's . . . cold. I just found her very cold. Lynne, he said, she's a doctor. I know, I said, but still, Don. *But still.*

Adela

MOM NEEDED TO BUY a bra for the dress she was wearing to dinner, so we went shopping after lunch on Thursday. Then we got in a fight in the dressing room, and I felt so bad . . . I don't know, everything started coming out. And then, afterward, we were standing on the street and I wanted to tell her when she asked what was going on, but I couldn't.

Then, when I tried to tell her about Ixnomy, of course she didn't know what I was talking about, which just made it worse. I said, Mom, sometimes you're so in your own world I almost wonder if you heard of this thing called 9/11? Dela, please, she said. And the truth is, I wanted to fight, so I said, No, seriously, I try to explain to people how shut off you are, and all I can say is that it's like you live in a cave — in the caves of New York. I mean, seriously, Mom, get a fucking life, will you? And it hurt her feelings — I could see it had. Honestly, I never speak to her like that, but then, all she said was, Dela, I'm trying, believe me . . .

Bobbie

ADELA FLEW DOWN Thursday, and we met at Japonica for a late lunch, but I could barely eat. What, are you on a diet? she asked, looking at my plate, and I looked at her: *please.* Relax, she said, waving off my nerves. You know what you need? she said. This should be good, I said, reaching for my wallet. You need some new lingerie, she said. Need, I said, smiling. Well, if you don't, I do, she said. Oh, I said, smiling. I see: *you* need some new lingerie, you mean? Want, need, same difference, she said, throwing out her hand in a dead-on impersonation of Joyce.

That reminds me, I said, pulling my coat off the back of my chair, we're meeting Joyce for brunch on Saturday. What? she said, wrinkling her nose. I said, She called and asked what we were doing, and I invited her to join us for brunch. *Mom,* she whined. What, Adela? What's wrong with that? Mom, I just wanted it to be you and me, she said.

I said, Then we'll go out alone afterward — Adela, she hasn't seen you in months now. And she says you never call her anymore, that you barely speak to her —. Mom, I'm busy, okay. I barely see my friends. I don't have time to worry about Joyce —. Del, I'm not accusing you of anything, I said, All I'm saying is that she just wants to see you.

Fine, she said, looking away. So, I said, do you need some lingerie or not? Wait a minute, she said, who's bribing whom here? You've got fifteen minutes, I said, and we walked across the street. Next thing I know, we're fighting in the dressing room, and then Dela's screaming at me on the street. She calmed down, but still. I should have known.

I wanted to stay with her, but the office called and I had to run. Don't be late, I said, as she held the taxi door for me. Eight o'clock, I said. Wait, she said, eight o'clock? Mom, I thought you said ten. I gave her a look. Don't. Be. Late, I said, closing the door, and she smiled: *Ixnay, Ommymay.*

Joyce

SONJA. MY MOTHER. That's what I call her, Sonja, *my mother,* yes. Anyhow, one of Sonja's favorite pastimes is collecting human conversation pieces that she can share with all her little bridge cronies and her biddies who lunch. For example: a second cousin whose ten-year-old identical twins both died of leukemia; an old colleague of my dad's who choked to death on a piece of gristle; a neighbor who lost one hundred pounds one year, and then gained two hundred pounds the next . . . And, last but not least, Bobbie.

For a good ten years after Bobbie graduated from medical school, my mother used to call her Mary, as in Mary Tyler Moore, she thought Bob was so pretty, such the career girl, you know. Such a pretty girl, that Mary, she'd say to my dad. Yep, she's a looker, all right, he'd say. *Not that I'm looking,* we'd say in unison, before he winked, then licked his finger and calmly turned the newspaper page. And smart as a whip, Sonja would say, as if she cared — please, she didn't care if Bobbie could *read* for chrissake. Very smart girl, Irving agreed, nodding on cue. But what a shame to be so pretty, when she's almost thirty and no husband, Sonja would sigh. And I'd just have to let it go, biting my tongue.

Well, needless to say, Sonja didn't know what to make it of it when Bobbie told her that she intended to adopt a Hispanic baby and raise the child, alone. A single mother — I think those words were spoken about as often as *cancer* in our house. Not by necessity, either, *by choice?* As far as Sonja was concerned, a baby was the last nail in Bobbie's coffin. Really, who would want her now? Thirty-one years old, with a baby — and someone else's baby, at that. And forget the racial issues, Sonja will never admit that single mothers are as capable at parenting as married mothers. She can't — it would shake her to the core.

Not to say Sonja doesn't absolutely adore Adela. Because she does. Trust me, Sonja dotes over her worse than I do. I mean, the woman will find some way of steering entire dinner conversations just so she can name-drop, telling everyone that her daughter's best friend's *adopted daughter* attends Harvard, then Sonja nods, solemnly . . . Harvard, yes: *that* Harvard. Most beautiful girl you've ever seen, too, she'll wave: ugh, such beauty.

But then, if she's in private company, she'll cock her head, adding, Single mother, too. And then all her little friends nod, knowingly, as if she had just told them Adela ran the New York Marathon with four prosthetic limbs — or none at all, she just rolled her way the twenty-six-point-two miles. I'm telling you, she's a real piece of work, that one.

Bobbie

THERE WERE TWO THINGS I made clear to my daughter from the start: one, that she was adopted, and two, my work, meaning the nature and extent of what I do for a living. Although we discussed abortion a few years after the sex talks, and I wasn't the one to bring it up — Dela heard the word on the news, which was embarrassing, obviously. But I just didn't want to push anything on her too soon.

I think she was six, at most, when we had the abortion talk. And even though I'd had the conversation thousands of times with patients, it didn't help any. Because it wasn't a patient, it was my daughter, and she was a child. Suddenly, words like *cells* and *terminate,* they made no sense, really. My explanation was accurate, but at that moment, I had no idea what I was saying, much less what I truly believed.

So your mom could have had an abortion, too? Grandma? she said, looking at me, so serious. And I said, No. Well, yes and no: abortion wasn't legal then, you see. But my other mom could have had an abortion? she said, so proud of her word; her big, adult word. Yes, I said, dreading her next question. Oh, she said. So you can only have an abortion if it's legal? Maybe she was ready for that conversation, but I immediately realized that I wasn't. When I looked in her eyes — she was trying so hard to understand me — I felt scared. Which wasn't the first time and wouldn't be the last, but it was harrowing.

I try to remember that conversation, how humbled I felt, when I speak to my patients. When in doubt, I tell the truth: I can't decide for you, I can only answer your medical questions to the best of my abilities. But faith, no. I can't answer that. And frankly, I wouldn't even if I could.

No. My daughter is the one person in this world I have ever allowed to watch me struggle with the questions she asked me then. Right or wrong, she's the only person I have ever answered to. But there are limits, of course: because I'm still her mother, yes. And I'll always have that trump card, I'm afraid.

Well, in any case, aside from my personal life, there are very few things I haven't shared with my daughter. I never hid the fact that

105

part of my job involves the termination of unwanted pregnancies: that I perform abortions, yes. I don't advertise the fact, but I have nothing to hide. There's too much hiding already. I won't be ashamed for the women; I won't be ashamed for myself: I refuse.

It's perverse, but the only shame I feel is the fact that I've never had an abortion. I might as well be a male doctor for all I know, and that shames me at times, it really does. I've heard every imaginable description, and I have no doubt I could convince my patients I know exactly what they're feeling, inside and out. But in that instance, the only way I know how to earn their trust is by having the decency, the humility not to pretend I know something I don't. I can give them that, at least.

Adela

I WAS SIX when I asked what abortion meant. Because I'd heard it on the news, and as soon as I heard it, I knew it was a bad word: people were screaming, holding up signs — something was up, right? And there were so few dirty words in our house, I thought I'd just struck gold — it was very exciting. I never got to be excited about stumbling across something sexual, because my mom had told me all that. So I got up and I walked into her office, and I said, Mom? And she looked up from her desk, and I said, What's abortion mean?

So she looks at me a moment, and then puts her elbow on the table and she rests her chin on her palm for a second, with her fingers rolled back, hiding her lips, and she says, Can you give me two minutes, and then we'll talk about it? And I said, Okay. But two minutes means two minutes, Mom, I said, knowing I had something good — anything that could pull my mom out of her office must be good. You go on, she said, I'll be with you in a second, and I was so excited, thinking, *Ooh . . . I've caught a big one!*

So she sits me down and explains about the sperm and the egg, and that in the first few months, if a woman chooses not to have a baby, she can have a procedure, removing the cells from her body, and then she won't have a baby. If I remove the cells from a woman's body, that procedure is called an abortion, she said. I said, That's what you do, Mom? Sometimes, yes, she said, perfectly calm, and I think I said, Oh.

Honestly, it didn't bother me any more than the day we drove to visit my grandfather, and I saw a cow in a field, and I realized we ate cows, just like that cow — who knows, maybe we'd even eat that cow . . . So I put it together pretty quickly that if my mother had had an abortion, I wouldn't be here. And that if my biological mother had had an abortion, my real mom could have performed the abortion, right? I mean, I didn't really think about it; I just asked her, straight out, and she said, Hypothetically, yes. I'm six years old, and that's her answer? *Hypothetically?*

Bobbie

I REALIZE I CAN PUT her on a pedestal, but she's far from perfect. And her teens were not the best years by any means. Once, when she was about fourteen, she met me at my office one night because we were going out for dinner — we ate out a lot because I never had time for grocery shopping, never mind cooking. Well, she walks in one night, drops her bag on the floor, and falls into the chair in front of my desk. Then she leans back and squints at the wall behind me, like she's scrutinizing my degrees, even though she's seen them a thousand times. I had no idea why, but she was itching for a fight, I could smell it on her like gin. I said, What's on your mind, Del? I was just wondering, she says, have you ever had a patient who had more than two abortions?

I wasn't exactly sure if she was asking if I had any patients who'd had three abortions or if I'd ever had a patient who came to me for a third abortion. In any case, the answer was yes. Yes, I said, sitting up. Why do you ask? That's dis-*gusting*, she said, making this vile face. Three times? she said, wincing. How can anyone be so stupid? Yes, well, I said, carefully setting down my pen. Can I ask you something? I said, taking off my glasses. Yeah? she said, shrugging, and I said, Who the hell do you think you are? Who do you think you are to judge *anyone*, Adela Hernandez? I said, staring her down, thinking, *Shame on you . . .*

It only infuriated me that much more to see tears welling in her eyes. You said one question, she said, pulling herself together. That was two, she said, cool as a cucumber. I was about ready to slap her, but instead, I said, I want you to wait in the waiting room so I can finish up here. I'll be done in five minutes, and we'll discuss it then. Five minutes? That'd be a first, she said, then she leaned forward, grabbing her book bag, and she walked out. We've had our moments, that's all I'm saying.

Adela

THERE WERE TIMES, when I hit the nastiest point of my teenage years, that I used to try so hard to put her on the defensive, to judge her, even just sitting down, eating dinner. I don't know why, but I wanted to fight with her for some reason. Once I even said to her, Mom, just out of curiosity . . . ? For the sake of debate, she said. Yes, I said, for the sake of debate, what if you're wrong? What if abortion is a mortal sin? Well, she said, putting down her fork, slipping that oversized wineglass between middle and index finger with such grace you'd think she'd just put on a ring. Then I suppose God will decide what to do with me, she said, not the least ruffled. I'd be all right with that, she said, wouldn't you?

Bobbie

I WAS STILL WAITING for the Vicodin to kick in, and then Joyce let out a dramatic sigh, watching this girl — excuse me, watching this *young woman* walk past us, then she says: Remember when I had an ass like that? Joyce, I said, you never had an ass like that. See! she says, pointing at me. You see? This is why you really need to do some drugs, Bob — because there are entire realities going on above your head, beneath your feet, staring you right in the eye, and you don't even see them. Even worse, you have no idea what a great ass I had, she said, slapping my forearm.

Well, if it's any consolation, I said, remember when I had an ass like that? Yes, she said. Vaguely, yes. And I remember I hated you for it, too. In fact, Bob, I've always hated you for your great ass. Oh, *now,* I said, laughing, finally, the truth comes out. Your tits, too, she said. Really? I said. That's so sweet, Joyce . . .

That's all you're getting from me today, she said. So what did you want to tell me, anyhow? Ah, yes . . . that, I said, suddenly losing my nerve. Let's have it already, she said. Don't you want to hear about Paul first? I said. It's bad, isn't it? she said. It's not good, I said. All right, then tell me about Paul first, she said. I need another five or ten minutes, anyhow. You got it, I said, patting her hand.

Lisa

SO THE THREE OF US are sitting in the dining room eating pizza, and I'm looking at Don and Lance, thinking, *Is this it? Is this what a normal, average life is?* Then the phone rang, and Don just stared at the table. You want me to get it? I asked, and Don said, Would you mind? I don't feel like talking right now. So I walked to the kitchen: Hello, Yaeger residence.

When I returned, Lance was saying, I just don't understand—, then he stopped and looked at me, obviously debating whether to drop the subject. But then, apparently, he decided I could be trusted. Seeing as I already knew the whole story and all.

Don looked at me for a moment, waiting to hear who called. Telemarketer, I said. I mean, I just don't understand what happened, Lance said. It's like they're saying Mom was tripping or something? he said, throwing up his hands in disgust. How could you look at Mom and say that?

And I tried . . . honestly, I tried looking him in the eye, but the whole time, I'm thinking, *Wake up, Lance.* I mean, I don't know what happened to him, really. He was such a good kid, and now . . . now, he's got the military crew cut and a collection of ill-conceived tattoos. I'm serious: Lance is the sort of eighteen-year-old who gets a hard-on watching those steroid-infused armed-services recruitment ads. Go Army! Go Navy! You can see it in his eyes, too: I want to fly a jet plane! I want to drop a two-ton bomb, *oh, please, oh, please . . .* I'm sorry, but it's true.

Lisa, seriously, you think she was on drugs? Lance says. And I flashed on the image of Lynne, bawling in the front seat, telling me how sorry she was. You'll have to ask her, I said, at the very moment Don bellowed, Well, hello!, drawing our attention to Lynne, who'd been standing in the door for who knows how long. What are you doing up? he says, and she looks at me: I needed to change the sheets in the guest bedroom. Lynne, I said, I could've done that —. No, Lisa, you're the guest, she said.

How are you feeling, Mom? Lance said. Thirsty, she said, reaching for the back of the chair and pulling it out. I'll get you some water, Lance said, standing. Sit down, I said, but she just looked at me. What time do you want to leave tomorrow? she said. Well, not too early, but I should get out of here as early as possible. By ten? I asked, and she said, That's fine. I'll take you to the train —. I can take her, Don offered, and she said, No, I'll take her. I was thinking we should stop and see Daddy first.

I didn't say anything, and then she said, I know how much he'd love to see you, staring at me, so I stare right back: you bitch. You crazy bitch, no matter what you just heard me say — all of which happens to be true, by the way — I was willing to forgive and forget everything that transpired over the course of the past few hours. So don't give me your self-righteous attitude, because you're in no position, lady.

Oh, she says, before I forget. We're thinking about leaving town at Thanksgiving or Christmas. So which would you prefer this year? Which what? I said, confused. Which holiday do you want to stay with Daddy? she said. We can't leave him alone, so you tell us what's best for you, she said, as Lance returned with her water and cleared our plates, leaving Don, Lynne, and I alone at the table. And then, for the first time in my life, I thought, *Come back, Lance — right here — drop your bomb right here . . .*

Jordan

EVEN UNTIL I was like ten or eleven, I thought Lance was like the coolest thing in the whole world. I'm serious, until I started junior high school, I used to follow him like *everywhere,* and whatever

110

Lance liked, I liked. Whatever Lance loved, changing his mind from like to love, trying to shake me, I loved. If Lance loved video games, I loved video games. If Lance loved pirates, I loved pirates, and the next second, if Lance hated pirates, I hated pirates, too, *pirates suck!*

So, of course, because Lance loved Godzilla, I loved Godzilla, right? And then, one night, I had a dream that Godzilla demolished our town, and then he stepped on our house, squashing my whole family. So after my dad had to wake me up — I was screaming so loud — after that, Lance wasn't allowed to watch Godzilla with me there. I think Mom was probably just pissed the house got squashed, but then Lance was always trying to get rid of me so he could watch Godzilla alone. And if I wouldn't leave, he'd throw things at me, telling me I was ugly or I had a cow butt or whatever. One time, he even punched me.

He goes, Jordan, I'll let you stay if you let me punch you in the shoulder as hard as I can. So of course I just nodded, like, okay. Okay, Lance, you're so cool: punch me. So he did — he punched me, hard as he could. It really hurt, too, and I tried so hard not to cry. Because the only thing that made Lance shut down was crying. I mean, he'd do everything he could to make me cry, but once he did, he'd clam up. Like he felt so bad, he couldn't even deal with looking at me, and that was almost worse than being punched.

Lisa

LYNNE, YOU SHOULD get to bed, you must be exhausted, Don said, but Lynne stared at me. Lisa, she said, do you mind sleeping in the guest bedroom, or would you prefer the couch in the living room? Why would I mind the guest bedroom? I said, and she said, Last night, while I was trying to sleep down there, I realized why I've always hated that room: because it reminds me of Daddy's office. Don just sat there the whole time, no idea what was going on, but that whatever it was, it wasn't good.

Hey, Aunt Lisa? Lance said, breaking the silence, returning to the dining room, and I'm thinking, *You know, Lance, calling me Aunt Lisa is one of your least endearing qualities of your many least endearing qualities.* Lisa's fine, Lance, I said. Oh. Okay, he said, shrugging whatever. Lance, I said, just out of curiosity, how old do you think I am? And he said, Honestly? And I said, Honestly, no, when a woman asks you her age, it's never honestly. What, were you born yesterday? I don't know, he said, twenty-five, twenty-six, maybe? Close enough, I said.

You were saying? I said, and he said, You ever seen *The Simpsons*? And I said, Durrh . . . Yes, I've seen *The Simpsons,* Lance. And he said, Well, don't you think Grandpa sounds just like Grandpa Simpson? And I had to laugh because he does. Don started laughing, too, and then Lynne looked up and said, We'll leave at nine, then? And I looked at her: I wasn't bad-mouthing you, Lynne. Perfect, I said.

Bobbie

So how did you two become friends? Paul said. I don't know, I said, I don't remember, really. Joyce remembers, he said. Like I said, she's a very loyal person, I said, and he waited. All right, I said. What happened was Joyce got the flu two weeks before Thanksgiving break, and I took care of her. It humbled her, me seeing her that way — she couldn't even stand in the shower, so I had to give her a sponge bath in bed. When I tried to get her to drink some water, she broke down, sobbing. Fragile . . . she was so fragile, and I'd never seen that person before. I'd never given her that much credit, I'm afraid.

For the next month, she behaved like my servant; she kept trying to buy me things, take me out. I didn't ask for anything, of course, but if I had, whatever I had asked, she would've done, gladly. I remember thinking, *Wow . . . is this what it's like to be a cute boy, to have a girl crazy about you?* Because I could see the appeal, certainly, I said.

It passed, of course, but everything changed after that. For one thing, I started to like her. She had the mouth of a sailor and the most vicious sense of humor, and I was never clever, really. But Joyce . . . Joyce always said exactly the right thing at exactly the right time, especially if it involved an insult. I remember my dad once saying, That girl has balls to make a bull blush. Just try to say that ten times, I said, laughing.

112

To this day, I can still see that room, our old dorm room, I said. The building's on West 116 and Broadway, and we had a double-occupancy, facing the courtyard, on the second floor. There was a phone at the end of the hall; dorm rooms didn't have phones, as a rule, but ours did — as Joyce's rule. She paid extra, or rather, Sonja and Irving paid extra. The price being that Sonja could call whenever she pleased, but still.

I thought it was obnoxious, of course, especially since the other girls would come knocking on our door every night, asking if they could use the phone, but they'd always leave a dime in payment. Some mornings, there'd be a dollar in change on the frame of Joyce's bed. *A dime*, can you imagine? I said. I didn't know it at the time, but that was the seed money of her drug fund, I said, laughing.

Joyce

NO, I'LL TELL you what happened, *both ends* justify the means: that's what happened. We're talking *The Exorcist* out my ass, okay. I mean, I couldn't even get up off the bathroom floor, and that's where Bobbie found me, passed out in the dorm toilet stall. Honestly, she stayed up all night taking care of me. She washed and changed my sheets — I mean, Jesus, she *bathed me*. I've never been so humiliated or so grateful. I'm not sure my own mother would've done that for me, at least not without wrapping me in a plastic shower curtain, but Bobbie did.

Bobbie

I DIDN'T FEEL comfortable, talking about marriage, his or Joyce's, so I tried changing the subject, asking Paul about his car, or I said his car was beautiful, something like that. I think I said, You have a beautiful car, and he said, Which one? And I said, You have more than one? Two: I have an International, and a '57 Chevy, he said. Ah, I said, nodding. So you have a thing for old broads, huh? Speaking of, he said. This doesn't bode well, I said.

Joyce tells me you've known each other thirty-five years, he said, and I smiled, thinking, *I'm going to kill her*. Since the day we were

113

born, I said, setting down my drink, and he said, College roommates, Joyce said. Yes, well, birth, college — it all happens in the blink of an eye, I said. Can I get you another? he asked, looking at my glass. So that's how you work, I said. Mention their age, and they're sure to need another drink. Another round, please? he asked, speaking to the bartender.

So tell me, he said, turning back to face me, what was your first impression of Joyce? he said, holding up an invisible microphone, and I said, Honestly? Yes, the cold, hard truth, he said, give it to me. All right then, I said. Honestly, I couldn't stand her. And why is that? he said, and I said, Well. She was loud; she was obnoxious; and for some reason, she seemed to think the whole world revolved around her, and then he started laughing. Why are you laughing? I said. Because I asked the same question about you, he said. Oh, no, I said, what did she say? But before he had a chance to speak, I said, Never mind, waving him off. I know, I said. You think so? he said. No, I said, I don't *think* so: I *know* so. Huh, he said, unconvinced.

A hundred bucks says I know exactly what she said when you asked her first impression of me, I said. A hundred bucks? he said, raising his eyebrow. I'll spot you if you're short on cash, I said, cocking my chin: put up or shut up. You're funny, he said, I like that in a —. You're stalling, I said. Says who? he said, taking out his wallet, removing a bill and putting it on the bar.

I sat up straight on my stool, and I said, You said, What was your first impression of Bobbie? Something like that, yes, he said. You said, What was your first impression of Bobbie, I repeated, and then Joyce said, First impression? I hated the fucking bitch. His jaw dropped.

Pleasure doing business with you, I said, placing my hand on the bill and sliding it toward my glass. Check, please, I said, folding the paper around my finger and raising my billed finger for the bartender. No, really, he said, that's —. Verbatim, I said, nodding. Incredible, he said, nodding. Not really, I said, raising my glass and finishing my drink. We do this all the time, I said, setting down the glass. Oh, I see, he said, laughing. That's why she wanted to set us up, it's a grift. Afraid so, I said. And I fell for it, he said. And you fell for it, I said with a shrug, standing up to leave.

114

We went outside, and Paul raised his arm, hailing a cab. Now can I — excuse me, *may* I ask you a question? he said, stepping around me in order to open the car door, and I smiled. Listen, Bobbie, you aren't going to be offended if I don't try to get you into bed tonight, are you? Not at all, I said, trying not to laugh as I got in the cab. And I hope you aren't going to be offended if I tell you that you didn't have a prayer of getting me into bed tonight —. Because I like to take my time with a woman, he said. Is that what you tell yourself? I said, laughing.

How's tomorrow night work for you? he said, cheeky bastard. Unfortunately, tomorrow night does not work, because I'm working tomorrow night, I said. Thursday? Working, I said. Friday? he said. You're staying in town all week? I asked. No, he said, I was thinking of inviting you to my house for dinner. Can you cook? I asked, avoiding answering. Can I cook? he asked, balking. Does the Pope wear a dress?

And you? he said, knocking on the cabbie's window and removing his wallet. Do I wear a dress? I asked, raising my brow. No, he said, I know you wear a dress — you wear a dress very well, thank you, but do you cook? he said. Oh, god, no — that's what men are for. So is that a yes? he said. No, that's not a yes, I said, trying not to laugh. We'll say ten o'clock? I'll pick you up at the train station, he said. You know . . . no wonder Joyce likes you, I said, and he smiled, closing the door and handing the driver a bill.

Then my phone started ringing. Joyce? he asked, and I smiled. You know her so well already, I said, genuinely impressed. You want me to talk to her? he offered, and I said, No, I've got it, silencing my phone. She wants the dirt, he said. Hope springs eternal, I said. Indeed. So I'll see you Friday night, he said, leaning over, and then he very gently kissed my cheek before he stepped back and patted the side of the cab twice.

Where to? the driver asked, and I gave him my address, and then he pulled out. I swear it was all I could do not to look behind me to see if Paul was still standing there. Fortunately, I could see him in the driver's rearview. Unfortunately, I realized he saw me, looking at him in the rearview, because then he held his right hand to his ear, gesturing, I'll call you. Damn, I said, out loud: caught red-handed.

Two blocks later, Joyce called back. He kissed my cheek, I said, looking out the window. Are you fucking kidding me? she said. You know how many hours I've put in on this evening? Seriously, Bob, you're like a one-woman Make-A-Wish Foundation, as much time as I've donated to this cause, and for what? For a kiss on the cheek?

We're having dinner Friday, I said. Getting warmer . . . depending on where he's taking you, she said, but I didn't answer, because Joyce can turn a fun little game of rate-a-date into blood sport in the blink of an eye. In other words, where is he taking you? she asked. His place, I said. In the city? she said, surprised. No, I said, his house upstate. He's making me dinner, all right? Well, she said, that's more like it. Call you tomorrow, I said. Yep, she said, and I hung up, resting my head against the window.

Jordan

WHEN LISA TOLD ME Dr. Myers called, I was just like, I love Dr. Myers — she's so cool. I mean, she's so beautiful, and the way she *dresses*. Like she's just so classy, you know? And Lisa goes, Yeah, I know, and I go, When we walked into her office, I was just like, ohmygod, I hope I'm like that when I get to be her age, then Lisa smiled and she goes, Me, too.

Of course, Mom hated her, I said, and Lisa was like, There's a surprise. And I go, Seriously. I heard her talking to Dad, I said, folding the pillow behind my head and resting my legs across Lisa's lap, and Mom was just like, Oh, she's such a type. She's one of those *New York women*, I said, wrinkling my nose, and Lisa just laughed, nodding her head and rolling her eyes, and I'm like, Right?

Lisa

THE PHONE RANG, and Don and Lance just looked away, so I offered to get it. I said, Hello, Yaeger residence. And a voice said, Hello, may I speak with Jordan or Lynne, please? It was a woman's voice, and then I knew: Dr. Myers?

Yes? she said, and I said, It's Lisa — Lisa Soutar, and she said, Oh,

Lisa. Hello. I said, Wow, it's like déjà voodoo all over again, huh? And she laughed. How are you? she said. Well, I've had better days. Haven't we all, she said, I heard your sister got sick this morning. Yeah, that's what I heard, too, I said. Lynne got sick, and here I am, upstate.

How's Jordan? she said. I tried her cell, but I got her voice mail. Oh, I have her cell phone in my bag, I said, but she's sleeping now. She's fine, I said, she's just worn out. Understandably, she said. And then I wanted to tell her, to say, I'm glad it was you, you know? But I didn't know how — I couldn't seem to form the words.

After I helped Don with the dishes, I went upstairs, and Jordan's light was on, so I knocked. Just me, I said, opening the door: Can I come in? When I went in, I have to say, I was blown away by how much her room had changed since I'd last visited. She'd taken down all the pictures of her and her friends; all those collages she made of the latest *Vogue* It Girls and Marc Jacobs ads . . . no magazines, nothing — her computer wasn't even open. It made me sad. Then again, it kind of reminded me of my old room, just without the graffiti.

I sat down on the side of the bed, and she had that hollowed-out look I knew all too well, so I decided to give it the old school try. I said, Imagine . . . Jordan, imagine the most lewd, disgusting, unspeakable sexual act . . . You got it? Got a picture? I asked, and she grinned, looking up, then quickly looking away, as though I might see it in her eyes. That's right: I really thought I was making my mark, building a reputation that would span the ages, because I was punk rock, motherfucker! Lord, I said, nodding. But I don't think she had any idea what I was saying. Well, she is Lynne's child, after all.

So I told her about the many, *many* stupid things I did over the years. I told her about Sally, infamous Sally, the girl I thought was the coolest girl in the whole world. I told her how the first night I met Sally in this scuzzy studio apartment on First, off Houston, she walked in, with her spiky platinum hair and her striped black-and-white tights with these gaping holes in the thighs that promised an even bigger hole at the crotch. Sally looked me up and down, and then she goes — she goes, I fucked Iggy Pop: who are you? And I . . . oh, god, I just crumbled.

Nobody, I said, my voice breaking. I'm Nobody, and I've never

117

fucked Anybody. Just the lead singer of a Poison cover band. I was just like, ohmygod, you fucked Iggy Pop? Granted, at that point, I didn't realize quite how many women could say the same, but anyhow. I was so starstruck, my mouth must've been hanging wide open. *Wow, you fucked Iggy Pop? Can I be your friend?* That's all I wanted, was to be Somebody. And if I couldn't be Somebody, I could at least fuck Someone who was. I didn't say that to her, of course, but still.

Who's Iggy Pop? she said, and I gasped. Who is Iggy Pop? I said, and she shrugged: I mean, I've heard the name —. My god, that's . . . that's like asking who Bobbie Kennedy was, Jordan! Where there was darkness, Iggy brought light. Where there was hopelessness, Iggy sowed hope. Iggy *is* punk rock, motherfucker — that's who he was! She smiled, laughing, as I shook my head. For shame, young lady, *for shame,* I said.

She's so young. I look at her, and she is so very, very young, and I want to say, Jordan, do you have any idea how many things I'm ashamed of? Do you have any clue how many things I've said and done that I wish I could take back? Because she looks at me, and she believes what she sees. She thinks Will's absolutely perfect. She thinks I've got this amazing loft and this beautiful baby and all these clothes and cars, so everything's just great, right?

Just to put it all in perspective, I said. You know, Jordan, the truth is, I was one of those skanky chicks who are always standing in the smoker's corner, rain or shine, with all the other rejects. One of those girls who fucked about half the guys in that group, and not even punks, either — heshers, okay? The guys who did a lot of acid and wore skintight black stretch jeans and slashed T-shirts and jacked off to Mötley Crüe videos. God, they were such waste cases, and I actually had sex with them, I said, almost shrieking. All of them — I mean, at one point or another.

Trust me, I said. You don't know shame until you've blown the lead singer of a Stryper cover band. Stryper? she said, furrowing her brow: I thought you said Poison —. I did: it was a long weekend, I said, and she laughed, and I said, That's my girl . . . I knew you were still in there. Then she screeched, hiding her face in her pillow: That's so *gross,* she said, shoulders shaking, and I said, Jordan, you have no idea how low,

118

low can get. Please, I said, I was crowned Blow-job Queen before I'd ever actually seen a penis, never mind opening my big mouth. So of course by the time I actually gave my first blow job, I had a reputation to protect. Really, you can't imagine the pressure I felt. You want to hear more? I said, and she did, but she shook her head no.

What can I say? When in need, repulse. I learned that from Joyce. You do what you have to do, and you go as low as you have to go, and at that moment, I would've said anything to make her smile, to remind her that she could still smile, no matter what. Then Lynne knocked and stuck her head in. Just making sure we weren't having too much fun.

Lynne

SO I LISTENED, yes. I stood there, eavesdropping, until I couldn't take it anymore, and then I poked my head in. As soon as I saw their faces, I knew that the minute I closed the door, they would start laughing at me, that they'd barely be able to contain themselves. It was humiliating, if you want to know, hearing them talk about me, but I knocked anyway. For one reason: because I wanted to look Lisa in the eye. So I did; I looked her right in the eye, thinking, *What right do you have to judge me? You — you don't even* know *me.*

Bobbie

WHEN DID YOU DECIDE you wanted to be a doctor? he said, pouring me another glass of wine, that first night at his house, and I said, When I was six. Six? he laughed. Yes. The year my mother died, my dad got me that game Operation for Christmas, and I was so excited that opening my present I screeched, I said, laughing. But when I opened the box, I took one look, and I said, Where's the ovarian, Daddy? Because my mother died of ovarian cancer, and I wanted to see it, thinking I could fix it for her. My father looked at the game as though it might rescue him, like, *The ovarian must be in here, some-where.* Then he came to his senses and said, I don't think this one has an ovarian — ovaries.

I said, Then where's its vagina, Dad? My mother taught me that word; it was a big-girl word and I had to be very careful when I used it, like my grandmother's china. Well, my dad turned the box over, and then he looked at me. I guess this one doesn't have a vagina, either, honey, he said, trying to console me. But it's still fun, right? You can still operate, he said, and then I became furious: Dad, you got me the *boy* one! How can I operate if there's no ovarian? For years, he used to love to tell people that story, but it pained him at the same time, talking about that first year after she died.

My poor dad, I said, realizing I was touching my lips, hiding, so I reached for my glass. He had to be both parents, and it's hard enough to be one, I said. You would know, he said. No, I said. I had help — I believe you've met my wife, Joyce? I couldn't have done it without her. You know, Paul said, I've been meaning to ask who was the . . .

Adela

I WANTED TO TELL HER, I really did, but she's been so happy, how could I do that to her? I mean, my mom's in love — how bizarre is that? But then every weekend I thought I'd go down and tell her face-to-face, she was upstate. She's barely home anymore, so I kept waiting for the right time, but the right time never came. Then, when we met for lunch, Thursday, I almost said something, but she was so nervous, I just smiled, thinking, *I want you to have this. I know you won't understand why, but this is why: because for one night, I want you to be happy and in love, and I want to remember that, too.*

Joyce

I REMEMBER HEARING a report on NY1 a few days after 9/11, when there was still hope of finding survivors. I remember they brought on this psychologist who said that when a loved one dies, the first thing you should do is save all their messages, anything with your loved one's voice. Something about how important our sense of hearing is, or I can't remember what, exactly, I just knew it was true.

Because then I remembered how my dad had left me several voice mails in the weeks before he was diagnosed. Of course I didn't think anything of it at the time, because he always left me the same message, in that droll, nasally voice of his, like . . . like Ben Stein. Seriously, he sounded just like an older version of Ben Stein: *Hello, Joyce. This is your father. Nothing's wrong, I'm just calling to say hello. All right, then, I've said it. Well, so, I guess this is goodbye, then. All right, goodbye.* I erased it, without giving it a second thought. And now . . . we have pictures, we have video, but still. I'd give anything to hear that message again, just once.

The odd thing is that my dad didn't look anything like Ben Stein, but now, every time I hear that man's voice on a TV commercial, I get sort of turned on. Which is completely perverse, I know — that's what I love about it.

Lisa

WHEN WE WALKED into his room, Lynne said, Look who's here, Daddy, look who came to visit you! And just as I was about to tell her to fuck off, she stepped aside. He didn't see me at first, starting in on her: Lynne? Lynne, where's my shirt? Someone stole my shirt, he said, and Lynne ignored him. Daddy, she said, look who's here, and I stepped forward. Oh . . . Lisa, he said, Is it you? He looked so happy, so childlike in his happiness; it broke my heart.

Yes, Dad. It's me, I said, stepping forward to give him a kiss. He's wheelchair bound now, and his chair was parked in front of the TV; some daytime talk show or other, I couldn't look. What a nice surprise. No one told me you were coming, he said, kissing me back. Well, it wouldn't have been much of a surprise if they told you, now would it? I said, and he laughed that raspy ancient laugh. No, I s'pose not . . . One thing, though, he said, turning back again.

Lynne, I told you, I told you. Someone stole it, he whined, and she said, Dad, it's in the wash. Once a year, we have to wash your shirt, she said, unruffled. What's the matter? I asked, and Lynne said, His shirt is in the laundry and he thinks someone stole it. They did! he said.

What shirt, Dad? My Mets shirt, he wailed. You know, Lynne said, lowering her voice, the one that says, I STILL BELIEVE. He won't take the damn thing off. Not even to let me scald the crotchety-old-man stink out of it — makes me nauseous, she said. I just looked at her. He can't hear me, she said, turning to look at him. There are certain registers of voice he can't hear, she said, looking at him, but he didn't blink.

I turned to him. I'll buy you another one, Dad, how's that? I'll send it Monday, first thing, I said, but that only upset him more. No, I don't want *another* shirt; I want *my* shirt, he said, almost in tears. Lynne, he snapped, I want you to, to speak to someone. All right, Daddy, she said. It's just not right, he said, people taking things that aren't theirs. Lisa, why don't I leave you two alone for a few minutes while I go file a report, Lynne said, turning and walking out the door.

Lynne

MY GOD, WHAT A SCENE: Lisa pulling me away, yelling, What do you want, Lynne? What do you *want*? And me, yelling back, screaming at both of them, I want him to say I wasn't messy! Say it, Daddy: say my room was never messy! And then she slapped me.

We didn't speak the whole way to the station, and I couldn't leave it like that, so I pulled up in front and turned the engine off. But I didn't know what to say, really, except, How's Will managing without you? Same way I manage without Will every day, I'm sure: Rosalee, she said, staring straight ahead.

What about Jordan? she said, finally looking at me, and I said, What about her? Lynne, please, she said, she has to get out of here — this town is killing her. So I was thinking maybe she should come and live with me for a while. And I said, I appreciate your concern, Lisa, but she's not going anywhere right now. Lynne, she said, be reasonable, will you? She's miserable here —. Yes, I realize that, I said, but, fortunately or unfortunately, Lisa, running away isn't always the answer. Well, fortunately or unfortunately, staying isn't always the answer, either, she said, grabbing her bag off the floor.

I said, Lisa, I know you think you and Jordan are just alike . . . and, in some ways, you are, yes. But in other ways, you're nothing alike, I said, looking out my window. Then she turned to look at me, and she

122

said, How's that, Lynne? And I told her — for once in my life, I told her exactly what I thought — I said, Because she's sweet and kind and she has a big heart —. Nothing like me, she said, and I said, No. Then she got out of the car.

Lisa

SO I GET OUT and I walk to the platform, and of course, because it's upstate, there's a man standing there smoking, because people here still smoke, thank god. But all I can think is, *Oh, a cigarette . . . I want a cigarette.* Seriously, I haven't smoked a cigarette in years — one, at least. *In fact,* I thought, *I deserve a cigarette, because it's been a long fucking weekend, you know? And it's only Saturday morning, for chrissake.*

So I walk over and ask if I could buy a cigarette from him, and he just laughed, removing the pack from his pocket. Keep it, he says, handing me the cigarette and winking. Thank you — you have no idea what this means to me, I said. And just as he's reaching for the lighter in his jean pocket, just as I'm about to smoke my first cigarette in sixteen months, I hear my name: Lisa? It's Lynne. Of course it's Lynne. Who else would have nothing better to do than to bust me, red-handed? All I can think is, *One word . . . you say a word about the cigarette in my hand and I'm going to slap you again, I swear.*

Yes? I say, thanking the guy before turning and putting the cigarette in my pocket, daring her. What is it? I ask, and she says, I almost forgot . . . I have something for you. She looked so shy, handing me a box. What is this? I asked, taking it from her. The whole box was wrapped in silk, and of course, instead of using glue or staples, or even double-stick tape, she's sewn the whole thing by hand. I mean, it even had a ribbon with my name sewn in this burgundy-colored florid cursive, LISA. It was beautiful.

But looking at it, I just couldn't get over the fact that she'd actually sewn my name on a ribbon. All I could think was, *When did she do this, last night? No, it couldn't have been last night, so when did she have the time to do this? What, did she actually have LISA ribbons just lying around?* It was insane. Open it, she said, go on, open it! But I didn't want to tear it; I just wanted to look at it.

Lynne, I said, starting to protest. Open it, she said, tugging my sleeve, so I did. It was a bowl. It was this delicate little black bowl — like a bowl Lynne might've made, had she been a potter in eighteenth-century Japan. It's beautiful, I said. It's for potpourri . . . or you can stash drugs, she said, in all seriousness, still looking at my hands. I was at a complete loss for words. I mean, I don't know your style, really, she said, but I thought it looked like you. You can always re-gift, if you want —. No, I said. Thank you, I know exactly where I'll put it. Well, I should go, she said. Bye, I said, trying to smile, holding the bowl in the crook of my arms. Bye, she said, giving me a little wave, turning, and walking around the corner.

I waited until she was gone before I gave it a closer look, and it was beautiful — I don't know what possessed her, but that had become the rule, not the exception. So I put the bowl back in its box for safekeeping, and then I walked back over to the man. Sorry, I said, peering around. Do you have a light? I asked, taking the cigarette from my pocket. *God I've missed you,* I thought, taking a deep, deep drag, and exhaling.

Bobbie

MY PHONE RANG, Saturday afternoon, just as we sat down at the table, and my first thought was, *If it's Paul, I forgive you; if it's not Paul, I don't forgive you.* Then I checked the number; it was my service; Jordan Yaeger had called. I'll be right back, I said, standing and heading for the door.

She worried me, when I spoke to her before the procedure. She's a beautiful girl who's been beaten down — I don't know why, and sometimes it's not any one thing, really. But still, there was something in her eyes that told me she thought she deserved to be punished, and that the abortion was punishment for what she'd done. Which made me so sad, but it also made me so angry that I wanted to shake her: You don't deserve this — no one deserves this! Really, how do you defend someone you'd just as soon slap across the face?

So I stepped outside and we spoke for a minute, then Jordan said, Can I ask you something, Dr. Myers? Anything, I said, shoot. Are you married? she said, and I had to laugh. Why do you ask? I said. I asked you first, she said. Yes. Yes, you did, I said. No, I'm not married. Now, my turn: Why do you ask? Two reasons, she said. One? I said. One, because Lisa bet me a hundred bucks I wouldn't ask you. I'll cut you in on forty. I said, And two? And two . . . I don't know, she said, I was just curious. Understood, I said. I want you to check in with me on Monday. Can I text you? she said. No, call, please. I don't text, I said. No husband, no text, huh? she said, and I laughed. Exactly, I said. Thank you for calling. You're welcome, she said. Monday, I said, and I went back inside.

Lynne

FRIDAY NIGHT, I SLIPPED into my studio — I know Lisa would never call it a studio, but it's the room where I work, so that's what I call it. Anyhow, I have an entire closet full of thick glossy white boxes I ordered from a place online, and I found the perfect size box. Then I took out a piece of silk that some friends of ours brought me from India; I'd been saving it for a special occasion, and I decided that this was it. So I cut and sewed the silk to the box by hand, carefully sculpting the material into rose petals, twisting and hand-stitching every last fold in place. Each flower took at least an hour, but it looked beautiful when I was done. Well, I thought so, at least.

Actually, I have an entire shelf of fabrics and papers I save just for Lisa's gifts, and you can always tell Lisa's gifts under the tree, because they're the most beautiful of all of the gifts I wrap. I knew she'd accuse me of martyring myself again, considering she'd been talking about me at my own table, and then I went and spent three hours working on gift wrapping a bowl. But I wasn't martyring myself; it was more of a peace offering, really. Knowing what I had to do the next morning. Knowing that after we saw Daddy, we might never speak again.

Adela

SERIOUSLY, THE LAST thing in the world I wanted to do was have brunch with Joyce. Of course, as soon as Mom left the table, Joyce asked what I thought of Paul. I said he seems like a great guy, but that

125

they must've had some sort of fight Thursday night, and Joyce waves me off, saying, I wouldn't worry about it.

Let me guess, Mom said, returning to the table, and before I could say anything, Joyce turned to me and said, So what about you, Señorita Thang? You must have a hundred guys on the line. No, I said, looking down at the table. No? she said. Don't give me that —. I have to get going, I said, smiling, looking away. Already? Mom said, disappointed I was running off so soon. Sorry, I said, giving her a kiss on the cheek.

God, I felt like such a shit walking out, because I was awful to her — I was short, I was mean — but Joyce's just so overbearing sometimes, and she wouldn't drop it, either. She kept saying, That's exactly what you need, Del: an older man. Trust me, I will introduce you to some of the most *amazing* men, and granted, they don't have the stamina of guys your age, but they can more than make up for it in other, very important ways. And I thought I was going to puke, honestly. Are you feeling all right, baby? she said. I'm fine, I said, I think I just caught something on the plane.

Here, have some water, sweetheart, she said. I'm fine, I said. No, here: take a sip —. Joyce, I said I'm *fine*. I'm sorry, she said, hurt. Please, just stop mothering me, okay. Seriously, one is plenty —. *Adela*, Mom snapped. No, she's right — she's absolutely right, Joyce said. She's a grown woman — I mean, look at her, Joyce said, defending me. It was so shameful, I couldn't even look at her, thinking, *Please, Joyce. Please don't let me do this — don't forgive me. I can't bear it.*

How was brunch? he said, as I dropped my bag on the floor, and I rolled my eyes, moaning: Unbearable. The whole time, I was just like, get me out of here, I said. Come lie down, he said, patting the bed. Did you tell her? he said, and I just rolled my eyes, as my mouth fell open, thinking, *Don't start — seriously, don't start in on me right now, you have no idea what you're asking . . .*

Bobbie

I WALKED OVER and sat on a bench in front of the Union Square dog run, and then a woman handed me a flyer. Normally I don't think twice about declining flyers, but not Saturday afternoon. Oh, no, I smiled, taking her flyer, because I was a free woman, and I wanted someone to see me smile so I could believe it myself. Then I started reading, and wouldn't you know it? A right-to-life pamphlet; I couldn't help but laugh.

Exactly one week ago, we were driving home from the grocery store, when the traffic started slowing down right before we hit that part of Route 9 that Paul calls the Pubic Triangle. Which is crude, yes, but then again, there's the Alight House, next door to Planned Parenthood, which is directly across the street from the self-proclaimed LIFE IS ABOUT CHOICES shack. It's this ramshackle hut where they display a poster of a supposed late-term aborted fetuses cupped in the palm of a man's hand next to the highway. Every time I look at that poster, I think, *You would actually hold an aborted fetus in your hand for a religious-right photo op, and you want to preach to me about morality?*

Well. Last weekend, there was some sort of protest at the Alight House; this tiny four-room house with a sloping lawn, facing the highway. There were about twenty people gathered, most of who were middle-aged to elderly, all standing on the front lawn. In front of them, there were approximately fifteen miniature white crosses pitched in the yard, signifying how many souls had been lost in Hudson that week, or who knows what.

The traffic slowed while drivers stared, watching the people begin to line up in a row, facing the highway, each holding a long white candle. Then a man started walking down the row, lighting each of their white candles, and Paul turned to me and said, You want to wait and see if they set the crosses on fire, too? Those must be the same people responsible for the billboard, I said, turning away.

Over on 66, there's a two-panel billboard facing the highway. On one panel, there's a nondescript Indian Fuel and Reserve ad, and sharing the bill, was an antiabortion billboard. It's a picture of that woman, that sixties television actress or whoever she is — Jennifer O'Neill, that's her name — failed actress turned right-to-life spokeswoman. The billboard is a picture of her today, and it says, I REGRET MY ABORTION. It was one of the first things I saw that day Joyce

127

picked me up, the weekend I met Paul. You actually bought a house here? I said, disgusted. I'm redecorating, don't worry, she said.

It was still there the first time I went up to spend the weekend with Paul. When we passed it, I said, You know what I'm going to do? I'm going to have a portrait of myself taken in my white coat, wearing a stethoscope, with my arms crossed, and I'm going to purchase the Indian Fuel and Reserve ad space. Then I'm going to have my picture plastered next to that woman, with my slogan: BUT I DON'T. I swear, I said, if that billboard's not down by Thanksgiving, I'm doing it.

Months later, looking at those people standing in that yard, my cheeks flushed: Unborn souls? What about the living? What about all those souls who are dying in Iraq every day? Why don't you take your candles and your crosses and charter a bus down to Washington to rescue them, you fucking hypocrites! Paul turned to look at me, and I said, I'm sorry, catching my breath, while he signaled, pulling off the road. I'm sorry, I said, I was just having a moment. You sure? he said, reaching over, grabbing the back of my neck. I'm fine, I said, nodding.

I rested my head against the window, and I said, There's a picture that was taken during the 1971 NOW convention in Houston. It's a picture of this young woman, with this dark, bone-straight hair parted down the center — the kind of hair you only saw in the seventies. Anyhow, she's holding up a sign that says:

IF MEN GOT PREGNANT
ABORTION WOULD BE SACRED

She's standing there, holding the sign high above her head with straight arms, so young and proud and . . . not defiant, no. She's not defiant: she's just standing her ground. She couldn't have been more than twenty, twenty-one, a few years older than I was. But when I saw that picture, for the first time in my life I wanted to be another woman: I wanted to be her. I knew then — I was a senior in high school, and I'd applied to Barnard as premed, thinking I'd become an oncologist, but looking at her, I changed my mind. To this day, I said, there are still moments when I want to remove all the diplomas from my office wall and hang that picture in their place.

I make my own choices in this life. I never encourage or discourage my patients: I have no right. All I can do is respect their decision. And be there, afterward, to sit with them — they don't need my medical knowledge at that point; they need someone to hold their hand. Sometimes they just need someone who will acknowledge that maybe everything won't be all right, but that they aren't alone, I said.

Come here, he said, pulling me to him, and I tried not to cry because I didn't want him to see me cry, but I did. It was only a minute before I became impatient, thinking, *This is ridiculous,* and I sat up, drying my eyes. I don't know about you, he said, but I hear the hammock calling me like the sirens. So let's get a move on, he said, stepping on the clutch and shifting the knob of the '57 long-bed step-side pickup that he'd rebuilt by hand. She had four on the floor, as they used to say, then he took the knob and ground her to shreds. Oh, he moaned in agony, oh, baby. Baby, baby, baby, I'm sorry, he cooed, petting the dash. No wonder your wife left you, I said, staring straight ahead, before I burst out laughing. Yeah, you're a real card, he said, staring straight ahead, but don't give up your day job.

When we got back, we took a long walk in the woods, and then we went home, crawled into the hammock, smoked a joint, and drank whiskey. We went to bed, and then, afterward, I said it. I said: I love you . . . I really love you, you know that? Paul looked at me, smiling, staring into my eyes, and then he took my face in both hands.

Lynne

BY THE TIME we got to Dr. Myers's office Friday, I didn't know what was happening; things were still moving, the walls, the ceiling . . . and then they put me in a room with all these women. There were about eight or nine women, girls — some were girls not much older than Jordan, and some of them were sobbing openly, and some were trying not to cry, but they were the loudest. And I know . . . I know it sounds crazy, but I could actually hear them holding in their sobs. There was just so much pain in that room; it was deafening, moving, taking shape in the shadows.

I don't know how long I'd been lying there when the woman next to me sat up, and when I looked up at her, I noticed there was a dark stain on her hospital gown near her crotch, and then the circle started growing bigger and bigger. Then her blood started dripping on the floor, one drop at a time, and it was screaming — her blood started screaming — and I panicked: Where's Jordan? What have you done to her? I could hear myself screaming in my head, but — but I don't know about my mouth. I didn't know what was happening. I just wanted my daughter.

Adela

FOR YEARS I HAD this nightmare I was sent back. I used to dream that I did something — I never knew what I did wrong, exactly, and I didn't know if my mom sent me away or I was just taken away because I was bad, but anyhow. It was a horrible place; it was dark and filthy and there were these people . . . these terrible people, this couple, who locked me up. And I'd beg them, I'd promise to be good if they'd let me go . . . I'd cry and cry and beg them to let me see my mom, and then they'd tell me she was never coming back, that she didn't love me anymore, and then . . . then I'd wake up screaming.

Bobbie

SHE USED TO HAVE nightmares and wake up screaming: Mommy, the cats, the cats! We didn't have any cats; I didn't know anyone who had cats; I had no idea where the fear came from, but she wouldn't let go of me after I woke her, so I'd carry her into my bed.

I once mentioned it to our friend Gordon, and he bristled: *Cats*? I had the same reaction, he said. Really, Bobbie, what on earth would possess you to take your daughter to see *Cats*? I looked at him: It was *Beauty and the Beast,* not *Cats.*

One of my patients gave me two tickets, and frankly, I would rather have been stoned to death than sit through a Broadway musical, but Adela was obsessed with *Beauty and the Beast.* So there I was, and Dela was so excited, just before the curtains opened, she looked up, squeezing my hand with both her hands, and she said, Mama, I've got ants in my vagina! I loved that—it was the best description I'd ever heard, and I'm not just saying that because she's my daughter.

Speaking of bad dreams, what is this? Gordon said, standing in front of my makeshift bar. What is what? I said, turning to find him holding a photograph of Adela that I took on our first trip to Costa Rica, our first family vacation. It's a black-and-white of Adela standing on the beach at sunset, brown as can be, and naked from the waist up. Except that her little burned meringue nipples are covered by dozens of seashell necklaces, which she insisted on wearing with her red polka-dot bikini bottoms, telling me she could dress herself, and slapping my hands away every time I tried to help her. All right, all right . . . you can dress yourself, I told her. But where's the dress?

Bobbie, it's *so* Save the Children, he said, making this pathetic face, holding the photo next to his cheek: For sixteen cents a day you can feed a hungry child—. Give me that, I said, taking it from him, but unable to keep from laughing. Taking another look, I had to admit she was all sticklike arms and legs, except for her big eyes and protruding stomach . . . For some reason, I hadn't noticed just how protruding it was, actually.

I *love* that picture, and Dela looks beautiful, I said, setting the frame back on the table. But, I admit, I took the photo to my office the next day. Where, I might add, not one person failed to mention what an absolutely beautiful daughter I have, thank you very much.

Adela

I DON'T KNOW what to say except that he was there for me at a time when I felt . . . I just felt so fucked up, and I didn't know what to do, and I couldn't seem to talk to anyone else. And he didn't make me talk about it, and he didn't try to make me feel like anything would get better. He just let me be, you know. And he knows I'm fucked up. And he's all right with that, far as I can tell.

I mean, people look at me and they're happy to leave it at that. No, really, all my life people have told me how beautiful I am. Of course my mother's response was, You are beautiful, Adela, but that's just the outside. The rest, you have to decide for yourself. And I'm trying, but I'm not the woman I want to be — I don't even who that is, really.

She talks the talk, you know — oh, she's all about free choice when it suits her, but then she'll rail against plastic surgery, saying, You have to learn to accept yourself — why can't these women understand that you just have to be yourself? And I think, *Just? Oh, is that all? And why is that, Mom, because you know who you are — because you think you know, we all should know, right?* I don't mean to be facetious because I like the sound of it, I really do. But the thing is, all the times I've fucked up, every mistake I've made, I *was* just being myself, and it's not pretty, no. But no matter how fucked up I feel or how fucked up I truly am, Michael still sees the best in me. And right now, that's more than I can say about my own mother.

Joyce

YOU KNOW I TOOK my mother to see *Sophie's Choice* one year. I thought it would be good for us — a little mother-daughter bonding, a little Judaica, a little reprieve from feeling obligated to speak to each other for three hours. So the first fifteen minutes of the movie, Sonja kept saying, Is she Jewish? She's not Jewish. What, you're telling me they couldn't find a Jewish actress to act Jewish? I'm telling you, people were hushing us; it was mortifying, okay.

So afterward, Sonja lets out this heavy sigh and says, That's why you should always have two, Joyce. I knew what she meant, but I asked anyway. And why is that? I said, baiting her. God forbid, but, she said, ducking her head beneath the high heavens: just in case, she said. Just in case? I said, Just in case what, Mom? Just in case you find yourself stepping out of a cattle car, arriving at Auschwitz in 1941, and you have to choose which of your two children is going to die in the ovens? You mean *that* just in case? Sonja, are you insane? Honestly, have you completely lost your mind?

I couldn't speak to her for weeks after that. And, fortunately or unfortunately, she couldn't speak to me, either. It was my dad who finally called to mend fences, telling me how distraught Sonja had

132

been. I didn't buy it, of course, but I felt for my dad, torn between us until the day he died. No wonder he checked out early.

One day at the hospital, my dad sighed, and then, in his sleepy morphine voice, he said, Joyce . . . if only you could have known her, if only you could have seen her. Boy, she had a smile. Let me tell you, she had a smile that could've solved an energy crisis. Quick, too — just like you, Joycie — the woman had a one-two punch like sunshine and lightning. She was so full of life, he said, riding off into the opium sunset again. And I knew, *I knew* he wasn't lying — I knew he was telling the truth, but I didn't believe him. I couldn't. I still can't, really.

Bobbie

I SAT BESIDE HER at the funeral. There was an incredible procession of cars — hundreds of people turned out in the pouring rain. Afterward, walking back to the car, I followed Joyce and Michael, who were following Sonja, and then Benjamin suddenly stopped in his tracks and said, Oh, no! I'll never forget that: Oh, no! He couldn't have been more than four years old and he spoke in a voice that was so Opie-earnest, you expected him to say something like, Gosh, darn it! Or, Dagnabit!

We all stopped, and then Michael, Joyce, and Sonja turned to look at him — they all had the same look in their eyes, as though they were all wondering if he'd finally realized what was happening, what this really meant. Then Benjamin looked up at Joyce and he said, I hope Poppy remembered his umbrella . . . Joyce looked at him, and she began to smile, but her eyes welled with tears. Then Sonja turned to look at her, waiting to see if Joyce would dare cry in public, so I said, Hey, Benjamin? Do you want to come with us? Yeah, come with us, Benjie! Adela said, luring him away. Which didn't take much because the boy had such a crush on her that it was comic.

Benjamin's coming with us, I offered, and then Joyce pulled it together. We'll see you at Nana's, okay? she said, speaking to him. Be good — hey, she said, grabbing his sleeve: I said be good. I will, he said, taking off, piling into the backseat with Adela.

133

I remember the driver closing the door, after I'd gotten in the car, and then I looked back at the grave one last time, thinking about Irving, Benjamin, my own mother . . . how, when you got down to it, Benjamin knew no more or less than any of us. But what he *did* understand was that every solemn occasion has a silver lining. Aunt Bobbie? he said, looking up at me with those big eyes. Yes, sweetheart? I said. Can we go to McDonald's? he said, as soon as I turned around. Adela just looked at me, sitting behind him, and I had to think about it, knowing he was playing me.

I leaned forward to speak to the driver. Listen, I said, a hundred bucks if you take us to McDonald's. McDonald's? he said, turning to look at us in the backseat. You want to go to McDonald's? Eeesh, he said, clenching his jaw, I don't know. I could get in trouble —. You won't get in trouble, I promise. I'll even throw in a Big Mac, I said, using the same smile that had just been used against me.

When we got there, the driver stayed outside to smoke, and the three of us went inside. We sat in a booth in front of the swing set, and Benjamin knelt beside me, mesmerized, staring out the window, chomping his french fries to the quick, watching the kids playing. Content for the moment, but mentally preparing himself to pounce as soon as he finished eating, calming himself by shaking his little butt back and forth, back and forth.

Benjamin, you want to go play? Adela asked, and he looked at me for permission. Ten minutes, I said, and then she took him outside, while I sat in the booth in my black dress and waved, watching Adela push Benjamin so high on the swings that he screamed in the most delicious terror, and I couldn't help laughing. Maybe it was inappropriate to take him to McDonald's, I don't know. What can we do but keep living?

We flew home the next day, Adela and I, but it was more than a year before I saw Joyce again — the person I knew, I mean. Standing at the grave, I remember holding Adela's hand, thinking, *Who knows? Maybe it's easier to lose a parent young — maybe I had it easy, who's to say?* Then again, the truth is that it's never easier: there's no such thing in love.

Joyce

HE GOT EXISTENTIAL at the end, old Irving. He kept stuttering, What, what if, what if this is it? What if there is nothing else? A week or two of that and I lost all patience. I mean, come on, I already had one child asking too many meaningful questions. Finally, I said, Oh, Jesus Christ, Dad, who died and made you Woody Allen? He smiled, then he said, Ah, Joycie, you're funny . . . I like that in a funny girl. Michael started laughing, shaking his head. Listen to the peanut gallery, my dad said, hiking his thumb at Michael.

Sure are feisty today, aren't we? I said. I got nothing left to lose, he said, staring at the ceiling like it was the Milky Way. You know what I always say, Joycie? Where's my change? I said. What's that, Irv? Michael asked, trying to find a more comfortable position in the hospital chair, and Dad said, I always say: It's not the size of the bitch in the fight; it's the size of the fight in the bitch.

You said it, Michael said, turning once again, looking as though he was actually about to try and plump the bedside chair. So I said, Michael, please, leave the chair alone; it's not hurting anyone but you. Besides which, these chairs are designed for maximum discomfort. Just another little way the hospital has of saying, Time is money: now get the fuck out, people.

Michael, you need to stretch your legs? Dad asked. No, no . . . not a problem, Michael said. You sure? Because the nurse, that little brunette, gives a great massage, he said, giving Michael a wink. And I just looked at Michael, like, where — where was he coming up with this stuff? He always said it's the size of the fight in the bitch? To whom? I was forty years old, with a child of my own, when a lightbulb exploded above my head, thinking, *My god . . . did he have a life I didn't know about? Did he actually have a life without me?* And another thing, he said: Just remember that *twat* is spelled with an *A,* not an *O.*

I looked at Michael, my mouth hanging open. This is my father speaking. My dear old dad, Irving Kessler, a man who had never once raised his voice or spoken a dirty word in my entire life . . . I'm telling

135

you, at that moment, I almost wept. *I knew you were in there, Dad, I knew there was a man in there, somewhere . . . I never gave up hope,* I thought, reaching for his hand. Then I saw he was white-knuckling the morphine drip. Oh, I said, disgusted. You lush. Gimme that, I said, taking his clicker away.

Hey, Irving, Michael said. What's it like, morphine? Oh . . . overrated, Dad said, looking sleepy again. And scratchy — it's very scratchy, if you want to know. I had some better stuff at home, but your mother took it. Actually, I took it, I said. But it was pretty good, thanks, I said, squeezing his hand. I'll be damned, he said, the truth comes out . . .

I hate to say it, but in some ways, those shifts together, those times when Sonja was home, taking her turn sleeping an hour or two, those hours with my dad were some of the best we ever spent together. Michael stayed with me the whole time, too. For two weeks he didn't leave my side. Which, of course, was only possible under the circumstances; we would've killed each other, otherwise.

But still, for some reason I thought my dad's death bound us in some way, not unlike our vows had. He adored my father, and vice versa. I mean, really, Michael took a lot of heat off the old man for a few years there — and to survive his death together, I was certain we would last.

Lynne

I REMEMBER STANDING at the grave, listening to the priest talk about what a kind and devout woman my mother had been all her life, as Lisa stood on one side of my dad and I stood on the other. I remember that when he said those words, kind and devout, Daddy put his arm around Lisa, hugging her — but not me. No, he didn't touch me. Then Don put his big arm around me, and, frankly, I wished he hadn't. I wish he'd just left it alone. Because the gesture was so obvious — sweet, yes, but so painfully obvious — it only made it more humiliating for me.

I was pregnant. I'd been planning on telling my parents I was pregnant for more than a month, but I wanted to tell them when my mom was well enough to express . . . well, anything, really, without coughing herself into a respiratory attack. I kept thinking I'd find the right time to tell my mother I was pregnant, but I never did.

Who wants a drink? my dad asked, as we returned to that infernal kitchen table. Lisa had gone out, no one asked where — myself, included. Not me, I said, but my father ignored me, taking out three glasses. So I repeated myself: I said not me, Daddy, as he started pouring. The truth, of course, is that he was almost deaf, so I'll never know if he heard me or not, but still. He turned around, gripping the three glasses together, and then I mouthed the words: No thank you. I can't, I said. Why not? he said. Because I'm pregnant, I said. My timing couldn't have been worse, and I knew it. Really, I was behaving like a child who found a new way to throw a tantrum: by acting like an adult.

No one spoke. Don just stared at his hand, wrapped around the glass, and in true fashion, my father said, Well, then . . . all the more reason to toast. And then I walked out of the room. I made it to my mother's old bedroom, the room Don and I had taken, and I started crying, finally realizing that he and I, Daddy and I, we just . . . we were never going to be close, were we? Honestly, until a few days ago, I don't think I'd ever felt so completely alone in all my life.

Joyce

AFTER WE GOT HOME from the funeral, people kept coming over and saying to me, Oh, your mother's so brave! And, Look how strong she's being for you, Joyce. And I just looked at them, thinking, *I'm sorry, but have you ever met my mother? Because if you had, you'd know that that's just utter and complete bullshit — I mean, let's get a few things straight. First of all, she's not being anything for me right now; and second of all, if she were so brave, she would've been the first to cry — she would've led the way, all right?* Thank you for coming. Will you excuse me? I said, smiling, heading for the bar I'd set up in the backseat of the rental car.

That's where Michael found me, trashed, knock, knock, knocking on heaven's door for the twentieth time, and by god, I wasn't leaving until somebody opened up. When he tapped on the glass, I rolled down the electric window; the volume practically blowing his hair. Can you believe this? Ninety-seven bucks a day, and no treble. I mean, I'm grieving here: give me some fucking treble, people, I said, turning the volume down. Don't try to make me go back in there, I said, looking up. I was going to beg you to let me in, he said, and I unlocked the door. He sat down, looking at me, and then he pulled me over, hugging me, before I lay down, closing my eyes.

I don't know how long I was out, but I remember hearing voices and then . . . and then I remember smelling french fries. I thought I must be dreaming. How long have I been asleep? I said, rubbing my eyes. Two and a half hours, he said. What? Why didn't you wake me, Michael? Because you needed to sleep, he said. But if you wouldn't mind sitting up, my legs went numb about ninety minutes ago . . . Thanks, he said, shaking out his feet and moaning in relief as I sat up. Are you hungry? he said. Starving, I said, fixing my hair.

Bobbie brought you something, he said, pulling a McDonald's bag off the floor. And I was fine for a minute, watching him pull a deluxe cheeseburger out of the bag, then I looked at the house and I remembered. I'd forgotten for a moment — for a second there, my dad was still alive, and then he was gone again. That's when I realized that this was going to keep happening over and over again, forgetting and remembering, and I thought, *Should I start counting? How many mornings, how many hours, minutes, seconds will I be punished, waking to think that everything is all right, only to remember that it's not, that nothing is right.*

But for that moment, for that split second, I still had him — he was still alive. The front curtains were drawn, but I could see Sonja's figure moving across the living room, probably heading to the kitchen. I felt numb, watching Michael taking fries out of the bag, then I had to reach across his lap and open the door just in time to retch on the driveway.

When I was able to sit up, Michael handed me his handkerchief. Where's Benjamin? I asked, wiping my mouth. Watching TV with Adela, he said. Did everyone leave? I said. No, he said, Lenny and Doris are still here. Sonja came out to check on you, he said, without the least trace of sarcasm. What did you tell her? I said, folding the cloth into a tidy square. I told her you'd gotten plastered and passed out, and she should do the same, he said. You did not —. Didn't I? he said, taking a bite of his burger.

Michael? I said, sighing, and he said, Yeah, babe? And I said, What do you think about having another? A kid, you mean? he said. Yes, a kid, I said, what about it? Well, I'm not opposed to the idea, but one of us would have to quit her job, he said. Would you mind? I said. Me? he said, laughing. Why me? Because I make more money than you do, I said, smirking, as he removed my head from his chest. Oh, come on, Michael, I was teasing — happens to be true, but I was just teasing.

To this day I still can't believe he just sat there the entire time, with my head on his lap, stroking my hair. I mean, it happened — I was there . . . But I still don't believe it.

Lisa

WHAT CAN I SAY? They're completely different relationships. With Greg, there was nothing I couldn't tell him about myself, nothing I didn't want him to know about me. We had no secrets, no shame. Granted, I was pretty shameless to begin with, but still. I'd never been interested in falling in love — honestly.

As far as I could tell, people just made such asses of themselves for three to six months and then they spent the rest of their time grieving that the asshole stage was over: oh, the romance is gone. When I looked around, seeing people mooning all over each other, I was just like, fuck that . . . no way. And then, when it happened, I thought I was going to be the exception — we weren't going to act like thirteen-year-olds, no way. I mean, I didn't act thirteen at thirteen, I sure as hell wasn't going to start at twenty-three . . . I thought wrong — wrong, again.

And with Will? she asked. With Will, it's different, I said. There are plenty of things Will doesn't know about me, and she said, For example? And I said, Well, for example, Will doesn't know anything about the year I was basically homeless, or that I've had two abortions — and

I'll never tell him that, either. One was more than enough for Will; one was excusable, but two? Two he'd never understand — which is fine, really. Honestly, I said, Will doesn't need to understand everything about me; and I don't need him to know everything about me. I mean, I had that once; it didn't turn out so well.

Bobbie

WELL, HELLO, GORGEOUS, I drawled, entering the exam room. Well, hello to you, Dr. Gorgeous, she said. We are fabulous, aren't we? I said, placing my hand on her thigh. We are, she agreed. It was a routine we did once a year, every year, before I grabbed the stool and took a seat beside her.

How are you, Lisa? I'm good, she said, grinning from ear to ear. You look good, I said. No, she said, throwing out her hand, as though I was embarrassing her. You do, I said, clicking my pen. No, she said, I look *fanfuckingfabulous*. I sit corrected, I said, smiling. Tell me, what's your secret?

Well, let's see, she said. I graduate next week. I've been offered my dream job at a salary that will allow me to work myself to death without starving first. And . . . and I have a boyfriend. She was absolutely beaming. And, I said, what's his name? Greg, she said, grinning from ear to ear. Where is Greg from? I said. *Detroit,* she said, pronouncing it with a French accent. He's from Detroit, Rock City, she said. And what does he do, this Greg from Detroit? He's a painter, she said. Well, no . . . he's a *fanfuckingbrilliant* painter. You watch, you're going to read his name in the paper one day: *Greg Malone is the best fucking painter of his generation. . .*

Well, he's obviously doing something right, I said. Oh, she said, raising one hand, bracing the air, trust me, Doctor G, there are things they don't teach you in medical school. You're telling me? I said. One last question: Where did you get this dress? It's fabulous, I said, admiring her style.

She had on some vintage A-line number, her hair in an updo or whatever they're called. Hot-pink patent heels and black liquid eyeliner. She was always a fashion plate. Two-dollar bin, she said, grin-

140

ning. Ugh, I knew you were going to say that, I said. Love it. Now, should we check out the rest of you? I said, standing again. I'll be back in a minute. The less-than-fashionable paper gown is right there, you know the drill, I said, wrinkling my nose at her and closing the door behind me.

I'd never seen her so happy. In fact, it takes a hell of a woman to look *that* gorgeous under the florescent lights of an exam room. I'd watched Lisa grow up; she'd been through so much, she deserved it — every hug, every kiss, every beat of her heart.

Lisa

WE MET AT the end of my first year at Columbia. Kate dragged me to this party in Tribeca, thrown by this chick Ulla, whom I couldn't stand — I mean, I could not *stand* the chick. She was some six-foot-tall German heiress in the MFA program, whose father was the CEO of Swatch or something like that.

Kate knew all those people because they were in the program together, but she didn't come from money. She was the last generation of middle-class kids who could still move to New York in the hopes of making it big. That's not possible anymore, and even back then, the chance was one in a million. Anyhow, on our way there, Kate told me that Ulla held salons, and I stopped in my tracks: You're fucking kidding me . . . *salons*? There'll be drugs, Kate said, pulling me along, and I said, Twist my arm, why don't you?

It was a warehouse on Duane Street, and a bit run-down back then. At least the original freight elevator was still intact. The elevator opened directly into the loft, which must've been three thousand square feet, easily. Nice life if you can get it, huh? Kate said, and I just glared at the room. I hated those people. I hated them for their privilege; I hated them, knowing they'd all be famous soon enough. Of course they'd all be famous — they'd never have to work a day in their lives, what else were they going to do?

That's why I wanted Kate to make it — I didn't know how, but then and there, looking around that posh spread, I decided I was going to make her a big star. For two reasons: One, to prove that it was still possible, because I had to believe it was possible for people like us. And two, in a close second, to flip my finger at everyone who was standing in front of me at that moment.

Then across the room I saw Greg talking to Ulla, and he caught me looking at him, so I looked away. Where's the booze? I said, and Kate led me by my elbow into the kitchen. A few minutes later, Greg sidled over, making himself a drink. Hello, he said. Hey, I said, turning away. I'm Greg, he said, but I just looked him up and down — I gave him the Sally, basically.

Let's try that again, shall we? he said. My name's Greg. What's your name? And I said, Lisa, taking a drink. And he said, Lisa? Lisa what? And I said, Lisa Barrett, that's what. I was in the Art History Department, but I knew who he was — everyone knew who Greg was. And unlike most of the painters in the program, Greg could actually draw. In fact, he was far and away the best draftsman I'd ever known — still, to this day. You know those specials you see on musical geniuses, little kids who can hear a piece of music — anything, Mozart, Monk — they hear it once, and then they can sit down at the piano and play the song note for note? That's how Greg was with painting.

First time . . . god, this is so corny, but the first time I saw one of his paintings — and this was early work, he was twenty-four, twenty-five, maybe — I remembered that saying, the one about how there are no atheists in trenches or delivery rooms. I just didn't know which I was standing in, delivery room or trench. Both, I guess.

Naturally, my next thought was, *I'm going to fuck you. Whoever you are, you're on . . . oh, you're so on.* Then, when Kate pointed him out one day, I thought, *Him? He . . .* he was *hot.* So good-looking, I thought there was no way in hell could he have any talent other than beauty, pure luck.

Well, good news was I'd moved up from starfucker groupie to bona fide starfucker. But when I saw him talking to Ulla, watching the entire room circle around him, waiting for his acknowledgment, that was all I needed to write him off. Honestly, the whole thing disgusted me in that way that made me want to fuck him and bite his head off, like some insect mating-death ritual, so I got out of there as fast as I could.

I turned and walked away, looking for Kate to tell her I was leaving. But when I got in the elevator, Greg got in with me, closing the gate behind us. You wanna see the roof? he said, and I said, No. Well, that's where this elevator is going, so you'll have to take it down after, he said, turning the handle.

Guess you weren't having a good time, huh? he said, looking upward. It's not my scene, I said, purposefully looking in the opposite direction. And what is your scene? he asked, opening the gate. I'll let you know when I get there, I said, staring straight ahead. Something to look forward to, he said, stepping out onto the roof, and I pretended I hadn't heard. Come see the view, he said, and I said, Thanks, anyway.

Lisa, he said, turning back to look at me. Did I . . . did I *do* something to you? And I shrugged: No. But just out of curiosity, do you enjoy having your ass kissed? I said. And here I was, thinking you didn't like me for some reason, he said, and I had to bite my tongue to keep from smiling. I was talking about all your Eurotrash jet-setter friends, I said, and you could hear the cat hiss in my voice, *rrrrerhrr.* If you don't like anyone here, why'd you come? he said, and I shrugged. Free drugs, I said.

At least you've got your priorities straight, he said. Yes, I do, I said, closing the outer gate, and then Greg took a vial out of his jacket pocket and held it up, wiggling it in the air. I ignored him, sliding the inner door shut, but then I just stood there, holding the freight handle, debating what to do. When I reopened the gate, Greg was standing there, his arm still in the air. Now give us a smile, he said, popping the vial back in his pocket and taking out a pack of cigarettes.

Bobbie

JOYCE ONCE ASKED me what I liked best about Paul. A few things come to mind, I said, but I think what I like best about Paul is that he doesn't judge me the way I judge him — or myself, for that matter.

Ah, that's sweet, Joyce said, patting my thigh. But let me rephrase the question: What's the *dirtiest* thing you like best about Paul?

By the way, I said, did you know he plays the ukulele? That's great, she said, but wake me up when it gets kinky, okay? He's quite talented, I said, smiling. It's true, though. One night the two of us were sitting at the table, and Paul was massaging my feet, when out of nowhere he said, Did I ever tell you I was once a semiprofessional ukulele player? Before I could respond, he moved my feet, got up, and left the room, returning to the kitchen with a ukulele.

Semiprofessional? I said, *Wow.* True story, he said, tuning the instrument, and I said, Did you ever think of turning pro, or is that too much to dream? Ah, you laugh, he said, but have I got a song for you. Then he started singing and strumming: *You are here and warm, but I could look away and you'd be gone, 'Cause we live in a time where meaning falls and sputters from our lives, And that's why* — oops, he said, starting again. *And that's why I've traveled far, 'cause I come so together where you are.* He stopped: 'Cause I come so together where you are, Bob, he said, lowering the ukulele, looking at me. Then I laughed — I laughed right in his face. I said, Nice one, Don Juan . . . and his face fell. It's *splinters*: where meaning falls in splinters from our lives, I said. Sputters, splinters — whatever, he said, cradling the instrument.

I know why he said semiprofessional, why he qualified his abilities. Because, early on, I asked him if he was a good architect, and I meant it jokingly, of course, but I expected a certain answer, a certain degree of confidence, I admit. Even the failsafe boast, *I do all right.* But in all seriousness, Paul answered: So-so, rocking his hand, side to side. Great carpenter, but so-so architect. I was never going to be great — I knew from the start, he said. He was so forthright about it, too — I was stunned. Why, does that turn you off? he said, tracing a lock of hair behind my right ear. I don't know, I said, smiling, trying not to think about it.

Don't lie, Bobbie, please. I can't stand lying, he said, and I said, Yes. Yes, it does turn me off, if you want to know the truth. Because I don't know how to respect a man who's satisfied with being average at his chosen profession. I'm sorry, but mediocrity isn't high on my list of turns-ons — no offense, I said.

He didn't speak for a moment, and then he said, None taken. But of course I felt horrible for saying such a thing because it wasn't called for. Hey, he said, dropping the subject by knuckling and shaking my chin: Look at me, he said, so I did. It's okay, he said, just don't lie to me, that's all I ask. All right? he said, and I nodded. All right, I said.

Lisa

THE DEAL WAS I WORKED. Yes, I worked; I paid the rent; I paid the bills. And, in exchange, Greg painted. That was our agreement. Seems crazy now, I know, but at the time, I would've worked seven days a week, three hundred and sixty-five days a year to support his painting. I've never . . . I've never believed in anyone more. I've never been so close to work that I thought was truly brilliant — right there, in our living room, too.

Place was a disaster, of course. One morning, I stepped into the tub and turned on the water, only to look down and start screaming, thinking my feet were bleeding . . . blue. I thought I was bleeding blue blood. Greg tore open the shower curtain, thinking I'd stepped in glass, I don't know what. But seeing that I was just standing in the overflow from one of his paint jars, he started laughing. Oh, he got a good laugh out of that.

He was a phenomenon at Columbia. Greg was a star, and, likewise, treated with reverence and contempt, depending on who you were talking to. Critically, he wasn't that well educated, partly because he'd had a learning disability as a child and was held back in school. But he didn't give a fuck about critical theory, semiotics — just the paint. The canvas and the paint, that's all he cared about.

I used to watch him, the way he inspected the work of other students — I mean, the way he walked up to a canvas was so confrontational, all but cocking his chin: Let's see. Come on — show me what you can do, fucker. I remember him doing that once with this friend of mine, this Japanese painter, Tomiko.

We went to her opening, and I watched Greg step forward, thinking to myself, *Oh, here we go.* I loved her work, too. I was getting ready for a fight on the way home, if he was the least bit condescending — but then Greg just looked. He looked and looked, becoming quiet, calm. He looked over, his eyes telling me, *This is fucking amazing — this woman can really paint.* Yes, he had a big mouth and an even bigger ego, but he just wanted . . . god, he was so young, he just wanted honesty. Truth, that's all.

Of course at the time, everyone was scrambling to get a gallery, and Greg just sat back, laughing. People came to see him, to meet him — galleries actually came to Harlem to see his work, and he told them, Thanks for making the trek, but I'm not ready. Sorry, I'm just not ready yet. I'm going to take a couple years and learn to paint. Really, last thing this world needs is another bullshit painter, hanging his two-hundred-thousand-dollar insect paintings on a wall in some shiny new Chelsea gallery.

Word got around. It spread like wildfire. Within five minutes of some famous gallery owner leaving the school in a huff, everyone knew Greg said his work wasn't ready to be shown. And they hated him all the more for saying that, for making them look like sniveling fools. Like the fucking dilettantes they were.

He did sell one painting, though, but just one. And then he surprised me with a trip to Paris as a graduation gift. I was twenty-four years old, and I'd never been out of New York State.

Our first day there, I saw a pair of shoes in the window at Christian Lacroix, and I stopped in my tracks. And for five, ten minutes, I stood there, motionless, covering my mouth with both hands, silencing my ecstasy. Look, I said, finally: Look at those *shoes*.

They were bright blue, robin's-egg blue satin and python, woven together, open-toed, with thin straps that wrapped around the ankle, and then, the crowning glory, one large ostrich feather, jutting at the back of the heel. Now *that* is a work of art, I said. Excuse me? he said. I'm just saying, I said, still staring at them.

What do you think? I said, Four inches? Five, he said, correcting my estimate. Greg was always more accurate with proportion. With five-inch heels, I said. Five-inch heels with real ostrich feathers. I'd never seen anything so beautiful in all my life. Should we kneel? he asked, taunting me. It's not a bad idea, I said, as he pulled me away.

I hate to say it, but Paris disappeared that day. Honestly, I couldn't think of anything but those shoes. One day, I would have a pair of shoes like that. One day . . .

Joyce

I JUST LOOKED at her, thinking, *A semiprofessional ukulele player? Dear Lord.* I said, Tell me something, Bob. Yes? she said, smiling that dopey in-love smile. Are you going to start doodling your name as Mrs. Paul Dr. Bobbie So-and-So? Because I'm gonna need reinforcements if that's the case —. Joyce, I told you to quit hitting me up for drugs, she said. I'm a doctor, not a pharmacy. Oh, honey, I laughed, patting her thigh. Is that what they told you at medical school?

But first, I said, can we just play a few rounds of I told you so, I told you so? Mmmh, I moaned, savoring the moment. Aren't those just the sweetest words in the English language? I said. Wait, what — what was it you said to me, Bob, he's . . . he's not my type? Fuck off, she said, beginning to blush. Ho-ho. My fair lady sullies her chaste tongue with the F-word? *Damn.* I knew he'd be good for you, I said. *Knew it.*

Bobbie

THEN AGAIN, THERE are times I think he spends his entire day doing nothing but getting high, strumming his ukulele, and forwarding me articles like "The Ukulele Is No Toy," and links to YouTube videos. Anyhow, Paul called me at the office one night, and I put him on speakerphone. I said, You know, if you keep sending me these e-mails, I'm going to start sending you the classifieds. Why? he said, and I said, Because you need a job, that's why. Which wasn't fair, I know. I make him sound like a prince when it suits me, and a fuckup when it doesn't — I was just tired, that's all. It was a long day, and I almost wept, looking at the stacks on my desk. Three partners, and I still have to work eighty-hour weeks to keep up with the paperwork.

Fortunately or unfortunately, he ignored me. For your information, I have a job, he said, I'm your personal trainer: we're in training here. I didn't call just to chat, you know. No, I called you to chat *and* waste your precious time — we're multitasking, you see, getting twice the workout. Speaking of, I said, I'm at work now, Paul. And what I usually like to do at work is work. And what I have to do at work even if I don't like it, is work, and I could hear him falling to his side, laughing. Are you stoned? I said. Well, that would depend on how you define *are*, he said, cracking himself up.

Please, Paul, I said, imploring him. Please, you have no idea how much —. Bobbie, he said ignoring me, Bob, let me ask you something. If I answer your question, will you let me work? I said. Come on, now — don't give up — a few more reps and we're done for the day. Deep breath, in through the nose, he said, inhaling, and I said, All right. What is it?

Just a little question that's been plaguing humankind since the dawn of time, he said, strumming a few notes or bars or whatever one strums on ukuleles. And it goes like this, he said, tapping as he counted off: Two, three, four: *Why's love got to be so sad . . . ?* Listen, I said, I've had a shitty day today, and it's far from over —. Which, he said, is exactly why you need a song to lighten your heart. One song, Paul. *One,* I said. Do you hear what I'm saying? Yes, you're saying one song, he said. All right, then, I said, how 'bout some Dylan? And he said, Keep your pants on, Doc . . .

I requested Dylan because no man can resist giving you his Bob Dylan impersonation. Honestly, I don't know what happens in the male brain, but it's like universal Tourette's; men simply cannot relax until they release the lyric from their lips. It's like the first time a five-year-old sees *ET* and spends the next day, week, month, year of his life raising his imaginary alien digit to the sky, croaking E . . . T . . . Sure enough, he let it go: *I want you, I want you . . . I want you so baaad.*

So I requested "Sad-Eyed Lady of the Lowlands." Come on, let's hear what you got, I said, thinking he wouldn't dare. Then he started singing. And at first, I couldn't stop grinning, I was so shocked, but then I started tearing up because — because it occurred to me that no man had ever serenaded me before. And because there are some people who sing with such honesty and such humility: voices that bare themselves, naked in a way the body can never be. Joyce taught me that.

So there I was, sitting at my desk, with tears in my eyes, listening to some middle-aged pot-smoking mediocre semiretired upstate divorced architect playing Dylan on the ukulele for me on speakerphone.

Jordan

BUT CAN YOU believe we actually had a fight about homecoming? Seriously, Mom asked if I wanted to go look for a dress, and I was just like, For what? And she goes, For homecoming, and I'm like, No, because I'm not going, and she's like, Why not? And I'm like, Mom, I have to work, and then we just got into it because she goes, Jordan, I really think you should go, and I was just like, Why? And she goes, Because I don't want you to regret it, one day—. And I was just like, Please, twenty years from now, if you ever hear me say, *Oh, I wish I'd gone to homecoming,* shoot me. Because obviously I don't have a life, anyway, and she was like, You sound just like Lisa, and she meant it as a slam, you know, but I was just like, Really? I sound like Lisa? Anyhow.

The strange thing was that I didn't want to go—honestly, I was so relieved I had to work—but at the same time, I was in a nasty mood because . . . I don't know, it's like I felt left out. Because no one asked me, that's why. The only good thing was that when Misha gave me a ride home that night, he didn't say anything about it, and I didn't know if he didn't know it was homecoming or what, but I didn't care. Because I *so* didn't want to talk about it, and then, just before we got to my house, Misha goes, Oh, I almost forgot, and then he kept driving.

So he parked on the dead end next to the river, and he turns around, grabbing his bag from the backseat, and he goes, I got you something, and I was like, Really? What is it, a corsage? And he goes, Better, and then he pulled this big pink bottle out of his bag and

149

handed it to me. Bubbles? I said, reading the yellow label. You got me bubbles? And he goes, They were damaged, but they seem fine now — open them. Now? I said. Yes — here, he said, offering to open them for me.

He twisted the cap and pulled out the plastic wand, holding it in front of my mouth, and he goes, Go on. And I looked at him, and I'm like, Are you seriously asking me to blow you?, and I started laughing. He just looked at me, totally unamused, right, then he goes, Oh, wait — there's something else, hold on . . . get this — check it out. Then he pulls out this kazoo, like the bottle came with one of those bubble kazoos, you know?

So he pulls out the kazoo and dips it in the bottle and then he just starts blowing bubbles everywhere. I mean, he had like thousands of bubbles going, and I started screaming, telling him to stop, because they kept popping on my face, and there was all this bubble spit flying everywhere, and then I had to roll down the window to get some air. But seriously, it was *so* much better than stupid fucking homecoming. So I was just like, Thanks for my damaged bubbles, and he just shrugged and he goes, No sweat, then he started the car.

Bobbie

WE WERE SITTING in the sunroom, after breakfast that first morning, when I got up to take a look around. Oh, I said, and what types of plants are these, Paul? That's what's commonly known as a pot plant, he said, and I rolled my eyes. Do you argue the medicinal properties of marijuana, Doctor? No, I don't, I said. Do you have glaucoma? No, I don't, he said, but my mother does. Honestly? I said. Honestly, he said. And even if she didn't, there's no way in hell the woman's moving a quarter of a mile from my front door without having drugs readily available for the both of us.

I laughed, walking back to the table, taking another sip of juice. What? he said. Why are you shaking your head? Because, I said, only Joyce would set me up with a pot farmer. Well, it's not exactly a farm, he said, returning to his seat, but I like the way you think. Is this where you made your money? I said. No, he said. I made my money getting dumped by my ex-wife. So it's not really your money, is it? I said — it just came out. He said, Have you ever been married, Bobbie? He knew I hadn't, but I answered. No, I said. Well, when you have, you can tell me what *ours* means to you, he said.

I'm sorry. That was — that was completely out of line, I said, thinking, *Shit, I just blew it. Things were going so well, and I had to screw it all up, didn't I?* Yes it was, he said, and —. And? I said. And, as you were about to say, you're more than willing to make it up to me in any way I see fit. Yes, I said, as he pulled me from my chair, that's exactly what I meant to say.

Adela

I DON'T KNOW why I called him, really. I was just walking aimlessly for hours and hours, and I needed someone to talk to — that's why, I guess. I just needed someone to talk to. So I called him on his cell. Hello? he croaked. Michael, I said, it's Adela. Adela? he said, sounding confused. Bobbie Myers's daughter? I said. Adela, yes, he said. But what . . . what time is it? Don't ask, I said.

He said, What's wrong, Adela? What is it? I need a drink, I said. Will you buy me a drink? When? he said. Now, I said. Adela, where are you? Downstairs, at the hotel bar. He got a laugh out of that. I'm sorry, he said, did you say you need a drink or you had a drink? Both, I said. Two minutes, he said, sighing.

I didn't know what to say when he walked in, so I said, What took you so long? Then the bartender said, What can I get you? Michael started to speak, then let out a yawn. Excuse me: bourbon, please, he said. You look tired — you want a coffee instead? I asked. Just because I'm twice your age and it's . . . oh, three o'clock in the morning, he said. Yes, but it's only midnight L.A. time, I said. Dear god, he said. You've got your mother's looks and Joyce's logic . . . that's a terrifying combination.

Do you talk often? I said. Who, me and Joyce?, he said, looking surprised. Who, Joyce and me, I corrected him. Yeah, yeah, yeah, he said. Know what, next time you want to give me a grammar lesson, bring your wallet, Harvard girl. Oh, man, he said, yawning again. I'm sorry, I said, I shouldn't have woken you —. No, no, I'm just stretching my mouth, getting warmed up, he said. Joyce and me . . . well, as a matter of fact, we speak every day, sometimes twice a day — through our lawyers, of course. Then again, he said, after eight years, they aren't just lawyers; they're more like family — Joyce's family, at least.

So, Adela. What seems to be the problem? he said, seeing the bartender approach with his drink. Thank you. Put these on my tab, room three-fourteen, will you? he said, and the bartender looked at me. I told him, already, I said, and Michael smiled, nodding. At least I asked, I said. Yeah, yeah, yeah, he said, nodding: *at least.* Correction: you've got your mother's brains and Joyce's balls — now *that's* a terrifying combination.

So why don't you give her a divorce? I said. Did she, he said, quickly looking over his shoulders, did Joyce send you here to ambush me? Is that what this is about? No, I said, I'm just curious. Adela, do you have any idea how disappointed she'd be if I threw in the towel after eight years of battling it out? I can't. Last time I broke her heart, I swore I would never let her down again, he said, raising his glass. *Salud,* he said, and I raised my glass, Cheers.

Now tell me, he said. What brought you to my hotel at three in the morning? It was one when I got here, I said. What, so you were going to drink and dash on me? That hurts, he said. Seriously, Adela, you want to tell me what's going on? I said, Michael, I just —. But it took a minute before I could say it: I just made a complete fool of myself — I completely humiliated myself, I said, covering my face with both hands. And here I am, I said, looking up, voila! This wouldn't happen to involve a man, would it? he asked, setting down his drink. No, I said. No, I wouldn't call him a man . . .

I woke the next morning, not knowing where I was or what happened. Then I remembered Michael showing me to his room, offering to let me sleep in his bed before he closed the door behind him. It was a gorgeous suite, and I really didn't want to go home, but I didn't want to put him out, either. It's almost six, I need to shower and get to work soon — just let me grab some clothes, he said, opening the closet. I remember sitting on the side of the bed, watching the sky change colors, that was it.

When I finally got up to see if he was in the other room, I noticed there were fresh flowers on the table in the living room. I walked over to look at them, and then I saw that there was a card, addressed to me:

> *Adela,*
>
> *Please order yourself some breakfast.*
> *If you haven't done so already.*
> *Michael*
>
> *P.S.*
> *You SNORE.*

It was the first time I'd laughed in weeks. Then I just stood there looking at the flowers — they were beautiful. And I felt so much better, I really did — I almost felt like myself again. But then, an hour later, I felt so much better, all I wanted to do was call Marshall; there must be a way to get through to him — I just . . . I just had to try once more.

Joyce

AND YOU KNOW what he says? He says, Oh, Joyce . . . there you are. And then I just looked at him. *Here I am? That's the best you can do, Michael, here I am? Are you fucking kidding me?* I said, Michael, I think that's what's commonly known as open mouth, insert dick. No, I didn't. I wish I had; I wish I'd said that and more — *much more* — but I was speechless. Second time in my life I have ever been speechless.

I was standing outside, in front of the hotel, when Joe found me. You feeling all right? he said. You look pale, he said, and I said, I just needed some air. You sure? he said, squeezing my arm. What are you talking about? I said, I've been looking forward to this dinner all week. But an hour later, I had to leave the restaurant. I'd ordered the filet mignon, and then, looking at the blood on my plate, I thought I was going to be sick.

Lisa

SATURDAY NIGHT, I told Will I'd forgotten about a baby shower, and that he'd need to watch the baby for a few hours. I said I'd be home by two so that he could get some work done, but he didn't ask. So I got up early Sunday, and I stuffed myself into the most body-slimming black number I had; I went to the storage unit, then I changed my shoes in the cab on the way.

I'd worn my best coat, too — my most flattering coat, a fur. Well, a fur collar at least, and when I saw my reflection in the gallery windows, I had to laugh; fifteen years ago, I would have spat on someone like me . . . with good reason, too. Then again, I forgot how beautiful those shoes were — I forgot how they made me feel, you know. They felt like weapons, ankle holsters, opening the front door of the Joyce Kessler Gallery for the first time in five years.

Jordan

I FINALLY WENT outside Sunday night, to get some air, and I just sat on the swing. It was nice out, but I was so dreading the thought of going back to school that I felt sick again. And then I remembered Misha asking me once, straight out. We were sitting in his car, and he goes, Jordan, you don't have many friends do you? And at first, I was just like . . . I mean, he wasn't being mean; he was just asking, you know. So I was just like, I used to, but not anymore. And he goes, Why's that? And I wanted to tell him, but I didn't know where to begin.

I mean, it's so stupid, but it's like all the girls who I used to be friends with . . . I mean, Chloe Schenck — we were best friends since kindergarten, and now we don't even talk. And what happened was, one day, freshman year, I'm standing at Chloe's locker, waiting for her to get her books, and then I see: *Jordan Yaeger is a HO* written inside her locker. And I was just like, ohmygod, what is that, you know?

So I asked her; I said, What's that? And Chloe goes, Oh, it's noth-

154

ing, and she closed her locker. And I was just like, *Jordan Yaeger is a HO* is nothing? I didn't know what to say, you know. It was Trysta Dodd, that's who wrote it. Because Topher Janssen asked me out at the beginning of my freshman year, when he was a junior, and I said yes, and then the next day I found out that he was still going out with Lexie Romberger, which I didn't know, I swear. So when I found out, I told Toph I couldn't go out with him, and he was such a dick about it, and then all the junior girls hated me, too. I mean, I didn't know about Lexie, and I didn't go out with him, but it didn't matter. It wasn't because of Lexie or Topher; it's like they just wanted someone to hate, and I was it. I mean, seriously, if there wasn't someone to hate, it wouldn't be high school, would it?

I mean, Chloe just wanted to be in with all the cool junior girls so she'd get invited to all the parties, right? Because it's like Chloe always got all the attention from the boys when we were in junior high, and then one day, the summer before freshman year, my mom and I were shopping in New York, when this woman came up to us on the street. We stopped to find out what she wanted, and she said she was a modeling agent, and she gave us her card and said she'd be very interested in meeting with me. So we talked to her for a while, and that night my mom called Lisa, and Lisa said the agency was a big deal and I should meet with them, right.

It was like a dream come true, you know? I mean, come on — if you're a foot taller than anyone in your eighth-grade class and even your own brother calls you Jordan the Giraffe, what else are you going to dream about? So when Mom asked if I was serious, I said I was totally serious, and we made an appointment to meet with the woman a week later. After we got back from meeting with her, I told Chloe that the woman wanted me to work on a portfolio, and Chloe promised she wouldn't tell anyone, but then she did. One weekend, I had to go to New York to meet with this photographer, and I had to miss Alex K.'s birthday party, and I guess that's when Chloe told everyone I was skipping the party because I thought I was going to be a supermodel or whatever.

Monday morning, everyone — all those guys like Tyler and Brandon, that whole group of guys — they all started calling me Giselle.

I mean, I'm just walking down the hall, like, Hey, Ty, and he goes, Hey, *Giselle* . . . How's it going, *Giselle*? The worst part is that I was so embarrassed, I couldn't even call her on it, Chloe, because that would've just made it worse. So I had to act like she was my friend, and nothing happened, even though I knew she just totally lied to me.

People started posting shit about me — I almost felt worse at home than I did at school. But the thing is, I mean, even if you aren't sure what's being said, you can still feel people making fun of you, laughing behind your back, you know? It's like you feel it when you walk in late to the cafeteria; you feel it when you ask permission to go to the bathroom, just to get out of sixth-period algebra for two minutes. But there's no escaping it — god, even when you're alone, you can hear it in the stall, after you lock yourself in.

After that, I gained like fifteen pounds. I mean, there was the modeling thing, and then my dad got sick; he had this heart problem, and I went from like one-oh-nine to one-twenty-two in like three months, and I felt huge — I mean, not just tall: *big*. And I know I'm not fat, but still, just before Christmas break, Sophie Joyner walked past me in the hall one day and she looked me up and down and she goes: *A plus-sized model, maybe,* and I'd forgotten all about the modeling thing, you know. And I knew she was just being a bitch, but it worked — it totally worked. I mean, I feel disgusting — I feel like a giant, walking down the hall, like I'll barely fit through the door, you know. But it's like the only thing I like to do anymore is sleep and eat.

Anyhow, I just quit going out with my friends. I stopped calling, I stopped going out, and if you don't go out, no one includes you. I still sit with them, but I know the score; I know they aren't my friends. It's like last month, we were all sitting at the lunch table, and Chloe started singing Aretha Franklin, and I listened to her for a moment, and I was just like, What are you singing? I mean, she didn't know the song "Respect," okay? She thought the woman was rapping the alphabet or something, like: *r-b-d-j-k,* whatever, and I was just like, ohmygod . . . and I'm *friends* with you? So when Misha asked me if I had any friends, I didn't tell him any of that because I can't deal with talking about it, but also because, that drive home on Friday night, that's like my one escape, you know?

So all weekend, I kept turning off my phone, hoping if my phone was turned off, he'd call, right. Then I'd turn it back on an hour later and check my voice mail, because I was so sure he was going to call me, but he didn't — he didn't call. And then every time I checked, it's like I could hear my mom saying Misha was just using me. And it's like, maybe she's right, but that doesn't necessarily make it true, you know? It's like, I don't know why you have to go through so much shit before you can admit the truth sometimes, but that's not how it was. The truth is he didn't want me, he just felt bad for me. And the worst part is that I thought I'd feel better if we had sex, but I didn't. I just felt more alone.

Lisa

SHE WAS RIGHT, though. As much as I hate to say it, I was furious because Lynne was right about one thing: I don't know how to be alone with him anymore. In fact, I can't stand to be in the same room with my dad anymore . . . because he's dying. And it scares me — scares the shit out of me, if you want to know the truth. So brave, right?

And then, once I got on the train Saturday, all I wanted to do . . . all I wanted was to call Greg. Just to hear his voice. I mean, is that wrong, if there are some people who — or . . . or even just that one person who understands you in ways that no one else can possibly understand you? I don't know, I said, thinking out loud. I don't know what I want, really. I used to, but not anymore.

I said, I know how I make him sound sometimes, but Will's a good man. He is. And he gives a lot of money to worthy causes. Such as? she said. Doctors Without Borders, Fresh Air Fund, Planned Parenthood, I said, putting an end to the discussion. He's generous, he's thoughtful in his own way. It's just that he's — severe, I said. That's what I used to understand best about him, but now it's what I understand the least.

What else attracted you to Will? she asked. Well, I sighed: he worked hard. He was ambitious. He knew what he wanted, and he wanted me. Which was a hell of a lot more than I could say for Greg.

But now — now, we're just very different people. We were always different, I suppose, but that's lost its charm. I'd probably leave, I said, but I can't leave him without risking losing my son, so I can't go anywhere. Not now, at least.

I look back and I know everything that happened, but I still have no idea how I got here. Have you considered couple's counseling? she said. Will would never go for it, I said. Have you asked him? she said. No, I don't need to ask; he's openly contemptuous of therapy. Why? she said. I said, Paying someone to listen to your problems is obscene in Will's view. Obscene? she asked. Yes, obscene. Anal sex, no; therapy, yes. He's a Freudian wet dream, all right, I said. Just out of curiosity, she said, where does Will think you go every Monday at eleven? Assuming he thinks, I said, I don't know, yoga? He approves of yoga but not therapy? she said, and I said, Tighter ass: go figure.

Adela

I WENT BACK on Monday afternoon, even though I knew she wasn't there anymore, Ixnomy. I mean, I knew I wouldn't be able to see her face, but I bought flowers, and I went there to pray, because I couldn't think of a better place. The only problem is that I don't know how to pray. I mean, we never went to church except for funerals, and then I'd spend the whole time flipping through the hymn book, trying to find the sermon or whatever because I didn't want to be the only one not holding a book.

And I know you're supposed to kneel, but I wasn't kneeling in the middle of the sidewalk. So I stepped back, and I closed my eyes, trying to picture her face . . . and I could almost see her, except for the people staring at me, walking by. After a couple minutes, I was just like, *Mind your own fucking business, will you?*

Bobbie

STILL STARING AT THE DOGS, she said, Honestly, Bob, I don't think it ever occurs to her that she's being cruel — because that's just who she is. That's just Sonja, she said. Love her or leave her, I said. I'm trying, she said, believe me I'm trying.

How's Benjamin? I said. Alive, she said, but wishes he were dead. Right where you want him, I said. Exactly, she said. You know what the Greeks did? They swapped —. Now those were the days, I said. Oh, not just wives, she said, children, too. When their children became teenagers, parents sent their kids away to live with another family. Clever people, those Greeks, I said. You wanna swap? she said. Your son for my daughter? I said, and she thought about it. You know, she said, I always wanted a daughter until now. I understand, I said. I always wanted a mother until I met yours.

Speaking of, she said, you should call Del —. I will, I said. When? she said. When I'm ready to speak to her, Joyce. Bobbie, at least give her a chance to explain herself, she said, and I said, Joyce, she's my daughter —. Then act like it, she said. Excuse me, I said, but I don't need you to tell me how to raise my child — you aren't doing such a bang-up job, yourself —. No, Bob, no, you don't need me to tell you anything. In fact, you don't need anyone, do you? she said. I wanted to say, That's not true, Joyce, and you know it: I need you . . . but I didn't. Because something snapped, and the words vanished.

3

Adela

SHE KICKED ME OUT. I told him . . . *I told him* she could do it. I knew *exactly* what would happen, and when I heard her walk through the front door, my heart stopped. What are you doing here? she said, flinching, seeing me on the couch. I came to talk — we need to talk, Mom, I said. I told you I would call you, she said, and I said, Yes, you did, but you didn't call, and I have to get back tomorrow morning.

She said, Honestly, Del, I think you've said enough for one day; and I said, You think? Yes, I think you've said plenty, already, she said. Or is there another relationship in my life that you need to ruin? I said, That's not fair —, and she said, How old are you? Really, Adela, you want to talk about fairness? she said, and I couldn't say anything.

I didn't think so, she said. You're wrong, I said — it was all I could manage, fighting the quivering in my chin, pulling me down, down. You've got a lot of nerve, she said. Now go — please go before I say something I'll regret, and I said, Like what? Adela, I want you to leave, she said, and I said, No, really, Mom. Have you ever regretted anything in your life? Adela, I'm asking you, she said, and I said, Sorry, guess I didn't hear the question — all I've heard is accusations, and you won't even listen to me. Not now, no: I've heard enough for one day, she said, as though that ended the conversation.

I just nodded my head and then I said, You know . . . you're right. You're right, Mom, I shouldn't have come — but it's not just because you won't listen, it's because you couldn't understand, even if you wanted to. You've never been there, so how could you possibly understand? I said, and then I walked out.

Joyce

HONESTLY, WHO KNOWS why one marriage succeeds and another fails? I mean, I look at Sonja and Irving, and I wonder, why did *they* last when we didn't? Michael and I — we had so much more in common than they did. I mean, we talked, we laughed, we danced, we sang — we had sex. What was it, then? Was it our jobs, really? I don't know.

I just remember standing there that morning, on the balcony, hoping against hope that he would turn around, but he didn't. So what can you do but put one foot in front of the other and start over? Which is exactly what I did, hopping right back into bed, where I promptly drank my juice, popped a couple of Percocet, and slept eight hours straight.

It was almost dark before I got around to calling Sonja and telling her that we'd need to put Benjamin on a plane the next day, and that a driver would be picking him up at two o'clock. When she started asking questions, I said we'd talk about it once I had a chance to speak to my son, and for once, she dropped it. I swear that kid is the one and only person in the world the woman has ever put before herself. Then again, I'm sure the same could be said of me.

Michael picked Ben up at the airport, and we agreed he wouldn't say anything about anything, including my cast, until they got home, and I waited for them on the couch in the living room. It was such a beautiful sunset, too, and I remember thinking, *What a spectacular view . . . this view should've been mine . . .* And then I realized, *Wait a second — fifty percent of this is mine!*

Watching Michael walk into the living room behind Benjamin, I just looked at him, thinking, *You don't actually believe I'm going to give you a divorce* and *let you keep this house, do you? Oh, no,* I smiled. *Oh, no, no. Mark my words: Hell hath no fury, and I will see molten pitchforks rammed up your tight ass before you get one square foot of this house.*

Hey! What happened, Mom? Benjie asked, running into the living room, and then stopping in his tracks, startled by the sight of my ankle cast. Skateboard accident, I said, shrugging. Nuh-uh, he said, searching my face for signs of deceit before quickly looking to Michael to see if it could possibly be true. She did you proud, Benj, Michael said, reminding me what a gifted liar he was. I don't believe you! Benjamin said, throwing his head back and grinning. Come here, I said, taking him in my arms.

How's Nana? I said, kissing his forehead, and he sighed, Oh, fine. I kicked her butt at Uno, he said. Yeah? I said, grinning. Yeah, he said, like *twenty times.* Mom, she kept putting the blue on *green,* he said, looking up at me. Sweetheart, your grandmother's color-blind and you saw an opportunity, I said, patting him on the back. I felt bad for her, Mom, he said, and I said, Benjamin, you know the rules. Rule number one: weakness is for the weak. And you know who taught me that rule? Nana, I said, nodding, that's right. Fact is you did her proud, Benjamin, I said, pulling his head to my cheek, smelling his hair. Long as I live, I'll never forget looking down and kissing my son's forehead, thinking, *I know we're about to ruin your life, but believe me, I love you with all my heart . . .*

A few weeks after I got back from L.A., Sonja came for Thanksgiving. So we get home from the airport, and she immediately starts nosing around the living room, like she always does. All but running her white glove across the tops of the picture frames, when she suddenly stops in front of a picture and leans over, inspecting it, and I'm thinking, *Jesus, let's just get it over with. What is it, Sonja? What?*

Then she turns to me and says, Joyce. *Who* is that *stunning* woman? I had to catch my jaw before it broke a toe, and then, finally, I said, Me. That's me, Mom. *I'm* that stunning woman, I said, and then she goes, You? That's *you*? she says, leaning over, squinting. And I was just like, what, you think I'd just put random pictures of beautiful women around my house, and claim they're me?

Michael took the picture. It was a few months after my dad died, and we rented a house in Maui for three weeks. Benjamin still talks about that trip—I think it was the happiest month of our life together as a family. We're both so tan in the photo, and I have to say, I look like a neo–Jackie O, throwing my head back, laughing, while Benjamin grabs my coral necklaces.

Who took that picture? Sonja said, still unconvinced. Michael, I said. Oh, she says, I didn't know he was such a talented photographer! That's when it began, at that moment. After ten years of vilifying the guy, never once having had a kind word to say about him, the day I tell her we're divorcing, suddenly Michael became a saint. Then she starts in on me with the, Oh, I can't believe you could ever leave your husband. She says this—she actually said that to me.

Of course at the time, I was so stunned, I said to her, I said, Sonja. Who else's husband am I going to leave? I mean, really, the woman had the *audacity* to say this to me, okay. She goes, Joyce, I just don't understand how you can walk away after all these years together, especially when you have a child to think of. And at the point she brought Benjamin into it, I was just like, that's it. Aside from the fact that the kid's in third grade, and he's started pissing his bed again at night, he's so strung out from all our late-night fighting, you crossed the line this time, lady.

I said, Well, Mom, here's a thought. Why don't you call the house that I paid for with blood, sweat, tears, and my father's body, and ask the twenty-three-year-old Swedish straight-to-video actress, playing the role of look who's sleeping in my bed with my husband, how I could possibly think of doing such a thing, huh? Because, you and me, I said, pointing back and forth, we aren't having this conversation, Sonja. And the reason why we aren't having this conversation is because *I can't fucking talk to you*, okay? So for once in your life, why don't you mind your own goddamn business instead of passing judgment on a situation that you know absolutely nothing about!

Oh, her nostrils were flaring like sails in high winds. No, it—it took her a good minute to regain her composure, and then, finally, she goes: You do realize this could be your last chance, Joyce. And that stung, all right — she drew blood with that one, but I was perfectly willing to trade blow for blow. Yes, I realize this might be my last chance, I repeated. But I'm afraid that's a risk I'll have to take, seeing as the alternative is to live the rest of my life bitter and resentful, like you did with Dad, I said, staring her down.

Well. Needless to say, Sonja . . . Sonja was speechless. We're talking pure glass-eyed catatonic shock, okay. She was absolutely shocked that I would dare speak to her that way, that I would dare say such a thing. Honestly, it was *fantastic*. And that was the last time we ever discussed my marriage — or hers, for that matter. Of course, hearing shouting from the other room, Benjamin runs into the kitchen to see what all the commotion's about. Then he stops, and he looks at her, he looks at me, waiting for someone to speak, and then I said: Let's eat.

Bobbie

MY PHONE RANG in the cab, on my way to meet Joyce, and I checked the number, hoping it was Paul, but it was Adela. I looked at her name, and I thought about answering, but then my cheeks flushed . . . Leave, I'd told her, Sunday. I said, Please leave before one of us says something we'll both regret, and she said, It's a little late for that, don't you think? I said, Adela, I told you that I was not prepared to have this conversation — you haven't given me twenty-four hours, what do you expect me to say? That you love me, she said, say you love me.

Then I silenced the ringer. I know it's cruel, I do. I know it's cruel of me not to call her back, but frankly, she's not my first concern right now. She made her decision; she's a grown woman, or at least she says she is. Well, then: here you go. Time to grow up.

I said, Sir, right here, please. Excuse me: *right here,* sir. I said I want to get out here, I said, unfastening my seat belt. What? he said, speaking to me in the rearview. I said, *Right here.* You can't get out here, he said, and I handed him a ten. Take nine, I said, ignoring him.

By the time I got to the park, seeing Joyce . . . Honestly, what could I say? That I felt sick to my stomach and I had no idea what to say for myself, my daughter? Then, when I saw her, sitting there, staring

164

straight ahead, watching the dogs, she looked so calm, so peaceful . . . And then the thought of Joyce never speaking to me again, the thought of losing her seemed worse than death.

So? she said. So what? I said. So cut the bullshit, Bobbie, and tell me what happened Thursday night. All right, I said. Well, we had dinner, and then we had a fight. She said, *We* meaning? We meaning: me. *I* had a fight, I said. I see, she said. And what did Paul do to start this fight? Nothing, really, I said. Of course not, she said.

Did he call to apologize? she said. No, I said. Not once? she said, looking surprised. Not one call since Thursday night, I said. And now it's Monday afternoon, she said. Yes, and now it's Monday afternoon. Bastard, she said. How could he do nothing, and then — and then *not* call you to apologize for what he didn't do, at the very least? Exactly, I said. Which is why I'm not speaking to him, even if he does call. Which you hope he does, she said. Yes, I do, I said. I hope he calls so I can not return his call. In fact, if all goes according to plan, he'll call me countless times, and I'll never speak to him again. Serves him right — he brought this on himself, after all, she said. Thank you, I appreciate the support, I said. What are friends for, she said, sighing.

Adela

I SCREAMED IT, too: *I said I'm sorry, you fat bitch!* And then my voice echoed up and down twelve flights of stairs . . . I didn't feel better, but I was finally able to stand, at least. When I got downstairs, I walked over to the front desk and I said, Lionel, I had to take the stairs. I know, Miss Adela. I'm sorry, the repairman is on his way, he said, and I said, Know what, Lionel? I don't want you to call me *miss* anymore. Oh? he said, raising one dignified brow. Are you getting married? Not if I can help it, I said, and he smiled in a way that assured me he'd call me Miss Adela if I lived to be a hundred.

Never mind, I said. Listen. That woman who just came through with the little —. Yes, he said, nodding, she's new. I thought so, I said, nodding conspiratorially. Seventh floor, he said, and I said, Well, her little dog just had an accident on the stairwell —. Oh, I'm so sorry, Miss—. No, no, no. I just don't want anyone to slip coming downstairs, I reassured him. No, he said, we can't have that. No, we can't, Lionel, I said, offering my hand. It's good to see you, I said. And you, Miss Adela, he said, shaking once and carefully placing my right hand over my left.

I turned to walk out the door, then it hit me and I turned back. I said, You know what I'm going to call you from now on? What's that? he said. I'm going to call you Mr. Lionel. *Ha,* I said. How you like them apples, Mr. Lionel? I like 'em just fine, he said, grinning and tipping his hat. I was pleased with that, pleased to know this man, pleased to make him smile at the very least. How bad could I be if I could still make Lionel smile?

Bobbie

THURSDAY NIGHT, I went home, and I was asleep before my head hit the pillow. And I hate to say it, but the next morning, I felt fine. As a matter of fact, I felt great. I got up on time; I walked to work — I even got into the office early, just like I used to. In the past few months, for the first time in thirty years, I've been showing up late. I've fallen behind in my work; I'm unfocused — and I'd finally come to my senses.

But it was a little ridiculous, the way I kept chirping, Morning, everyone! *Morning!* With my patients, especially. Making a point to take an extra minute to talk with each of them, woman to woman. Putting my arm around their shoulders. Holding their hands. Telling jokes and asking about their lives, their boyfriends, girlfriends, husbands, families. Really looking them in the eye, focusing my undivided attention on their every word. And I do care, honestly, but it was a bit much.

I know what the staff thought — they might as well have had GUESS WHO GOT LAID written in permanent marker across their foreheads. I even caught Sarah shooting Donna a look at the front desk. It's not what you're thinking, I said. Oh, yeah? Sarah said, swiveling around in her chair to face me. What am I thinking? I don't know, but whatever it is, you're wrong, I said, laughing as I walked away, because I do like to keep it professional. Which is hard with an office full of women, but still.

It was a good day, all in all. There were the usual problems, of course; the mother of one of my patients got sick, and they had to put her in the recovery room, which was a mistake — I still don't know what happened, exactly, but anyhow. After work, I went to yoga, and then I picked up some take-out, and I felt . . . I felt in control again. I felt like myself, basically. The best part was that it felt so much better than I remembered.

Of course I thought about Paul throughout the day. Except that every time he came to mind, I felt sick. I was physically repulsed — it was that violent. But otherwise, I kept thinking, *This is great, because now I can have my life back.* Besides, what did I want with this man, anyhow? What, for him to tell me he loved me, and . . . and what? Really, what was I going to do, sell my apartment and move upstate? I thought about it, certainly. It's beautiful up there, and I can't remember the last time I felt so peaceful, and Paul's a fantastic guy . . . but that's not my life.

Lynne

NO, I WASN'T SLEEPING, but I thought I was doing all right. All things considered, I thought I was managing pretty well, really. But then, last week, when I heard my mother's voice talking to Delphine . . . Honestly, my whole life I swore *not me.* Because what a sad, lonely woman my mother must've been all those years, turning a blind eye to everything happening right beneath her nose, in her own house — not me, no. That would never be me. And then, there she was, talking to Delphine Schroeder in the cereal aisle at ShopRite, acting as though things couldn't be better . . . It's true, I'd become my mother. Really, if that's not a case for drugs, I don't know what is.

So sometime around two, Friday morning, I decided to get started in the guest bedroom, seeing as it's my least favorite room in the house. And as much as I hate to say it, the potpourri bowl had to go. Which is such a shame, really, because it's this beautiful black bowl with this delicate strand of cherry blossoms hand-painted on the outside, and it looked so pretty on the bedside table . . . But the question was: Do I need this bowl, really? No, not anymore — I think it's served its purpose, so out it went.

Because those were the rules, and if I started bending the rules in the guest bedroom, then there's no point, now was there? Besides, the only reason I bought the damn thing was because I thought Lisa would approve, even though she never visits us. So why I imagined she would ever see it, I don't know, really. Hope springs eternal, I suppose.

Anyhow, that's where I hid the pills: in the potpourri bowl. Because I knew that one day, when Lance checked his pockets and realized the pills were gone, he'd never think to check the bowl in the guest bedroom: not in a million years. But I wasn't snooping. Honestly, one morning, last September, I couldn't find my car keys. I looked everywhere, and Don had already left to take Jordan to school. Then I remembered Lance had a spare set, so I went in his room to look, but they weren't on his desk. So then I checked his coat pockets, and that's where I found the pills. Someone must've given them to him, and he couldn't take them because of his physical; they drug test.

At first, I thought about flushing them down the toilet, but I didn't. Because I liked having them, I liked knowing they were there, at least. I suppose I'd always planned on taking them, and I just couldn't admit the fact. Really, the only reason I waited so long is because it took me two months to come up with an excuse. I mean, I couldn't just say, Oh, well, let's see, my life is in shambles, let's pop a couple of pills and see what happens. I mean, isn't that what they say? That the best salesman actually believes his own bullshit?

The worst part is that I knew I might be making a terrible, *terrible* mistake, because who knows what might happen? I mean, I had to get up in the morning; I had to drive Jordan to the city; Lance was flying home — how could I even think about doing this to my family, and now, of all times? But for the first time in my life, I thought, *You know what? Screw it: I want them, I'm taking them.* Which was completely unconscionable of me, I know, I do. Then again, honestly, I had no idea how pleasurable that could be.

Lisa

I WAS TRYING not to laugh, I really was, then she caught me smiling. It's not funny! Lynne said, practically shouting. You don't know what it's like, Lisa, and I said, I do, Lynne, believe me, I know—. No, Lisa, no, I'm, I'm crawling in my skin here, and I—I just don't know what to do anymore—. Lynne, breathe, okay? I said, Just take a deep breath.

Then, completely out of right field, she says, Did you know he cheated on me? *Don?* I said, realizing I was speaking out loud. Yes, Don! With a woman named Barbara, she said, slapping me across the seat. And the thing is, she said, the thing is, I thought—I thought if I stayed active, kept busy, he wouldn't tire of me. But you know what? I tired of him. I hate to say this, but I am so fucking bored with him, I could scream.

And what's worse is that I bet they could've been happy together, too—isn't that awful? It's terrible, I know, but I almost wish he hadn't had that heart attack just so that maybe he would've finally picked up and left me for her. I don't know, she sighed. All I know is that it's not working anymore. My life: it's not working, she said. What I finally realized last night is that I need to get out of here. Maybe even out of this marriage. But where would I go? What would I do?

Anyhow, thank you for being there for me today, she says. I know we aren't close—. We're very different, I said. Yes, we are, she said. You've always known who you were. I've always envied you that, and I'm sorry. I'm sorry I wasn't there for you, she said. I'm sorry I resented you for so many things over the years—. It's all right, I said. No, she said, no, it's not all right, Lisa, because I've done . . . I've done terrible, terrible things, and I'm so . . . I'm just so ashamed of myself. Lynne, why don't we stop and get you some water? I said, looking around, then she looked at me and said, Where? She was right—it's not like we could just pull over on the Taconic State Parkway.

Well, maybe we'll just stop so you can get some air, I said, stretch your legs. No, she said. I need this, I do. I mean, I've been — I've been living in fear for so long, you have no idea, Lisa. You're brave, you're ballsy, you do whatever you please, no matter what — you, you have no idea what it is to live in fear of the truth every fucking day of your entire life.

You know it, too, she said. You've always known it, and you held it over me. That's not true, Lynne — I don't judge you. You don't *judge me*? she says, shaking her head in disgust. Don't lie to me, okay? Please, Lisa, for once in your life, just listen, will you? Because I'm not preaching, I'm not criticizing you.

You know why, Leese? You know why I married Don? Because you loved him, I said. And she said, Yes, because I loved him. And one of the reasons I loved him was because I knew Don would never leave me. Talk about a mixed blessing, huh? I just wish I were more like you. Why is that? I asked, laughing. Because then I could leave him, she said. What makes you think I could do that to Will? I said. Because I know you, she said, and you always do exactly as you please. I always envied you your freedom, Lisa. I always envied the fact you never cared what anyone thought —. I did care, I said. I just didn't show it the same way you did.

Okay, so we've gone down and we're winding back up the psychedelic roller coaster, and any second now, she's gonna start bawling again. Lynne, I said, trying to speak very calmly, checking on Jordan once more before asking, What were they? Who? she says. What did you take? I said, trying not to lose my patience, and she said, Oh, I don't know. Well, how many did you take? Three, four, I can't remember now, she says.

I let her down today, she says, looking at Jordan, asleep in the back. I did, she said, turning back. I let her down. She needed me and I wasn't there, she said, her voice breaking. I was too . . . High, I offered. You were too high, I said, and she thinks about it for a minute, staring straight ahead, and then, in this squeaky little voice, she finally says, Yes, I let her down because I was high. Then she starts sobbing again.

Adela

WHEN I GOT BACK to the hotel Saturday, he asked where I'd been all afternoon, and I told him I needed to walk, get some air. I wanted to tell him about Ixnomy, but I didn't know where to start, so I told him about that girl in the orphan pageant.

I said, She was just so homely, you know? I mean, she was bucktoothed, and she had these splotches of freckles and fatty boobs beneath her cheap polo shirt. And I pitied her, I did. Because she was the most pathetic thing I'd ever seen, walking down the catwalk, jiggling in every direction as she turned and walked back. And then . . . and then, I don't know why, but I actually wanted to hurt her for being so pitiful — I mean, can you imagine? You're only human, he said, putting his hand on my thigh, shaking me, telling me to lighten up, I don't know what.

I said, You know I love when people say, oh, it's only human, as if that excuses anything. Because sometimes it doesn't, you know? Sometimes it doesn't excuse a damn thing, I said, and he thought about it. Agreed, he said. But on the bright side, I bet you looked pretty hot in your little panties. It's true, I said, nodding, but don't try to make me feel better, okay? I wouldn't dream of it, he said, still looking at me, and I thought, *How can you look at me?* I don't know how, but he can — he does. And never looks away.

What a beautiful and shameful thing, to be seen for exactly who you are.

Jordan

SO THEN I turned over on my side and I go, Hey, Leese, remember that time we visited you at the gallery? And she goes, Of course, and I said, I go, We were late, remember? And she was like, I remember, and I go, But you know why — you know why we were so late? And she goes, I thought you guys got lost on the subway, and I was like, No, we didn't get lost. Mom was so nervous; she had to pee like four times before we got there, and we kept having to go in and wait in

171

line for the bathroom at Starbucks, and Lisa just laughed, nodding her head. I said, Seriously, she really cares what you think, you know? And Lisa was like, *Why?* Dunno, I said, because you're you, I guess.

Lynne

YES, ACTUALLY. YES, I am proud when people notice and comment on what a beautiful house we have. And I am hopelessly crafty, it's true. I can knit, sew, crochet, I make stained glass — I can matte and frame pressed bouquets of wildflowers that I planted, grew, and picked myself. I even make baby clothes as gifts for friends, and to be honest, several people have approached me about starting businesses over the years.

Of course I don't talk about that in front of Jordan because I know what she thinks of my taste. I know how she sees it, and how Lisa sees it: just slightly amateurish, or — or *quaint*. That's how Lisa would describe me, I'm sure, as quaint. And I realize how small it is in the grand scheme of things, and I know it's silly, really, but it's my silly — it's me — I'm sorry, but that's *me*. That's all I want them to see . . . just to look, to see me for who I am, because it's the only thing I know how to do well, you see. No, honestly, I can make anything look prettier — that's just how I am. Is that such a bad thing, really? To want to make something more beautiful, more — *more*?

It's not just about the house, either. No, I always wanted a place where my kids could feel creative and free-spirited. And I tried — I really *tried* to encourage them to draw and color, and then, when they were older, I took the kids down to visit Lisa in New York, and she gave us a tour of the gallery. I wanted them to know about art, I really did. And Lisa looked so — so chic, showing us around, catching people's eyes. Frankly, I couldn't help thinking, *Wow . . . my juvenile delinquent of a little sister is all grown up. Will wonders never cease?*

That night, on our way home, I asked them. I said, Remember when we hung your paintings on our walls? The kids looked at me, the two of them, and Lance said, *What* paintings? I said, When you were about five or six, and we hung all your paintings on the walls, don't you remember? He wasn't interested, but I told them, anyway. I said that one day, when they were little, Jordan got hold of a Magic Marker and scribbled all over the front hall. So finally, I decided that instead of painting over their scribbles, I would let the kids color on the walls, anywhere they liked. Why not?

Well, next morning, poor Lance didn't know what to make of it when I handed him a marker and told him to draw me something in the living room. Really, he just didn't know what to do, because I'd scolded him so many times for doing exactly that, but it didn't take much convincing, really. Sometimes when they'd actually draw a picture — and not simply scribble frantically on the same spot twenty times in purple, green, brown, and black — I'd stencil frames around them. I remember there was one with a gilded frame, and then I gave one this sleek silver frame, and once I even did this old-fashioned western-looking frame that I painted to look like dead wood. We had fun with it, the kids and I, we really did, but it got a little ridiculous after a while. Because there was this ten-inch-wide band of scribbles that ran through the entire house, four feet off the ground, until Don finally put his foot down a few months later.

They just looked at me. You don't remember that? I asked, genuinely surprised, and then Lance went back to his video game. And Jordan . . . Jordan made this, Sorry, Mom, face. I smiled at her and turned away, watching the river. Nobody remembers those things about me now, do they? No. They don't. They don't remember. Which just . . . I'm sorry, but that just blows, it really does, because that's what I remember. I had no idea that memory would become such a lonely place to be.

Joyce

IN MY ENTIRE LIFE, Irving and Sonja argued once that I'm aware of. Once: in 1970, the first and only time my mother ever decorated the house. She chose brown for my father's study and insisted he stay out of the room until her masterpiece was finished, so of course he did as he was told.

I was in my room during the unveiling, one floor beneath my bedroom. I heard the study door open, and something like a, *Ta da!* Then I heard my father's voice, then my mother's voice sounding shrill, and then my father's voice sounding perturbed, and then my mother's voice taking on an accusatory tone . . . And finally I heard my father say, Dear god, woman, you don't actually expect me to work in a room the color of shit brindle, do you? There was a moment of silence, and then fury. I had to bite my tongue — I literally had to bite my tongue to keep from squealing with laughter.

Shit brindle . . . ? Had he actually said the color of shit brindle? Well, Sonja was just beside herself. Seriously, the closest I'd ever heard the man come to swearing was that benign bellow of his, *Jesus Christ, the carpenter!* I'll never forget that . . . Honestly, I could not imagine where the old man came up with that. What, did he make it up, or had he heard it someplace? Did it matter? No, not really.

But the best part was that he'd nailed it: the color Sonja chose for that psycho-chromatic study was a most disturbing combination of brown, rust, and mustard — it was a slightly metallic dark-gold puke color, basically. No, it was shit brindle to a T. Genius — I mean, it was a genuine stroke of genius, and I thought, *I want to do that . . . I want to be able to describe something like that.*

I can't be certain, but a moment later it sounded as though Sonja began weeping, and I almost, *almost* felt sorry for her, because it was the first and only time I'd ever heard my father object to anything the woman said or did. But then, not a minute later, I heard my father break, followed by muffled tones of apology and indignation, as Sonja became increasingly incensed with his criticism of her grand decorating scheme.

So I tiptoed downstairs, just in time to hear my dad promise that he would never speak to my mother in that tone of voice ever again. Or use that sort of language, Sonja added. Or use that sort of language, he repeated, sweetly, like an obedient child. What my mother said then, I couldn't hear, but then my dad said, You know how much I love you, Sonja? *Do you?* At which point I ran back to my room. It was his chance to finally put the woman in her place, once and for all, and he'd caved. And it disgusted me, it did.

Lisa

SHE BROUGHT THE KIDS to visit me once at the gallery, when I first started. Before they arrived, I went to the girl at the front desk and I told her. I said, My family is coming by today, so be sure to smile and say hello to *everyone* who walks through that door, you understand? Her name was Auden, and I hated her on principle — the principle of her spoiled rich ass. Seriously, on her first day she took a two-hour lunch, and returned loaded down with Miu Miu and Chloé bags. As far as I was concerned, she was just another Ivy League girl whose parents had connections and old money, also known as patrons of the arts. But apparently Joyce had some new friends.

So they showed up, Lynne and the kids, and I showed them around, introduced them to everyone, including Joyce. Well, I should get back to work, Joyce said, giving me that I'm-not-paying-you-to-throw-a-fucking-family-reunion-here smile. It was so nice to meet you all, she said, and I really hope you can make the opening next month — it's Lisa's first show. Oh, we'd love to, Lynne said, so impressed, so intimidated by Joyce that I winced. I walked them out, then I stopped at the front desk, and I said, Just for the record, Auden, Mary Boone hails from Michigan. She looked up, mouth agape; no fucking clue what I was talking about, but I'd already turned and walked away.

You know I can still see the black-and-white photograph of the ravishing Mary Boone, sitting at a restaurant table with Julian Schnabel and David Salle and Eric Fischl, like it was a family photo. I must've stood in that corner for ten hours, easily, just staring at that picture. Then again, I had nowhere else to go. That was my home.

Jordan

I WISH I was like you, I said, and Lisa goes, I wish I was like me, too, and I was just like, No, seriously, I could never do that. Do what? she said, and I was like, Any of the things you did. And she goes, Why not? And I was just like, Because I'd be too scared, that's why! And she goes, Scared of what? And I was like, Scared of people finding out, scared of people saying nasty things about me. Then she turned

175

me around and started brushing my hair, and she goes, Jordan, it's the same thing, just from the opposite direction. I was too scared *not* to do those things, and too scared not to leave. Doesn't make me any braver than you are, doesn't make me anything.

And I said, Yeah, but just once, *just once* I'd like to shave my head, and she goes, *Don't you dare,* and I turned to look at her, and she goes, Excuse me. What I meant to say was, great, do it, Jordan. Shave your head! First thing tomorrow — in fact, why don't you come see Grandpa with us, and we'll pop into the barbershop before I catch the train —. And I was like, No, seriously, Leese, and she goes, Oh, I'm serious. And I go, I know, but I told you, I can't do that — I'm not like you. No? she said.

And I go, No, and she said, Well, tell me this: are you happy here? And I was like, No. Half the time, I think I'm going to die, and the other half, I think I'm going to kill myself. I mean, I hate school, I hate the kids at school, I hate everyone in this fucking town —. *See?* she goes. You see how much we have in common? And I started laughing.

Then she goes, Jordan, what do you want to do? And I was just like . . . I mean, when she said that, I started thinking about it for real. Like how I could move to New York and get my GED, like Lisa did. Maybe I could try modeling, or I could just get a job, and meet people — it's like I could do anything. And for the first time in so long, I felt really excited, but like two seconds later, it was gone. I was just like, *Who am I kidding? I can't do any of those things.*

Then someone knocked — Mom — I knew it was Mom before the door opened. Hey, she said, trying to sound all sweet and cheerful, and I was just like, Hey. Just checking to see if you need anything, she said, and I go, I'm fine, and she goes, All right, and I was just like, Thanks, looking at her like I was just waiting for her to close the door. Then I just looked at Lisa, trying not to laugh, before mouthing: *Busted.*

Lynne

AFTER I FINISHED Lisa's flowers, I turned off the light, heading to bed, at the very moment Lisa walked out of Jordan's room, and then

I just stood there, looking at her. She doesn't believe me: she thinks I'm lying about Daddy. I could see she was half expecting me to say something, but I didn't. I just looked at her, thinking, *Yeah, well, we'll just see about that. I mean, really, how could you believe what I told you, if you don't even know what you're capable of doing, yourself?*

I'll never forget this. As long as I live, I'll never forget the day when the kids were little, and Lance had his best friend Tyler over to play. Jordan had been pining for Lance all afternoon, but the boys were in this terrible no-girls-allowed stage and excluding Jordan had become a sport. Anyhow, I was in the kitchen starting dinner when I heard the boys kick Jordan out of Lance's room and close the door again. So Jordan stood at the door, pounding and hollering, Let me in! Let me in! Then I heard her slamming herself against the door, trying to knock it down — of course we didn't have any locks on their doors, so the boys must've braced the door with their bodies to keep her out, and that went on for ten, fifteen minutes, maybe.

Finally, I yelled up, Jordan? I said, Jordan, leave them be. They need some time to play alone, I said, and she stood on tiptoe, looking down at me over the rail, and she said, But Mom, they've played alone all day! When do I get a turn? I said, Here's an idea . . . why don't you go play in your room without *them*, huh? She stared at me with this excruciating look on her face: But I don't want to play without them! Well, then I don't know what to tell you, I said, and I went back to the kitchen.

Really, it was six o'clock. I'd had three kids for three solid hours; I had to make dinner, and it had been another long day alone with my daughter, and . . . and I was tired. I mean, *I* was tired, *they* were tired, we were all getting hungry, cranky. It was that awful hour when everyone in the house starts crying, so I didn't think anything of it, really. At most, I thought Jordan would sit and pout on the top stair like she always did until, sooner or later, her brother remembered her name and made a peace offering by saying, Hey, Jojo, look at this! Look what I can do! And then she'd go running, like the little dog her brother had trained her to be.

So I started putting away dishes, and then I heard more pounding. I shouted, Jordan, I'm warning you: stop! And I thought — what

177

I thought I heard was the sound of the boys opening the door to let Jordan in, followed by this shriek, like a hand being caught in the door. What is going on? I said, running upstairs, and then, just before I reached Lance's door, I heard a metallic thwack that made my hair stand on end, and I thought, *Ohmygod, one of the kids is dead!* When I got to the doorway, Jordan was holding a baseball bat in her hands; and Tyler was standing there, paralyzed, waiting for the scream to finish traveling from his sternum to his vocal cords; and Lance stood, frozen, like a child of Pompeii. I took one look, and I knew exactly what had happened.

They kept pushing — the boys kept pushing Jordan. They were being mean to her, leaving her out, and she just snapped. She picked up the baseball bat and she hit Tyler over the head. Finally, seeing me there, Tyler began to squall, and I was so relieved that he was alive, I wanted to cry. Screeching in pain is tolerable, but hearing no sound — to hear *nothing* coming from a child's mouth is to die a little death. Then Jordan turned to me, shouting, He slammed the door on my hand! And then *I* snapped. I took the bat out of her hands, threw it on the ground, and dragged her into our bedroom — dragging her so hard that she could barely walk — and then I slammed the door and paddled her.

Don returned home an hour later. Where are the kids? he asked, looking a little spooked, the house was so quiet. Tyler still here? he said, looking up, listening for the boys. No, I said, Shelley had to pick him up early because we had an accident. And then I told him. She did what? he said. She swung a *baseball bat* at his head? Does she *know* — does she have any idea? I shouldn't have spanked her, I said, covering my mouth to keep from crying. So Don went upstairs to speak to her, and then I heard Jordan's wail echoing through the entire house: I just, I just . . . I just wanted to, to *play,* Daddy. But all I could do was sit there, hiding my face in my hands.

When he came back to the kitchen, I hadn't moved a muscle. But what . . . ? What would *possess* her — what on earth would possess her to *do* such a thing? he said. Don, I told you: they wouldn't let her play. I know, but, he said, not understanding a damn thing I'd said. She's four years old, he said, furrowing his brow, and then I nodded, betraying my own daughter. As though I didn't understand perfectly well.

I used to bathe them together, and if I dried Lance first, Jordan used to become so impatient to run after him; all she wanted was to chase him, to be near him again. And not . . . not even knowing what to do with herself when she finally caught him, not wanting to end the chase by touching him, she would hesitate for one last delirious moment. He would watch her, too. Lance would wait to see what she was going to do, letting her get closer and closer, and then, just before she could touch him, Lance would slip past her and tear down the hall. Then that ear-piercing shriek as Jordan set off to hunt him down once more . . . What I realized at that moment is that I had never felt that hunger, that yearning for my own sibling, my own blood. No, Jordan was born feeling something that I would never know or feel, and I'd actually thought I must've done something right.

Well, Don sighed, you didn't do anything I wouldn't have done. Don, I said, I dragged her down the hall, I threw her over my knee, and I beat her, for chrissake —. Lynne, he said, it's not like you went after her with a belt —. You weren't *there*, Don. You weren't here! I know, he said, and I'm sorry —. No, I said. No, you tell me, Don. How can you expect a child never to raise their hand if you hit them in anger? I don't know, he said, and I said, You're right: you don't know — because you weren't the one who hit her, *I was,* I said, starting to cry.

I beat her, I did. To this day, I still believe that. Because you don't beat a child with your hand, you . . . you beat them with your chest, you beat a child from something in your bowels, something unspeakable and merciless. Sitting there, I could still see myself, screaming, Don't you ever, *ever* . . . as I kept spanking her. I didn't — I didn't even try to control myself — God help me, my rage felt like ecstasy. Then and there, I swore I would never raise my hand against either of them ever again. Because there is something wrong with me. And who can forgive you for that?

So, yes, I look at Lisa, and I think, *Because you have a six-month-old son, you think you know what parenting is all about? Well, remember that, Lisa, and you will. Because the day will come when you, too, will*

*be shamed by your own ignorance, your hubris, and by your own fail-
ure as a parent . . . Yes, even you.*

Just me, I said, sticking my head in the door Friday night, and then
Jordan stopped talking. You need anything, honey? I said, and she
shook her head. Call if you do, I said, doing my best to ignore Lisa,
and Jordan said, Okay, thanks. All right, I said, smiling and closing the door, and then I just stood there, arms crossed, holding my
breath on the other side of the door.

Lisa

I WENT OUTSIDE to call Will, and we almost got into a fight, which
isn't surprising. Anytime we speak these days, a fight can't be far behind. So after we hung up, I just stood there, staring at the sky, wondering for the umpteenth time why it's so easy to forget the stars.
Come to think of it, maybe that's the greatest sin of New York — not
the wealth, the greed, but the simple fact that you can't see the stars
at night. So you never have to be reminded that there's something far
greater than you in this life.

We went on a vacation one summer, just after my mom got sick.
We rented a little house and spent two weeks in Mystic. My dad and
I went down to the beach one night to check out the full moon — my
mom wasn't feeling well, so she stayed home. And at the time, I
was happy to be alone with my dad. It was just easier without my
mom around. Which is terrible, I know — I knew it then, too — but I
couldn't help it.

We built a bonfire and it was just the two of us, lying in the sand,
watching shooting stars. I remember the Big Dipper was so low, it
hung right above the water. I said, Wow, Dad, *look* . . . And he looked
for a moment, and then he said, Guess even God needs a sip of water
now and then, and I smiled, because that's exactly what it looked like.
Like God was leaning over for a sip of water, and I couldn't have been
happier if he'd just handed me a bouquet of flowers.

So I tried to find another constellation — my dad knew all the con-
stellations, but for some reason I could never remember their names.

180

Then Dad said, Lisa? Yes? I said — he looked so serious, too. Then he shook his head, like he'd just changed his mind, and he said, Nothing. Whatever he had wanted to say was gone, and I knew I couldn't bring it back any more than those flashes of light, falling in the sky. I wasn't curious, really, just sad that I'd missed that moment. I mean, who knows, it might've changed my life.

Lynne

MY FATHER HAD a group of drinking buddies who used to come over once a week, and they'd stay up half the night, playing cards at the kitchen table. One night, I was upstairs, and I stopped in my tracks, hearing my dad's voice. He started laughing at a joke someone made, and then he said, Yes, but Lisa is the son I never had. Then a voice said, And Lynne? I think it was Jim Malone, I'm not sure. I just remember gripping the stairwell, holding my breath, as my father took a sip, and his exhale: Lynne . . . he said, Lynne is her mother's child. And tears started streaming down my cheeks.

She was meek, my mother. So quiet, I'd never know if she were home or not when I'd return from school, even before she got sick. My last year of college, I went home for Christmas, and it was torture, listening to her coughing all night — worse because she tried so hard to muffle the sound, so not to wake anyone.

Three years later, Lisa stole a car, and the cops found her and her boyfriend in Massachusetts. They were charged with grand theft auto and crossing state lines. My father pulled strings; he called in favors from everyone, *everyone* he knew, and the theft charges were dropped. But there was still the matter of driving underage and crossing state lines — in two states.

My mother was in the hospital, but she went to court that day. We all tried to talk her out of it, but for once she stood her ground. It was a beautiful courthouse, with all the original woodwork, cherrywood, I think, and the shiny wooden benches reminded me of pews, built back in a time when courthouses were treated with the reverence of churches. It was cinematic, really — such a handsome setting, you almost expected Gregory Peck to walk out at any moment. The judge was stout and double-chinned, with a bulbous red nose that looked like a shattered pane of skin — a gin nose — and these tufts of gray hair curled up in the hangar of each nostril like two miniatures bales of dried hay. One look and I thought, *Oh, Leese . . . oh, are you ever going to get it now.* Finally, the day had finally come.

So there we were — Mom, Dad, Don, and I — sitting behind Lisa and her public defender, or whoever he was, telling her to stand for the verdict. My mother bit her thumbnail — nerves, I'm sure, but also to muzzle herself in case she started coughing — while the judge looked down at a piece of paper that would decide Lisa's fate. Then, in his rusted baritone, he said, Miss Barrett, I have decided it would be wrong to sentence you to serve time in juvenile detention *at this time.* But, he added, were it not for the extenuating circumstances, I assure you, I would sentence you to no less than six months in a juvenile detention facility. So let this be a lesson to you, he said, and then Lisa said, Excuse me? The judge honestly thought she hadn't heard him, so he repeated himself: I said let this be a lesson to you, young lady.

Lisa stared at him, then she said, I said, Excuse me, but I don't need *you* to tell me my mother's dying, okay? I swear a silence cracked through the room like a whip, and Mom — my mother blanched, and I had to grab her arm, steadying her, thinking, *You little bitch.* In the end, Lisa was sentenced to one hundred hours of community service. That's it.

That night, Don and my father sat at the kitchen table, drinking Calvert and 7Up, my father's drink. Well . . . she certainly speaks her mind, that one, Daddy said, nodding and exhaling through his clenched teeth. The way Don nodded in agreement, I'd swear he was afraid of her, my little sister. In that way some men fear women who will do things they will never dare, things they would never dream of doing, themselves. Because Lisa wasn't simply a bad girl, Lisa was a real-life hellraiser, like some mythic creature he'd read about in a book. No, Don was afraid of Lisa, but it was a fear indistinguishable from admiration, and it sickened me, truly. We left the next day, first

182

thing in the morning. Two weeks later, we returned for my mother's funeral.

Lisa

WHEN MY MOTHER DIED, all I could think was, *Not me, not like this . . . I want to be somebody. And that's not going to happen here. If I don't leave this place, I'm going to die here.* So I ran away, and they found me, and then I ran again. I remember a cop driving me home one night — just your average upstate New York hick, who'd found gainful employment in law enforcement. He didn't say a word, but the whole way he kept looking at me in the rearview, staring at my hair — whatever color it was that day.

Finally, I looked him right in the eye — well, in the rearview, but still. I said, You smell that?, sniffing the air. I almost said, Smells like . . . smells like bacon, doesn't it? I didn't — I wasn't that bold just yet, but it was a rush, seeing his face turn red, and I thought, *This is good . . . I like this. Yeah, I like this very much.*

Why didn't I fit in? I don't know, really. And it used to bother me — it really upset me, how to fit in, why I didn't belong. And then, one day, I just didn't give a flying fuck anymore. Because whatever the reason was, it wasn't gonna change a damn thing.

Joyce

YOU KNOW, AS much as I hate to say it, before too long, people won't ask if I have a boyfriend or a partner or if there's a man in my life, they'll say *male companion* and speak of me in some neutered third person. As in, Does your mother have a male companion? I mean, what a horrifying thought that is. And personally — this is just me — I'd be far less offended if they just came out and said, So who's she fucking these days?

In fact, maybe that should be my epitaph. That's not bad, actually: SO WHO'S SHE FUCKING THESE DAYS? Wait, I've got it, next group show: epitaphs! I see it already: this could be *huge*. Especially since the art world will have a sneak preview of my own.

Bobbie

DOWNSTAIRS, IN PAUL'S living room, there's an incredible painting hanging on the wall. It's huge: fifteen by fifteen, maybe, I don't know. I was so stunned, it took me a moment, the first time I saw it, and then I recognized the work. Did you buy this from Joyce? I asked, taking the glass he offered me.

No, it was a gift from the artist, he said, standing behind me. A gift? I said. I helped Joyce remodel her barn, he said. She lets her artists come up and use the house; that's why she bought the place. Anyhow, Greg came up for a few months last spring, Paul said, nodding at the painting, and we got to know each other. Do you know him? No, not personally, I said. It was so tacky, but I couldn't help thinking, *Do you know what this is worth now?* I think he's looking to buy up here, Paul said. Well, I said, he can certainly afford to buy; he's a big star now, Joyce's Golden Boy. I'll introduce you sometime, Paul said, but I smiled, thinking, *I don't think so.* What? he said, reading me. Nothing, I said.

Why don't I believe you? he said. Because you're frighteningly perceptive for a man, I said. You're stalling, he said. I know someone who knew him, I said, that's all. In other words, he was a real shit to a woman you know. Really, I said. I can imagine, he said, and then I turned to look at him: Is that so?

What I mean is that there are plenty of people who knew me when and could say the same about me, Paul said. I mean, I can't say, because I didn't know him then, but he's done some growing up the past few years. You know he thanks Joyce for helping him get clean, he said. After all, I said, her middle name is irony. She's been a good friend to him, he said. Yes, I said, and he also happens to be an investment. Well, he said, as Joyce would say, Since when are the two mutually exclusive?

You have great taste, I said, after he'd given me the full tour, heading back to the fireplace. Was there any doubt? he said, and I said, No, you were aesthetically prescreened. Prescreened? he said. Didn't Joyce tell you? Ah, I said, reading the expression on his face, you thought she brought over an expensive bottle of Scotch because she doesn't like to drink alone? What a fool I've been, he said, shaking his head, and I shrugged.

I said, You know when you asked me my first impression of Joyce?, and Paul nodded. I said, To be perfectly honest, my first impression was that she wasn't very pretty. Because she really thought she was something special, and I looked at her — this is so bitchy, too, oh, my word — but I looked at her and I thought, *Why do you think you're so special? Obviously you've never taken a look at yourself in a three-way mirror* . . . Although, I have to say she's gotten much prettier, and she's aged better than any woman I know —. But, he said. But still, I said, Joyce had something a million pretty girls in this world don't have: confidence, good old-fashioned chutzpah. I'd never known anyone like her in my whole life — I've always envied that, I said. Well, maybe *envy* isn't the word, I said, and he smiled. You tell me, he said.

Lisa

I WARNED HER — visiting my dad, I warned her, but she wouldn't stop. She kept saying, You don't believe me, do you? Do you, Lisa? I said, I'm not listening to this because this, this is *insane* —. If you don't believe me, let's ask him, she said. And I said, Stop — *stop*, Lynne . . . I mean, what are you trying to prove? I'm not trying to prove anything; I'm telling the truth, she said.

Daddy, she said, kneeling before him, do you remember when I was little and you got angry because you said my room wasn't clean? Remember when you used to tell me what a messy little girl I was? This is fucking insane, Lynne —. Maybe, she said, but I'd rather be delusional than a liar. I'm tired, Lisa, I'm so sick and tired of being afraid.

Daddy, remember what you used to say? Remember when you used to tell me, Lynne, sweetie, you know how much I love you? I love you more than anything, but I want you to be a good girl. I want you to keep all the pretty things I give you nice and clean, she said, but he just looked at her, confused. Lynne, I said, what do you *want*?

What do I want? she said, standing. I'll tell you what I want: I want to hear him say my room was never a mess, that's what I want! Say it, Daddy: my room was never a mess, was it? she said, practically shouting at him. Lynne, I said stop, I said, grabbing her arm, pulling her away from him. Why? she said. What scares you more, Lisa, that I'm telling the truth, or that you've always known something was wrong? Drop it, Lynne, I said, and she said, No! No, I won't *drop it* — you asked what I wanted, I told you! And then I slapped her, open-handed, even.

Once we got into the car, after we left my dad, she just sat there. Finally, Lynne goes: You still don't believe me, do you? You'll never believe me, will you? I said, You know, what I find especially disturbing is that you've decided to talk about this now, seeing as the man is senile and can't even defend himself. She said, He's not senile, Lisa. That's just what you tell yourself to ease your conscience because you never come to see him. Lynne, do you actually think he's going to remember any of this? I said, and she said, I hope so.

The whole ride back, all I wanted was to talk to Greg. My stomach was in knots; I wanted to call him so badly. Just to say, Hey, it's me. Listen: my sister's lost her mind; my niece got herself knocked up; my father is dying; I'm stuck in a loveless marriage; and the worst part — the worst part is that Jordan doesn't even know who Iggy Pop is. Oh, and by the way, I still don't forgive you, you spineless bastard. Got a minute? What's crazy was, I knew he'd answer, that he'd listen to me. If he could get to his phone when I called, I knew he'd answer. But then, of course, I'd have to tell him that he was about to make the biggest mistake of his life by marrying that girl — which was true, but still.

I didn't know him anymore, and he didn't know me, and it was an impulse I'm sure I'd regret for the rest of my life. So for once I did the smart thing and put my phone away. I turned it off, put it in my purse, and kicked my purse beneath the seat. The rest of the way, I just sat there, watching the river, which was becoming increasingly choppy, and as we got closer to New York, clouds were moving in.

Adela

I TOLD HER I wasn't hungry, but she didn't listen. She just wouldn't listen to me. It's tradition, she said, then she ordered us the huevos and the cornmeal pancakes. I nearly gagged — the smell of green chilies literally made me gag — so I pushed the plate away. One bite, she offered, holding out her fork. Just one bite. And I said, Joyce, I said I'm not hungry, okay? Would you listen for once or is that too much to ask? I said, disgusted, looking at her still holding her fork midair, stunned, scolded. God, you're more like Sonja every day, I said, twisting the knife. Silence.

I picked a fight I knew she couldn't win, because she wouldn't fight dirty with me. So I thought of the cruelest thing I could possibly say to her, and I said it, just like that. Joyce immediately looked down, returning the fork to her plate, and I thought, *Well? Let's have it — the great Joyce Kessler, the woman who always gets the filthiest last word: let's go, already . . .*

Adela, my mother said, mouth agape. Mom, I said I wasn't hungry; I said it twice before she ordered for me, and once more after the two times she didn't listen the first time. If I'm not hungry, I'm not hungry, I said. What more do you want me to say? Well, she said, how about I'm sorry I'm in such a foul mood today? I said, I didn't come here to be lectured or given unsolicited advice on my sex life or force-fed pancakes —.

You're right, Joyce said, looking at me. I'm sorry, babe, you're right, she said, reaching for my hands. You said you weren't hungry, and I didn't listen. I was out of line; I haven't shut my trap since you sat down, and I'm sorry, she said, placing her hand over mine. But all she did was make things worse: I couldn't even look at her. I couldn't look at her anymore than my mother could look at me at that moment.

Well, Joyce said, finally breaking the silence, not to change the subject, but get this, she said, and then she told us about Benjamin and his spy cams. Which, of course, I already knew — I mean, I knew he was in trouble for something. Because I was there when she called.

Bobbie

I CHANGED THE SUBJECT; it was too awkward. Because we got in a fight on Thursday, after Adela talked me into taking her shopping — or I talked her into taking her shopping, whichever. But she came into my dressing room, just as I'd finished trying on the third or fourth bra. I think this is the one, I said, looking at myself in the mirror. What do you think? I said, looking at her. Hot, she said.

Yeah? I said, uncertain. Oh, Mom, are you kidding? Lady, you put the hot in hotsy-trotsy, she said. That's what I'm going for, I said, still inspecting myself. Well, you got it — you've got it, all right, she said, sitting down on the chair in the corner, while I continued tugging a bit here and there. Mom? Look at me, she said, so I turned around, and then she pointed her phone at me, and it clicked.

I was stunned. I didn't know what she was doing at first, and then I realized she'd just taken my picture. Adela, what are you doing? I asked, covering the lens with my hand. I'm sending Paul a postcard, she said, grinning, looking at the image and speaking to her phone, as she typed: Wish You Were Here —. Adela, that's not funny, I said. Oh, he'll love it, she said, staring at her phone, pushing buttons, scanning her address book. I forgot that I'd given her his cell number in case of emergency.

Give that to me right now, I said, reaching for the phone, feeling my face flush. Mom —. I said *give it to me*, Adela. All right, here, she said. Where is it? I said. Mom, just push the button, she said. Which button? I said, getting increasingly angered. Here, let me show you, she said, reaching for the camera, and I said, I don't want you to show me, and I don't want you to take my picture without my permission. What were you thinking?

She said, I thought you looked —. No, Adela, the answer is you weren't thinking. Because had you stopped for a moment to consider what you were doing, you would've realized it was an invasion of my privacy to take my picture while I'm half naked, I said, grabbing my sweater. I wanted to hide — in front of my own daughter. First time in our lives I'd felt the need to cover myself in front of her.

I'm sorry, she said, as I turned around, unhooking the bra. Mom, I said I'm sorry. I was just checking my messages, and — you're right, I wasn't thinking. I believe that's been established, I said. Now would you let me finish getting dressed, please? All right, she said, then she stood up and left the dressing room.

When I finished dressing, I stepped outside and the saleswoman

188

said, Isn't that set amazing? So amazing, I'll take it, I said, smiling. Dela? I said, turning to look at her. Yes? she answered, still browsing. Are you getting anything? I said, and she shook her head. Are you sure? I said. I'm fine, she said, almost in a whisper, which is about as close to contrition as you'll get from my daughter. That's all, then, I said, handing the young woman my card.

When we got outside, she said, I'm sorry, Mom. It was wrong and I'm sorry, okay? I hate when you don't talk to me —. I said, Adela, don't do that ever again. Don't do that to anyone — I can't even believe I'm saying this to you —. I know, I know, she said, I'm sorry, how many times do I have to apologize? That's enough: it's done, I said, reaching for her, pulling her to me and kissing the side of her head. I have to go, I said, and she said, Me, too.

By the way, I said, don't forget we're having brunch with Joyce on Saturday, and she started whining: *Mom* . . . Don't Mom me, I said. She's your godmother —. She's not my godmother: I don't have a godmother, she said, and I said, Then why don't you give back the diamond earrings that she's-not-your-godmother gave you?, and she rolled her eyes. Honestly, she's still fourteen — I look at her roll her eyes sometimes, and she's still fourteen years old. And, honestly, there are times when I'm in awe, seeing her so grown up, and then there are times I still want to slap that fourteen-year-old girl in her.

I said, Adela, what . . . what's going on? Nothing, she said, I just don't have any time this weekend, and I need to see my friends. I said, Joyce is family, Del. You need to see your family, too —. I know, *I know* . . . Then I don't want to hear anything more about it, I said. All right, she said. What time are we meeting tonight? We have an eight-thirty reservation, I said. Want me to pick you up? No, she said, I'll pick you up. Good, I said.

I'm excited to meet your boyfriend, she said, smirking. I'm excited for you to meet Paul, I said. I couldn't even bring myself to say the word — I swear I'd been on the verge of blushing for four months straight. It was ridiculous. But you know I'm going to grill him, right? she said. Funny, he said the same about you, Del. But I have to go, I said. Hey, Mom . . . ? she said. What, baby? I asked, stepping back as a cab pulled over.

Adela

I SAID, MOM, Ixnomy, the little girl who was killed last winter. Remember? And she just shook her head. Mom, it was in all the papers — it was front-page news, how could you have missed it? And she said, I'm sorry, and I said, Come on, Mom, *Ixnomy* . . . ? I said, becoming so irritated, I wanted to shake her.

No, honey, I don't remember, she said, and I said, Mom, are you blind? Increasingly, yes, she said. But I really don't know whom you're talking about —. Please, Mom: last winter. There was a little girl named Ixnomy who was murdered by her stepfather. Ring any bells? No, she said. She was killed last winter, and afterward, they said there were all the signs of abuse: she was absent from school all the time; she had black eyes and bruises — they saw it, but no one did anything — no one helped her . . . *Ixnomy,* Mom, Ixnomy!

She kept shaking her head. Adela, I'm sorry, she said, and then I couldn't take it anymore, so I shoved my hand in my purse, removing a folded sheet of paper.

Joyce

I SAID, DEL, he's *very* handsome, don't you think? For an older man, she said, shrugging and looking away. What's that? Bobbie said, returning to the table. Actually, I don't want to know — I can tell by the look on your face, she said, taking a seat.

Speaking of, I said. Roberta, I can't help noticing what a dewy youthful glow orgasm has brought to your complexion — seriously, sex has taken years off your face. She looked at me, giving me her we-are-not-having-this-conversation look, so I gave her my then-I'll-have-this-conversation look right back. No, really, I said. I don't know if you caught that piece of the *New England Journal of Medicine,* but orgasm not only increases a woman's bone mass, it works wonders for her epidermis. All things considered, you'd think *I'd* look like a teenager, but no wonder so many women suffer osteoporosis, huh, Doc? I sighed, taking a sip of coffee.

Bobbie

THE FIRST DAY I took the baby to meet Joyce, she had a stack of gifts waiting on her coffee table. It was obscene. I took one look, and I was almost speechless: *Joyce . . . what have you done?* Then she took a tiny box off the table and handed it to me: Open it, she said, taking the baby from me.

When I opened the box, there were . . . earrings. She'd bought Adela a pair of diamond earrings. Joyce, I told you I didn't want my daughter wearing earrings, I said, aghast. No, she said, you told me you didn't want your daughter wearing fake diamond earrings — these aren't fake, trust me. Joyce, you *didn't* —. Tell that to AmEx, she said.

She said she wanted to give them to Adela on her eighteenth birthday, that she'd bring a bottle of champagne, and we'd toast before Adela opened her earrings. And that's exactly what we did.

It was always Joyce, though. It was Joyce who bought Adela her first Barbie. It was Joyce who took her shopping. And it was Joyce who took her for her first manicure-pedicure — just as she'd taken me, many years prior. I didn't know about all those girlie things; Joyce did. Even if I had known, I never had time for those things, and Joyce did. And if she didn't, she made the time. No, Joyce was Adela's second mother, and a much better mother in many ways than I ever could have been. Joyce should have had a daughter of her own; it's true.

Now as to why my daughter has suddenly regressed into a snot-nosed fourteen-year-old, I don't know, and frankly, I don't care. What I do know is that we're going to have a little talk, because this is unacceptable: she's a grown woman, and it's time she started behaving like one.

Lisa

I MET WILL at an opening a few weeks before Greg and I broke up. And Will . . . he was so obviously looking to buy, you know. I mean, you can always spot the Wall Street guys by that cocky gleam, because they know, and they know everyone in the room knows, that they can afford to buy anything they like. Then again, what they never seem to understand, doing their best to appear as though they're coolly inspecting the work, is that galleries decide who they want to own their work — I just find them laughable. *You really think you're all that, don't you?* I thought, looking at him. And that's how we met: I stood there, laughing at this guy, and then he looked up, seeing me laugh at him.

Are you the artist? he asked, walking over and standing beside me. No, I said, are you? Only in my dreams, he said. Oh, bullshit, I said. No? he said, amused I'd called him on it. No, I said, your wife or girlfriend or whoever is the artist — in your dreams, you're exactly who you are now.

Will Soutar, he said, turning to face me and holding out his hand. And? I said, shrugging. You want my blood type, what? he laughed. I want another drink is what I want, I said, handing him my glass.

I had my hand down his pants before we got in the cab, and two hours later, I crawled into bed beside Greg. I mean, I screwed around with Will, knowing I was pregnant, and somehow I justified it — all of it, everything. My rationale was that Greg had been cheating on me for years, and that you can't cheat on a junkie, really, because they always beat you to the punch. Far as I was concerned, Greg was hurting himself more than I ever could, so what did it matter?

Joyce

I GOT HOME Saturday afternoon around four, four thirty; did some work, got cleaned up for dinner, and had a few minutes to spare. So I sat down on the couch and spread out all the pamphlets I'd spent the afternoon collecting on the coffee table. I rearranged the stack a bit, debating the layout, then I stood up to take a look. Oh, Benjamin, I called. Oh, my poor, poor son, let's see those cojones, big boy.

Bobbie

YOU DON'T TALK about your mother much, Paul said. I don't remember much, I said. I was six when she died, so it's been a few years,

I said, trying to lighten the mood. I'm sorry, he said, reaching for my hand. Most of all, I said, you tire of people feeling sorry for you all the time. In that case, he said, I take it back: I'm not sorry. People die, tough luck, kid. Thank you, I said, smiling. You're welcome, he said.

I said, I started first grade a week after she died, and the first day of school, my dad had to help me get ready. My mom had already picked out the outfit; she had my aunt June buy it for me, so I had my new dress and my new patent Mary Janes . . . which just left my hair. So I asked my dad to help me with my hair, handing him the brush and two ponytail holders. He brushed my hair almost methodically, then he tried to pull it into pigtails, and I said, No, Dad, braids: I want *braids*.

So he tried braiding my hair, and I kept jerking my head away, saying, No, Dad, *no* — do it the way Mommy does it. I want French braids, up here, I said, pointing at my hairline. My dad didn't know what French braids were, but he tried — he was really trying, even though I kept whining no . . . but he wouldn't stop. Let me try, he said, just let me try, but I kept telling him he wasn't doing it right. He kept starting over until finally I said, No, Dad! I want it the way *Mommy* does it — I told you I want Mommy to do it! Then he let go of my hair and stepped back.

She can't, Bobbie, she's . . . Mommy's not here, he said. He couldn't bring himself to say the word, and that's when she died — it wasn't in a hospital room, a week earlier; she died in the kitchen, the morning of my first day of school, I said. I realized Paul was stroking my hand, but I didn't feel it until I stopped talking. All those times I was forced to sit by my mother's bed and tell her about my day, I was so scared of her dying, all I wanted to do was run as far and as fast as I could so she couldn't leave me first. I was so angry at her, and that's all I had, I said. Children get angry when a parent dies, he says, that's natural. Yeah, well, tell that to the kid, I said, changing the subject.

It was harder for my sister, Liz; she was only three; she can remember bits and pieces, but not like I can, I said. About a month after my mom died, a bird flew into the front window and must've died upon impact. We didn't see it happen, we just found a dead bird on the porch one morning, and Liz went over to inspect it. She thought it was sleeping, so she reached to touch it, and my dad said, Liz: don't

193

touch. Then she stood up straight and she looked at him, and she said, Daddy, look at the bird. Is it sick? My dad said, No, it's dead, Lizzy. And Liz said, Oh. Dead . . . ? Like Mommy? My poor dad, I said.

Are you close, you and your sister? he asked. Which is a perfectly normal question, but I had to think about it for a second. Yes, in a way, I said. In what way? he said. I love her — in that way, I said, smiling. In what way aren't you close? he said. Well, I said, we have nothing else in common, really. She's kind and sweet and gentle —. Nothing like you, he said. Different, I said, smiling, different from me. There are many things I admire about my sister, but, frankly, they're things I don't give much thought to except when directly questioned about her, I'm afraid. Liz is content. Lizzy has always been content in a way I found . . . alarming, frankly, I said, laughing. She has a nice husband, a nice house, three nice kids — they're a perfectly normal, happy family.

There was a turning point, though, I said. One Christmas we visited them in San Diego, and Liz wore a Christmas sweater with a . . . with a snowman, I said, wincing. At first, I thought it was a joke — I thought she was being ironic, but then I realized she wasn't. All I could think was, *Jesus, Liz, when did you become such a mommy?* I'm sorry, but she even had a mommy butt to match the sweater, and I was stunned, completely stunned, thinking, *My little sister has a mommy butt?* Which is unkind, I know, but still. We spent the first fourteen years of her life in the same house, and all I could think was, *I don't know you.* Anymore, he said. Exactly, I said.

I said, You know the first time Adela asked about my mother, she was about three, maybe. She said, Mama, what was Grandma like? So I told her what every little girl wants to hear. Really, it's the whole reason, the only reason they ask that question — and we all ask, hoping to hear the same answer. So I told her: I said, She was very, very beautiful . . . like *you.*

Jordan

When I was little, like once a year, my mom and I went down to New York, and we'd spend the night, just the two of us. My dad

194

would drive us to the train station in the morning, and once we got to Penn Station, we'd wait in line and take a cab to our hotel. And after we checked in, my mom would redo my hair, then she'd put on some lipstick, and we'd head out. But first thing, we always went to Carnegie Deli for pastrami on rye and matzo ball soup.

And I felt like such a big girl, you know, sitting there, with all those New York people. I used to look around, thinking, *One day, I could be rich and famous and all these people will know my name, but they'll never know they were sitting right next to me!* After lunch, we'd go to Macy's, and FAO Schwarz, and then, after we got back to our room, Mom would call room service for grilled cheese and tomato soup. And as a special treat, she'd always ask them to send up a bottle of ketchup for my grilled cheese: that's what I remember most. New York was the place with all the people and the big buildings, but most of all, New York was the place where you could have all the ketchup you wanted.

And after we finished, we'd crawl into bed and watch old movies, like those ones where the women always wore hats and gloves, you know. I remember this one time — like this one time I asked her — I go, Mommy, was it black and white or color when you were born? I thought the movies were black and white because the world was black and white then, like I could never figure out what day it was the world turned color, you know? But she just thought I was so funny, and lying there, I thought she was the best mom in the whole world.

Adela

I WASN'T GOING to save it: I just wanted to see if the camera was working, honestly. Then she goes, Adela, how would you like it if I took a picture of you half naked? And I said, Actually, would you mind —. Then she told me to let her finish dressing, and I was expecting her to give me the silent treatment.

She gets so angry, she can't speak — it scares me, as far back as I can remember, it's always scared me. When I was little and she used to get angry with me, I would have nightmares that she sent me back — back to strangers, people I didn't know. I used to wake up screaming, begging her, I'm sorry, Mommy, I'm sorry . . .

Then I lost it, telling her about Ixnomy, and she had no idea what I was talking about. And what I was trying to say — what I was trying to tell her is that I don't know if I can do this. I don't know if I'm really cut out for relief work, you know? I wanted to say, Mom, you've spent all this money for me to go off and do these things I'm supposed to do — god, Mom, if you could just see yourself when you tell people I'm going to save the world. But the truth is I don't think I've got the guts to do it because it scares me — when I hear stories, like the one about that little girl, I don't think I can, and that's just one girl, just one. I'm sorry, but the truth is, I'm scared all the time, and I don't even know how to tell you that because you don't fear anything, do you?

And I want to be tough and strong and ballsy — I so much want to be the sort of woman you admire, but the truth is, I'm not. I'm not that woman. There was so much I wanted to say to her, standing there, on the street, but none of it came out right. I mean, I couldn't even tell her I'd dropped out because I knew what she would say. She'd say I was wasting my life. And if I was wasting my life, I was wasting her life and everything she's ever done for me, everything I was spared, not having to spend eighteen years in foster care. And it shamed me to think she would feel that way . . . it shames me, and it always has.

Lynne

WELL, I THINK she liked it, but I can never tell with Lisa. If I'd turned back five minutes later, I might have found the bowl in the trash, for all I know. Really, the whole morning was so exhausting, by the time I got home on Saturday, I felt like I was about to collapse when I walked through the door. Don was in the kitchen when I walked in, and he offered to make me something to eat, but I said no, heading for bed.

Hey, babe? he called, as I was heading upstairs. Yes? I said, and he said, What do you want me to do with all the stuff in the garage? Just leave it for now, I said, and I'll deal with it later. Lynne, he said, standing at the foot of the stairs, can I get you anything? He's trying — he's trying so hard to keep us together, but I don't know if that's what I want anymore. No, I said, turning away, just sleep.

I crawled into bed and closed my eyes, but I kept seeing Lisa's face, how much she despises me, and for once she didn't hide the fact. You don't believe me, do you? I asked, standing beside Daddy's chair. You don't believe I'm telling the truth, do you, Lisa? No, she said. No, Lynne, I think you're full of shit, if you want to know the truth —. Then let's ask him, I said. Dad . . . Daddy? Lynne, stop it . . . *stop,* she said, but I wouldn't. I didn't stop.

At that moment, I was angrier with Lisa than with Daddy, really. Because I'd finally told the truth, but she didn't believe me. And because I was willing to look him in the eye, to face him, to give him a chance to speak, and she refused to listen. But it was cruel of me, what I said to her in the car. I said, She's nothing like you, Lisa. She's kind and she has a big heart —. Nothing like me, she said, staring straight ahead. No, I said.

Maybe not, she said, pursing her lips. But if you knew Jordan half as well as you think you do, we wouldn't be here right now, would we? And she was right. I was lashing out at her for taking his side — and for being his favorite. Because no matter what I do, Lisa will always be Daddy's favorite, his prodigal daughter . . . I started crying in bed, and then I finally fell asleep.

When I woke up, there was no one home; Jordan, but Don wasn't there, Lance wasn't there. I checked the garage, and both cars were gone. I knocked on Jordan's door, waking her, and she growled, What?, not bothering to look at me, cocooned in her duvet. I'm sorry to wake you, sweetie. Do you know where your dad is? I said, and she said, No, pulling her pillow over her head, and then I closed the door.

Adela

FRIENDS? I CAN'T tell her we're friends. She won't understand how I could even speak to the guy — because she doesn't. Not after

197

whatever he and Joyce have been through. But whether she can understand or not, Michael's the only person who's been there for me. He's the only person I don't have to pretend with — pretend like I'm so bold and brave and I've got my shit together. And you know, sometimes I feel so fucked up in my head — about everything — and I don't know why. But Michael's the only person who seems to understand that.

Weeks later and I was still pining after the guy, and Michael knew it. He took me out to dinner one night, and I jumped out of my skin when my cell rang. It's Ana, I said, pretending I'd been scared by the sound of the phone. Michael looked at me, then he said, Adela, you really think he's going to call? I'd like to think, I said staring at the table. It was all I could do, feeling like I'd just been slapped. Because he treats you so well, he said matter-of-factly, before taking a sip of wine. Then I wanted to hurt him for that, for knowing what I was thinking, what was really going on. And because he was right.

I looked up and said, Who are you to talk? You know, Michael, we don't even say your name in my house. Did you know that? Mission accomplished: I'd hurt him; it hurt. I'm very sorry to hear that, he said, because I admire and respect your mother very much. Unfortunately, I said, the feeling is not mutual. Which was mean, I know, but it also happened to be true. My mother considers any discussion of the man beneath her. Point taken, he said, dropping it, and we never discussed Marshall again.

New York Magazine

IN THE SPRING *of 2000, Kessler found herself embroiled in a bitter divorce with her Hollywood action–movie producer husband, Michael Petrucci, a divorce of such epic proportion that one insider described their blood feud as the Uncivil War. (Petrucci, the dark, lanky Tinseltown Casanova whose knack for record-breaking box offices and red-carpet It Girls has earned him the nickname Goldfinger, refused to comment for the story.) Entangled in hand-to-hand courtroom combat, and having just relocated from a second-floor space on 20th Street to a 3,000-square-foot ground-floor space on 22nd Street, Kessler found*

198

herself near financial ruin—incredibly ironic for someone obsessed with shoe culture.

On the brink of closing her doors, she took a large gamble, turning away from the celebrated conceptual artists of the late '70s and early '80s upon which she had built her reputation, in favor of young talent— complete unknowns. To date, her discoveries include the likes of Columbia grads Katherine Gaines, Tomiko Mori, Mila Koslowski, Gavin Prince, Chelsea Kim, Lane van der Wahl, and, most recently, Greg Malone. The risk paid off, to say the least. Though Kessler rarely does.

"Some curators tell you it's instinct, that they feel a little twitch in their nose . . . not me," she says. "Believe me: I never twitch, and if I do, it's certainly not in my nose. That's not art; that's hay fever, okay. When I look at a painting," she continues, "here's my rule of thumb, so to speak: if it makes me want to spread my legs, I know. And that, my friend— now that is what I call a work of art. A twitch in your nose? Puh-lease. I mean, not to name names, but no wonder some of these curators exhibit the shit they do at their shitty museums and they're always in the red, running back to their board of trustees, begging for more money, claiming no one cares about art anymore," she says, her five-karat Fred Leighton diamond ring gleaming as she strikes a spot-on, forgive the pun, Macaulay Culkin–esque pose, mocking her detractors. "The Philistines are coming! The Philistines are coming! Oh, give me a break," she says, snapping back to attention with her hip thrust and Leighton hand akimbo, "because that's just bullshit with a capital fucking dollar sign."

Kessler was a former fixture of CBGB back in the day, when the Bowery was a punk outpost that few dared brave even in broad daylight. Today, friends with the likes of Lou Reed, Laurie Anderson, David Johansen, Chrissie Hynde, and Patti Smith, Kessler is largely responsible for the rock-star treatment lavished on many young painters, having single-handedly bridged the gap between rock & roll and modern art as a young curator at some of New York's most prestigious galleries. Enter Kessler's latest gamble, the upcoming show of the art world's latest and baddest of bad boys, Greg Malone.

With his runway looks, his Bruce Weber physique, full smirking lips, penchant for suave Dries Van Noten ensembles, and his open disdain for publicity, critics, and journalists alike, Malone's large-scale

199

paintings have created an eardrum-piercing buzz among those in the know—namely, Kessler's A-list friends and longtime buyers. A former star of the prestigious Columbia master's program, Malone all but disappeared from the art-world radar for several years, first by choice, then by necessity, repeatedly in and out of rehab.

Malone has added nine treatment programs to his CV in the past four years alone in his attempt to overcome a heroin addiction that had landed him in the emergency room more than once, and in jail several times. Though no one contests his talent, Malone's bad habits and erratic behavior also caused him to burn several bridges, upon failing to deliver the work promised for no less than two major and highly publicized shows. By which point no gallery in New York would speak to him—except for Kessler, whom he credits for his recovery of the past three years.

Kessler remains fiercely loyal to Malone and his talent, despite both his history and her own inability to get the artist to deliver his work on time. Or to appear at his own openings on time. Or to appear at all, period: rumor has it Malone skipped his first opening at the Kessler Gallery in order to stay in bed with twenty-three-year-old Brazilian-born Victoria's Secret supermodel Raquelle del Soto, to whom he is now engaged. Likewise, he credits del Soto with keeping him sane through the vitriolic, here-today-and-later-begone culture so prevalent in the art world.

Malone repeatedly refused requests for an interview, until, months later, Kessler called to say he would be willing to sit down and discuss his work for one hour, "And that's it, not a minute more, got it?" she told us in her typical restrained-yet-possibly-about-to-crack tone. Upon arriving at Kessler's ten-acre house upstate, Malone meets me at the door of a picturesque, newly renovated Dutch barn, and we enter, only to find all the canvases in the studio covered by tarps. Malone then takes a seat at a cluttered worktable and begins the interview. "Let's get this over with," he says.

Since he refuses to show his work, claiming that it's unfinished, and asked, instead, to describe his work, Malone reaches for a cigarette, lights it, and then exhales a cloud of very expensive-smelling brown smoke with a heavy sigh, hunching over the table with an ironic beaten-down power. "I would describe my work as neo-retro-abstract-expressionistic-impressionistic-photo-realistic-figurative-art landscapes . . . It's the next wave," he says.

"Come on," he says, "give me a real fucking question, will you? Seriously, dude, is that the best you can do? How do I describe my work? The answer is, I don't. Because that's not my job, that's your job, and I don't intend to do your job for you: sorry. I paint, that's how I describe my work. That's what I like to do, paint, and what I don't like to do is waste my time talking to journalists who've arrived at my door, having already decided the angle of the story, because their editor told them the angle, before I've even opened my mouth, and they don't have the balls to say so. Present company excluded, I'm sure," he adds.

"So why don't you save us both some time and write what you were going to write, no matter what I say. And if that's not good enough, why don't you just tell me what you want me to say, and I'll say it, loud and clear, so you've got your quote on tape," he says, grabbing the tape recorder. "That way, you can catch the next train to the city, which is in, oh . . . fifteen minutes. How's that sound?" he says, abruptly standing from his chair and walking toward the door. Is it confidence? Is there something to be hidden? The secret still seems to be skulking behind his Alain Mikli frames.

When asked what transpired from his heyday at Columbia to the doors of Betty Ford, Malone pauses. "I broke up with a girlfriend, I lost my apartment; I had no money, no place to live, and I lost my shit for a while. That's it, really." Asked about the rumor that he failed to appear at one of his own openings because he couldn't be bothered to get out of bed with his fiancée, Malone returns to the table to stub out his cigarette in the overflowing ashtray. "Have a wonderful day—it's been such an incredible pleasure talking to you," he says, rolling his icy blue eyes, holding out a knuckle-scarred hand. Apparently, the interview is over. Ms. del Soto's agency did not return our calls.

Slightly more diplomatic, Kessler dismisses the rumor. "For the sake of argument, let's say it's true, he skipped his opening because he wanted to shtup his girlfriend, instead. Even if, even if that were true, could you blame him? I mean, personally, there'd be very few openings I wouldn't skip, gladly, given the same opportunity," she says, tugging at the middle part of her ironically feminine Diane von Furstenberg blouse.

When pressed, Kessler admits she has seen few of the paintings that will appear in Malone's upcoming show, but shrugs, undaunted by the fact. "I know Greg, I know his work, I know what he's capable of, and I know he's going to deliver. And what I have seen gives me more than a twitch in all the right places."

Lisa

OUR FIRST APARTMENT was on Second Street, which is now Joey Ramone Place — and a complete misnomer in my book because it should be Way: Joey Ramone *Way*. Joey Ramone Place sounds like a destination for Japanese tourists — which is exactly what it is. Whereas Joey Ramone Way would've been — well, the *way*, you know. Like the way of the punk samurai — the way of the Joey.

Anyhow, Christmas rolled around, and we finally rolled out of bed, whatever time it was we got around to rolling — literally. Greg took out the tray, ready to wake and ho, ho, bake, while I put on some warm clothes, hat and scarf, and then we sat cross-legged beneath our Charlie Brown Christmas tree. Greg said, You first, and he took out a box, wrapped in plain brown construction paper and twine. I thought he'd bought me a new pair of Converses, because the sole of my old pair wagged its tongue with every step.

So I started smiling, wondering what color he'd chosen — I was hoping for the hot-pink high-tops — and then I tore open the box to find . . . the shoes. *The Shoes.* He bought me the Christian Lacroix shoes. I didn't even believe they were real, so I had to rip all the paper off, inspecting the box, just to be sure it was true. Then I just looked at him, speechless . . . Somehow, he managed to buy them and hide them from me for six months. *Six entire months,* and not one word.

We were just sitting there, on that nasty old Persian rug, and Greg kept looking at me, waiting for me to show some sort of response, you know, and then I started crying. I did. I couldn't — I couldn't even begin to imagine how much they must have cost, and . . . and I'd never owned anything so beautiful in my whole entire life. Well? Do you like them? he said, grabbing my hand.

Yes. I love them, I blubbered, trying to get a grip. I love these shoes more than anything in the whole world. And if you get one speck of paint or gesso on these, I said, wiping my nose on my glove, I'll kill you, I swear. Ah, yes, he said, reaching for the biggest box under the tree. For you, mademoiselle, he said, and then I ripped it open to find a shoe case.

Greg had built me this gorgeous Lucite display case for my shoes. It had a large antique glass brooch for a doorknob, and he'd even made me several sets of freestanding steps, of various heights and angles, so that I could display the shoes different ways. Thank you, I said, leaning over to kiss him, it's beautiful. I love it, I do.

Your turn! I said, crawling over and pulling his present out from beneath the couch. Since I won't let you have any posters in the house, I said, handing him his gift, waiting, as he grinned in wonder. Just before we moved in together, I told him I had a rule: no posters — no rock posters, no posters, period. No rock posters? he said, and I said, No. I mean, it's your choice, of course, but I do *not* have sex with boys with posters on their walls —. Anymore, he added. That's what I'm saying, I said. Not even Bob Marley? he said, and I said, Especially not Bob Marley! Jesus, do you know how many times that man has seen me naked?

So I waited, watching his face as he opened his gift, watching him piece it together. I got him a silkscreen of Jamie Reid's *God Save the Queen* cover art for the Sex Pistols. Look, babe — *look, look* — it's an original, I showed him, pulling out the papers. Of course it was completely absurd that the artwork of a renown situationist would have documentation vouching for its legitimacy, but that's the age we live in. You know . . . you know what this is worth? he said, looking up for a moment. You bet your sweet ass, I do, I said, grinning, but he was still staring, dumbfounded.

I'd bought it from a dealer in England. I'd been saving for over a year — well over. But how? he said. He meant how could I afford it. Easy, I said, I sold one of your paintings. He looked up at me, alarmed. No, I would never do that, I said, just my body.

203

Do you like it? I asked, kneeling behind him, putting my arms around his waist. I love it, he said, kissing me. That's all I wanted to hear, I said. Aren't you going to try them on? he asked, watching me as I took off my glove to pet my feathery shoes with my index finger. No, not yet, I said. I can't. I just have to look at them for a while, get used to them. So I arranged them in their dollhouse shoe case, while Greg hung the silkscreen on the nail I'd hammered into the wall, then we placed the case, with shoes and all, on the marble mantel. I got up and stood beside him, both of us, speechless.

Finally, Greg let out a heavy sigh. Would you like to say a few words, Leese? And I said, Yes, as we bowed our heads: Dear God, thank you for letting us buy each other the most beautiful presents I could ever imagine, even if we just ruined our credit rating for the next seven years and don't have any money to eat for the next six months, we love you. Amen, Greg said.

The phone rang. It's probably my mom, Greg said, walking over to answer. Because we know it's not mine, I said, biting my thumb, debating whether or not to display the shoes differently. Hello? he said, and then he said, No, she's not. May I take a message? I turned and looked at him, then he held his hand up, pointing an index-finger gun at his head, before pulling the thumb-trigger: Joyce. The woman actually called me on Christmas, okay, and it sure as hell wasn't to wish me a Happy Birthday, Baby Jesus.

All right. Merry Christmas to you, too, he said, hanging up. *You're fucking kidding me,* I said, ready to start screaming. What did she say? She said to ask you if you could go in for a few hours tomorrow—. *Fuck no!* I said. Did you tell her I said fuck no? I was going to, he said, but it didn't seem in keeping with the Christmas spirit, honey. It's in keeping with my Christmas spirit. I swear that woman is killjoy incarnate, I said, inhaling a deep breath through my nose, trying not to let her ruin my day.

Well, good thing I saved one little present under the tree, I said, trying not to squeal. Ah, but first, he said, I should put on a little holiday music, don't you think? How about "Little Drummer Boy"? I asked, watching him run into the bedroom and return with a record. A real live vinyl album, boy, those were the days. No, I've got something better, he said. That's my favorite, I said, singing in my best baritone: *Come, they told me, puh rump pum pum pum . . .*

Wait, he said, close your eyes, so I did. He dropped the needle, and then "White Lines" started playing. That's right, he said, it's a Grandmaster Flash Funky Christmas, and guess what else I've got, he said, disappearing into the kitchen, and removing a bag from the secret stash. I just sat there, on the couch, bouncing and clapping my hands. This is the best Christmas *ever!* I said.

Can I ask you one thing? he asked, an hour later, standing in front of our display. What's that? I said, getting up and standing beside him, while he put his arm around me. Why? he said, looking at the placement of the nail I'd hung. And this is not a criticism, okay — I'm just asking — but why did you hang the nail so far to the left? Oh, I said, relieved he reminded me. Here, I said, pulling out another gift from under the couch. Almost forgot to give you your big gift, I said, handing it to him; it's actually a re-gift, but it's the thought that counts, right?

Your mother sent it, I said, unsure how he'd take it. He probably didn't even know she'd kept it all these years. She was a great lady, Greg's mom. Janet was an unwed teenage mother. Not much more than trailer trash from Indiana, who'd taken a bus to Detroit to live with an aunt in a one-bedroom house, where she left her son every day and night, off to work at a fast-food joint before she went to night school. It took her six years to get her bachelor's, but she got her degree. Tough cookie, I liked her a lot. She was so pretty, too, even then.

I met her at graduation, and she told me about Greg's first painting from sixth-grade art class. By the age of eleven, he'd already been held back two years, before they put him in special ed. He'd been called a retard so many times and returned home with so many black eyes that his mother signed him up for boxing classes. Greg was the first and only guy I'd ever dated that had been in more fights than I had, but that only helped after school, really. So he started skipping school every other day, and then, finally, one day, someone thought to stick him in an art class.

His first assignment with acrylics was to choose a record cover and copy it. Naturally, he chose the Sex Pistols, and he was given his

205

first A in nine years of schooling. Janet showed the painting to everyone she knew. She even took it to work with her and hung it above her desk, she was so proud. Her son got an A in art. Her son had talent. Her son was not retarded, like they'd been telling her since the day she enrolled him in school.

God, I remember, he said, sitting down, probably looking at the painting for the first time in ten, fifteen years. What? I said. Nothing, he said. It's just that I remember it being so *good*, so —. It is good, babe, I said. It's very good — in a special-needs-child sort of way. So, to answer your question. See this? I said, showing him the tiny *X* I'd marked on the wall. That's where it goes. Right there, I said.

So we hung Greg's first painting, the one and only painting of his that he would allow to be hung in his own house. Ach, I almost forgot the best part, I said, turning the canvas over and showing him. In case you forgot, I said, reading the words he'd scrawled on the back: *Greg Malone, Second Period Art, Mr. Whitman,* and *PUNK ROCK RULZZZZZZZZZ!* Unfortunately, your spelling hasn't improved any, I said, cracking myself up: *Rulzzzzz!* Oh, that's funny, he said. Reminds me Santa left a note saying some naughty little girl needs a Christmas spanking. Then I ran for the other room, screaming.

It wasn't just the happiest Christmas I'd ever had; it was one of the happiest days I've ever known. Just the two of us, alone together. For one day of my life, the rest of the world could go fuck itself, as far as I was concerned. *Including that old hag, Joyce Kessler,* I thought.

Bobbie

HE TOUCHES MY FACE sometimes, in the morning, just before I wake. I'll feel his fingertips on my forehead, around my eyes. Paul likes to trace the lines — and not just the wrinkles on my face, but still.

The first time he started tracing my crow's-feet, I flinched: Paul, *don't* — don't do that, pulling away. Bobbie, there's something I need to tell you, he said, staring me in the eye. There are lines on your face, he said. I was so incensed, I pulled my arm away from him, but he wouldn't let go. Let me finish, he said, pulling me back. If you knew — if you only knew, he said, holding my hand, how beautiful you are, it wouldn't matter what I touched or where. In fact, you might even like it, if you could just let go, he said, releasing my hand.

Maybe he's right, but I don't know what I want, really. I thought I would know by now — I've spent years thinking I would know what I wanted by this point in my life, but I don't.

Joyce

WHEN WE GOT TOGETHER that week, after their first date, I watched her walk through the door and I said, My god, woman. What? she said, giving me her innocently surprised face. Don't what me: you're grinning like a Cheshire cat in heat, that's what, I said.

Well? I said, waiting. Well, what? she said, practically giggling, and I said, Well, how about, Thank you, Joyce; or, I love you, Joyce. Or, how's about, You were so right, how could I have been so stupid, so wrong, and most important, how will I ever repay this enormous debt of gratitude, Joyce . . . Feel free to stop me anytime, I said. Bobbie smiled and puckered her lips just slightly, as if to say, ahh, then she dropped her head to one side. I love you Joyce, she said. That wasn't my first choice, I said, but it's a start.

Bobbie

THE NEXT MORNING, he sat, naked, on the side of the bed, reaching for his watch on the bedside table. I lay there, watching him, and he smiled at me. He didn't say it, but his eyes asked, What? There's just something extremely sexual about watching a man removing or putting on his watch, I said, folding the pillow beneath my head. Really? he said. Because I have several, I can try them on for you —. You had to ruin it, didn't you? I was being serious, I said, rolling over: it's men at their most sensual. Then he fastened the band and leaned over me, kissing my shoulder. Thank you, he said.

Hungry? he asked. Famished, I said. That's what they all say after a night in my bed, he said, but he was already laughing before I could give him a look. Make you an omelet, he said. I'll make coffee, I offered. You can make coffee? he asked. Yes, I can make coffee, I said. That's all I can make, but I do it *very* well, thank you. All right, then, you're on coffee duty, he said. Hand me my shirt, will you? I asked, propping myself up. He looked at me, and he said, No, before walking out the door. Just like that. No.

Then, just as I was sitting up in bed, he poked his head back in and said, Well? You coming or not? Yes, I'm coming, I said, trying to twist my body into a more flattering pose. Bob, he said, I hate to break it to you, but you aren't going to show me anything you didn't show me three hours ago — and quite happily, I seem to recall. So let's go, he said, clapping his hands, *hut to,* but I didn't move.

You want me to hold up a towel so no one can see, or what? he said. Look, lady, I'm sorry, but I'm fresh out of Vaseline lenses — used them up on the last old broad I bedded —. Bastard! I said, throwing the pillow at him. Ahh, look at that: you're blushing, he said, and then I threw a second pillow at him.

And feisty, he said, catching the second pillow, as well, standing there, gloating. I like that in a —, and then I reached to throw another, but there weren't any pillows left. As a matter of fact, there was nothing left on the bed. Just me.

When he left, I laid back, stretching in the sunlight . . . I couldn't remember the last time I'd smiled like that. A minute later, Paul stuck his head in the door: You coming? When I'm ready, I said. Oh, I see, he said, when you're ready. Well, if you're going to force me, he said, stepping into the doorway, buck naked, holding the ukulele. I started to laugh, thinking he couldn't be serious, as he cradled the instrument, and then he began: *I'm looking for a hard headed woman* . . . It was absurd.

One who will take me for myself . . . Should I continue? he said, or are you ready to come down to breakfast? Because I will — I'm warning you, don't do it, Bobbie — don't make me pull a "Peace Train" on your ass. Because I've got all the time and Cat Stevens in the world —.

No wonder your wife left you, I said, laughing. Ouch, he moaned, lowering his ukulele. And no wonder you're Joyce's best friend, he said, turning to leave.

Adela

I KNOW HOW I ACT, and how I talk, but it's just a show, really. I mean, I know how to perform — and I can grind with the best of them, believe me — the problem is I don't know how to stop acting, you know? He calls it fucking for the camera.

The first time we had sex, I was on top of him, and I was — I was fucking him with a vengeance, it's true, and then he suddenly grabbed my hands: Stop, he said, stop that. So I stopped, and looked at him, thinking, *What's wrong? What am I doing wrong?*

Not like that, he said, and I turned away, feeling like a total idiot. I was just like, fine, and I started pulling away, and then he grabbed my arms; he wouldn't let me go. And I wanted to cry; I really did. I felt that quivering in my chin, and I tried moving away — I mean, his erection's jabbing me in the groin, and I feel like I'm being scolded, and I just wanted to grab my clothes and run away. Then I started twisting, knowing I was about to throw a fit if he didn't let me go — and then he said, Look at me.

So of course I immediately looked away, and then he said, Adela, look at me, and then he let go of one of my arms, turning my chin to face him. All I mean is stop posing for the cameras, he said, it's just you and me here. And you don't have to prove anything to me, he said, pulling me back on top of him, reinserting his cock.

Joyce

FOURTH TYPE WAS huge . . . *huge* show. Benjamin gave me the idea, as a matter of fact. Honestly. One night, I got home from work and Benjamin was in his room, doing his homework. So I went to ask about his day, and I see this sex ed booklet, right. And it wasn't a big deal — we've always been very open with him, especially if you consider the sexual discussions we had in my household, growing up. Which was none.

Anyhow, Benjamin had already told me they were doing a unit on sex ed in his public health class, so I started leafing through the booklet, curious to see what was being taught — what, considering how much kids see everywhere else. So I'm flipping through the chapters on abstinence, AIDS, STDs, types of sex . . . and then, on page fifty-three, I come across a bullet-pointed header that says: THE FOURTH TYPE OF SEX.

Well, needless to say, I was stunned. I mean, imagine my shock, learning that there are *four* types of sex. So I took a quick count, and no — unless they've invented a new orifice, I got the same number on the fifth count as the first. So I'm just staring off, thinking, *What the hell could it be . . . ?* They aren't actually counting Internet porn, are they? Because I might take issue with that. Seriously, what are we teaching our children: keyboard, asshole, separate but equal? Crazy.

Then I realized, *Well, no wonder I've always felt so incomplete — there's a fourth dimension missing in my game!* A minute later, Benjamin finally looks up from his math book — the kid's all of twelve years old, right. So he looks up at me, and then he says in all seriousness — I mean there's a look of compassion on his face as he says to me, You can borrow it, if you want, Mom. I said, Thank you, sweetheart, don't mind if I do.

Bobbie

I'VE BEEN THINKING about a lot of these things since I met Paul. Just all the things I thought I could control. All the ways I've tried to bully and out-clever life, thinking that I, alone, could spare and be spared the petty cruelties we all must suffer. Of all the things that scare me, and everything I hide from myself.

That's what I wanted to tell him last weekend, after our hike. Saturday, when we got back, we kicked off our shoes and lay down in the hammock, drinking whiskey and smoking a joint. Lying there, I don't think I'd felt so comfortable in my own skin, in my body, my life — not like that, not with a man. Then I remembered those guys on the street — those derelicts who ran into me — how I'd started to feel invisible, and I hadn't even noticed it, really, until that moment. I wanted to tell Paul about them; I wanted him to know so that he could truly understand how good it felt to be lying there, beside him.

Just before I was about to say something, he said, Let's go inside, and he put his hand on the ground, keeping us balanced while I sat up. He took me upstairs, into the bedroom, and the light was so beautiful up there, and granted, I was pretty high by then, but still. It was so pink and warm, with all these shadows of arching branches and leaves stenciled on the white walls. By the way, he said, did I ever tell you my gynecologist fantasy? Ooh, sounds kinky, I said, and he said, You have no idea, doctor . . .

He took my hand, pulling me around to face him, and it's the craziest thing, but I still get shy with him — there are still moments, yes. And that was one of them, as he sat on the edge of the bed, facing me. He began unbuttoning my shirt, and then he unsnapped my bra, in the front . . . I could feel my boobs sagging, while he ran his index finger down my sternum, and then I started chattering. Because I could feel it coming, a split-second before it hit, this surge of blood, heading straight for my face. You know what my grandfather used to say? I said.

What's that? Paul asked, unzipping my pants. He said there's nothing as beautiful as watching a woman blush from the tits up, I said, and Paul smiled that big open smile. So that's what we always called a real blush in my family, tits up. I like that, he said, that's good. Now take your pants off.

Afterward, I was resting my head on his chest, staring out the window, and for once, I didn't mind the light on my face. You know what I love about you? I said. What's that? he said, rubbing my cheek. That you're exactly the sort of man who could date a woman half his age, but you don't . . . I mean, that's, that's so admirable. You actually choose to date a woman your own age: I *love* that, I said. Babe, he said, taking my face in his hands, that's the nicest backhanded compliment anyone's ever given me. I started laughing, and then he pushed me off, getting up.

Water? he asked, heading for the door, and I had to laugh. I'm sorry, but a spent penis only gets funnier with age. Yes, please, I said, before rolling over on my stomach to face the window, sunning my- self in the sunset. I was so content, lying there, but even so — and I don't mean to brag — but *god* I wish the man had seen my tits at twenty-five . . . because they were fucking amazing. I'm sorry, it took thirty years before I could say such a thing, but it's true: I had *great* tits. Sometimes I still look down, expecting them to be there, but they've moved on, I'm afraid. The trade-off, of course, is that you take less for granted. And you learn to let go. Which is a powerful combination, but still.

Who knows, maybe there are times Paul wishes I could've known his body when he was twenty-five. Which would make two of us, ac- tually. Does that constitute fantasizing about another man during intercourse? No . . . I love his body, I do.

Sure, he's little softer, a little looser in the chest, a little fuller in the waist: just slightly. But then there's this gentle hurricane of gray hair on his chest that makes me want to bite his clavicle, and sink my teeth in to the bone sometimes. Well. Who knows, maybe he sees some- thing extraordinary about me, too, as is. I don't know that I truly be- lieve that, but it's a nice thought, certainly.

Adela

I SAID HE was just some guy, and it's true, more or less. But there was something magical about him — honestly, he had this charmed life, and you could feel it the moment you met him. I mean, we met at the end of my first year, and he was connected to all these mov- ers and shakers; celebrities in certain circles, I suppose. He was from Louisville, from a good family, old money.

It wasn't just that, though. I thought he looked — this is so stu- pid, but I thought he looked exactly like the Little Prince, I did. An- gelic, truly. His name was Marshall, and when he introduced him-

212

self, I said, Marshall — like the Marshall Court? He said, One and the same. It was a family name — that Marshall, yes.

What can I say? I was obsessed with the guy, I really was. And the less he wanted to know me, the more I felt . . . the more I felt it could change everything, my whole life. I thought he could make it right, that if he loved me, everything would be all right for once. I mean, really, how . . . how stupid can you get, you know?

I kept calling, and then, finally, I went to see him. I waited in front of his house for almost an hour in the pouring rain — naturally, it would have to be raining. I even smiled when he pulled up in his truck and parked, steeling his face, seeing me on his front step. Can I talk to you? I said, and he didn't answer. I just need five minutes, I said, please? Five minutes, he said, and I said, Why don't we go across the street? There was a café on the corner, and he followed me, making a point of walking as far away from me as he could.

There was no one else there when we walked in, and then the waitress came over to take our order. Nothing for me, he said, smiling at her. I'd like a coffee, please, I said, and she took our menus, leaving us alone. Marshall looked at his watch, and then he said, Well? I didn't know where to begin. All I could say was, I wish you would talk to me . . . I don't know what I did wrong, but you should tell me — honestly, I just want to understand. But he simply stared at me, with his arms crossed, unmoved.

He didn't care. He honestly didn't care if he ever saw me again. I didn't say anything; I just waited, hoping he'd soften. I thought if he could see how much pain I was in, he'd be decent, at least. Not kind, but decent. The waitress brought my coffee, and he thanked her, and that, alone — that he could be polite to her, sweet even, but not to me — made me think, *How? How do you do that . . . ?* I still forget sometimes that I know how — I know exactly how.

You have thirty seconds, he said, looking at a large antique clock above the bar. I just sat there, looking at him. Looking into his eyes, trying to find some trace of kindness or compassion, and he looked at the clock on the wall once more, counting the seconds. Then he grabbed his gloves and got up. Goodbye, he said, and that was it. He

213

walked out the door, crossed the street, and I watched him open his front door and disappear inside.

I felt queasy . . . not just my stomach, my entire body — stomach, head, limbs. I couldn't seem to focus; couldn't see two inches in front of me. Everything — air, sound, time — became so slow, so thick, simply standing from the table brought me to the verge of tears. I'd blown it — it's like all I ever did was fuck up. I made it to the end of the block, and then I suddenly wanted to call my mom, but I couldn't do it. I mean, even if I could've brought myself to tell her what an ass I'd made of myself, she was working — it wasn't the time. Besides, if I told her how many times I called him, texted, e-mailed, wrote him — proper letters . . . I begged him to talk to me, I did. Never . . . no, she would never understand.

I walked for hours, and then, finally, I called Michael, because . . . because I had to tell someone. Because Michael was as good as a perfect stranger, and far from perfect, from what I'd heard. Who better? So six hours later, I finished my fifth drink and I told him the whole story.

Lynne

I SAT IN my studio until ten o'clock Saturday night, just staring at that damned Mets shirt, trying to decide what to do. It was wrong — not just wrong, it was heartless, really, and I knew it. Yes, I knew how cruel it was to steal Daddy's favorite shirt, but I knew I wasn't giving it back to him, either. Finally, I went to say good night to Jordan, ask if she needed anything, and she said no. All right, good night, I said, turning away, and then she said, I know about Dad. And I froze, standing there, with my hand in the air.

I didn't know what to say to her, except sorry. I said, I'm sorry, Jordan. Then she looked at me — she finally turned her attention away from the television for a second — and she said, Don't be sorry for *me* — I'm sorry for *you,* she said, returning her attention to the TV, dismissing me. All I could do was nod; I just stood there, nodding, then I realized I was biting my lip, and, finally, I said, See you in the morning.

Lisa

SOMEWHERE ALONG THE WAY Greg lost his confidence, and I don't know why. But I thought I could believe for the two of us — I tried, too. But that only made it worse, like he wanted to prove me wrong. About a year before I left, he quit painting, and he started getting high before I'd even left for work, like he was throwing it in my face, my faith. I wish I could blame the drugs for that, too, but I can't. I mean, why does anyone lose their confidence? I can't even answer that question for myself, and I know all the reasons. But still, I supported his ass for five years while he spent his money getting high all day, so what the fuck is that, a girlfriend?

He asked me to marry him. He wanted to get married, have the baby, and move out of the city. He said he wanted to find a place where he could get some workaday job, and he'd paint in the morning, after work, weekends — we'd figure it out, he said. And I said, Figure what out? What would we do, Greg? And he said, Leese, we'll do what people always do: we'll raise our kid and live a normal, average life.

Normal, average life? I winced. What's so terrible about that? he said, and I said, Normal, average lives are for fucking losers, Greg, that's what's wrong with it. Well, as long as we have each other, right? You and me? he said, reaching for me, trying to pull me to his waist, and I couldn't answer. I wanted to pat him on the shoulder: you poor, poor man . . . but instead, I just pulled away. I'd rather die, I said, same difference.

Adela

HE ASKED ME once if I was curious, if I'd ever tried to look for her family, and I said no. No, I'm not curious, I said. I mean, she wasn't some Latina *Pretty Woman*. She was a crack whore who left me to go out and score: end of story. I know who my mother is; I know who my family is; I don't need to look, I said. And I was angry — angered to be talking about it, angered to be questioned, angered at the thought that he was judging me — but he didn't say anything. He just let me be. I'm sorry, I said, calming down, and Michael shook his head. Don't be sorry. Please, he said, anything but that.

Bobbie

I FINISHED AN ENTIRE BOTTLE of wine before Adela called Saturday night, and then I finished a second bottle after we spoke. Not surprisingly, I woke Sunday morning with the worst hangover I'd had in at least ten years. Even more painful: for a moment, I thought I'd been dreaming. I thought it was all some terrible dream, and then I remembered that it wasn't. It was real. It was true. Then I closed my eyes again, wanting nothing more than to go back to sleep, but I couldn't. I had to go to the hospital.

Adela

THE WHOLE NIGHT, Saturday night, I just lay there, awake in bed, and then finally I got up at seven. When Michael got up and walked into the living room three hours later, I was still sitting on the couch, staring at the wall. I have to go see my mom, I said.

What are you going to tell her? he said, and I said, The truth. Which is? he said. That it's just — it just happened, I said. Adela, running into an old acquaintance on the street just happens. Having sex with a man for three months doesn't just happen, he said. He had a point.

So what about telling the truth? he said. Which is what? I said, raising my voice at him. You tell me, he said, and it sounded — it almost sounded like an accusation. I have to go, I said, standing. I'll be here, he said. Thanks, I said, grabbing my coat, heading out.

Lynne

SUNDAY NIGHT, I stood at the window, watching her swinging, debating whether or not to go out and talk to her, tell her the truth. Which is that I went to see him, I spoke to him — Misha, yes. I went to see him during the day, when Jordan was in school. I don't shop at

Price Chopper's, so no one recognized me when I told them I wanted to speak to the assistant manager, and they called him down to customer service. I'd never laid eyes on the man, but somehow he knew who I was the moment he laid eyes on me. Because the first thing he said was, Why don't we talk in my office, Mrs. Yaeger?

So we went upstairs, and I sat down, and before he'd even had a chance to sit, I told him I'd charge him with statutory rape if he saw or spoke to Jordan ever again. He looked at me, reaching for his chair, and then he sat down, very calmly. You have two children of your own, so maybe this would be a good time for you to remember that, I said, and I braced myself, expecting him to retaliate, but he didn't. No, he just sat there, looking at me, slouched in his chair, with the fingers of both hands buttressed like the frame of a house.

Which only infuriated me that much more. Just out of curiosity, Misha, is this what you wanted for yourself? To be the assistant manager of Price Chopper's and live with your common-law wife and your two kids in low-income housing, while you're having a fling with one of your teenage checkout girls? I said, and then I waited for an answer. Finally he said, Is that what you came to say? No, I said.

No, I came here to tell you to stay away from my daughter. And unless you're ready to give up what sad little life you've managed to create for yourself, don't ever see or speak to her again — in person, on the phone, via e-mail, text, I don't care. If you don't believe me, call my bluff, I said, and he opened his mouth, then he changed his mind. Something you wanted to say? I asked. No, I was just noticing the resemblance, he said, referring to Jordan and me. Goodbye, I said, walking out the door.

Adela

I WENT THERE to explain — as much as I could, at least — but as soon as I told her I'd dropped out of school, she went ballistic. Mom, I have the money — I withdrew in time, and I'll pay back the rest —. I don't care about the money, Adela! I can't believe — I cannot *believe* that you're just . . . you're just going to throw it all away. Everything you've worked for —. No, I said. No, Mom: everything *you've* worked for.

She said, Then what was that bullshit you told Paul about the Sudan, that you'd leave tomorrow if you could? It was for you, I said, meaning I said it because I thought it would make her proud. God, if she could've seen the way she beamed, hearing me say those words — nothing I do, nothing I really am could ever make her as proud as that Sudan story. No, she said, don't you dare say you lied for me — don't you *dare*.

Mom, I'm not blaming you for anything, but it's my life, and she said, Yes, it is: and this is what you want to do with your life? I said, You know, I haven't agreed with all the decisions you've made, but at least I respected your right to choose. Isn't that what you always told me: freedom of choice means the right to disagree? What do you want, Adela? she said. Honestly, what do you want from me? And I said, I want your support. I'm sorry, she said, but I don't support this decision, and I have every right to disagree.

How, Adela? Really, how could you be so stupid? she said, and I said, Don't speak to me like I'm a twelve-year-old. Then stop acting like a twelve-year-old and grow up. Start by thinking about someone beside yourself for a change, she said, getting up to leave the room. Where are you going? I said. I'm going to bed, she said. I'm not through, I said. I am, she said, walking away.

Lynne

I WATCH THE NEWS every night and I'm horrified by the fires and floods, the sight of people losing everything they have, and I don't know what I'd do if we lost this house. Then again, it doesn't take a hurricane, really, sometimes you can lose everything you have simply by answering the phone or opening a door. Four weeks ago, the school nurse called me at work. She said Jordan wasn't feeling well and I needed to pick her up, and there was something odd about it. I don't know what it was, but something wasn't right.

Fifteen minutes later, I walked into her office, and Jordan seemed fine, but the nurse didn't look well. What happened? I said, and the woman asked me to sit down. I'm fine, thank you. But I'm sorry, what's this all about? I said, and Jordan stared at her hands, nodding.

Finally, the nurse said, Mrs. Yaeger, Jordan's pregnant, and I said, I see. That was my response: *I see.* Turns out, the nurse didn't bother to test her: she simply took one look and asked the question, and then Jordan told her everything. I looked at Jordan, sitting there, thinking, *Who are you? And what have you done with my daughter?*

We didn't say a word in the car. Once we got home, Jordan went straight to her room, then I called the office to say I'd be out the rest of the day, and then I called Don. I told him it was an emergency, and that he needed to come home, and we'd talk about it then, I said, cutting him off. Then I called Lisa, before I finally sat down at the kitchen table and waited for Don.

Half an hour later, Don walked through the door; and he came right at me, like, what the hell is so goddamn important you insist I come home and won't even tell me what's going on? So I told him. Jordan's pregnant, I said, and the way he threw his head back, it was like he'd just run right into my fist: pop! It took him a good minute to speak, but of course I couldn't answer his questions because I had no idea what was going on myself, so we called her down. There we were, the three of us, sitting across from one another on the matching sofas, separated by a square glass coffee table I'd spent weeks choosing. Yes, there we were, and for the first time, I looked around the room and thought, *What is all this crap, anyhow?*

Of course Don didn't know what to say, so very calmly I said, Well, for starters, why don't you try explaining what's going on, and Jordan said, Why? You aren't going to understand anyway. Maybe not, but you still need to tell us what the hell is going on, and I am in no mood for your attitude right now, so cut it, I said, trying to control my voice. Because I was ready to slap her, I really was, looking at her, thinking, *Don't you* dare *speak to me in that tone.* Fine, she said, sitting up straight, and then she told us the whole story. Oh, she told us all right.

Well, turns out it's not even some high-school boy. No, oh, no . . . Jordan's been screwing her boss, the assistant manager at Price Chopper's, and I was speechless. I don't think that's irony, I think that's just a cruel joke. I mean, really, she sat on her butt all summer, moping about, doing nothing but eating junk food and watching *The Hills* reruns, with her computer in her lap, IMing god knows who. Really, all summer, that's all she did. So one day I said to her, I said, Jordan, why don't you put your computer away and try spending some time with your real friends? I am, she said, continuing to type.

Finally, one night I returned home to find her in exactly the same position she had been in when I left for work that morning, and I'd had enough. I told her that if she had that much free time on her hands, it was time for her to get a job and start earning her own spending money. So she gave me that snotty, Fine — not even bothering to peel her eyes away from the television for one second — Fine, she said.

Next day, she applied for a position at Price Chopper's: just to spite me, yes. I wasn't suggesting that she start looking that second, and I certainly thought she could find something more suitable than Price Chopper's, and I told her so. Jordan, I'm just saying you could look for something more interesting —. What, like working for the chamber? she said, with a little snort of contempt. It was such a slap, but what could I say? Really, what could I possibly say? She'd made her point, belittling my job and exposing my snobbishness in a single stroke, so I turned and left the room. But when she interviewed a day later, I thought, *All right, then, let's see how far you want to take your little joke.* Well, here's my answer.

If that wasn't enough, he's thirty — this person she's seeing, or whatever they've been doing together, he's thirty years old. And he's married — oh, excuse me, no, he's not married, he just lives with the mother of his two children, as Jordan said. One other thing: his name is Misha and he's African American. Which we know because Don, in his stupor, actually said, Misha? What's that, Russian? No, Misha's not Russian; Misha's not even Black Russian; he's just black. He's black? Don said, as though he hadn't heard her correctly. Then Jordan started screaming, telling us how racist and small-minded we are. Jordan, I said, I don't care if he's blue; he's thirty years old, and he's your boss. And then she stopped, reduced to glaring at me, as though I had done this to her.

So there we were, Don and I, sitting side by side, the weakest united front in history, and then Don stunned me, asking her: Jordan, what do you want to do? Because I hadn't thought to ask, no, I didn't even know there *was* a question. She couldn't seriously be thinking about keeping the baby. I don't know yet, she said, shaking her head, I haven't decided. *She hadn't decided . . . ?* That was the last night I slept, four weeks ago now, even though, for the first time in twenty-four years, Don's finally stopped snoring because he isn't sleeping, either. No, we just lie there, staring at the ceiling, night after night, because neither one of us knows what to do anymore.

A few nights later, I managed to fall asleep, and then, in my dream, I remember hearing all this crying and screaming; and then I realize Don was shaking me, telling me to wake up, and I knew something terrible had happened. It was one of those moments when you search every corner of your life, like you would, checking your body parts after an explosion, and they're all there; everything's still there. You're in shock, of course, but even then, you know for certain that whatever it is, whatever just happened will never make any more sense to you than it did at that moment.

Joyce

SATURDAY NIGHT Joe walked me outside, and I told the driver to take me home. My phone started ringing a minute later, and I turned it off. I didn't even look to see who it was; didn't matter. I just wanted to be alone. The driver tuned in a station on the radio and I yelled at him: Turn that shit off! But when the silence fell, I almost wanted him to turn the music on again.

I never told him — I never told Michael I got pregnant. No, the only person I told was Bobbie. Not that it took a medical degree to help me polish off a couple bottles of wine and piss on a stick the week before I left New York. That's blue, right? That's not pinkish-blue? I asked, walking into the living room, handing her the plastic stick.

So when I called her from L.A., all I had to say was, I didn't tell him, and she said, Do you want to think about it? I did, I have, I said.

How soon can you get me in? Friday? she asked, and I said, Okay. But make it as early as possible, will you? I don't want to wait in line, and she said, I'll put your name on the VIP list, and I almost started to cry, and she said, I'm so sorry, babe. And then I finally managed to reel it back in, and I said, What can you do, right?

So we got back to New York on Thursday night, and Bobbie handled everything. She met us at the airport, then she sent Benjamin home with Adela; Adela took Benjamin to school the next day, picked him up that night; and Bobbie got a sitter for the weekend. I had a car pick me up and drive me to the Upper East Side first thing Friday morning; I was home by noon, and that was that. Done. Adios. I wasn't coming back, either.

But still . . . ah, fuck me: but still nothing. I wanted a daughter so badly, it killed me; it did. I wanted . . . I wanted a beautiful, precious little girl like Adela. I mean, they have the most amazing relationship, those two — not perfect, but amazing. Adela calls Bobbie almost every day — they actually *enjoy* talking to each other, and I . . . I just wanted to feel that bond. Yes, of course I have Benjamin, but that's not what I'm talking about. I'm talking about what I never had with my mother: just once, you know?

For a few years there, before Michael came around, I used to take Adela for overnights and weekends when Bobbie had to work those thirty-, forty-hour shifts. So I got to live out this entire fantasy I don't think I'd admitted having since I was about ten years old. And for several years, the only thing that got me through was pretending Adela was mine, and I remembered that so vividly, on the way to my appointment that morning. How I used to dress her up and making peanut butter–chocolate chip cookies and giving her Mr. Bubble bubble baths — everything. I could almost feel her head, the way it bobbed backward, as I combed her wet hair, and that sweet smell of Johnson and Johnson No More Tears.

I wanted all those things: I wanted a daughter of my own. But there was no way in hell I was bringing a child into the world as a forty-three-year-old divorcée, about to enter what promised to be a very long and extremely bloody war. That's not a child; that's a human sacrifice.

Lynne

SUNDAY, WHILE DON and Lance were watching football, I took my sharpest pair of scissors and I shredded that goddamn Mets shirt, thinking, *Fuck you, I Still Believe!* And honestly, it was . . . it was excellent. Take *that.* And *that,* and *that!* At one point, I became so violent, I actually — I dropped the scissors and started tearing the damn thing with my bare hands, screaming: I hate you! I hate you, I hate you, I hate what you did to me!

I stopped, suddenly, hearing the television muted. I stopped and held my breath — I didn't realize how loud I was. I still must've had some drugs in my system, but then the sound returned, and I took a breath, finally looking to see what I had done. You know we once had a cat named Pepper that used to do that to the toilet paper, shred it to pieces if we left her alone for too long. Don used to walk in, holding the shredded white mound with both hands, like, would you look at this? It was insane — completely insane, but completely understandable at the same time.

Joyce

I MEAN, MY PHONE was ringing off the hook all day Sunday. First Bobbie, then Michael, Bobbie, Michael . . . About three o'clock, I picked up the phone to check the number, and it was Adela. I just sat there, looking at the phone, like it had the answer.

Lisa

AT LEAST I'D HAVE the element of surprise. I mean, when I walked through the door, shaking in my plumed heels, all I could think was, *Well, if Joyce is here, she's going to be a hell of a lot more shocked to see me than I am to see her. Bet she's gained weight, too.* Which was small consolation, but wasn't the first time I took what I could get.

The place was just as I had left it — plus or minus my ex-boyfriend's artwork covering every wall. Enormous — I mean, *ginormous* canvases. No more than three per wall, but both sides of the gallery. I finally got up from the bench in order to take a closer look, then I stopped and glanced at his artist's statement, then I took a quick look at the titles, before looking up, taken aback. Damn you, I said.

I had to sit down again, and then a voice in my head said, *Say it . . . say it louder . . . Come on, scream,* the voice said, *let me hear you scream! What happened to you, Lisa? You used to be brave, Lisa — you used to be bold, you used to be so fucking punk rock, now let's hear you scream!* And then I did — I screamed: *Goddamn you, you motherfucker!*

I screamed until there was no air left in my lungs, and I leaned forward, feeling my chest collapse. I sat up again, taking a deep breath, and then, for a moment, I didn't know if I was going to start bawling, or — or scream again . . .

Joyce

SO I GAVE THE KID a choice, and option B was: get a job. I can't get a job: I'm underage, Benjamin said. Then lie, I said. I can't —. Oh, yeah? Since when? I said, and he — get this, he says, I can't lie about my age —. Because you'd never do something so underhanded, would you, Ben? No, he said, because you've got to show ID. We have these things called child labor laws in this country to protect us against parents like you.

I said, Yes, you've got a point, Ben; you can't work legally, no. And since you can't work legally, you'd be lucky to make, oh, five dollars an hour, under the table. So I took the liberty of running the numbers for you, I said, sliding him a piece of paper. I calculated, basing my estimate on the style to which you have grown accustomed these past fifteen years. Or, just think of it as one hour per year. Fifteen hours? he said, thunderstruck. Per week, yes, I said. That's two nights a week, after school, and one day every weekend — Saturday or Sunday, take your pick. I, I can't work after school! You know my schedule, he said.

I said, Yes, I do. Which is why I know you've got Monday and Friday nights free every week, don't you? Anyhow, they're flexible; they're willing to work with your schedule. Don't worry. One way or another, you will have a cell phone again, I promise. Then again, if you want to make more than that, I can give you the name of a nice urinal uptown, I said, sliding the application across the table. So what'll it be, Benjamin? What's your poison, Señor Swanky or Señor Swankier's? I said it with a straight face, too. I'm telling you, sometimes I even amaze myself.

And as far as the homework you weren't doing until now that you suddenly want to do your homework goes, guess you'll have to use the school computers, I said. The *school* computers? he said, turning up his spoiled little nose. Well, yes, I said, you're in school, and you need a computer, and your school has computers that you can use. You've got to be kidding—I wouldn't use those shitty computers if you held a gun to my head, he said. Benjamin, I said, I haven't ruled out the possibility.

But, I continued, knowing how limited your time is, I spoke to the manager at Señor Swanky's on your behalf, and he said he might be willing to make an exception. For the right candidate, of course. Unfortunately, since it'll have to be off the books, he'll only be able to pay you $5.50. Tough luck, I said, flapping my cheek. But, again, it's not like you don't have a choice, I said, and he looked up, glaring at me.

Oh. And while you're thinking about it, let me help. Listen—just listen to this: pure poetry. *Presenting evidence that we are not alone,* I said, reading aloud, before closing the glossy pamphlet. And look at these pictures, I said, opening the brochure again. I mean, can you imagine that *divine* piece of technology in your bedroom—can you *just imagine* having all your friends over, kicking back, watching the BeoSound 4?

So, I said, pulling out another piece of paper: To answer my question for you, minimum wage in the state of New York will be $7.15 as of January 1, 2007. Which you could check on your computer, if I hadn't given it away to a far more deserving kid. Really, just because life isn't fair doesn't mean it shouldn't be every once in a while, don't you think? *I hate you!* he said. Yes, I'm sure you do, I said. But, on the bright side, further evidence that we are not alone.

Lisa

WHEN I LOOKED at her, when I looked her in the eye, I could see she believed what she was saying; she was sober, at least. But I can't—I can't believe her, no. And, and . . . I mean, why now? Why tell me now? Because he loved me best? I said, Can't she let me have that? Can't she let me have one person who loves me more than anything in this world?

Lisa, she said, what did Lynne say he did, exactly? Doesn't matter, I said. Then why don't you tell me? she said. Because I don't need to repeat her drugged-out delusions, all right? What if she is telling the truth? she said, and I just sat there. Lisa, if what she's saying—. Honestly, I don't really care, either way, because I will never believe her, I said.

I mean, what's the difference? She's believed plenty of things about me that weren't true. And you can look at me like that as long as you like, I said. Because you don't know him, and she doesn't know him—she never knew him like I did. What did your father say, when she confronted him? she said, and I glared at her: *Confronted* him? One more, I said, trying to control my voice, one more word about my dad, and I will get up, walk through that door, and I will never return. Do you understand? Yes, she said, I understand.

Joyce

AND YOU WONDER why men don't understand women, he said, and I practically snorted. No, I said. As a matter of fact, I don't wonder, Paul. The fact of the matter is that men don't understand women because men are just plain stupid, that's why. Jesus Christ, a fucking sea anemone knows more about women than men do.

Seriously, Dr. Phil knows more about women than men do, all right? Which reminds me: I need a drink, I said, looking around. *And you wonder . . . ?* I thought, practically slapping the table. Finally he said, You want to tell me what's going on? And I said, Oh, no—I brought you here, the rest is Bobbie's job. I'll let her fill you in on all the gory details of the past three, four days . . .

226

Bobbie

THAT NIGHT, the night Paul serenaded me on speakerphone, I'd had a terrible day, and I was exhausted. I'd seen one patient, a teenage girl, who was scheduled to have an abortion the following week, so I sat with her after her exam, and I explained the procedure again. I went through it very carefully, wanting to be certain she understood everything I was telling her.

She was so tough, but you could see it took all the energy she had, simply holding up her chin — as though she would have broken down sobbing if you'd poked her with a pin. Like Lisa. She reminded me of Lisa, exactly.

Then, finally, I said, Do you have any questions, Jordan? She started to speak, and then she shook her head, she understood the procedure — that wasn't it, her jaw said, contracting in pain. What is it, honey? What's wrong? I said, almost kicking myself for asking such a stupid question. Then she finally spoke, almost laughing.

She looked up at me, and she said, He didn't call . . . I just checked my messages in the bathroom, and he didn't call. I pulled over my stool, and took her hand in mine. He knew — I told him I was coming in today, I left him a message, and I've had my cell phone on this whole time, and he doesn't . . . he doesn't even care, she said, tears running down her cheek. What could I tell her? Nothing. Not a damn thing. So I didn't; I just listened.

Adela

I CALLED HER twice Sunday night and once Monday morning, but she didn't answer. So I ended up staying at Ana's Sunday night after all, and then I went to see Ixnomy on Monday afternoon. When we walked past the mural on Wednesday, Ana and I, there were just a couple of cheap Mexican candles, the kind with purple-and-yellow swirls, half burned and faded by the elements, and a few tacky plastic flowers hanging limp over the lip of a Heineken bottle. So I decided to take her some real flowers.

But instead of leaving them, I decided I'd give her flowers to that little woman in Tompkins. I thought I'd go look for her, and then I'd give the old lady the flowers and tell her, These are for you. They're from Ixnomy. And she'd say, Bless you. Christ, what is the world coming to, when the only person who thinks to bless you is crazy?

Anyhow, I went to see her, to ask her forgiveness for how selfish and thoughtless and unkind I've been all these years. So I spent forty bucks on flowers at that stand on the corner of Sixth and Second, because that was all I had on me, and then I walked over, taking Sixth to C. But when I turned the corner, she was gone. When I got there, she was gone — Ixnomy — her mural was gone.

I thought I must've been confused, so I walked to Fifth, but she wasn't there, and she wasn't on the corner of Fourth or Third . . . so I walked all the way up to Ninth, and she wasn't there, anywhere. She was gone, and for a moment I almost started crying because I honestly thought I'd lost my mind . . .

Joyce

HER PHONE RANG; she checked the number, then turned off her phone, moving her purse from where it had been resting between us on the bench to her other side. Which told me that Adela was calling and Bobbie wasn't speaking to her. I waited, but she just stared straight ahead. Finally I said, Can I tell you something if you promise not to tell? I promise, she said. Because I promised I wouldn't tell, I said. Joyce, I'm your best friend —. Lotta good that's done me, I said, and she gave me the look. Fourth of July, I said, when you were supposed to come up for the weekend? Yes? she said. Then, at the last minute, you canceled, remember? Yes, Joyce, yes, I remember. What, already?

Paul threw the party for you, so we'd have an excuse to get you over to meet him. Took him the whole week to cook all that food, and then, at the last minute, you canceled. So he threw *another* party the very next weekend. Just for you, I said, but she didn't say anything. He was so embarrassed; he made me promise not to tell you . . . he even bought the flowers that were on the picnic tables, you remember? He asked me to stop by that first Friday night to make sure they

228

looked just right, and then he went and bought them twice, I said, but she didn't blink. She does this — she disconnects.

Finally she said, And your point is what? Of course I was too high to respond, but were I in my right mind, or at least sober, what I would've said was, You know, I can be a real cunt, but god . . . you make me so sad sometimes, you know that? *Your point is what?* Oh, I don't know, that you're being an asshole? But all I could say was, Jesus Christ, Bobbie, do you know how much I wish someone would do that for me?

Joyce, she said, what do you want me to say, thank you? All right, thank you for the potato salad —. Forget it, I said, I don't want you to say anything. But you're in the wrong here, and if you were a man, I said, if you were a man, I'd tell you to be man enough to own up to it and call him to apologize. But, fortunately or unfortunately, you aren't a man, and fortunately or unfortunately, you never make mistakes, do you, Bob? At least Adela has the balls to keep trying to get through to you —. We're not having this conversation right now, she said, and I said, We're not? Then go, I said, *go.* Or better yet, I'll go. Because if you aren't interested in continuing this conversation, I'm not interested in sitting here any longer, I said, getting up from the bench.

4

Lisa

I HAVE TO SAY, I was really enjoying watching her sob and plead and beg for my forgiveness. I'm sorry, but I was just sitting there, in the driver's seat, thinking, *How many times, Lynne? How many times have you looked down your nose at me?*

She knew, too. She remembered — I knew why she felt so guilty, and she should. I mean, the reason I hit her up that last time was because Greg told me he'd help. He said he'd pay me back the three hundred bucks he owed me, but a couple of nights before, I returned home to a note that said, *Sorry. Tried, but I can't come up with the dough,* and I just stood there, shaking . . . Goddamn you! I screamed, loud enough for the whole building to hear. Then I just hid my face in my hands, trying to keep it together. Now — *now* he tells me? I've got forty-eight hours to come up with another two hundred bucks when I've already borrowed money from everyone I know.

I had no choice, so I picked up the phone and called Lynne. I asked about the kids and she said the kids were fine, and I asked about Don, and then she said, Really, Lisa, what is it this time? And I said, I need to borrow some money. No kidding, she said. Lynne, I swear I'll pay you back. Lisa, she said, that's what you swore last time, and you still haven't paid me back. Lynne, please, I said.

I know, I know, she said, you're desperate. Why don't you ask Daddy? He's got money, she said, and I said, I can't. I don't know why I couldn't ask him, really. No, I know why I didn't ask my dad: because, believe it or not, I couldn't lie to him. And I couldn't tell him the truth, either, so I just couldn't ask. I said, Lynne, we're talking two hundred bucks, and she said, No, Lisa, we aren't talking two hundred bucks, because I'm not loaning you any more money until you pay me back the two grand you owe me.

Lynne —. Lisa, I'm sorry, but we've been through this. It's like give a mouse a cookie with you, and I said, It's like what? Give a mouse a cookie, she said. Lynne, what are you talking about? And she goes, If you give a mouse a cookie, he'll ask for a glass of milk —. And then I lost it.

I said, What the fuck are you talking about, mice and cookies? I'm eleven weeks pregnant, Lynne — I've got one week, you understand? And Greg — Greg swore he'd come up with half, but I just returned home to a note saying he tried but no luck. And now you're telling me about mice and cookies and I've had it — I'm so fucking sick and tired of your preaching and your goddamn judgment all the time, Lynne, *fuck*.

Neither one of us said anything while I caught my breath. Finally, she said, I'll send you a check tomorrow, and I closed my eyes, squinting in gratitude, feeling the blood return to my body. Then I winced, asking, You think you could wire it to me?

Lynne

I HAD TO — no, I had to — I just . . . I just couldn't take it anymore, so I told her everything . . . Absolutely everything, it all spilled out. And I told her, I said, I'm sorry, Lisa, I'm so sorry I was never there for you. I've been a terrible sister —. Lynne, she said, you're tripping. No, I said, no. You don't understand. Oh, believe me, I do, she said.

I understand all too well, she said, and in the morning, this will all be a bad dream — a bad dream that you'll remember in vivid color, but a dream. I promise, Lynne. Everything will return to its proper place; tomorrow morning, everything will look better, or however it looked before. And I said, No! No, I don't *want* everything the way it was before, because I can't do this! I can't do this anymore, Lisa — I'm so tired of all the lies. I'm sorry, but I'm so tired of living one big goddamn *lie*, I can't — I just can't do it. All right, she said. All right — calm down.

I said, You aren't listening to me, Lisa! You aren't *listening!* Lynne, she hissed, checking on Jordan in the rearview again. I said, Please, Lisa, would you just listen for once? I'm listening, she said, looking genuinely concerned. I'm sorry, I said. I'm sorry, okay? Please, just know how sorry I am to have to ask you this. All right, then, she said, tell me, already. And I said, Lisa, did Daddy —. Dad, she said. Please don't call him Daddy, I can't stand that, she said. I'm sorry, I said. Lynne, stop apologizing, all right? she said. Did Dad what, Lynne? Did Dad, I said, did Dad ever touch you?

Lisa

WE GOT TO their house just before dark. I got out of the car, and an Irish setter came running. Is that Red? I asked, guarding myself as he jumped. No, Jordan said, sighing, that's Rusty. Can't you tell? Red was Red, but Rusty's so obviously Rusty. Get down, she said, Rusty, *get down.* And the dog obeyed. What happened to Red? I said. Red's dead, she said, perfectly matter-of-fact. Then Don stepped out the front door.

I stretched my arms for a moment, taking in their yard: the autumn leaves; the weeping willows; an apple tree; a porch swing I'm sure Don made by hand. The perfect house. The perfect yard. It was idyllic, just before sunset. But then I felt that same tightening in my chest I always felt coming back: claustrophobia.

Don came over, and Lynne, who'd stayed in the front seat, staring at their house, finally gathered herself and stepped out of the car, unsteady, balancing for a moment. You all right? Don said, walking over to help her. I'm fine — I'm fine, she said, finally getting out. Jordan, your brother's home, Don said, just as Lance stepped out the front door.

Hey, he said, as Jordan approached the door. Hey, she said, walking right past him into the house. Hey, Aunt Lisa, he said, and I winced — hate it when he calls me that. Hey, Nephew Lance, I said. Lisa, Don said, why don't you come in? Sure, I said, I just want to look at the river first, okay? Of course — you go on, then, he said, following Lynne inside.

I walked to the end of the backyard, and I stood there, watching the last few minutes of the sunset, standing on the edge of a cliff with one of the most spectacular views I know, but still. All I could think was, *I should love this place. It's where I was born, where I was raised; it's in my blood. But I don't . . . I don't.*

I walked across the lawn, heading for the swing, inhaling that fresh, clean air I had spent so many years despising. *So much . . .* I thought, nodding my head, climbing into the tire. There was just so much Will didn't know about me. And I wasn't sure if it even mattered anymore.

When I was little, I remember staying outside, playing with all the neighbor boys until my mom called, and then she made my dad call me inside. It wasn't until I finally went inside that I even noticed that my arms were numb. There was nothing better in this world than staying outside until that last sweet second of the day. I had a gang back then — I was gang leader, too. I initiated all the games; I chose the teams; I passed judgment and rewrote the rules to serve my purposes. And then one day I was kicked out — founding member kicked out of her own club. For almost three years, I had been king and queen, judge and jury, coach and player, field marshal, fair maiden, warrior princess . . . Christ, in the course of a single afternoon, I could play anyone from Snow White to George Patton and back again. I was the chosen leader of our gang: it was agreed, unanimously.

I'll never forget that moment, showing up late one day, after school, to find my gang peering over something I assumed to be dead by the fascinated tilt of their skulls. Then their four heads opening like the petals of a spring tulip to reveal a magazine. It wasn't a dead animal; it was *Penthouse.*

Right there, right beneath their noses: tits, bush, everything, right there. A woman, a naked woman, but not like my mom — god, no. She was like a woman from another planet, like nothing I'd ever seen before. And the worst part was that she was real — or she looked pretty real. I couldn't take my eyes off her pubic hair, that dark, downy seventies bush, but most of all, I remember her airbrushed, lip-glossed mouth, the tiny tip of her pink tongue curled back, barely touching her parted upper lip.

Whose desire I felt at that moment, theirs or my own, I don't know. Both, I'm sure. But all I remember is a pang so sharp that I wanted to cry out, *Who did this?* Who brought this into my world? A day before, I would have demanded an answer, but I knew then, at that moment — I knew everything had changed. My reign had ended. My paradise was gone. It was mutiny, my fall from grace.

Worst of all, for some reason I couldn't begin to understand, my arrival sealed my fate. In the course of what seemed like nothing more than seconds to me, our paths split. And for weeks after I hoped it would simply pass, that moment, but it didn't; the separation had only just begun. I was so lonely without my friends; I had no one to play with. I mean, I didn't even know how to talk to girls, really.

I became convinced that if I hadn't gone to the dentist, if I had only been there, I could have suppressed the mutineers. Disaster could have been avoided, were it not for a semiannual teeth-cleaning my mom insisted on. Which meant it was her fault: *she* did this to me, my mom; it was all her fault. And that's what she had wanted all along, to make me into a girl. And what did she care? She'd never known anything better. But still, this was all her doing, and I glared at her as she poured milk into my glass. How could she have engineered this whole crisis but still be too simple-minded to understand her own actions? She was the child, not me.

For weeks I tried again and again, approaching with caution, beseeching them. Hey . . . *hey,* you guys, I've got matches. Let's build a campfire, I said, using that same irresistibly mischievous voice that had lured them a hundred times before, but they didn't want to play with me. So finally, one afternoon, after school, I brought a stack of my dad's old *Playboys*, offering them that cotton-candy porn like a cat proudly dropping a dead mouse at its owner's feet. And they took them, of course, but it changed nothing.

A few years later, when I heard the rumor that I was a lesbian, I knew exactly when and where it got started — with one of those four heads: either Brandon Foley, or one of the Daves, or Scott Yancy aka Schmancy. It didn't matter who it was, really. Alone, they were harmless; together, they were hyenas.

One day, in seventh grade, I just sat there, watching as Schmancy and Dave Auerbach walked by me at lunchtime. Take a picture, Schmancy said, and I tried to ignore him as the two of them started snickering. For the smallest guy in our class, Schmancy had the biggest mouth; he was a prick with nothing to show for it. So I turned to walk away, deciding to take the high road for once, then, hearing them whisper behind my back, I changed my mind. I walked right up to the two of them and I said, I'm sorry, what did you say? Humored, Schmancy looked at Dave, then he looked at me: Or do you only like pictures of girls? he said, and I smiled. That's what I thought you said, I said, and then I turned — not to walk away, just to give myself a little room — and swung back around: *pop*. I punched him right in the nose.

The kid was down before I'd even lowered my arm, but I just stood there, motionless, watching him writhe in pain. If you have something to say to me, say it to my face, I said, trying to shut my mouth, but I couldn't before kicking him in the ribs with the dirtiest word I knew echoing through the halls: You *pussy*. I didn't break his nose, but I got two weeks' suspension. I wasn't exactly popular before, but I was completely ostracized after that. And so began my famous career as a preteen lesbian.

I walked over and stepped inside the swing, holding the tire's rim as I turned in circles, twisting the chain around and around, and I smiled, remembering the sight of little Scott Yancy, doubled over in agony, holding his bloody nose, looking up at me, scared. I started laughing, and then I lifted my feet and threw my body back, letting go, twirling like a dervish beneath the first stars.

When I went inside I found Don alone in the kitchen, pouring a glass of water. Lisa, can I get you anything? he said. And I said, Xanax, please, and he laughed, but I waited. Give me a minute, he said, holding his finger to his nose, *hush*, before heading upstairs. He returned a minute later and pointed his clenched hand toward my waist. You didn't get them from me, he said, in all seriousness. Get what? I said, opening my mouth and popping the pills toward the back of my throat, before taking a sip of water. You know how Lynne feels about medication, he said, and I just held my tongue.

Guess you've had quite a day, huh? he said, nodding and solemnly exhaling, and I had to laugh. Let's talk about that later, okay? I said. Sure, he said, no rush. Well, Leese, he said, looking around, seeing as we had nothing to talk about other than what we were avoiding discussing. I'd offer you a drink, he said, but —. But nothing, I said. Scotch, please. Lisa —. Listen, Don: it's been quite a day, I said, nodding my head. Besides which, I've got the night off breast-feeding — which is far more than you need to know, I'm sure, but still. I'm ready to par-*ty!* For a moment there, he looked scared — genuinely scared. Don, all I'm saying is that I'd like a Scotch, please. And then he nodded, heading to the liquor cabinet for our drinks.

Lance returned with a pizza, and the three of us were sitting at the table, talking about what had happened, when Lynne walked in. Hey, what are you doing up? Don said, looking contrite, seeing her standing in the door. I needed to change the sheets in the guest bedroom, she said, walking into the dining room. I said, I could've done that, Lynne —. Oh, no, you're the guest, she said, and I knew what she was thinking. Lynne, why don't you sit down? Don asked, always trying to keep the peace. Well, when he's not fucking the help, I suppose, but still.

Whatever mistakes he's made, Don loves Lynne, he does. You can see it in the way he looks at her every time she enters the room — he truly cares about her comfort, her feelings. And I bet if she'd have sex with him every few months, they could probably work things out. God, I wish I could say the same about my own marriage . . . Were it only so simple.

Lynne

THERE MUST BE something wrong with me. Honestly, I don't know what it is, but something happens every time. I mean, at first I want to, and then . . . and then I don't. Last week, or maybe a couple of weeks ago, I can't remember now, but anyhow, one night, Don was lying in bed, watching the news when I walked in, and I sat down on the side of the bed. And for a moment, there was a part of me that wanted to walk over to him, pull back the covers, and straddle him, just like that, sitting upright in bed . . . But, of course, no sooner had the thought crossed my mind than I felt repulsed.

The last time Don touched me, I was standing in front of the bathroom mirror, taking off my makeup. I was wearing my nightgown, and he came over, and he reached around with one finger, and he began rubbing my left nipple. He didn't touch me anywhere else, just his left index finger, barely even touching my skin, and I watched us for a moment, feeling aroused, turned on. Then he leaned against me and started rubbing his erection against my butt, and before I realized what I was saying, I snapped: Don't! Don't do that, I said, and he stepped back — hurt, angry, I don't know, really. I left the room and crawled into bed, pulling the covers over my shoulder.

And it's not because of my dad, either; it's because of me. Really, a few minutes later when I felt Don walk into the bedroom, I still wanted to slap him. But not half as much as I wanted him to slap me back, thinking, *Make it stop, Don. Just make it stop.* But I just pulled the duvet over my shoulder, turning away, as he crawled into bed beside me, thinking to myself, I've known Don since I was nineteen years old . . . and what does he know about me, really? Doesn't he have any interest in knowing what I think about when I close my eyes? He'd be ashamed, if he knew what I think about when we have sex. Well, fortunately or unfortunately, he never asks.

Jordan

AFTER THAT NIGHT he stayed over, he blew me off for weeks — didn't call me, didn't talk to me at work — and then, suddenly, it's like he wants to talk, right. One day Misha caught me outside on break, and he came over and he goes, I'd like to talk to you sometime —. So talk, I said, and he goes, Not here. And I was just like, Then forget it, and I started walking away, and he goes, Listen, Jordan — listen, I'm sorry, okay? So I stopped, and then he goes, I was wrong to let it go that far, and I go, You mean you're sorry you had sex with me? He goes, *Jordan* — I mean, he just looks at me like he's trying to let me down gently or something — and he goes, Jordan, you're such a cool chick, and then I just cut him off. I was like, Misha, how would you know? Oh, what, because you're so cool, right?

He didn't know what to say, and I was just like, *why are you doing this,* you know? So I go, Was it because I wasn't any good? He just looked at me, shaking his head, and he goes, Good . . . ? No — no, Jordan — you don't understand, and I go, No, Misha, no, I don't understand. For two weeks, I called, I texted, I e-mailed — nothing. So how could I understand? You said you're my friend — I thought we were friends, Misha, and I looked at him, and he reached to touch my arm, and then he stopped.

He goes, Jordan, look: I've got . . . I've got two kids, okay? And I have to live with their mother just so I can keep up on my child support. I've got a job I hate, but I can't afford to lose, and you've . . . you've got your whole life ahead of you —. You know what, Misha? I go, You know what? You're just like everyone else. Because whenever someone says, *Oh, you've got your whole life ahead of you,* what they really mean is, it doesn't matter what you're feeling right now, and he goes, That's not what I'm saying —. I was like, Then don't talk to me like some fucking high-school counselor, okay? And he just stared at his feet, then he goes, You're right. I'm sorry.

I mean, can't you at least tell me you wish you could? I said, and he thought about it. Then he said, I don't know if I can say that. And you might not believe me, but I really do care about you —. Gee, thanks, I said, rolling my eyes to keep from crying. Then he goes, Jordan, I can't — I just can't fuck up again, and I was like, Well, why didn't you think of that before? Why'd you offer me a ride and hang out with me all this time? Because. He goes, Because. And I said, Because what?

And he goes, Because you looked so alone —. Fuck you, I said, and I felt so embarrassed, all I could do was repeat myself. No, *fuck you,* Misha, and he just looked at me. And then, finally, he goes, I'm sorry, and he turned, heading back inside.

Lisa

I TOOK A SEAT and turned off my phone as soon as I got on the train. The rest of the way, I just sat there, staring out the window, watching the reflection of the sky and clouds on the river, remembering what I used to think every time I took the train to New York. Looking at the water, so tranquil, so exquisite: something only God could paint. And how I used to dream of climbing on top of the train, taking a running leap, and cannonballing right into the Hudson River, shattering it into pieces. It was such a beautiful image, and all I wanted to do was to destroy it. Jordan thinks I was so brave, but it's not true. That's my best-kept secret: I have never been brave, just scared.

I've got to get her out of there, that's all I know. I've got to find a way to get Jordan out of that house, that town . . . I can't bear to think of her returning Monday morning. When Jordan talks about My-Space and Facebook and LiveJournal and DeadJournal and all this shit she has to deal with, all I can think is, *God, I thought I had it bad.* I mean, at least teen warfare wasn't simulcast when I was her age. No, I can honestly say I hated absolutely every day of school I can remember.

I mean, I was bored. I didn't have any friends. Boys didn't like me. I only liked the boys who didn't like me. Those were the most miserable years of my life. And then I learned a little trick, I said. What's that? she asked. To leave, I said, just leave; turn around, and walk away. In fact, run; don't walk. So that's what I did — I ran away. I ran away nine times before my dad finally agreed to let me drop out.

One day, it hit me, and I realized, *Wait a minute . . . I don't have to be here. I don't have to do this.* I could just get up and leave at any second, and who's going to stop me? It was the first moment it occurred to me that maybe there's an alternative to suicide. Running away, she said. I preferred to think of it as living elsewhere, I said, and she smiled. So one day, when the bell rang at the end of second period, I walked out the front door, I walked down to the train station, and I bought a ticket. The woman gave me a strange look, but she let me go. Three hours later, I was sitting in Tompkins.

How long did you stay? she said. Five days, I said. I might've lasted longer if I'd thought to pack some food — but at least I had my Joan Jett T-shirt, I said, laughing at my lack of foresight. What did your parents do? she said. Well, my mom had already died, but even before then, she left all the discipline to my dad, and then my dad said if I ever worried him like that again, he'd belt me: *I swear to god, Lisa Barrett!* he bellowed. Then you might as well do it now, because I'm not staying here, I said, turning toward the table and unbuttoning my jeans, leaning over on the table and clasping my hands, waiting for him to remove his belt.

You hate it that much? You really hate it here that much? he said, dumbfounded. Yes, I said. Stand up, he said, and I did. All right, he said, I'll give you some money to get yourself a place to live. And that was it. I was all he had, and he let me go. I mean, there was Lynne, but it was different. It was just the two of us, and I was leaving him. We just stood there, and suddenly, for the first time in my life, I felt terrified. But I think he saved my life that day, I really do.

Jordan

THAT NIGHT — I mean, on homecoming, after we put the bubbles away — I go, Hey, Misha . . . what did you think you were going to be you grew up? And he thought about it, like he really gave it some thought, you know, then he just shrugged and he goes, Better. And I was like, Better how? And he goes, I don't know, just better — better than this. So I thought about it, and I was just like, Yeah . . . me, too, and then he just laughed.

And I was like, Are you laughing at me? And he goes, You got time . . . you got plenty of time —. And I was like, So do you, but *I'm* not laughing in *your* face. Then he turns over the ignition, and he goes, Jordan, is this where you get your feelings hurt and you don't speak to me for two weeks? And I just gave him a look, like, fuck off, and he started the car.

When we pulled up to my drive, he goes, Hey, Jordan, can I ask you something? And I was just like, Yeah? And he goes, So what do you do in your free time, Jordan? You one of those girls who lives for the Internet? Then he hunches his shoulders, raising his hands, sarcastically air-typing, like, *Der, I'm Jordan, and I'm such a dork,* you know? And I was just like, One of those girls, and he was like, I don't know, throwing his hands up in the air.

Then he goes, What I'm trying to say is do you have any friends? And I said, Yes, Misha, I have friends. And he said, What, here, at school? And I bit the inside of my lip for some reason, smiling at him, you know, and then I just started — I don't know. Tears just started rolling down my cheeks. Then he said, Jordan, when's the last time you had a good cry? And then I remembered what he'd said the night that guy stood me up, like when he asked me what I thought would happen. I said I didn't know, but I did — I mean, I don't know what I thought would happen with that guy or anything, but I just thought . . . I don't know, I just thought maybe I'd like being me for a couple of hours. I mean, I used to like being me, but I don't anymore . . . I hate being me now, and as soon as I thought that, tears just started rolling down my cheeks.

I mean, I don't even know why, but there was just something about hearing it out loud, you know? Because until he said that, I didn't know it showed. I didn't know anyone could see it, like it was just waiting for someone to notice. Finally, I sat up straight, wiping my cheeks, while Misha looked for Kleenex in the glove compartment. I didn't mean right now, he said, handing me one.

I took a deep breath, and I was just about to open the door when he goes, Jordan, listen . . . And I could tell it was serious, so I was like, What's up? Then he goes, Maybe this isn't the right time, but I don't know if we should hang anymore. And I was just like, Why not? And he said, Well, for one reason, I'm your boss. Sort of, I said. And second of all, he goes, second of all, I'm thirty, and you're sixteen, and

I'm a guy, and you're a girl. And I thought about it, but I was just like, Misha, I know what you're saying, but the thing is, girls are much more mature than guys are.

I mean, at sixteen, I'm more like twenty-two, and at thirty, you're more like twenty-four, I said. So really, we're practically the same age, you know? Okay, he goes, okay, but you know you're crazy, right? And I just smiled, and I go, You know what they say about the crazy ones, and he goes, Good night, Jordan. That's what I say about the crazy ones: *good night*. Good night, I said, but I was just laughing the whole way inside, and then I was just like, ohmygod . . . I forgot what that felt like, laughter. I almost forgot.

Bobbie

I WAS TELLING him about the surprise party I threw Joyce for her fortieth, and Paul said, I've got a big one coming up pretty soon myself, and I said, Oh, yeah? Fifteen? Well, the five's right, he said, and I gasped. I literally gasped. Fifty? He's only fifty?

Hey, do that again, he said, do that again! Do what? I said, annoyed. Bobbie, I've been trying to get that exact sound out of you for four solid months, and all I had to do was tell you my age —. You're . . . you're younger than I am? I said, stunned. Paul, why didn't you tell me? Bobbie, it's just a year, he said, shaking his head at me. Come on, age is not a venereal disease —. It sure as hell is when you're my age, I said, and you're . . . I couldn't even bring myself to say the number out loud: You're *years* younger than I am, I said. I would've thought it would be a notch in your belt, he said, grabbing my hands before I pulled away, snapping my wrists back. I was smiling, but I was far from humored. You're confusing me with Joyce again, I said, shaking my head at him, feeling something flare in my brain.

And at that moment I felt overwhelmed, knowing that I had the choice, the ability to calm myself down and leave it alone. Or, I could make an issue out of absolutely nothing for no better reason than the fact that I could. Naturally, I chose the latter. Bobbie, he said, you can't be serious —. On the contrary, I said, I can be very serious.

Come here — come on, let's sing, he said, reaching for me. No, I said. Come on, now — we'll sing a song, and everything will look much brighter, he said, wrapping both arms around me, while I kept my arms pinned to my side. What should we sing, huh? Oh, I know: here's a good one, he said, but I looked away, not the least humored.

Bobbie, he said, turning me around to face him: I've gone out with many older women. Yes, I said, but you didn't marry an older woman, did you? No, he said, I happened to marry a younger woman, and then she left me for a younger man. So now it's older women, I said, because they're much less likely to leave, right? He started to speak, then stopped, inhaling through his nose.

When you want to have a real discussion, I'll be in the barn. But I'm not doing this. Not for you, not for anybody. I adore you, Bobbie, but I don't do this, period — that's how old I am, he said, then he opened the screen door and walked out. Life's too short, Roberta Ann, he called, finally turning back, halfway to the barn. So come out when you're ready.

Joyce

MICHAEL TOOK BENJAMIN on a surfing trip to Brazil the year we split. When Benjamin got back, he went to his room, and a few minutes later, he called me: Hey, Mom, come here. So I walked in, and Benj asked if I wanted to see the pictures he took on the new camera his dad bought him. *Over my dead body*, I thought, but I took a seat beside him, pretending I couldn't wait to see his pictures from their father-son vacation.

Naturally the first was a shot of Michael and Benjamin, standing on the beach, and I said, Oh, that's nice, who took that? Inka, Dad's girlfriend, he said, showing me the next shot, and I knew — *I knew* I shouldn't ask, but I didn't listen to myself. Oh, really, what's she like? I said, and Benjamin thought about it. Well, he sighed, she's tall —. Never mind, I said, it's none of my business.

Listen, I said, standing, we're going to eat in an hour. Which gives you just enough time to clean your room, I said, heading for the door, and he moaned, Mom . . . and he just looked at me like, duh.

Benjamin? I said in the same tone. Mom, that's what we have a cleaning lady for, he says, and then I looked at him, smiling, sweetly. No, Benjamin, I said, I have a cleaning lady to clean *my* room, and we have *you* to clean your own. Now get to it.

Adela

WHEN I GOT BACK to the room on Saturday, Michael was working on his computer in bed. How was brunch? he said, looking up. Unbearable, I said, dropping my bag on the floor: unfuckingbearable. I'm sorry, he said. Thanks, I said, shrugging. Adela, when are you going to tell her? he said, and I shook my head, dunno. You want me to tell her? he said. No, I said. No, tomorrow. I'll tell her tomorrow. She's staying in town, and . . . And? And what? he said. And I'll tell them both, I said, and he nodded, all right.

You know my mom's never going to speak to me again, I said. Give her time —. No, you don't know her, Michael. You don't know what she's like when she gets angry, I said. She's your mother, Adela, she loves you, and I said, Yeah, *like I said.*

I had no idea what I was going to say, or what the truth was, really. Because the thing is, when Joyce said that, about how I must have a hundred men on the line, it hurt — I mean, my chest *hurt.* Because I didn't want a hundred men: I wanted one, but he didn't want me. Even so, deep down, I still want Marshall to change his mind, because if he did, I'd leave Michael, and there'd be nothing to tell. Honestly, there's a part of me that's been hoping that all along; that I'd find a way out of this mess — if you can call that hope.

Bobbie

THAT AFTERNOON, the day we argued at Paul's, I stood at the screen door and watched him walk the entire way to the barn. To be honest, my eyes were burning holes in each of his shoulder blades, but he didn't turn around, didn't turn back again. Then again, I didn't call his name, either, which might have something to do with it, I suppose. So after giving it some thought over a glass of wine, I de-

244

cided to surprise him. He was still outside, working, and I knew he'd be coming in soon because it was getting dark, so I poured myself a bubble bath in the claw-foot tub upstairs. Ugh, I love that tub: it's *huge.*

Anyhow, while the bath was filling, I put on the kimono Paul bought me, then I went downstairs and poured myself a quick glass of wine, as Joyce would say. I even lit candles — after a long debate, because I really don't care to think of myself as a candle woman, but still. Last thing, I pinned up my hair, thinking how sexy and seductive I would look when Paul walked in.

Well, my timing couldn't have been better, because ten minutes later, Paul came inside and called my name, and I yelled, Up here! Then, hearing his steps on the stairs, I jumped into the tub, only to discover the water was *scalding.* I tried sitting down, but then I started screeching, Ow, ow, ow! So instead of walking in to find me looking sultry in the tub, Paul walked in to find me crouching down, scratching my freshly boiled ass, yelping like an abused puppy. It was absurd — that's what I get for trying.

Are you okay? he asked, genuinely concerned. No, I'm not *okay,* damn it! I said, finally able to sit, but still scratching my legs. I was going to surprise you, I whined: I wanted to look sexy in the bath, but it's too *hot,* I said, covering my lips with my fingertips, feeling my cheeks blush. Then he walked over and kneeled down and kissed me. Not just with his mouth, he kissed me, grabbing my skull with both hands. Like he couldn't get enough of me if he tried . . . And I'd waited so long to feel that, I almost started crying. What's the matter, babe? What is it? he said.

But I didn't want him to know, of course, so I said, For the record, I'm not a candle woman. I'll keep that in mind, he said, nodding. And by the way, I said. Yes? he asked. You *stink* — ohmygod, you stink! Do I really? he said, before sniffing both pits, first left, then right. Don't even, I said, then I looked away, knowing he was going to shove them in my face, and sure enough, he did, then I splashed him, and he splashed me back before he got in with me. You know, he said, pulling me back against his chest, next time, you could just say, I'm sorry. Yes, I said, but what fun would that be?

Adela

THE TRUTH IS I initiated everything. Seriously, I was the one who came on to him last August. And I knew exactly what I was doing, too — or so I thought. I got on top of him, like a real pro, right, and then, a few minutes later, Michael said, *Stop . . . stop fucking the camera, Adela. It's just you and me here, and you don't have to prove anything to me.* And I felt so embarrassed; I wanted to hide under the bed.

I started to climb off, suddenly pissed, and then he grabbed my arms: Calm down. You don't have to get angry just because I'm right and you know it, he said. I just had to bite the inside of my cheek: *bastard.* Yeah, yeah, yeah, he said, reading my face, but I take it you don't mind your boyfriends taping you —. Oh, *get out!* I said, trying to climb off. No, I mean it literally, *get out,* I said, falling off him, and then, as I withdrew, my pussy . . . my pussy made the most *mortifying* farting sound. Video killed the porn star, he said, laughing at me, because he knew I knew I was *so* busted.

I'm serious, he said. You know what the problem is with kids today? I said, Michael, if you want me to call you Daddy, just —. The problem with kids today, he said, is that you don't know how to stop posing for the camera. Ohmygod, I just realized something! I said, slapping his stomach with the back of my hand: Were you in Nam?

Then I started laughing so hard Michael had to grab my biceps to keep me from falling off the bed. When I finally stopped, I wiped a tear from my eye, and I fessed up. I said, You know I used to have the biggest crush on you? Yes, he said, completely matter-of-fact. You mean you knew — all this time, you *knew*? I said, covering my mouth. Adela, he said, pulling me to him, it was your greatest charm.

Joyce

SO I WALK into the lobby, and there's this knockout standing near the front desk, and I stop, cold, staring at her, when I realize, *Wait a minute . . . I know that ass!* Sure enough, it's none other than the

Latina bombshell better known as Adela Myers — my very own gift-from-God goddaughter, who just happened to be wearing this slinky, backless lamé number that was just *to die*. So of course my first thought is, *Where did you get that dress?* And I'm thinking, *What a coincidence . . .* Because I'd just had brunch with her and Bobbie that morning, and here she is.

So I sneaked up behind her, ready to dry hump her perfectly toned thighs, and then I leaned over and whispered in her ear, What's a girl like you doing in a place like this? She turned around, almost jumping out of her skin, and her face . . . she turned to look at me, and her face — Adela's face — I'll never forget it as long as I live.

Then who do I see, turning away from the front desk, but . . . Michael. And here's the best part — you know what he says? He looks at me and says, Oh, Joyce . . . there you are. Between that and the look on Adela's face, I knew all I needed to know.

I took a huge step back, and then he buried the two of them, alive: Well, what a coincidence — look who I ran into, he says, and I just look at them, at the two of them, together. Will . . . I'm sorry, will you excuse me? I said. Then I turned and walked outside. By the time I came to, I turned around and glared through the front door, at the spot where he'd been standing, thinking, *There you are? Is that the best you can do, you self-fellating cocksucker? Oh, Joyce, there you are?* But of course they'd gone.

Lisa

THE DAY BEFORE my appointment, I finally broke down and called her office. She was in private practice by then; the first time I got pregnant, when I was sixteen, she was working at the clinic. Which is what I could afford. So when she called me back, I said, Dr. Myers, is there any way to cut the cost of the procedure? And she said, Well, you could skip the anesthetic, and we'll just give you a leather strap to bite on.

I thought about it for a second, and then I said, How much would that save me? Lisa, she said, I was *kidding*. But I wasn't, I said. I thought I had a dark sense of humor, she said, sighing, Listen, we'll work something out, all right? Look, I said, I don't need your charity—. Good, she said, because I'm not offering it.

And that . . . that he thinks he *knows*—he actually had the audacity to say he knows how I must feel. I was just like, how could you, Greg? You weren't there, remember? No, of course you don't. Because you fucking bailed, asshole. You left me hanging. So fuck you and fuck your new fucking best friend, too—*fuck you both.*

I'm sorry, but I told the woman three times, okay: three. The minute I made the appointment, a week before I went in, I told her. I went straight to her office and I knocked on the door, and I said, Joyce, I'm really sorry, but I have to go to a doctor's appointment, and the only time they can get me in is next Friday. And she said, Well, then, do what you have to do, Lisa. But remind me next week, please, and I said, Of course. So I reminded her the following Tuesday.

Then I reminded her *again* on Thursday morning. I said, Joyce, I just wanted to remind you I won't be in until noon tomorrow, and then she goes, What? And I said, I have that appointment tomorrow, and she said, What appointment? I said, The doctor's appointment I told you about. And she goes, Not possible. You know how much work there is to do between now and tomorrow night. And I said, Joyce, I know, but I can't—I can't change the time, and she said, You can't or you won't? And I said, I can't, Joyce, they need to run some tests—. And she just looked at me, and then she goes: That's not what I asked you, is it? And I—honestly, I was about to start crying.

She goes, Lisa, you pushed for this show. You were the one—I mean, correct me if I'm wrong here, but weren't you the one who said you'd do anything, absolutely *anything* to make it happen? That you believed in this artist so much—wasn't that you? Yes, I said, and I do believe—. Good, she said. Because this is your baby, and now you tell me you can't be here the morning on the day of your best friend's opening?

I said, Joyce, I'm sorry, but I have to go in tomorrow; that's the only time they can see me. And she said, I heard you the first time. So what time can you be here? And I said, By noon. And she said, Make it eleven. And I said, I'll get here as soon as possible, and she said, We'd appreciate the help.

I thought, *You cunt. You are such a fucking bitch.* So I stepped outside to have a cigarette and pull myself together, and automatically, I reached for my phone to call Greg, and then I realized, wait: What am I doing? I closed my phone, hearing this voice inside my head say, *Deal with it.* Because that's the moral of any story involving Joyce Kessler: don't tell me about it, just deal with it. So I did. Oh, I dealt with it, all right.

Jordan

WHEN WE GOT to school Monday, Mom was like, Are you going to be all right? And I just looked at her and shrugged like, what choice do I have, you know? So I went in and . . . and everything looked exactly the same — I don't know why I was surprised, but I was. Seriously, whoever it was that said, Nothing stays the same forever — or whatever that saying is — well, they never went to high school, okay. Trust me.

Then I ran into Chloe before second period, and she goes, Hey, I saw Lance Saturday night. Why didn't you come to the party? And I was just like, I had the flu, and she goes, Oh, I'm sorry, babe, it was off the hook, and then I almost started laughing, right in Chloe's face. Because I was just like, ohmygod, I've got to call Misha and tell him I missed the party Saturday night, and it was off the hook. I mean, I say that, too, sometimes, but I'm not as dumb as Chloe, okay. And because that's the sort of thing we would've made a joke, like, *Dude, did you see that Dole pineapple display? It was off the hook.* And then I remembered I can't — I can't call him. Because we aren't friends anymore, and then my chest just went, mnhhh, you know?

I mean, I couldn't breathe for a second, because it's like the only thing that's been getting me through all this fake-o bullshit was knowing I'd get to hang out with Misha on Friday night, that there was one hour I could just be myself every week . . . So I made a face, and I was just like, Oh, I'm so bummed, and then I went to French. But you know what I want to know? What I want to know is what happens when you stop being friends? Like what happens to those people, the people you were?

Lisa

SHE WAS SO AMAZING. I mean, they always ask who's meeting you, who's picking you up afterward. And I told her Greg was meeting me. Which wasn't true, of course, but they keep you longer if there's no one to meet you. So I slipped out of the office, first chance, and I went to wait for the bus on First Avenue, because the posh Upper East has no fucking subway, the morons. Anyhow, there I am, standing in the rain, when I hear someone call my name, and I turn around — and there was Dr. Myers.

I thought I might find you here, she said, catching me in my lie, red-handed. Oh, I was *so* busted . . . but she didn't say a word. She just stepped to the curb and raised her hand, hailing me a cab. I'd rather take the bus, I said, and then a cab pulled over. Really, I pleaded. I know you have to work, but will you call me and let me know how you're doing? she said, opening the door and grabbing me by the arm, putting me in the cab.

Dr. Myers, I can't — I can't take a cab, I said, so ashamed to have to tell her that that was how poor I was. Angry, too, angry to be put in that position — by Greg, by Joyce, by my own stupid, fucking care- lessness. You aren't listening to me! I yelled — I mean, I actually yelled at a doctor. No, I'm not, she said, just completely unfazed. Then I bit my fingernails, because I'd started crying, as she calmly opened the front door to speak to the driver.

She handed him a twenty, told him to take two bucks and give me the change. Bring me the receipt, she said, smiling and closing my door and patting the window before turning around and running back inside, pulling her white coat over her head.

Joyce

WAIT, WAIT, I SAID, elbowing her because it was that shot of Diane Keaton, standing in the doorway . . . Then I joined in, speaking in

250

unison: It was a boy, Michael—it was a boy! Bobbie looked up at the screen, and I said, Hey . . . *that's it.* That's my new motto, I said: It was a boy, Michael, it was a boy! Joyce, she said, looking at me sideways in that calm, clinical way of hers. You need help, she said. I need chocolate, is what I need, I said, looking around the bed. Hand me the M&M's, will ya?

Ah, Al Pacino . . . Once upon a time, I thought Michael looked just like Al Pacino. Of course Sonja never openly acknowledged the fact that he was Italian—she preferred the term *Mediterranean.* All the more shocking, first time I told her about him, in a single phone conversation the woman went from a lifetime of fretting I'd wind up a spinster to worrying herself sick that Michael was going to piss in our kosher gene pool.

I swear I'll never forget the time I called to tell her I'd met this guy, and she goes, What's his name? And I said, Mom, I told you: his name is Michael. And she goes, Michael what? And I go, Michael Petrucci, and she pauses a moment, and then she goes, But that's not a *Jewish* name, Petrucci? And I go, Probably not, seeing as he's not Jewish. Honestly, what does it matter? And she goes, Well. Nothing, I suppose. Just that it's part of our heritage, she says. But it's your life, Joyce. And I'm thinking, *But it's my life? I'm thirty-two years old, I make more money in a year than my dad earned in ten, and you're still using the old, it's-your-life line?* Unfuckingbelievable.

I said, Hold that thought, Sonja. Second of all, heritage? You mean the one or two times a year you drive to temple, *that* heritage? And she goes, Oh. So now you're telling me I'm not Jewish? We're on the phone, right, but at that point, I just held up my hand, like, okay, that's enough. Seriously, we're what my father fondly referred to as McJews: the type of Semite who had to rent a yarmulke, but still bickered about the price.

I said, You know what, Sonja? You know what? Forget it. And before she could interrupt me, I said, No, really—just forget I said anything about finally, *finally* having someone in my life who I wanted to introduce to my parents. Because I've decided I'm not bringing him home after all. No, I won't bring Michael home; you won't have to meet him; he won't have to meet you; and we'll all be happy, how's that? And then my dad got on the phone, like a hunched, balding ref trying to break up a couple of boxers. What can I tell you? It's always been this way with us, always. And without my dad around, we just kept throwing punches, waiting for one of us to fall.

Lisa

I TOOK A SEAT next to the window, breathing that same sigh of relief I'd been breathing for twenty years every time I felt the train pulling out of the station, but poor Jordan. She's so alone; I hated leaving her there. And it pains me that she thinks I was so brave when I was her age . . . because I wasn't.

Some nights, passed out on someone's hardwood floor or the flea-infested couch of some lousy squat, awoken by someone or some two, three guys, pulling down my pants, thinking, *Just let me sleep, okay? That's all I care about — do what you want, but let me get a few hours of sleep, will you? I'm tired. I'm just so tired . . .*

I've never been brave, just desperate, and most people can't tell the difference. But still, Lynne's got it all wrong — she's wrong about me. Because the fact is I thought very little of myself. The only way to make it bearable was to believe in something better, that I could be something better. How else do you survive?

I crossed my legs, catching my foot on my bag and almost knocking over the bowl. I pulled it out from under the seat, and set it down next to me. She'd wrapped the box in blood-red silk, and the sides and the bottom of the box were seamless, hand-stitched, but on the top, she'd gathered the silk into these origami-like roses — three roses tied with a bright pink ribbon, and on the ribbon, she'd stitched my name. It was so beautiful, I didn't want to open it — I wanted to take a picture, actually. I didn't tell her that, though.

No, I didn't believe her — I don't — I can't . . . But she was right about one thing: it's not fair. I'm not pulling my weight, it's true. One other thing: I don't give her any credit, and I owe her an apology for that. But I don't know what else to say, really. All I know is that I couldn't get on that train fast enough, but then I didn't want to go home, either. So where's that leave me?

252

Joyce

HERE'S A SURPRISE. A few months before he died, I was sitting in the living room with my father, and he said, You know, Joyce, she's an amazing woman, your mother. After a fashion, I'm sure, I said. There's a lot you don't know about her, you know, he said, and I said, No kidding.

For instance, he said, turning to face me, did you know your mother was a concert pianist? Who? I said, looking up. Your mother, he said. Dad, what are you talking about? She was a concert pianist, he said, and I go: Oh, pshaw . . . What are you talking about, concert pianist? I'm telling you, Joycie. I'm telling you, he said, raising his hand.

First time I ever laid eyes on your mother, she was practicing in a recital hall in Pittsburgh. My father, your grandfather, worked as a janitor there on weekends, and I heard this music in the hall, and I went to see who was playing, and there she was. Most beautiful girl I had ever seen was sitting at a grand piano, playing it like an angel — she looked like an angel, too, with her long black hair.

What happened? I said, completely blown away. A few months later, she was playing a recital in San Francisco, I believe, and for some reason, right in the middle of a Bach fugue, she decided she didn't want to play anymore. She stopped playing, stood up, and walked off the stage. But what — what happened? I said. I don't know, he said. Well, did you ask her, Dad? For years, he said. For years, I tried to get her to play again — even a song or two at a party, if there was a piano, but I couldn't get a note out of her. Whatever happened, it's private. It's her business, Joyce. A woman has to have a little mystery. But she could have been famous, you know. And instead, she married me, he said, closing his eyes.

I didn't know what to believe. My mother, okay . . . My mother, who I never once heard sing or hum a single tune, who didn't even own a fucking *radio*, who I spent my last three years at home torturing with my record collection . . . A *Bach fugue*? I could ask her, of course, but I know what she'd say. She'd look at me, then her eyes would dart across the room. It was a long time ago, she'd say, finding something else to re-tidy in the kitchen. I don't remember anymore, she'd say.

But to this day, it still bothers me, that conversation. I mean, what . . . what did he see in her? What did he see in her that I couldn't see?

Lynne

WHIRLPOOL . . . ISN'T THAT a great word, whirlpool? Well, but that's . . . that's the beauty, you see. That's what was so beautiful, because after I took the pills, for once — for the first time in my life — I wasn't worried anymore, and I could see *exactly* what needed to be done, too. So I threw off the covers, because I was suddenly burning up, and I felt smothered in my sweatpants. Off, off! I said, kicking my way out of each leg . . . I don't know why the sweatpants made me so angry, but when I finally got free of them, I looked around the room — honestly, one look, and I realized, *I hate this room.* I said it, too; I said it out loud, I *hate* this fucking room!

I mean, it, it just felt like, like I suddenly realized that it wasn't just that room, either — no — oh, no, the whole house was drowning in all this stuff, everywhere, just stuff and more stuff, and all of a sudden, I felt so sweaty and — oppressed, really. I mean, I couldn't breathe . . . And that's when I realized, *Ohmygod, it's not just this room; the whole house is full of shit.* Well, chop-chop, I thought, slapping my hands together.

So I got straight to work, throwing on the nubuck slippers Don keeps by the garage door, or I make Don keep by the garage door, all fucking nice and tidy. *But no time to worry I about that,* I thought, running into the garage to get a bunch of those industrial trash bags he keeps out there on a big metal roll. And then I just started grabbing them like Kleenex, pulling out four, five, six at a time, and then I ran straight back to the guest bedroom, and I knew exactly what I needed to do. All I had to do — the only thing I had to do in the whole world — was ask myself one simple question: Need it or pitch it? Because if we didn't really need it, well, it was gone, bye-bye. So that's

254

what I did, working from one end of this house to the other. Need it? *No.* Need it? *No.* Honestly, I don't think I've ever felt as happy as I felt at that moment, throwing out half of everything we own. It was . . . I mean, I'm sorry, but it was fucking joyful like I have never felt on Christmas Eve, okay. Really, I wanted, I wanted to sing and dance — I even thought about waking Don, letting him in on the secret, which is: It doesn't have to be this way, you see? It doesn't have to be like this anymore. We can change all this — and it's, it's so *easy,* really.

I mean, you know how sometimes you get those flashes, think-ing, *Ohmygod, have I been out of my mind all this time? I mean, have I been wrong? Am I wrong? Is it really* me, *like everyone's been saying?* Well, guess what? You're right: it *was* you. But, see, the good news is you don't have to be sad, you don't have to be ashamed — no, not any-more. Because things simply don't have to be this way . . . that's right. You see? You see what I mean? Isn't that just so, so fucking beauti-ful, you could cry? *Ohmygod,* I thought, feeling all teary and over-whelmed, squeezing my face with both hands, wanting to scream like some hysterical teenage Beatles fan . . . Well. Once I finished cleaning out the house, I just felt so alive, I sat down for a second in the living room, and I decided the first thing we need to do is to sit down and talk — I mean, really talk. All four of us, yes. All four of us, each one having the chance to really talk.

Really, let's, let's just put everything on the table. No more lies, no more bullshit: I say what I think; you say what you think; I listen to you; you listen to me. I'm serious, no more accusations, no more name-calling, no more swearing and hating each other — enough — enough of that. What's important is that, no matter how long it took me to get here, I see everything so clearly now, and what I know now is that something's got to change. Yes, something has got to change, because I won't live this way anymore. No, I refuse.

Bobbie

I REALIZE THIS is a little odd, but personally, I never understood why people fussed so much about sex. Don't get me wrong: I like sex.

I would even say I love sex, but as a driving force, much less the underlying force of my life? No. For better or worse, it's just never had that pull on me. But now — now there are times when I'm sitting at my desk in a trance, and then I realize I've just chomped my front teeth together, fantasizing of biting the back side of Paul's hand as I'm about to come. Then there are times when I'm afraid it's going to eat me up, and I don't . . . I don't know what to do with myself.

Really, what happens to me when and if this doesn't work out between us? What happens when something better and/or someone younger comes along? Or he suddenly decides he does want children — I don't know what. It could be anything. And what do I do then? Hope I get struck by lightning twice and keep myself busy in the meantime? Christ, that's how I got here in the first place.

I'm sorry, but it took a good fifty years for me to feel this way, so I don't imagine it's going to happen again. And that scares me to death sometimes, it does. If I stop for a moment, it's there, just waiting to pounce. The voice that says, *You're alone. And no one loves you — no man, at least.* So I don't — I don't stop. No, I go to work and I shop for groceries and pay bills and call my patients — I do the same things I've always done, and all that fear and confusion gets kneaded into the day, just like every other day.

And there have been plenty of times I've felt unlovable and unsexy and all the shit you go through, being alone most your life. Or just being human, I suppose. But then I'd be reminded there were more important things than my self-pity, and how lucky I was — I had my work; I had a child; I didn't need anything else, really. I don't know if Adela realizes how much I owe her for that, but I pray she does.

Shortly after we got out of bed last Saturday night, Dela called me on my cell to say she was coming down for the weekend, that she was flying down Thursday and wanted to spend some time with me, if I was staying in town. Which we weren't, but of course I said we were. Because Del's in Boston now, so I hadn't had a chance to introduce the two of them. And I knew — I'd known for months — that I needed to deal with it, because I was beginning to worry that she wasn't going to like him. In which case, I didn't know what I would do. Which was why I'd put it off as long as possible, you see.

256

So we made a plan for Thursday night, and then I told Paul as soon as I got off. I knew I should've asked him first, so I tiptoed around it, saying, Hey, babe, I'm sorry, I should've asked first, but do you think you could come to town Thursday night to meet Adela? Well. Not only did he drive down, he offered to take us out — somewhere nice, he said. I gotta impress the kid, you know, he said. Oh, I know. Believe me, I know, I said. And just so *you* know, she's not easily impressed, but give it your best shot. Is that a challenge? he said, puffing up like a blowfish. I suppose one could take it that way, I said, if one were male, yes.

Lisa

WE BROKE UP, or rather *I* broke up with Greg, the week of Kate's opening. And when I got home from the gallery that night, I walked through the door and the first thing I saw was a note on the table — second note in a week. I knew what it said; I didn't need to look. So I walked straight past the table, and sat down on the bed. I'd worn a long-sleeved black minidress — skintight, to show off my weight loss; hair in a tight bun, bright-red lipstick and no other makeup. Nothing.

Exhausted, emaciated, and chic as hell. Looking at myself in the mirror in the gallery's employee bathroom, smirking, thinking, *I must say, abortion becomes me.* I pinched my cheeks a couple of times, and then I went to get a drink. But of course it wasn't so funny once I got home and took off my glass slippers.

So I sat on the bed, carefully removing my shoes, wishing I'd thought to bring home a pair of white gloves from work, unbuckling the right strap, so pleased that no one — *not one person* — failed to mention my shoes. I'm serious, all night I kept catching people staring, doing double takes at my heels. And I was just about to put them back in their case, when I changed my mind. Fuck it, I said, throwing them across the room; one exorbitant thud, then another . . . One at a time, just to make it that much more painful.

I'd waited four years — *four years* — before I could allow myself to wear something so beautiful, and that was the night. Kate's show was my baby, like Joyce said, This is your baby, Lisa. But what she really meant was head: This is your head, Lisa. Then again, she was right: it was my baby. And my baby was a smash success. Greg just couldn't stand to see me succeed while he floundered in his self-pity . . . *Well, fuck him,* I thought.

I got up, walked barefoot across the floor, picked up my beloved Lucite shoe case, opened the front door, stepped out into the hall, and hurled the damn thing down the stairwell. I teetered over the banister, watching it fall six flights before splintering into shards on the dirty tile on the ground floor. When I finished staring at my own crime scene, I stood up, and then I noticed blood running down my legs. *Oh, fuck* . . . Chic, yeah. I was incredibly chic, and a bloody mess.

I went to the bathroom and opened the cupboard beneath the sink, but I was out of OBs. I tore through the apartment, checking the crevices of every purse, bag, tote: nothing, not even a pad. Unreal. Unfuckingreal. The cab got stuck in traffic on my way back to Chelsea, so I only had two dollars left out of the money Dr. Myers gave me.

I thought of calling Kate, but I knew she was out celebrating, being feted. I should have been there with her, too, but she understood. She asked me if I wanted her to stop by, after, and I said no. No. I just wanted to be alone.

I slept three, four hours, at most, and when I woke, I stuffed a wad of fresh toilet paper in my underwear and walked across the street, to the deli, bumming a couple cigarettes off the Lebanese guy behind the counter, before asking if he had any empty boxes. When I got back to the apartment, I made some coffee, lit a smoke, and then I lit that last letter Greg had left me with his grandfather's old Zippo. Just burned the fucker — and he'd written two pages, even. But I was so proud of myself; I sat there, twisting the sheets this way and that, shooting every angle of that moment for posterity. Sadly, those grand romantic gestures don't always age so well.

Anyhow, I spent the rest of the day packing, keeping my ear peeled for the front door. But Greg didn't come back — not that I expected him to. Coward. So I cleaned the place out. I mean, I took everything — canvases, brushes, paints — *everything.*

Once I had it all in the truck, I went back inside to leave the keys, and then I debated long and hard about the silkscreen. I stood there, holding a box cutter to the Queen's throat. I could kill you, you know? I said, before standing back, looking around that sad, old naked apartment one last time. No, Greg, you: *you* will regret this, I said, needing to hear the words out loud, and then I closed the door behind me, leaving the open blade on the mantel, propped against the silkscreen.

He made me a promise, and he lied, so I kept all his work, everything he'd painted for almost four years. I mean, I knew I had no right to keep his work, but then again, he owed me money, and he never asked for the work back, either. Of course I rationalized it, telling myself that he wanted me to have it, to keep something of him. Maybe I was a cunt for doing it, but at least I wasn't a martyr. And I sure as hell wasn't anybody's victim.

They're still there, too, all his drawings, paintings, everything. I pay the bill once a year and I keep the key in a shoe box at the back of my closet. So Sunday morning, I took out the box, grabbed the key, and hailed a cab to the East Village. Then I opened the storage locker door in a basement on Avenue D for the first time in three years, and there they were, balancing on top of a stack of boxed-up drawings almost as tall as I was, right where I left them: the shoes. My beloved shoes. Hello, Sunshine, I said, taking the right heel in my hand, rubbing its regal plume beneath my chin.

When I put the shoes on in the taxi, I realized it was only the second time I'd ever worn them. I thought I would wear them on my wedding day, with a simple white sheath dress, and then without. But things don't always work out the way you want them to, do they?

What can I say? Once upon a time, on a very, very cold day in hell, I walked back into the Joyce Kessler Gallery, took a seat on the black leather bench in the center of the gallery, and then I screamed at the top of my lungs: *Goddamn you! Goddamn you, you motherfucker!* A genuine, honest to god, heaving-forward-in-my-seat-and-doubled-over-with-no-air-left-in-my-lungs scream . . . I screamed until I had nothing left inside of me except tears welling in my eyes. And then the voice inside my head was quiet, at last.

Damn, I forgot how good that felt. Besides, galleries always make me want to scream. Like churches. The silence is just so fucking sanctimonious, you know.

Adela

She wasn't angry; she was just — shocked. I've known her my entire life, and I've never seen that expression on her face . . . hurt. I'd never seen her look so hurt, no. And betrayed. And then I finally understood what I'd been denying all along. That I would hurt her willfully, knowingly — I knew better, but I didn't care. I mean, I did care, I do — just . . . just not enough, I guess.

Then Michael goes, Oh, Joyce, there you are, and I had to think the words through several times, before I realized, *Are you fucking kidding me?* We went back to the room, and then I lost it. I just started screaming — at him, at me, at us . . . An hour later, I called my mom, and she all but hung up on me, and then I just broke down, sobbing.

I called her Sunday morning, and I left her a voice mail before I tried her at home. She didn't answer, of course, so I spoke to her machine. I said, I'm sorry, I'm so sorry. Please let me apologize — please just let me explain — it's not . . . You don't have to say anything, but please just give me a chance, that's all I ask. And if you never . . . if you never want to speak to me again, I understand. Joyce? I said, Please pick up — please just speak to me . . .

Jordan

I mean, that's all he said — he was just like, Sorry, Jordan, then he started walking away, and I was like, Hey, Misha? And I was just so pissed, you know? I mean, I was so pissed, I was like don't just walk away, so when he turned around, I go, By the way, I'm pregnant. And his face — ohmygod, the look on his face . . . I mean, have you ever

260

dropped a bomb like that? Seriously, do you know what it's like to say something knowing you're about to ruin someone's life — maybe not forever, but long enough? And you do it on purpose, too, because you want to hurt them, you want them to know how *you* feel, and you want them to remember — and they will. When you look at them, you know they'll always remember . . . but the thing is, you'll remember, too.

I knew I was late, but I just couldn't believe it was true . . . I mean, *pregnant?* What does that *mean,* you know? It's like it was just so unreal, I tried not to think about it, but then I started getting sick all the time. Like this one morning, last month, I walked into the library before first period, and Trevor Johnston walked in — and it's like he leaves me alone, pretty much, because he played football with Lance, but he's a total dick.

Anyhow, he sat down on top of these two other guys, just like all the jocks, who always sit in the chairs in the middle of the library, and then he let out this fart, just like this long, wet fart. So everyone starts moaning and turning away, right, and next thing, Trev starts telling everybody, I mean, he's practically yelling, telling the whole school that he was going down on Trysta Dodd — *god, I hate her* — but anyhow. T.J. starts telling everybody that he was going down on her Saturday night, and that she had dingleberries, right, and then all the guys fell over, groaning on the carpet.

It's like there are fifty things like that that happen every day, but it made me sick. I mean, I literally had to run out the door, covering my mouth, and I could hear all the guys laughing at me, thinking I'd just gotten grossed out, and then I just puked, like right in the water fountain next to the computer lab. It was so awful, too, because all these sophomore guys saw me, and I just started crying.

Then I got sick in chemistry class a few weeks ago, and my mom came to pick me up, and it all came out. So that night, when my parents called me downstairs and asked me who it was, I told them it was a friend. I said it was a friend, and things just went too far, and for a moment my mom looked like she actually understood what I was saying. So when I told them his name was Misha, Mom goes, Who's

Misha? And I told her who Misha was, that he's the assistant manager, and then my mom just totally ignored everything else I said.

She never asked, you know? She never asked me what I want. I mean, I don't . . . I don't want to have a baby. I just wanted my mom to admit that it's not her choice: it's not *her* life: it's mine. It's *my* life. I just want to hear her say the words, What do you want, Jordan? Or, Tell me, what you want to do, just so I could tell her the truth. Which is: I don't know. I don't know what I want; I just don't want to feel so alone all the time.

Adela

AS SOON AS I found out, like the second week of September, after I took a test, I didn't call Michael for weeks. Didn't call; didn't return his calls: nothing. And then, when I did, I asked him if he could meet me at Café Pamplona. I made sure to get there first, and then Michael walked in and took a seat. Then he came right out with it: Where've you been? Why haven't you returned my calls? he said. Because, I said. Because why, Adela? Because I'm pregnant, I said, and his face fell. Don't worry, I said, it's not yours. Well, he said, raising his brow, scratching the side of his nose, in that case, I feel much better, thanks. Don't mention it, I said.

Adela, he said, shaking his head, trying to figure out where to begin. I knew it wasn't mine, he said, I had a vasectomy five years ago. Oh, I said, surprised that that was the first I'd heard of it. We didn't speak for a couple of minutes while the waiter brought my café au lait and Michael ordered a beer. Does he know? he said, after the waiter left. Have you told him? No, I said. Why not? he said, and I said, Because it's none of his business, that's why.

It's none of his business? he said, but I didn't answer. Adela? No, it's not, I said, shaking my head. But wouldn't you want to know? he said. If he were pregnant? I said, and he looked at me, not the least bit amused. Would you? I said. Yes, he said, absolutely. Well, fortunately or unfortunately, he's not you. Adela, I'm just saying that maybe you should give the guy a —. And I'm just saying you don't

262

know what you're talking about, I said, feeling my cheeks flush, suddenly furious.

I said, Michael, why does it matter to you, one way or another? Because I care about you, he said. Thank you, that's very sweet of you to say, I said. I mean that, he said, I care about you very deeply —. Please stop, okay, I said. Trust me, this is not where I wanted the conversation to head. What did you want, then? he said, leaning back. I wanted to tell you to your face, I said, and he just looked at me, waiting . . .

Because I slept with him after I started seeing you, and I thought it was only fair to tell you to your face, I said, feeling nothing at all, really. He knew when it happened, too. The weekend he went up to Maine to shoot, when I'd told him I was going out with friends. Which was true just not the whole truth.

That weekend Michael was away, I went to a party with some friends, because I knew Marshall would be there. And he was. And he was fucked up — fucked up enough to talk to me. Enough to hit on. So I did. And we had sex, but it changed nothing. Apparently the laws of physics don't apply to sex.

I'd told Michael about humiliating myself in the rain, standing on Marshall's doorstep. But I'd never told him what happened before that, about that day, last summer, when I was lying in bed, naked, and Marshall looked at me — he looked so tender and sweet. So I turned over, and I looked at him and said, I think I'm in love with you. He looked at me a second, then he pushed me off, standing up and putting on his pants. But before he'd even finished buttoning his jeans, he turned and started yelling at me, You have no respect! Once the words were out, he became all the more furious, yelling at me, louder and louder, You have no respect! You don't know anything about respect! Then he grabbed his shirt, opened the door, and left.

I was just lying there, naked, and I'll never forget this — there was the most beautiful light, and I suddenly felt terrified by the sunset, the light fading in my room. All I could think was, *What . . . what have I done? I just ruined everything.* I grabbed my robe, and I went downstairs to speak to Mia, my roommate. Did he leave? I said, panicked. Yes, she said, no idea what was going on. Did he say anything? I heard you talking, I said, and she said, He asked what I was cooking, he said, Smells good. What's wrong, Del? she said, seeing the look on my face.

I couldn't believe he could do that. That he'd shout at me, and then he'd stop to smell her cooking? I called him. I called him twenty times. I sent e-mails, I texted . . . he wouldn't speak to me, wouldn't explain — he wouldn't even tell me what I did wrong, so I could apologize. I mean, I couldn't even say I'm sorry, you know? I'm so sorry I said that — I'm sorry I said I was in love with you — I didn't mean to disrespect you. Believe me, you have no idea how much I wish I could take it back . . . I kept trying and trying.

I didn't tell Michael the whole story, but he knew the gist. He looked at me — Michael looked at me as though he understood, and I thought, No . . . no, you don't understand. So I spelled it out: I had sex with him while I was sleeping with you, and I told him — I even told him I was in love with him, I said, waiting. But he didn't blink. And only then did it occur to me that he did understand me, truly. Maybe that was the real reason I called him that night, because I knew he would understand. And because he could never judge me, because Michael was no better than I was.

What else? he said, waiting for me to finish. I don't want to see you anymore, I said. I see, he said, leaning back in his chair. Who else knows you're pregnant? he said, seeing the waiter approaching. No one, I said. You haven't told your mother? Not yet, no, I said. Well, don't you think you should? he said. I think I'm an adult, and you aren't my boyfriend and you aren't my father, so butt out, all right? No, I'm just your friend — or I'm trying to be, he said, but I looked away.

Adela? What, Michael? *What?* I said, completely annoyed. What did I do wrong here? What have I ever done but try to be a friend to you? he said. Michael, give me a fucking break: we aren't *friends*. You're my mother's best friend's ex-husband, or will be, if you ever get around to giving her a divorce. Seriously, we go out to dinner, we fuck around, nothing more, I said, glaring at him, but he didn't blink.

Look, I said. I tried to tell him, but he wouldn't give me the time of day. But I tried, okay? I waited for him in the rain for a fucking hour, so don't give me that look like I'm a bad person —. Adela, I never said you were a bad person, and I never would. I don't judge you, he said. At least not while you're still fucking me, no, I said. Is this why I'm here? he said. Is this why you asked me here? So you can yell at someone, preferably male? I don't know, I said, shrugging. Maybe.

Know what, he said, sighing. I've had a hell of a day, so if you need a punching bag, maybe we can schedule something this weekend. Sure, I said, furious, watching him pull out his chair. No problem, I said. Would you like to schedule that before or after we go to bed? Adela, he said, reaching for his wallet, maybe one day, you'll learn that you don't have to say the ugliest possible thing that comes to mind just because you can, he said. Then he dropped a hundred-dollar bill on the table and left. Take care, I said, opening the leather credit-card case, reading the tab. Then I put the bill in the check, and raised the binder for the waiter.

But I felt shitty, too. Because he was right: I just needed to yell at someone. Fifteen minutes later, I got a text from Michael. It said: *On second thought, I'm thinking before and after. Another thing: you can bring me my change then, too.* I laughed out loud. It was the first time I could remember laughing in two weeks. Right, again: I left the guy a ten-dollar tip, and pocketed the rest.

God, it was so tacky; I couldn't help myself. And he knew that about me — oh, he knew me, all right. I saw it all over again, the entire scene from the point where he stood and removed the bill. *You bastard,* I thought, laughing: because the whole thing was a setup, just so he could prove he had my number. And for once, that was all right.

Bobbie

IT WAS TORRENTIAL, really, and as soon as I got back inside, I called Joyce at the gallery, and they told me she was in a meeting. So I told them it was urgent, and they put me through. Bob, what's wrong? What's happened? She was panicked.

Joyce, I said, I have a patient here, her name is Lisa Barrett, and she's having what you might call a bad day. So if you should happen to see her, you're going to tell her she looks a little peaked, and then you're going to send her home for the rest of the day, understand? But she didn't answer. I said do you *understand* me, Joyce? Am I making myself clear? Crystal, she said. Gotta go —. Me, too, I said, hanging up. We never spoke of it again. That was, without a doubt, the single most unethical thing I have ever done in my entire career, that phone call. And to be honest, I'd do it all over again, without giving it a second thought.

Joyce

COME ON, I FELT terrible when I found out — of course I did. Then again, I was just like, give me a fucking break, you know? I'm running a gallery here, not a women's shelter; I had my own problems to deal with. And Bobbie — of all people, Bobbie should've understood that.

But I didn't treat her well, it's true. I didn't give Lisa the time or attention or praise or credit she deserved. And I have no excuse. All I can say is that I was almost bankrupt, and it was the worst years of our divorce. Michael was threatening to sue for full custody, and I couldn't — I *couldn't* — lose my son. It would've killed me. By the time I realized how I'd treated her, she'd quit and disconnected her phone.

I will say one thing, though: Lisa was special. I mean, gorgeous girl, of course, but she had the best eye, the strongest gut I've ever known. Tough, too. She liked to fight, she liked rolling up her sleeves and getting her hands dirty. Lisa believed in art; she believed in transcendence. She had such faith, and I'd strayed, and she reminded me of that every time I looked at her. But still . . . she *was* special, and I'm sorry I never told her that.

I thought about asking Kate Gaines, but Kate never said a word, so I left it alone. I'd always planned on giving her one hell of a recommendation when the call came, but it never did. Lisa never called, and no one called on her behalf. She just disappeared.

266

Lisa

THAT NIGHT, at the opening, she comes over, all smiles, and she says, Where's Greg? And I said, I don't know, Joyce. He's not here? she said. Guess not, I said, looking around. Isn't he coming? she asked, and I said, Joyce, we broke up. And she said, I'm sorry, I didn't know. Well, why would you? I said, and she said, Because we're having lunch on Wednesday, and he didn't mention that when we spoke. Best of luck to you both, I said, heading back to the bar.

Monday morning, first thing, I knocked on her door and walked into her office. Lisa, she said, looking up from her desk. May I have a word? I said, and she nodded at the chair, and I sat down. Two words, actually: I quit, I said, effective immediately. She didn't blink.

I'm sorry to hear that, she said, sitting back in her chair. Would you like to share your reasons? I said, Just one: you. Then I got up, closed the door behind me, and cleared out my desk. No one said a word — everyone watched, but no one spoke, as I walked out. I heard the phone ring three times before Auden finally answered, stuttering, Hello, Joyce Kessler Gallery. But even then, I never turned around.

I made it halfway home before realizing I didn't live there anymore.

Bobbie

I GOT HOME around five on Sunday, and all I wanted to do was take a couple of aspirin and go to bed. When I walked in, I dropped my bag in the hall with such a heavy sigh that you'd have thought I was carrying the weight of the world on my shoulders. I dropped my keys in the bowl and walked to the end of the hall, and then I gasped, finding Adela, standing up from the couch. Jesus Christ, you scared me —. Can we talk? she said, and I said, Not now — please, Adela, I can't talk right now. She said, When? When can we talk? Adela, I'll call you once I get some sleep, but now is not the time, I said, walking to my room.

Fine, she said, but it's not what you think, and then I turned back: Are you sleeping with Michael? I said. Yes, she said. That's what I thought, I said. Mom, it's not his — it's not his child, she said, and I looked at her. The word alone, hearing her say the word *child*, was almost too much, but that . . . There's someone else? I said, and she nodded. I said, You were seeing someone else, while —. Yes, all right? Yes, she said, there was someone else. Who? I said, and then I stopped, changing my mind.

I said, Does Michael know? Yes, he does: he knows everything, she said. I said, And you love Michael *so much*, you —. I didn't say that, she said, and I finally stopped. No. No, I said, you didn't, did you?

Joyce

I'LL NEVER FORGET seeing Bobbie's face, standing there, as they wheeled me out of the plane. Aunt Bobbie? Ben said, throwing my carry-on bag over his shoulder. Yes, Benjamin? she said, ruffling his hair. Who's J. F. Joplin? he asked, reading the handwritten sign Bobbie had been holding up like some car-service chauffeur at baggage claim. A famous composer, I answered, like J. S. Bach.

Is this *really* necessary? I asked, as people looked, then turned away, trying not to stare at my cast. Airport rules, ma'am, the man said. Appreciate the concern, I said, but honestly, I feel like an asshole here —. Never stopped you before, Bobbie said. Oh, and another thing, I said, turning to face her as we slowly made our way down the concourse, remind me to kick your ass when my ankle heals. Welcome home, she said, handing me my sign.

Adela

HOW FAR ALONG are you? she said, and I said, Almost twelve weeks. Baby, she said, listen to me —. I said, Mom, I know you think it's a mistake, and maybe I am making the biggest mistake of my life — but it's *my* mistake, and she started to speak, then she stopped.

Please, just listen, she said. I know you're scared and confused — I know, but it's not too late. I said, Mom, you aren't listening. *You aren't listening to me.* I'm keeping the child. I'm having the baby, okay. I'm having it, because I want it — you don't even know, do you? I said,

268

No wonder it's so easy for you to do what you do, day in, day out: because you've never had to make the decision. Do you believe in anything, Mom? Anything at all? She looked at me for the longest time, and then she said, I did, once: I believed in you.

I spoke to Lionel when I got downstairs, but then, when I stepped outside, I suddenly had the strangest feeling; it was like a panic attack, thinking I might never see him again. I don't know why, but it was this terrifying pang in my chest, and suddenly I wanted to go back inside and tell him I loved him — and I did, I do — but it wouldn't make sense. I mean, I didn't even understand it myself.

So I turned around, standing in front of the door, and I blew him this big old Hollywood kiss, kissing my fingertips and throwing out my arm. Lionel smiled and nodded his head, tipping his hat, and then I walked down the street, out of sight. And then . . . then I just stood there, a block from my house, not sure where to go.

But I couldn't go back to the hotel; I just couldn't. The thought of seeing Michael suddenly disgusted me so much; there was no way. He would see it, too. He would know — somehow — I don't know how, just that he'd take one look at me, and he'd guess.

Jordan

IT WAS NICE, hanging out in the TV room. It was like when I was little and Sunday night always felt so warm, lying on the couch with my head in my dad's lap, watching a game. At commercial, Lance got up to go to the kitchen, and he goes, Jojo, you want anything? And I was just like, *Ohmygod, you haven't offered to get me anything since I had my appendix out in fifth grade. Wow, you must feel really bad, huh?*

No, thanks, I said. You can get me a beer, Dad said, calling after him. And then I sat up and I was like, Hey, I'll take a beer, too, I said, waiting to see what my dad would say, but he didn't say anything. So Lance brought us beer, and we all opened our beers, and then Dad leaned forward and he goes, Let's toast —.

Then he froze — like he just totally froze, realizing what a stupid thing that was to say, like what are we toasting to, my abortion? And I knew he didn't mean anything, but it was just totally awkward, you know. Then Lance came to the rescue, and he goes, To the Jets, holding up his beer, so we all toasted, To the Jets! Then Lance set down his bottle, hunching forward in his chair and clapping: Now come on, you motherfuckers, *let's see some D!*

Joyce

SIX, SIX THIRTY, Sunday night, Benjamin got home and went straight to his room, while I sat on the couch, waiting. Listening, waiting . . . Then his door slammed, as he stormed into the living room. Hey, he said, threatening to shout, where's my stuff? What stuff? I said. *All my things* — everything!

Oh, I said, you mean all the things I bought you and/or gave you the money to buy for yourself, that stuff? In that case, I gave your stuff to a deserving child. You *what*? And I sighed . . . Benjamin, I gave them away, is what I'm saying. You did not, he said. No. You. *Didn't*, he said, glaring, and I just looked at him, like, who do you think you're talking to here?

I . . . I hate you, he said. Excuse me, I said, what . . . what was that? I said I hate you, he said through clenched teeth this time. I'm sorry, what did you say? I said, tugging at my earlobe. I *hate you*, he said. Oh, come on, Benjamin, you can do better than that, let's hear, give it to me. I — I, *I hate you, you fucking bitch!* he screamed. There: that's my boy, I said, clapping for him. Bravo! Then I walked over; I got right in his face, and I said, Now shut your mouth before I wash it out with soap. Because that, I said, that is what's called a *gimme.* In other words, that was the first, last, and only time you will ever speak to me like that. Because next time you do, Benjamin, you will be out on your ass so fast you'll be lucky to walk again, because you do not *speak* to me like that, *ever.* Got it?

Adela

I CANCELED MY FLIGHT, Monday morning, and I waited . . . but no call, nothing. No, I was being shunned, and I have to say, it's torture. Finally, Monday afternoon, I bought some flowers and I went to Tompkins to look for the old lady and ask her to bless me. I'd pay, too — I'd pay top dollar for a blessing — but I couldn't find her. So I sat on a bench, and I tried calling her again. *Please, Mom . . . Please answer . . .*

Bobbie

Joyce had just finished telling me about calling Sonja when my phone rang again, and I almost jammed my finger silencing the ringer, reminded again of what she'd said. One thing, Adela said, grabbing her bag and heading for the door, before turning around to look at me: If you've never been there, she said, you can't know how difficult a decision it really is. Adela, I said, you know I never wanted you to have to make that decision. She nodded her head, looking at me, and she said, I know you didn't, Mom. But I still have to make that decision, she said, and then she walked out. I sat down on the couch, and I hid my face, waiting for tears that couldn't seem to find their way.

You want to get that? Joyce said. No, I said. You sure? she said. Positive, I said. Water? Joyce asked, offering me her bottle of Evian. No, thanks, I said, and then she opened the paper bag, popped another pill in her mouth, and took a swig. Really, so thoughtful of you, she said, taking a deep breath and sighing. Least I could do, I said. Yeah, well, keep it coming, because I don't think we've seen the worst of it yet, she said, and I winced. What's wrong? she said, and I said, That's what I wanted to talk to you about, actually. There's more? she said. Depends, I said. On what? she said. On how much you know, I said, a fresh wave of anger causing my cheeks to flush.

She said I wasn't being fair, I said, clenching my jaw. Joyce shrugged: Well. Are you? Excuse me? I said. Bob, what I mean is, did you give her a chance to explain herself? Joyce, I said, I told her Saturday night that I needed time to think, and then she came over on Sunday —. In other words, Joyce said, no, you didn't give her a chance to explain. In other words, I said, it wasn't the time. All right, she said. Let's drop it, I said. Done, she agreed.

Well, I think I'm good to go, she said. What did you need to tell me? Adela's pregnant, I said. I know, she said, completely matter-of-fact. By the way, what's that saying — the shoemaker's children have no shoes, or is it the shoemaker's wife? Same difference, I said, and what do you mean you know? I mean it's like that, the gynecologist's daughter has no birth control —. Joyce, I understood you the first time.

I said, What do you mean *you know*? I mean she told me, she said, and I said, *When?* Yesterday. You spoke to her? I said. She called me, she said. Joyce, why didn't you tell me you spoke to her? I just did, she said, and I said, Well, I hope you told her, at least. Told her what? she said. That she's throwing her life away, for starters, I said. I think it's a little late for speeches, Bobbie.

Joyce, you cannot possibly *support* this. No, she said. No, I don't, but I can still support her. She's my goddaughter, after all. And she needs me, but not half as much as she needs you right now. She said you promised you'd call her back, Bob. *Stop,* I said. Stop, all right? Besides which, she's not your goddaughter, so please stop. Bobbie, all I'm saying is that you should call her and give her a chance to explain herself —. And I think you should mind your own business for once in your life, I said.

Bob, honestly . . . why are you angry with me? Because you've been talking to my daughter behind my back; because I don't need you meddling in my relationship with her; because I did nothing wrong and I had no idea what was going on, and you wouldn't return my calls, but you'd talk to Adela? How many reasons do you want? She said, Believe me, I had no intention of speaking to her, but she called my cell, then she called me at home, and I didn't think there was any way I could speak to her — until I heard her voice. I couldn't *not* speak to her: she was crying. She wasn't the only one, I said.

I think you should talk to her before we have this conversation, she said. Joyce, I called you at least six times in the past two days — *six times.* I've been so upset, worrying about *you* —. Oh, bullshit, Bobbie, she said. Don't lie to me, okay — if you want to lie to yourself, that's your choice, but don't even try that with me. No, she said. No, you're just using me as an excuse. Just like you used her as an excuse for not having a relationship for the past twenty years.

Speaking of excuses, I said, maybe if you stopped living vicariously through my daughter and me, you might actually have a life of your own, Joyce. Yeah, well, she said, there's a thought. But really, how is it you're the only one who doesn't seem to know that she's been putting on a hell of a face for you for the past three months? You know maybe if you could stop thinking about yourself and *listen* to her, you'd realize that your daughter's a fucking mess, and she needs you. I mean, Jesus, Bobbie, you're a doctor, I would think you, of all people, would know how short, how precious and —. Precious? I said.

Oh, fuck you, she said. No, really: *fuck you.* I'm sorry, I said, I didn't mean —. Bobbie, she said, you call her and you listen — you at least hear what she has to say, because that's the agreement you made when you took her home as your daughter. I said, Excuse me if I don't share your views on parenthood — you aren't exactly mother of the year, J. And as for promises? I said. What, like the promise you made to your dad to look out for Sonja?

Don't you ever, she said, don't you *ever* mention my father again. Because I really don't think you want to get into a discussion of dead parents right now. Meaning what? I said, and she said, Meaning, you want tough love? Well, then, here you go: all you have is your sad little workaholic existence, trying to save women's lives as though you can bring your mommy back and tell her you're sorry when you won't even apologize to the people right in front of you —. What an *awful* thing to say — that was low even by your standards, I said. *My* standards? she said, and I said, You think I don't know the things that people have said about you over the years? I do, believe me. And I have defended you every time, Joyce — every fucking time.

Gee, thanks, she said. And just so you know — just so you don't accuse me of going behind your back — I'm meeting Dela for coffee tomorrow, before she heads to the airport. She's staying an extra day in the hopes you'll deign to speak to her. I said, Do what you have to do —. Yeah, I'll do that, she said. But whatever problems I have with her are between Adela and me, not *you,* okay? So leave me out of it, she said. Fine: then leave, I said, and she did.

She got up and she walked away, while I sat there, watching her go. The thought of losing her had terrified me not an hour before, but at that moment, it seemed perfectly plausible, likely even, that I was about to lose my best friend. And the truth is I felt nothing.

5

Jordan

YOU KNOW WHAT the worst part is? The worst part of every day, right after waking up, is getting dressed for school. It's like every morning I sit on my bed, staring into my closet, thinking how much I hate my clothes — I mean, just getting dressed is enough to make me want to off myself, and then it's all downhill from there. And then, for like an entire month, I couldn't even get out of bed, I felt so sick every morning.

Seriously, Thursday I felt so nauseous, putting on my jeans, I had to run to the bathroom. After I gargled, I went back to my room and sat down on my bed, then I checked my messages again — and there was a message! I was just like, *He called!* I was so happy, I pressed one, holding my breath, and then a voice said, Hello, Jordan. This is Donna calling from Dr. Myers's office. I wanted to remind you that you have an appointment at ten, tomorrow morning. No, he just . . . he didn't call, and no matter how hard I tried, I couldn't stop believing he would. You know how fucked up that feels? I mean, seriously, they have all these drugs for depression, why doesn't someone invent a drug to make you quit hoping for something that's never going to happen? Because I know I'd take it, like every day.

So I just sat there, and then Rusty came in and he started licking my hands, and I just wanted to be left alone. So I tried pushing him away, but he wouldn't stop; he just kept sniffing me. So I said, Stop it, Rusty. Go on — get out, I said, pushing his nose away from my crotch. I mean, he just wouldn't leave me alone, so I said, Get out. *Get out!*

But he wouldn't budge, so I got up and I dragged him by the collar, and then he started whimpering because I pulled him too hard, and I heard him whimper, but it made me so angry, I slammed the door on his tail. On purpose — I did it on purpose, because he'd whimpered, and it was such an awful sound, the way an animal feels pain without knowing to try and hide it. The way that makes them better than we are, you know.

What kills me is that I choked him and then I almost broke his tail, but like ten minutes later, when I opened my door, he was still there, waiting to see me off to school. Looking up at me like he was asking for my forgiveness for hurting him. I could see it in his eyes, too: he didn't know what he'd done wrong, but he was sorry. Whatever it was, he was so sorry and he wouldn't do it ever again. I almost started crying again, but I got it together. I walked downstairs, and I put on my coat, and then my mom said, Jordan? What? I said. Come here, please, she said. So I closed my eyes and I took a deep breath.

Adela

I TRIED TO TELL HER after lunch — even just . . . I don't know. Just to explain something about myself, something she didn't know about me. But then she smiled, like it was a joke. You think that's *funny?* I said, and she covered her mouth, shaking her head. No sweetheart, that's not it: that's not why —. A little girl is raped and tortured and dies in a bathtub, bludgeoned with god knows what, and you smile? You disgust me, I said, and she reached for my arm. *Don't!* I said, stepping back as she tried to put her hands on me. Don't — don't touch me, I said, unfolding the paper so I could read it to her, aloud:

January 12, 2006: Bound, Beaten, Starved, Killed: Nixzmary Brown's . . . and then I stopped. Her name was Nixzmary, not Ixnomy.

276

Ohmygod, I said, covering my mouth, beginning to cry. Ohmygod, I got her name wrong, that's why Mom was smiling: I pig latined her name. Baby, she said, Dela, I'm sure she'll forgive you —. No, I said. No, Mom, you don't understand. Let me finish, I said, and then I held the paper up again, and I read it to her, because I had to. I had to finish it. I owed her that.

> Nixzmary Brown's tragic life of unimaginable physical and emotional agony ended at 4:30 a.m. yesterday when the 7-year-old's battered body was found in her Brooklyn "house of horrors."
> The second-grader had been bound to a chair, tortured, sexually molested and starved for weeks before being killed by a savage blow to the head — even after child welfare authorities dismissed charges of abuse.

Adela, she said. Let me finish, I said.

> Trapped inside a makeshift, barren bedroom, Nixzmary missed weeks of school — and was forced to use a cat's litter box as her bathroom, sources said.
> No expense was spared on flashy stereo equipment, perfumes, and soft toys for the parents . . . even while Nixzmary was forced to eat cat food . . .

I couldn't go on. That was my nightmare — I had one nightmare, over and over, when I was little: a nightmare about being sent back, and being cold, and there were all these cats. She lived my nightmare — I could have been her. I was, deep down. I said, She was so alone — she had no one. How, Mom? Tell me how someone could do that to a little girl, I said, sobbing.

Bobbie

SHH, I SAID, putting my arms around her, shielding her from the foot traffic. She just wanted something to eat — *fucksake*, Dela sobbed, she was hungry, and he clubbed her to death because she took a container of yogurt out of the fridge? I said, Sweetheart. Del, you know that's not why. But you haven't answered my question, she said, answer my question!

I said, I can't, sweetheart. I can't answer your question, Del, because I don't know the answer. But I do know who Nixzmary Brown was. And I know she was a beautiful, sweet little girl, and I'm sorry—I'm so sorry for how much she must have suffered.

Then she stood up straight, shaking her head no, rolling her eyes and flapping her lips. I'm sorry I got so angry with you, she said, drying her eyes. Del, what's the matter? What's going on? I said. Nothing, she said. Because I'll call the office—. No, go on, she said. I'm just worn out. Look at me, I said, you promise? Promise, she said, I'm just tired. She'd calmed down, but I knew something was wrong. Del, I said, if you don't want to go to dinner tonight—. No way, she said. *No way* am I letting you get out of this. And she was right. I half hoped she'd cancel, I was so nervous.

I got in the cab, heading back to work. Don't. Be. Late, I said, closing the door. Ixnay, Ommymay. Okay, I said, kissing my hand and waving. There was no getting out of it; the moment of truth had finally arrived.

Joyce

So I WENT HOME early Thursday, and I waited for Benjamin. I got up to get something to drink, and then I stopped to look at that picture of the two of us in Maui. I still smile every time I look at that picture. Because we were so happy, then—Benjamin still talks about that trip as the best vacation of his entire life. And I have to say I do look gorgeous.

Then again, it doesn't look anything like me, really. I'm so thin and tan, it's unreal. And the way I'm laughing, you'd never know my father had died a few months earlier. Then again, I didn't eat. Didn't sleep. It was grief, endless grief. And a large supply of cocaine. I put the picture down, trying to figure out what to do with myself, feeling spooked in my own house.

I'd already tried Michael; I'd practically hung up on Sonja; I couldn't call Bobbie. But honestly, at that moment, sitting on the couch, I didn't want to talk to any of them. Sitting there, the only person I felt I could really talk to was my dad. I mean, Jesus Christ, fifty-three fucking years old and all I wanted was my daddy.

But who else could I ask? Who else could I possibly say the words: I'm his mother . . . what did I do to make him want to humiliate me? The only person — he was it. Because I knew my dad would know exactly the right thing to say to me, even if that was nothing at all. When I heard his key in the door, I realized I was holding my mouth and shaking my head, thinking, *How can I still love you when you do this to me? But I do — I still love you, you little bastard, and you're still my son.* Then I dried my eyes, hearing the door open, and I cleared my throat, waiting. Benjamin, I said, come here, please.

Bobbie

·DEL PICKED ME UP Thursday night, and we met Paul at the restaurant, eight thirty on the dot. And I have to say Paul went all out, he really did. I have no idea how he got the reservation, but he wasn't joking when he said he wanted to impress the kid. The two of them really seemed to be hitting it off, too, and I was so grateful for Adela to see me happy with a man for once.

The waiter brought our dessert menus, and then Adela stood, excusing herself to the ladies' room, and Paul stood, while I returned my attention to the menu, giving it a once-over. Just as I was about to say, Guess what I'm having . . . I looked up, but Paul wasn't reading his menu, he was watching Adela walk away. He was checking out my daughter on the sly. Ogling, I should say.

I looked at him, I watched him, how he looked at her, up and down and up again, and I knew without looking — I knew what he saw. I know her body; I bought her that dress, as a matter of fact; it's stunning. But I'm staring at the man for a good five, ten seconds, maybe, and he's just completely oblivious. It's like I'm invisible.

Do you have any idea how shameful it is to feel jealous of your own daughter? You hear about those middle-aged women who compete with their daughters for attention, and you can't imagine how a woman could be so pitiful. But then it's you: you're pitiful. Of course I couldn't have admitted it at the time, but I see it now. Then again, that doesn't change anything, I'm afraid.

When the waiter brought the check, I smiled, handing him my card and giving him the eye, telling him to be on his way, before Paul had a chance to reach for his wallet. Which I did to shame him, yes — that's exactly why I paid. He looked at me, and then Adela looked away, embarrassed for him, but I just smiled, looking at him, thinking, *Don't feel like such a big man now, do you?* Shall we? I said, standing.

We put Dela in a cab and sent her off to meet her friends sometime after eleven, eleven thirty. Then we took a few steps down the street, before Paul stopped and turned. Do you want to tell me what's going on now? he said. I was so surprised by how quickly he reacted that I almost giggled, like I'd been caught red-handed, which I had. Nothing's going on, I said, except that I'm exhausted; I have a hideous day tomorrow; and now I just want to go home and go to bed, all right? And the look on his face . . . Honestly, I'm in love with this man, and he's the best thing that's happened to me in a long, long time, and I'm lying, staring him right in the eye.

He nodded his head slowly, clearly at a loss for words, before he turned and shoved his hands in his coat pockets, ready to continue walking. Then I'll see you home, he said, throwing out his right elbow, offering me his arm. Which was extremely generous, I admit. Except that I didn't want his generosity or gentlemanly behavior or anything else from him. *Spare me,* I thought, crossing my hands in front of me. Well, he said, looking off, why don't you call me when you feel like talking, because I don't know what the hell is going on with you, I really don't, Bobbie. And suddenly I felt so confused — I, I was just so hurt and angry and self-righteous and . . . and moved, watching him struggling.

So naturally I started denying the whole thing — and then his hand shot up and he patted the air a couple times, somewhere between asking and begging me to stop, just stop. All right, he said, looking down the street. You get some sleep. Good night, he said, leaning over and giving me a kiss on the cheek, then he turned and walked away.

It was sharper than a slap, and such a cold night, I swear you could hear an echo down the street. I could've called or run after him, but I just stood there, holding up my chin, in case he should change his mind and suddenly turn around to say something, yell something, even just to swear at me on second thought . . . But he didn't, of course, because that's not Paul's style.

I waited a moment longer before I turned in the opposite direction, and then I slammed my head down: *Fuck,* I said out loud, so disgusted I slapped my own forehead with the palm of my right hand. Because this happens every time: somehow, someway, I always manage to screw it up. That's my style, I'm afraid.

Lionel was standing at the ready, when I got out of the cab. Good evening, Dr. Myers, he said, opening the door for me, as I gathered my collar around my neck. Good evening, Lionel. How are you this evening? I said, smiling graciously. Oh, very well, thank you. And you, Dr. Myers? he said, before adding, You look very lovely this evening, if you don't mind my saying so. I said, Mind? No, Lionel, I don't mind: thank you. Good night, he said, so genteel, so dignified, and he immediately stepped away; even the slightest hint of intimacy was well outside a code of conduct that Lionel had instituted and maintained for almost forty years.

When I got home, I hung up my coat and went to my closet to undress, taking off my earrings. I hung up my dress, and then, for some reason, I went and stood in front of the bathroom mirror. Four hours earlier, I'd spent an hour dressing for dinner, expecting Paul to see me this way — the bra, garter belt, stockings, high heels . . . But at that moment, looking at myself, it seemed sad. Flesh giving way, the lines on my face . . . *Who was I kidding?* I thought, closing my eyes before I walked away.

I didn't even tell Joyce what happened — I couldn't even tell my best friend, I was too proud and too ashamed to tell her what happened last weekend. But Saturday afternoon, after we got back to Paul's place, we were lying in bed, and I said it. I said, I love you, you know that? I really love you, I said, laughing, feeling . . . feeling delirious, free. Then he took my face in his hands, and he looked at me, staring into my eyes for what seemed an eternity, and then, finally, he leaned forward and kissed me, leaving his lips on my cheek, before whispering in my ear, Thank you.

That was his response, Thank you. I was shocked. I mean, he — he said he adored me — he . . . I was sure he'd say he loved me, too, or I would never . . . I never. Why didn't he say it? He stood back, looking at me, and I smiled. You're welcome, I said, grinning at him, trying so hard to laugh it off, trying so hard to save face, I practically skipped away, getting out of bed. But at that moment, all I wanted . . . I wanted to go, to get the hell out of there and return to my own home. Most of all, I wanted him gone. All week, I was waiting for the moment, some excuse, and then I found one Thursday night.

Lynne

THAT NIGHT, after Don woke me, we got up together, and Don knocked on Jordan's door, asking her to let him in, and she started shouting at him. By the point she finally let us in, she was crying so hard that she was making herself sick, so we got her to breathe and then we took her downstairs. But of course Don was the one to comfort her, sit with her and hold her, not me. I can't hold her like that now — not anymore, no.

Well, apparently, this person — excuse me, Misha — his name is Misha. Well, apparently, Misha's wife or whatever she is, somehow the woman got hold of Jordan's cell phone number and called her, and since it was the middle of the night, Jordan answered, assuming it was Misha. Then Jordan told us that this woman had called her a slut and a whore and god knows what else. Jordan, Don said, hugging her, trying to calm her down.

I looked at the two of them, and then I said, Really, Jordan, what did you expect her to say? That's enough, Don said, looking at me, aghast. That's enough? I said, Wake up, Don: Jordan is in the wrong here, and not once have I seen her express any concern for anyone but herself, and you're telling me that's enough? I mean, Jesus Christ, in three days, the life I spent twenty years building has been razed to the ground by our daughter's stupidity, I said, but he couldn't look at me. Then again, I guess it's not too surprising that you feel so sympathetic, I said.

I was referring to the fact that Don had an affair with his secretary a few years ago. Barbara, yes. And she was from Ohio, for chrissake. I mean, the joke was on me, really, because I interviewed her — I always handle the interviews because Don's such a pushover. Anyhow, the moment she walked into the office, I distinctly remember thinking, *Oh, poor woman, who would ever have sex with her?* Now I know . . . why, Don, of course.

I was shocked, but not because my husband had been having an affair; I was shocked to realize that that was the first time I had ever allowed myself to think, *Wait a second . . . what would my life be like without Don? What would I do if I were on my own again?* All these bells and whistles went off in my head, and then it flashed before my eyes: this could be my out. For a split second I actually thought I could do anything I wanted — and then I remembered that I couldn't, really. I can't just pick up and walk out on him: because this is my home, my family, my life. This is all I have. And frankly, that's what enraged me the most.

No, it wasn't Don screwing around that made me feel screwed over, it was the fact that I couldn't leave, and I wanted to — I wanted to leave him so badly. But that was simply out of the question because that's not me, I'm afraid. I wished it was, but it's not. Instead, I did everything in my power to convince myself that I was heartbroken by his betrayal because it was so much easier than facing the truth.

So all these things bled together, looking at the two of them, sitting side by side, like accomplices. And for a moment, I had no idea who I was anymore, or who any of us were, really. Then time snapped back, and a moment later, I wished I could take it all back, everything I'd just said to Jordan, but I couldn't. No, you just have to move forward.

Next morning, I called the doctor Lisa had recommended, and I said my daughter was eight weeks pregnant. But the words — I can't explain how strange it was to say those words — standing there, I thought, *My god, last month, I was making her dentist appointment, and now . . .* Ten days ago, we drove down so the doctor could examine Jordan and discuss our options, as they say. And now . . . now all I know is that I'm tired, I'm just so *fucking tired.* Because I was up every night last week, thinking how I was going to tell Jordan the truth, how much she deserved to know the truth. Which is that I spoke to him, Misha. The night after that woman called, his wife or girlfriend or whoever she is, I drove to Price Chopper's during my lunch hour, and they haven't spoken since. No, I'm sure of it.

Jordan didn't tell me. She doesn't need to, I can tell. I can see it in the way she almost winces, simply taking her eyes off the ground. Wednesday morning, in the car, we both happened to look up at the same time, fastening our seat belts, and there was so much pain in her eyes that it knocked the wind out of me. I mean, I . . . I remember the moment the doctor handed her to me, when she was born, and I saw her face, and I thought, *How could I have made anything so beautiful?* Sitting there, in the car, I could feel that moment like it was yesterday, and I wanted to take her hand, but then she looked away.

Honestly, I was going to tell her I spoke with him, but then a day passed, and then another, and when Misha didn't call . . . well, it began to seem like a good idea if I just kept my mouth shut. I mean, really, if she can make a clean break of it now, isn't that best? I don't know anymore.

All I know is that it seems like I'm the only one holding this family together: like everyone expects me to be the one to keep it together, but then they don't like the way I do things, and . . . and that's fine, really. I understand. The only problem is that I can't do it anymore. So if the day comes that my son discovers his drugs are missing, and my husband and children sit me down, demanding to know what on earth would possess me to pop a few pills in my mouth not even knowing what they were, I'll tell the truth. Which is: Because I wanted to. And because I was desperate. Same difference, really.

Jordan

AND THEN FRIDAY MORNING, it's like she just kept hugging me and petting me, like pushing my head against her shoulder, and I was just like, Mom, are you sick? And she goes, No . . . no, I'm fine, baby,

I'm just fine. So we got in the car, and she backed down the drive, and then, when we got to the road, she stopped and she just let out this huge sigh, resting her head on the steering wheel. And I was just like, what is wrong with you? Then she goes, Jordan, you drive, honey; and I go, Mom, I can't. And she goes, No, it's better . . . it's better, she said, and then she opened the door and crawled into the backseat and she just collapsed. I said, Mom — I go, Mom, I can't drive — I don't know how to drive in the city! She goes, You'll be fine, sweetheart, it's just a city. It's all the same . . . I just need to lie down. I just need to rest for a minute, okay?

So I drove — I mean, I just got my license, and I made it the whole way there, but once we got to the city, I didn't know where I was going, you know. So I pulled over and I tried waking her; I said, Mom, *wake up*. I don't know where I'm going! But she kept saying, It's fine, baby, it's fine . . . everything is going to be fine, and I was just like, *Stop saying that*, you know. Then I turned on a one-way, and people were looking, shouting at me, like, Hey, you're going the wrong way!

So I pulled over, and I tried not to cry, but I was so angry with her, and like — I mean, all these people were just *staring* at me, you know. So I tried shaking her, like, Mom, wake up — wake *up!* But she was passed out. So I called the office, and I almost started crying when the nurse tried giving me directions, because she's like, Do you know where Lex is?, and I'm like, No, I don't know where Lex is, what the fuck is Lex?, you know? So she talked to me the whole way there, and I got to the building, but then there was no parking. So I kept circling and circling, and we were late — I was already twenty minutes late, when I saw a spot, so I tried parallel parking, but it was too close, and then I heard this scraping sound, and I was just like, *fuck,* you know.

So I got out to see what I'd done, and there were two guys, just standing there, watching me. The other car's side mirror was fine, but I scratched Mom's car, just like this huge scratch across the passenger-side door. So I got back in and I drove to the parking lot at the end of the street, and I gave the guy the keys, and I just pulled my mom out of the car, yelling at her the whole way, but I don't know if she even heard me.

Once we got inside, I sat my mom down in the waiting room, and then I walked to the front desk, and I said, I'm Jordan Yaeger, and the nurse said, Oh, Jordan, we were getting worried —. And I didn't know what to say, you know, so I was just like, I'm sorry, my mom got sick, and then I just started crying. I mean, there were all these women in the waiting room, looking at me, and then I heard one of the nurses say, I'll get Dr. Myers, but I just stood there, covering my face with both hands.

Lisa

IT'S FUNNY, YOU KNOW. I mean, yesterday — yesterday morning, I woke up and, and I had a husband, and I had a son, I mean, I had a life. As a matter of fact, I had a very good life — I liked my life, I really did. Couldn't stand my husband, but I liked my life just fine.

I took the baby with me to meet Kate for lunch, then we went for a manicure-pedicure and the baby slept the entire time — just completely conked out. And of course all the Malaysian girls were cooing over him, oh, what an angel. And he was an angel, but then I just had to press my luck, deciding to pick up some fish for dinner.

I stopped by Whole Foods, the one on Twenty-fourth Street; the one on Union Square sucks. I hate that place, but anyhow. I walk through the electronic door; I grab a basket; and then the baby wakes. Oh, but he doesn't just wake, he wakes squalling so loud they must've heard him in Central Park. And the thing is, it's impossible to get out of that place without walking all the way around.

I'm standing there, bending my knees, shaking the baby up and down, trying to quiet him, thinking, *Here's what we'll do: I'll just get the fish and we'll be out of here in two minutes, okay? Just give me two minutes, and I promise we'll be out of here.* I mean, I'm trying to cut a deal with a screaming infant, right? Bad idea. Because I make it as far as the cheese station, their little kiosk or whatever, and then *blech* . . . Lee pukes everywhere.

So I take him out of the snuggly, and I hold him, and he was fine. Course I'm covered in puke, but Lee's just fine, cooing again . . . And then, I hear a voice: *Lisa?* Lisa Barrett, is that you? I hear it just a second — I mean, *a split second* before I hear a voice in my head shout, *Run! Run for your life!* Too late.

I turn around, and there's Greg. Who's asking? I said, and he said, Oh, just an old friend of the family. Yeah, whose family? I said, and he said, Exactly. How are you? he says, answering his own question: You look great. Healthy, he says, immediately amending his compliment. Healthy? I said, What's that supposed to mean? No, really — you smell like vomit, but you look great, he says, and I said, Never stopped you before. I see your manners haven't improved any, he says, and I said, *Excuse me?*

Aren't you going to introduce us? he says, grabbing a handful of napkins from the cheese display and offering them to me. Thanks, I said, smiling. You might need another, he says, looking us up and down, and I just looked at him a moment, like, piss off. So, he says, looking down at Lee: Is he yours? I said, What, you think I'd let someone else's baby puke on me?

Who's this? Greg said, reaching for Lee, and I said, Careful. It's fine, I'll just hold him out, like this, he said, extending his arms a foot in front of his body. Lee's little stuffed-sausage legs dangling in the air. Isn't that how men hold babies? he said. That's pretty good, I said. So how've you been? he said, fastening Lee to his hip, bouncing him. I was surprised the baby didn't start howling; he's afraid of most men.

What's his name, anyhow? Greg said. Lee, I said. Lee . . . ? William, I said, tilting my head at Greg's raised brow, and he said, William, the fifth, sixth . . . ? Fourth, I said, cocking my chin at him, watch it. Of course you wouldn't want to give a kid his own name, he said, and just then, some six-foot Amazon, wearing six-inch platform heels, steps toward us, looking me up and down, before territorially cooing, Greg? Oh. Lisa, I'd like you to meet Racquelle. And this is William Something Something the fourth, he said, turning the baby to face her. We call him Puke, for short, I said, and Greg turned, trying not to laugh.

Puke? says Racquelle, the humorless six-foot-six Brazilian bra model, and I'm thinking, *Oh, right, she's foreign.* Of course, she is. Greg got the cover of *New York* magazine, and as a little reward, he went to the supermarket and picked himself up a bikini model named Racquelle, who doesn't get our vomit jokes. Well, guess you can't have everything.

Yes, I said. Puke: it's like Puck, but with an *E*. They had a little accident, he said, giving me the eye, trying to smooth over my sarcasm. Oh, no, I said, he had an accident, and it was anything but little. I look at her, smiling, and she's beautiful. She's beautiful in the way that you can do nothing but gawk. Unhuman, really.

On the bright side, at least she has enough brains to know something is up, or at least that she is not being included in this little joke of ours. And I smile back: no, you aren't included in our little joke, because I knew him long before you did, sweetie. And trust me, I know him better than you ever will. So then, of course, she smiles and coos at the baby, in that disgusting oh-Greg-I-want-one tone, at which point, I'm just like, get your hands off my son, you fucking meat puppet.

How old? she says, in her thick Portuguese accent. Twenty-three weeks, I said, catching myself only after saying it. Twenty-three weeks, *wow*, Greg says, and it's all I can do to keep from saying, Fuck off, will you? You see, Greg, I said, smiling, turning to him, leaving the centerfold out of the conversation: The thing you never quite understood about the stroke-and-kick method is that you're supposed to stroke, and, technically the stroke comes first, I said. Ah . . . I see your point, he says. But remember, Leese, you taught me everything I know. Oh, no, I said, I think you've learned a few tricks on your own. Congratulations, by the way. I hear you're a big, big star now, I said. You hear? he said, laughing.

What can I say? I keep my ear to the ground, I said. And what's the ground say? he said. The ground says you have a waiting list of what, four, five hundred? Thousands, actually — five thousand, he said. That's what I meant, I said, and he smiled. You're doing some amazing work, I said. Thank you, he said. That's probably the highest compliment anyone has every paid me. No, actually, that *is* the highest compliment anyone has ever paid you, I said, laughing at him.

So things are going well? I said, finally returning my attention to, or at least nodding at, the model-girlfriend. Yes, he said, And then

Racquelle turns and raises her hand to touch the baby's shirt. No, actually, then she raises her hand to touch the baby's shirt in order to show me the rock on her left finger. Which is not my style, but some people would be impressed, I suppose. And just as I'm about to snatch my child from her arms, Lee looks up and smiles, reaching for her, and I'm just like, *oh great — that's just great, now you're turning on me, too? Yeah, well, we'll see whose tit you're sucking tonight, little man. Because it ain't mine, and trust me, she's really not that interested in you, so don't come crying to me at two thirty in the morning, because you are officially weaned, my friend. Party's over.*

Then someone called Racquelle's name — some well-dressed Euro couple, who looked like they'd just been teleported from Milan, approached and pulled her aside, giving her a kiss-kiss after checking me out. And apparently having decided I was no threat. She absently handed the baby back to Greg, excusing herself.

So you saw the show? he said, and I said, No, but I saw you got written up in the *Times*. He smiled: The work's a little bigger in real life, you know —, and then he stopped, and I just had to smile. I said, No, Greg, I didn't see your show. And this might come as a surprise, but I'm never stepping foot in that place again. Leese, he said, I know you aren't going to believe me, but she's changed. You're right, I said, I don't believe you. No, it's true, Leese, she's not the same person she was five years ago.

Greg, I said, do you really believe people change? I believe they can, he said, I mean anything's possible, right? Maybe, I said, but not Joyce. That woman will never change, I said. What was it you called her? Cunticus Americanas, something like that? And Greg looked at the baby. Don't worry, I said, he doesn't speak Latin. Anyhow, you've certainly changed your tune —. She's been a good friend to me the past couple years, he said, and I held up my hand, meaning, I don't want to hear this.

I know what you're thinking, he said. No, I don't think you do, I said. Then why don't you let me buy you a drink and you can tell me? A drink? I laughed. Coffee, a cup of tea? Just to add insult to injury, I said. Well, since you're nursing —. Oh, you noticed, I smiled, pulling my shoulders back, proudly displaying my tits. Yes. They're fantastic, he said, laughing at us both. They really are, aren't they? I said, smiling and wrinkling my nose, inspecting my chest. Unfortunately, they're just loaners.

Yes, well, what I meant to say was, since you're nursing and I'm on the wagon —. So I read. Congratulations, I said, sounds like you finally got your shit together. Thank you, he said, I think. And you — congratulations to you, as well, he said, speaking to the baby. And looking at the two of them, I nearly said it: *And to think, all this could've been yours, Greg.*

So is that a yes? he said. No, I said, but I couldn't help smiling. I have to say I was certainly savoring the moment, seeing him again, talking, listening to him asking me out and denying him the satisfaction. Come on, we'll grab a cup of coffee, and I'll take you to my studio, how's that? I could show you what I'm working on now, and you can be your old merciless hypercritical self, he said. What about it? Look, if you think I'm going to meet you for a cup of coffee and forgive you —. No, he said, I know you better than that. No, I said, you knew me: past tense. All the more reason, he said. Greg, I don't really have time these days, I said, reaching for the baby, taking him back.

Then call me when you do — I'd love to see you again, catch up. Here, I'll give you my number, he said, pulling out his wallet, handing me a card. Gee, thanks, Slick, I said, giving him the eye. He pursed his lips, ready to fire right back, and for a moment, it was just like old times . . . then the Brazilian bimbette returned, grabbing his arm. Good seeing you, Lisa, he said. And meeting you, he said, patting the baby's cheek. You, too, I said, trying to smile like the proud mother, cooing at my son. Say, bye Greg, bye Rachel, I said to Lee, waving his fat paw at them, turning away. Of course it was petty and calculated, calling her by the wrong name: that was the point.

Hey, Greg? I said, turning back. Yo? he said, turning around; Raquelle turned as well, clearly annoyed, but I ignored her. Say hello to your mom for me, will you? I said, and he stood there. He just looked at me and smiled; didn't say a word. And I wished — I wish, *I wish* he would've said something, anything, really . . . but what was there to say?

I don't know what happened, or why — I mean, I know what happened, of course I know what happened, I just don't know why. He could've had everything — everything he'd ever wanted, everything we'd ever talked about, lying in bed, whispering our dreams in the dark — it was right there, nine years ago. But he got scared or . . . I don't know what. I don't know. And I wanted to ask; the way he was looking at me at that moment, I wanted to ask him, Whatever it was, why didn't you tell me, Greg? I thought I was your best friend, and you didn't tell me. Bye, I said, turning back around.

I managed to get out of the store, but once the doors closed, and I walked around the block, to make sure he wouldn't pass by, I couldn't breathe. I couldn't breathe, I smelled like vomit, and I wanted to scream, cry — I don't know what. It all came back again — not like it was just yesterday, like it was that moment, right there, on the street.

We got in such a fight after I told him I was pregnant — I knew I shouldn't have told him, but I did. For old time's sake, I guess. Then, of course, he started in, saying he could clean up his act and we'd have the baby. He said he'd go cold turkey, quit everything, which only infuriated me. Then quit, Greg, quit! Why do I have to have a kid for you to get your act together? And how can I believe you, when you've been telling me that for the past five years? You'll quit? *Right*, I said, just like you used to tell me it wasn't a problem. Honestly, I don't even care anymore, but you know what? I'm not having a kid. I've worked too fucking hard to have a kid and live in an East Village tenement with some unemployed junkie dilettante.

Leese, listen to me, he said, completely unfazed by what I'd just said. We could *leave* — let's just say — let's just *say*, he said, grabbing my arm, because I was turning away in disgust. Let's say I cleaned up my act and we moved somewhere —. Somewhere *where*? I said. Where would we live? Upstate —. I don't want to live upstate, Greg! I lived there for sixteen years and I hated every fucking second of it. I'm not moving anywhere, because I live here. *This* is my home. *This* is my life, that I've —.

Marry me, he said, and I just looked at him: What? Marry me, he said. Oh, fuck you! If that isn't about the most pathetic proposal ever, I said. How low will you stoop? No, really, how low, Greg? Look, he said, I know my timing could be better —. Ohmygod, I said, laughing, sitting on the bed. Lisa, I *know* my timing could be better, but I love you. And I want to spend my life with you. And I want to have this child and raise it with you — wherever you like. We don't have to go upstate, we could move somewhere else — Maine, I don't know. But we could have a good life, he said.

You seriously want me to believe we could leave New York, move to Maine, and raise a baby? I said, and he said, Yes, I do. I believe every word — so long as we have each other, right? I couldn't even — I, I didn't even know where to begin, at the thought of living in some sad little house in Maine, buried in snow, with a squalling brat, *oh* . . . but *at least* we have each other. What was he thinking? He hadn't even worked a day in —. No, I said, covering my mouth with my finger, in some professorial pose. I'd rather die, I said, same difference.

It was heartless, but what can I say? I wanted to hurt him, yes — but mostly, I just wanted him to go away, to leave me alone and take all our problems with him: buh-bye . . . Don't do this, he said, *please.* Greg, it's a child, not a life preserver, I said. No, that's exactly what children are, Lisa —. No, stop. It's not going to happen, I said, raising my hand, end of discussion.

So I don't have any say in this, is that right? he said, becoming angrier by the second. And I said, No, you absolutely have a say in this. Thank you, he said. But the decision is mine, I said, holding up both hands: What can you do? Go fuck yourself, Lisa, he said, and I looked at him a moment. I didn't yell, but I said it in the most brutal tone I was capable: I'm sorry, but I'm not having a kid out of *your* fucking desperation —. And then his hand flew back; his fist was cocked before he even realized what he'd done.

What, you're going to hit me? I said, more amused than scared. Yeah, you're father-of-the-year material, all right, I said, practically laughing in his face. You fucking *touch me*, I'll have your ass in jail so fast. And believe me, I won't be there to bail you out this time, either.

Lisa, do you even care — do you even care how *I* feel? he said, lowering his hand, completely demoralized. I looked at him, and then I said, Honestly, Greg, it's too little, too late — we've been through this so many times, I lost count years ago. Don't do this, he said; he was begging, but I just glared, moving to walk past him. I hope you regret this as long as you live, he said, getting out of my way. Greg, I regret ever meeting you; this is just icing on the cake, I said, grabbing my coat and heading out.

I didn't ask for money that night. Not because I wouldn't throw that at him on top of everything else but because I thought I had enough to cover it on my own. But then Greg's check to ConEd bounced — I'd finally told him if he wasn't painting, he'd have to pay his share of the bills — so, big surprise, we got shut off and I had to pay the entire balance. Of course I didn't say, hey, I need you to pay your share of the utilities from the past three months so I can pay for the abortion, but he knew why, and he promised me he'd get the money. I don't have any proof, but I'm certain Greg spent the money on drugs. He had money that weekend — I saw it in his wallet, and then it was gone.

After that last fight, I returned home to find him smoking — fucking freebasing right in front of me, right in my face. I took one look at him, and he said, I'll leave you cash on the table tomorrow. That was Monday night, four days before the opening of the first show I ever curated — my first and last, but who's counting. The next night, I returned home to a note, and I had no choice but to pick up the phone and call Lynne, begging for money. Five years later, here we are again.

No, I thought, standing on the street, inhaling a deep breath. *I'm not going to cry for you.* But I definitely wanted to scream, to look up at the sky and scream at the top of my lungs, I hate you, you fucking bastard! But I couldn't — my rib cage had collapsed, and I could barely raise my arm for a cab, and then the baby started fussing again, and I said, Please, Lee, not now. Please don't start fussing, because I can't take it right now.

I tried everything — everything I could think of. I started bouncing him; bending my knees, bouncing, bouncing, bouncing. Let's sing, Lee — come on, let's sing a song: Baby's on, I hummed. Shhh, shhhh . . . come on, I said, swaying back and forth and back and forth, we'll sing your song: *Baby's on fire, Better throw her in the water . . .* And he stopped for a moment, then he started screaming even louder than before.

The more I tried to comfort him, the louder he wailed, slapping his arms at the air, and I couldn't take it. So I took him out of the snuggly, and I said, Stop, Lee. Stop. That's enough, that's *enough*. And then he just shrieked at the top of his lungs, and I said, Stop. Stop it, Lee, *stop it!* I said, shaking him once. I was so angry, I started shaking him — and he couldn't breathe to scream. Then I stopped. I stopped, removing my hands so quickly that I almost dropped him, right there, on the sidewalk.

I was so furious with Greg, I — I started shaking my own son in re-taliation. Then I started crying, holding him: I'm sorry, I'm so sorry. It took a while, maybe ten minutes before I managed to pull it to-gether and hail a cab.

After we got in the cab, smelling his sweaty, milky cheeks, I thought, *I'd give my life for you, you little pain in the ass.* I smiled at him, cooing, Totalfuckingcunt, that's right. Can you say, total-fuckingcunt? Who loves you? Who loves you more than anything in the whole world? I said, blowing a raspberry on his fat cheek, but it brought tears to my eyes again. Not because of what I'd done but because I knew it was true. Thirty-six years old — it took thirty-six years before I realized I could love anyone like that. So how could I do such a thing?

When we got home, I handed Lee to Rosalee, and then I went to the bathroom and bawled. I felt like such a monster, shaking him — when I hear about women who do that, I never thought I could be one of those mothers who would shake her own child, I said. Has that ever happened before? she said, and I was so ashamed, tears came to my eyes. No, never, I said. But how do you know if you are one of those women if you've only done it once? I asked, but she didn't answer. Well, I said, drying my eyes with a Kleenex: seeing as I didn't feel bad enough, after I washed my face, I turned on my computer.

Bobbie

THEN, ONE DAY, she didn't say it back. I walked into the exam room and I said, Hello, Gorgeous, and she just smiled, pained. Hey, she said, which was odd. I said, Leese, you know how I value our time together, but didn't I just see you a few months ago? Ah, well, she said, a girl can't have too many Pap smears, I always say.

So, Lisa, I said, taking out my pen, what seems to be the problem? Well, for starters, I think I'm pregnant, she said, raising her eyebrow. Did you take a test? I said. Yes, she said, but I'd like a second opinion. All right, then, I said, looking at her. You're pregnant, I said, and she laughed. I wasn't kidding, though. She looked much too thin, but she was definitely pregnant — I can see it a mile away. I see women on the street who probably don't even know they're pregnant yet, themselves.

Are you sure? she said, her voice gone wispy. Yes, but I'd like a second opinion, as well, I said, grabbing her chart. Then I asked about her dream job, and she said it was dreamy, except for the fact that she had a real nightmare of a boss. She said, Pardon my French, Dr. Myers, but the woman gives *cunt* new meaning.

I finished my note before looking up, and then I said, You know what I love about you, Lisa? Well, at least *someone* cares, she said. Lie back, I said, and she laid back. What? she said. Relax your legs, I said. Let's have it already, what do you love about me, Dr. Myers? You don't pull any punches. Anyhow, where is it you're working now? Which gallery? I asked, taking a seat in front of her, and she said, Joyce Kessler — the Joyce Kessler Gallery. Oh, I said, my heart missing a beat; I'd never seen her there, but I went to the gallery about as often as Joyce came to my office. As Joyce said, Openings aren't my scene. If Joyce really wanted me to see something, she'd take me when the place was closed.

I've heard of it, I said. Oh, yeah? What did you hear? she said, and I said, It's one of the best, right? She started laughing, and I said, What's so funny? I knew better than to ask, but I did. My boyfriend, Greg, she said, and I nodded. He's the brilliant painter? I asked. No, she said, he was the brilliant painter, but anyhow. Greg always says, Joyce Kessler wouldn't know a work of art if it fucked her up the ass. Personally, I'm not so sure that would make any difference, she said, looking down at me, her face foreshortened by the exam table.

I'm sorry, she said, but honestly, she has other people do all the work for her — her only talent is knowing who to hire. Well, she hired you, I said. Like they say, she said, you can't rape the willing, right? She just uses me, she said, but one day . . . one day, I'll use her back. One day, I'll open my own gallery, and when I do . . . I'm going to put her out of business, she said, sighing, staring at the ceiling.

For a moment, I felt . . . I felt sickened, defensive, angry, and — fearful. Strangely fearful, yes, as though my own judgment . . . I don't know. Well, look on the bright side, I said. Which is? she said. You came to New York to make a name for yourself, and —. And here I am, she said. Yes. Deep breath, please, I said, waiting for her to inhale.

Lisa

WHEN I GOT THERE, I saw Jordan, sitting in the waiting room, and I sat down beside her, and then, seeing me, she started crying. I asked her what was wrong. I said, What happened, baby? And she just kept saying, He's going to kill me, he is — he's going to kill me when he sees what I did! Jordan, he's not going to kill you: I promise. And if he does, I'll kill him. Okay? I said, and she nodded.

Okay, then. Now, let's go find your scratched car, I said, teasing her, and then she started bawling all over again. Come on, let's go, I said, helping her stand. What about Mom? she said, and I'd almost forgotten.

I told Jordan to stay put, and then I walked to the reception desk to ask what was taking so long for them to release Lynne. The receptionist said, Your sister will be right out — we had to give her something to calm her down. To calm her down? I said. She was very upset, the nurse said, and I was like, yeah, well, I'm very upset, are you going to give me something, too? Is Dr. Myers available? I asked, and she said, No. Just no.

A few minutes later, Lynne came out, practically blinded by the fluorescent light, and I said, Lynne? *Lisa?* she gasped. Oh, Lisa, I'm so sorry you had to come — I never meant for this to happen, for any of this. Jordan, I said, handing Lynne over, I'm going to get the car. Can you stay here with your mom? She nodded. That's my girl, I said, knuckling her chin, smoothing her hair.

Adela

MICHAEL WAS ON THE PHONE when I finally got in the shower, and he was still on the phone when I got out. And he promised we'd have some time together on Friday. So when I got out of the shower, hearing him talking in the next room, I put on the plush hotel robe and walked into the bedroom, whispering, Duh *nuh-nuuh* . . . duh *nut-nuh-nuh* . . . He shook his head no, but I just kept going, shimmying my shoulders, removing the belt, singing: Duh *nuh!* Duh *nuh!*

Yeah, yeah, yeah . . . listen, I'm sorry I haven't had a chance to call you back, I just got into Palm Springs, Joyce, he said, and I winced, gritting my teeth — oops — pulling the robe back over my shoulders and retying the belt around my waist. Then he shook his head again; rolling his index finger, telling me to continue. I flipped him off and walked back to the bathroom, sat down on the toilet, and thought about showering again.

Lisa

SO I GET THE CAR; I get the two of them in the car; I make sure Jordan's sedated and comfortable in the back, but Lynne won't shut up. Not just that, by the time we get on the road, she's on the downward spiral: she's sobbing, going on and on about what a terrible sister she's been to me and how much guilt she had, leaving me alone like that. It was her jealousy.

I swear that's what she said. She goes, I was so jealous of you because you were always Daddy's favorite —. Lynne, I said, he loved us both, and she said, No, he didn't love anyone like he loved you — not me, not Mommy —. Lynne, please. It's true, Lisa, it's true! I was so jealous of you, because you were the only thing Daddy cared about!

I said, Lynne, do me a favor, *don't* — don't call him that. What? she said, scared. Please, Lynne, you're forty-five years old, don't call him Daddy, okay? I'm sorry, but that word makes my skin crawl. Then she nodded; she had the most agonized look on her face, nodding, trying to muffle the sob at the back of her throat. Go on, I said, returning my attention to the road. You were saying? I said. No mercy:

I showed her no mercy. I waited thirty-six years for this day to come, and I was going to enjoy every last second of it, too.

Lisa, did Daddy — Dad — did Dad . . . I said, Did Dad what, Lynne? I'm sorry . . . I'm so, so sorry, Lisa, but I have to know. I have to know the truth: did Dad ever touch you? she said. *What?* I said, looking at her. She said, Did he ever touch you? Did he ever —. Lynne, what are you saying? I'm saying, did he ever . . . did he ever rub himself against you, or —. Are you out of your mind? Lynne, are you out of your fucking mind? I hissed, trying to keep my voice down. Of course he didn't touch me. He would never do that — he could never do that, I said, pulling over.

I was sure I misunderstood, that she'd tell me I misunderstood. What are you saying? I said, feeling the blood surge through my cheeks, my ears. Lynne, are you actually asking me if I was sexually abused by our father? I said, Honestly, what — what is this about? She didn't answer, and I waited. I said, What is this *about,* Lynne? What are you trying to say?

He never penetrated me, she said, staring straight ahead, and I almost gagged, reaching for my throat. Lynne, please — stop talking, okay. You don't know what you're saying; you've been tripping all night, and —. He'd come into my room and tell me to go downstairs and wait for him in his office, she said, and then he'd let me sit there for hours, waiting, knowing he was coming . . . I'm not listening to this: stop, I said, checking the rearview, making sure Jordan was still asleep.

She said, Then, when he finally came in, he'd lean me over the chair in his study, and rub his dick against my butt. And he'd rub and rub until I'd feel this damp spot on my butt, she said, staring straight ahead. And then I finally turned the car off, thinking I was going to be sick. But he never touched me, she said, looking at me: I mean he never fingered me, never made me jerk him off —. *Stop it!* I said, grabbing her wrist, yelling at her through clenched teeth. That's all, she said.

That's all? I said. You know what, Lynne? I'm sorry, but you're coming off some bad turn in this life-changing trip of yours, and you don't know your asshole from the moon. You've been hallucinating

298

for the past twelve hours, and that's all it is, I said. No, she said, completely calm: no, I'm not lying. Well, I don't believe a word of it, I said. I knew you wouldn't, she said. I've always known . . .

Let me ask you something, okay? If that's true — if there were any way that could possibly be true — why did he single you out, Lynne? Because our father never *ever* touched me in any way that was inappropriate. So why you, Lynne? Why, because he loved you more? Because you were prettier, what? I don't . . . I don't know why, really — I've never understood why, she said, starting to cry again. He said it was because I was messy, and my room was messy . . .

I couldn't look at her. I know my father, I said. I know my dad a hell of a lot better than you do or ever will, and he is *not* capable of doing something like that, I said. Lisa . . . have I ever lied to you? she said. I mean, I know I didn't tell you the real reason I needed a referral, but other than that, have I ever lied to you? I said, Lynne, honestly, I don't care, one way or another. But I think your life's been falling apart for a long time, and you've spent so much effort trying to hide the fact, now you finally see what's been going on.

And I feel sorry for you, Lynne, I really do, I said. But don't *ever* say that to me again, because if you do, it will be the last time we speak, understand? Do you understand me? I said, and she said, Yes. I swallowed, hard as I could, and then I pulled back on the road.

Lynne

WHEN I WENT DOWNSTAIRS, Friday night, I heard them talking — Don and Lance and Lisa, they were talking about me, and I'd had enough. Ask me what? I said, walking into the dining room. Hey, Don said, trying to hide his surprise, what are you doing up? Hey, Lisa said, as I took a seat at the table, across from her. You want some pizza? Don said. You should eat something, Lisa said. Maybe later, I said, looking at her. What did you want to ask me?

I thought, *Say it, Lisa — go on — here's your golden opportunity. I'll even make you a deal: if you ask, I'll tell the truth.* She stared back at me, and then she said, Feeling better? I almost said it, too, I almost said, What happened to you? The Lisa I used to know would've just nailed me, but you? Tired, I said. Don told Lance to get me a plate, and suddenly I wanted to cry, thinking, *This is my family?*

But even then, I kept trying to bait her, practically cocking my chin, daring her to take a swing, begging her to put me out of my misery. Lisa, I said, would you prefer to sleep in the guest bedroom or on the couch? Why wouldn't I want to sleep in the guest bedroom? she said. Because I hate that room, I said, and she laughed, hearing me criticize my own home for once. Why? she said, and I said, It reminds me of Daddy's office. No, I'm sure the guest room will be perfectly cozy, she said, smiling, staring right back at me.

No: her answer was no. For once in her life, Lisa didn't swing. And the truth is that I've never been so disappointed in her. But less than an hour later, I was in my studio, wrapping Lisa's gift. And I have to say, it calmed me down, stitching; it felt like the only thing that I know how to do right anymore. When I finished, I sat there looking at the flowers I'd sewn, making sure there were no loose threads, wondering what Lisa would think when I gave it to her, of all the things she will never say to my face. And vice versa.

Jordan

THE FIRST WEEK of October, my parents had to go to this wedding in Pennsylvania, so I invited Misha in, after work, and I gave him the official tour. This is some place, he said, whistling, as we went back downstairs. Then he goes, Your folks give you the lecture about throwing parties while they're away? And I was like, Oh, right. What am I going to do? Microwave a pizza, drink a six-pack of Diet Coke, and watch cable until three in the morning? I was just like, woo-hoo, you know.

So we went into the kitchen and I offered him a beer, and he said no, so I drank one, and he said he should probably be going, and I was just like, Why? And he goes, It's getting late, you know, and I was like, Misha, we always hang out late on Friday night, what's the difference? And he goes, Because your parents aren't home, and I was like, What, you want to hang out in the car?

So he was like, he goes, Half an hour, and I said, Fine. You sure you don't want a beer? And he said, I'm cool, and I just shrugged, like, okay then, and I turned on the TV. I mean, we were just sitting on the couch, and then I starting surfing channels, and then I stopped on *I Love New York*, and he goes, Let me have that, and I was like, No, and we started wrestling for the remote, and then . . . I don't know. It's like we just started kissing or whatever. It's like one thing led to another — and it wasn't my first time — but anyhow.

We fell asleep on the couch, and then sometime around four or five he woke up, and then he just started freaking out, like, Oh, shit! Oh, fuck. *Fuck, fuck, fuck,* and then he started fumbling for his clothes, and he was like, I have to go. I mean, he wasn't even talking to me, really, like he just kept saying, I have to get home. Ah, *shit.* And then he grabbed his keys off the coffee table and he was like, I'll call you, all right? And I was just like, It's fine, go on, trying to act cool with it, you know. Honestly, I didn't know what I felt, but it wasn't like sex at all — I mean, it wasn't fun, it wasn't sexy — and I thought . . . I just thought maybe if we had sex, I'd stop feeling so needy on the inside, but I didn't. It was just more of the same, really.

Lisa

IT BROKE MY HEART to see that vacant look in her eyes, so I sat down on the side of her bed, and I said, Why didn't you call me? I would've gone with you —. Because, she said. Because why? I said, and she shrugged. Why didn't you tell me, Jordan? Because you're the only person who ever believed in me, she said, swallowing back the tears.

Jordan, I said. Even if that *were* true — which it's not — but even if that were true, what? Did you think that would change if I found out you got *pregnant*? She nodded yes, and then she began sobbing. Shhh, I said, shhh . . . what else? What aren't you telling me? I said, but she kept shaking her head. Oh — don't even try to pull one over on me, I said, you're talking to the pro here, you know?

Listen, I said, I want you to think about something, okay? What if you came down and stayed with me for a while? I could talk to your parents — your mom, I said. No, she said, taking the Kleenex and blowing her nose. Another? I asked, and she nodded. Well, don't say no before you think about it at least, all right? We have plenty of room, you know. No, I don't want Will to know, she said, starting to cry again, afraid I'd tell him. I said, Jordan, Will doesn't know — Will doesn't have to know anything. Trust me, there's plenty I don't tell the guy.

What about this afternoon? she said. I told him your mother was in town and she'd gotten sick, some kind of medical emergency. I didn't say anything about you —. You swear? she said. I *swear*, Jordan. Will doesn't know. And trust me, even if he did, he's no one to point fingers, okay? Look, I said, you don't have to stay with me if you don't want, but don't ever say you had no other options.

Well, I'm not going back to school, she said, almost defiantly. Then don't go, I said. Just like that? she said, laughing, hearing me agree with her. Jordan, you're the one who just told me you weren't going, I said, almost laughing. No, I have to, she said. No, you don't *have* to, I said. That's the hard part, see: you don't have to do anything. You know I fucking hated high school. I hated high school so much that my skin still crawls every time I think about it. So don't go, I say. Drop out, get your GED, and look into taking classes at a community college instead. Of course she started shaking her head. I'm not that brave, she said. Well, maybe not, I said. But you're obviously crazy enough.

I meant it as a joke, of course, but it just made her break down crying all over again. Jordan, come on, I said, pulling her over, so she could rest her head on my lap. Honestly, why didn't you tell me, Jordan? I said, stroking her hair. I didn't tell anyone, she said. I didn't want it to happen — I just . . . I just didn't care if it did. I didn't think it would happen, but if it did, what did it matter, you know? I wanted him to want me, and he just felt sorry for me — it was so pathetic, she said, biting her lip.

Jordan, I said, do you think you're the first girl to get pregnant, trying to force the issue, not even knowing what the issue is? Well, you aren't. I just hope you don't do it again, that's all. But if you do, call me next time, huh? She sat up to blow her nose again, and then she took a big breath, slowly exhaling. She'd calmed down. Of course she had a lot more crying to do, but not with me there.

You should get some sleep, I said, and she nodded, staring at her mushy Kleenex. You're going to see Grandpa? she said. Let's not talk about that right now, I said, stiffening. What happened? I heard you yell at Mom in the car, she said. Your mother's out of her mind, you know that? I'm beginning to think everyone in this house is out of their mind, I said. Yeah, well, you know what she did? Jordan said, starting to laugh. No, but I can tell this is going to be good, I said, sitting down again.

This morning — she came into my room at like five this morning, and she sat down on the side of my bed, like right where you're sitting, and she starts tapping my shoulder, saying, Jordan, wake up. And when I opened my eyes, she was sitting there, wearing a pair of underwear and nothing else. Ohmygod, I said, laughing, and Jordan said, *Right?* What did she want? I said, and Jordan almost squealed: She wanted to *dance* — she said she wanted me to dance with her. I mean, have you ever seen my mother dance? she said, laughing.

I said, Jordan, I want you to call me Monday, all right? I'll leave my cell phone on — anytime, night or day, all right? And she nodded. Okay? I said, and she smiled, looking up. Don't just nod your head —. Yes, she said. All right, I said. I love you, baby. I love you, too, she said. When I closed the door, Lynne was standing at the top of the staircase. I froze, expecting her to say something, but she just looked at me . . . Then she said, Good night, Lisa, walking to her bedroom. Good night, I said, heading downstairs.

I waited until we got in the car the next morning to say anything. In fact, I waited until we got to the senior citizens home to say a word to her. We never have anything to say to each other, and for once, I didn't care to pretend otherwise. As soon as she cut the ignition, I said, Honestly, Lynne, I'm more than happy to visit Dad, but all things considered, I really don't need you reprimanding me in front of your husband and son.

Seeing as you've only been to visit once this year, she said. Lynne, I said, I shouldn't have to explain this to you, of all people, but I have a baby —. Oh, Jesus, Lisa, don't give me that, like you're the first woman in the world to have a baby, spare me, please. And for the last

time, she said, just because I live here doesn't mean he's my responsi-
bility. He's your father, too, isn't he?

I ignored the comment. Fine, I said, let me speak to Will, and I'll
let you know by Monday if I can look after him at Thanksgiving or
Christmas, all right? Is that acceptable to you? Yes, Lisa, that would
be acceptable — if you actually do as you say for once, she said, opening the door and getting out of the car. I just sat there, watching her,
thinking, *Thank God . . . thank God I'm not you.*

Lynne

I LEFT THE TWO of them alone while I went to speak to the nurse
at the front desk. They'd changed his medications again, and Daddy
had been complaining all week. The sad thing is that this is the closest we've ever been, but that's all we have to talk about, really, his ail-
ments. Sometimes, even now, when I walk into his room, I expect
him to look up and smile, say a kind word, like, what a pretty dress,
or don't you look nice today . . . but he never does. I try to forgive
him for that, every time, I really do. Just like I try to reconcile the
abusive drunk I knew growing up, and the helpless old man he is
now . . . but I can't.

I knocked before I went back in. Lisa was sitting in a chair, across
the room, and if I didn't know any better, I'd almost say she looked
relieved, seeing me return. Then Daddy said, What did she say?
Daddy, I said, we have to give it some time — you know there are always side effects, I said, and he said, Not that — my shirt, what did
she say about my shirt? Lisa looked alarmed; he gets upset very easily
and starts crying over the smallest thing, really. She said they're looking everywhere, I said. Oh, what's the use, he said, angrily shooing
the air and turning back to Lisa, like I'd failed him again. *Time,* said a
voice in my head, and that was it.

I walked over and kneeled down beside him, looked him in the
eye, and I said, Daddy, do you remember when I was a little girl, and
you used to call me upstairs? He just looked at me, waiting. Do you
remember? I said. When I was a little girl, you used to call me to my

bedroom, and you'd say, I told you to clean up your room. And I'd say, I did, Daddy. I did clean my room. And you'd say, You call this *clean*? Lynne, Lisa said, but I ignored her. No, listen to me, I said, putting my hand on his. Then you'd take my toy box and you'd turn it upside down. You'd dump my toys all over the floor —. *Lynne,* Lisa said, stop. Well, he said, if I lost my temper with you sometimes, I'm sorry —. I said, You're sorry?

I almost smiled, hearing that, and I said, Daddy . . . frankly, I don't give a *flying fuck* about your half-assed sorrys. Sorry only *means* something to me if you can remember what you did —. I can't believe you're going to do this, Lisa said, standing, but I just continued. When I was five, six years old, no higher than this, I said, raising my hand to his eye level, measuring, you used to lean me over the chair at your desk, and then you'd rub against me, you remember that? And then one day, you dropped your pants. Do you remember now? I said, leaning over him, squeezing both his hands in my own, and he looked scared of me — *of me*. Let go of him, Lynne. *Let go,* Lisa said, taking my arm in her hand.

No! I said, jerking my arm back. You don't have to believe me, but I'm not lying! He used to bend me over the chair, and I can describe every knick on that chair, right down to the burn mark where Daddy must've dropped a match, lighting a cigarette at his desk once. He used to lean me over that chair, dry humping me, and the whole time — the whole time, he'd keep saying, Naughty girl . . . oh, such a naughty girl, aren't you? Lisa, he has a beauty mark on his penis, toward the top —. That doesn't prove anything; you might've —. Seen it, changing his diapers? You don't believe me, check for yourself, I said, turning around, and then she grabbed my arm, pulling me away from him. *Stop it!* she screamed.

I said, You know he used to drink until he'd black out — like you, Lisa. He'd get drunk and call me into my room to scold me, and then he'd say, Wait for me in my office, sending me downstairs. Then he'd let me sit there, waiting and waiting . . . Show me your bottom — remember that, Daddy? Do you remember how you'd say, Show me your naughty bottom, and I would? I'd stand there, with my underpants pulled to my knees, sobbing, but he didn't care. No, he'd drop his pants, and he'd press his dick against me, saying, You're a naughty girl . . . oh, you're such a naughty girl — say it, say what a naughty girl you are. He wouldn't stop until I said it, either, so I'd say it. I'd say, I'm a naughty girl, Daddy. I'm a *dirty, naughty girl.* Then she slapped me.

It cracked through the room, the sound of her hand against my cheek, but I didn't feel it — I mean, I saw her hand, but I didn't feel the slap. I almost wished she'd do it again, but Lisa just stood there, silently panting. Are you proud of yourself? she asked, nostrils flaring. I said, No, Lisa. No, I'm as ashamed of myself now as I was then. And the worst part is that for the past eight years, I've looked at that man and smiled and wiped the tomato soup off his chin, where his face was paralyzed by his stroke, and I've smiled, every day. I never stood up to him, and I should have, and I know that. But don't tell me I'm lying, because you weren't there. You weren't even born yet, Lisa, you . . . you were their second chance; their clean slate: *you,* I said, almost laughing. She hadn't lowered her hand, and it looked like she might slap me again, then she turned and walked out in a fury.

I stood there, watching, while she tried slamming the door behind her, but the doors in the nursing home don't slam — they're hydraulic. I hate to say it, but she didn't visit often enough to know that. After a minute, Daddy finally spoke, Lynne? Yes? I said, keeping my back turned, so he wouldn't see me on the verge of tears. Where . . . where's she going? he asked, and I started laughing — I couldn't help myself. Honestly, I think that was the funniest damn thing I'd ever heard the man say. So I sat down on his bed, on the crocheted afghan my mother made thirty years ago, and I laughed and laughed, until I started sobbing.

The whole time, my father sat in his chair watching me, silent. And the way he looked at me, he looked so frail, so confused by everything that had just happened, all I could do was sigh. Then I got up to grab a Kleenex. I don't know where she's going, I said, blowing my nose. You'll have to ask her when she comes back, I said, sitting down, the two of us staring at the door.

Lisa

HE'S A GOOD MAN. He's—he's, he's kind and generous and he would never do such a thing, no. She's out of her mind—she's out of her fucking mind, that's all there is to it. I mean, if it's true, why didn't she say something sooner? Like when he still had his wits about him? I mean, now . . . now she can say whatever she wants, and there's nothing he can do to defend himself. Which is just so—that's just so *cowardly*. But that's Lynne. That's just Lynne.

I went to the end of the hall, turned, and took a seat in the dining room. Nine thirty in the morning and the place was empty, sad. There was nothing wrong with it, really, but it looked like a cheaply remodeled visitor's lounge, with bland beige hotel-hallway wallpaper, bloodred carpeting with gold hexagons, and tables standing at wheelchair height. There were various large-print newspapers on the bookshelves, and I thought, *So this is where you come to read before you die.*

I took a seat at a table near the windows, but my ears were ringing; I could still hear her, talking in the car, saying, You, you had *such fire* . . . I didn't think anything could stop you—. Lynne, I said, enough. No more talking, all right? And she said, I'm sorry, Lisa. I'm so sorry . . . And then she told me that he'd sexually abused her . . . My father.

I thought I was going to be sick. It was the most disgusting, evil, *evil* thing I could imagine. How could she . . . how could she say such a thing? Why? *What have you done, Lynne?* I thought, hiding my face in my hands, and then a voice said, Ms. Barrett? It took me a moment to realize she was speaking to me, and then I looked up to find a nurse standing in the door. Your sister's looking for you, she said. Thank you, I said, and she turned to walk away.

Excuse me? I said, and she stopped. My father lost a shirt, I said, a Mets shirt? A what's shirt? she said. I Still Believe, I said, running my finger across my chest. Oh, yeah, his shirt, she said. He said it's missing, I said. I don't know anything about that, she said, but I'll ask around. Thank you, I'll be right there, I said, I just needed some air.

Then what are you doing in here? she asked, and I had to smile, nodding, yeah, well . . .

She comes here to visit him every day. She sits with him. Reads to him. Talks to him — every fucking day. Who knows, maybe it gets easier, but I couldn't see how. And then, getting up from the table, I heard that old familiar voice; the voice that said, *Run!* Run away! But I can't. I can't run anymore. I have a child now: I have to go home.

Funny, one day, you wake up and . . . you wake up. The day you finally realize all those dreams, all that ambition, and in the end, you're just another person trying to keep it together, and that you aren't so special after all. And I don't know if that's a sign of defeat or maturity, really. I guess that remains to be decided.

Joyce

I SAID, Listen, Del. What you need is an older man, someone who knows how to treat you right, and Dela said, Yeah, well, if you're so hot for Paul, why didn't you go out with him yourself? Because he's not my type, I said. Which is what, exactly? Bobbie said, looking up, smiling, and I said, Talk, dark, and cocksucking, apparently.

Speaking of. Did you talk to Michael? Bobbie asked. Oh, I said, *I* talked all right. And? she said. And he was very polite, I said. Polite? she laughed. Precisely, I said, pointing my finger at her. Which can only mean one thing: he had some little chippie in the room with him, and he was trying to show her what a great guy he is, and how well he behaves, even after the fact. Yeah, I said, that's Michael, all right, a real stand-up guy —. I have to go, Dela said, pushing back her chair. I said, What's the rush, baby? But she didn't answer me.

She doesn't talk to me anymore. I don't know why — I don't know what I said or did. I try calling her, and she doesn't return my calls. And I'm sorry . . . whatever it was, tell me. Let me apologize. Because I miss you: and you're my girl. Bye, she said, giving me a peck on the cheek.

Well, anyhow. Bobbie wanted me to go shopping with her, but I couldn't. I told her I had friends in town and I needed to run some errands before dinner, which was true. So I made the rounds, and when I got home, I sat down on the couch, and I removed an envelope, overflowing with pamphlets and literature.

Let's see, I had Apple, iPod, Samsung, Sony, Treo, BlackBerry, Bang & Olufsen, Nikon, Leica: you name it, I got it. That's right, Benjamin, all this could be yours, but first. *First,* you gotta show me the cojones, I said, talking to the room. That's right, son, show me. Show me, I said, then screaming at the top of my lungs: *Show me the cojones!* Ah, man. I started laughing so hard that I fell back on the couch.

Shit, I said, checking my watch. I have to get moving; I'm going to be late.

Adela

HOW'S JOYCE? he said, closing his laptop. She sends her regards, I said, removing my coat and kicking off my shoes. Regards, my ass, he said. For starters, I said. Yeah, yeah, yeah, he said, giving me that look. Adela? he said, and I said, *I know.* I'm not convinced, he said. Look, I thought I was going to have some time alone with my mom, but I didn't, and I just . . . I just want her to be happy, okay? Just for a few days — is that so much to ask? I said, and he looked at me, still unconvinced.

I'm going to tell her about us — I am, I said. What are you going to tell her? he said. I don't know, I whined, that's the problem. Well, he said, how about: Please don't kill me? She's going to kill *both* of us, you know, I said. Yes, I realize that: by me, I meant don't kill *me,* he said. You really are a selfish bastard, I said, kneeling on the bed, reaching for the pillow so I could hit him. I never said otherwise, he said, raising his hands and ducking.

He grabbed my wrist, and I pulled away, steadying myself. Then I got up and ran to the bathroom, but I didn't make it to the toilet in time. I puked right on the tile floor. I heard Michael get up, following me. Still? he said. Yes, still, I said, it's not the fucking flu, you know. And then I started crying — waterworks, out of nowhere. I just felt so disgusting, in every possible way. I'm sorry, he said, stepping around the puddle of bile. Come lie down, he said, leading me back to bed. He got me a bottle of water, and then I passed out.

When I woke, it was almost five o'clock, and I still felt exhausted. God, I'm just so *tired* all the time. I could hear Michael on the phone; then I got up and walked into the other room. Yeah, yeah, yeah, he said, smiling at me, as I hiked my thumb at the bathroom, heading to the shower. When I walked in, I turned on the light, and the floor was spotless.

I just smiled, nodding at the tile, because he'd cleaned up my mess, and because he's always thinking of me. I mean, he loves me — I know it, I feel it — so why . . . why do I still feel so alone when I'm with him? I don't know. I honestly don't know. So I turned on the water and stood beneath the showerhead, hiding my face in my hands, thinking, *What's wrong with me?*

Lynne

WHEN I WOKE UP, Saturday afternoon, I couldn't believe how long I'd slept — it was almost four when I opened my eyes. An hour later, I heard the garage door, and then Don walked into the kitchen and said, Get some sleep? A little, thanks, I said, grabbing his arm for some reason. Where were you? At the shop, he said. I had Lance follow me in your car. I spoke to Bill and he's going to work on it —. Go back, I said.

Don't worry, Don said. Bill said it'll be ready by Monday afternoon —. Go back, I said. Go back and get the car — it's *my* car, Don. I was just trying to help, he said, holding up his hands. I didn't want Jordan to see it, and —. I said, She's already seen it, Don, I said go back. *Go back and get the car,* I said, almost shouting at him.

He looked at me, angry, confused. I said, Don, we . . . we can't do this anymore. Really, I don't want him to fix the scratch, okay? Leave it be — it's just a scratch. Okay, he said, all right. I said, God, I'm just so tired . . . I'm *so tired* of the lying and the hiding and this perfect fucking house, I said, swirling my hand in the air. I can't do this anymore, I'm sorry, I said. He didn't say anything, and then, finally, he nodded and said, I'll go get the car. Thank you, I said, walking out, heading for my studio, and closing the door.

She didn't believe me — Lisa. I can't say that I blame her, but then again, I do. Because I told the truth: because I think she knows I'm telling the truth, but she still won't believe me. And I don't know why he chose me, really. All I know is that my mother walked in one day, by accident — she didn't think he was home, and then she walked into his office, looking for something, while he had his pants down, rubbing against me . . . She just stood there, frozen, and then she said, Oh. I'm sorry — I'll never forget her voice — I'm sorry, she said, then she turned around and walked out the door. She just left me there.

You're sorry? I'm your *daughter,* you're supposed to protect me. She never said a word about it, either. No, my mother never said anything; never did anything — like it never happened. Then, one day, she called me into her room and closed the door behind me. She told me to sit down, and I almost started crying; I didn't even know why . . . trouble. That's all I could think, staring at my hands, so ashamed . . .

Then she knelt down and told me I was going to have a little sister or brother. I didn't say anything, staring at my hands, and then she asked me if I was happy . . . I don't remember what I said. I can't remember anything after that: the memory stops there.

Joyce

So I WALK into the lobby, and who do I see but Adela. Well, well, I said, sneaking up behind her: What's a girl like you doing in a place like this? And then, just as she turns and this look of horror comes over her face, who do I see, turning away from the front desk, but . . . Michael. I said, Michael, what are you . . . I didn't finish the question, looking at him, and then I looked at Adela — and I believed, I believed in her until the last second, then I knew. But here's the best part: you know what he says? Michael looks at me, dumbfounded, and he says, Oh, Joyce . . . there you are.

I took a huge step back, and then he just started burying the two of them alive. Well, what a coincidence — look who I ran into, he says, and I just looked at them. Will you excuse me? I said, turning and walking out. By the time I came to, I turned around and glared through the front door, at the spot where he'd been standing, but they'd gone. Then Betsy and Joe stepped off the elevator.

An hour later, I had to leave the restaurant. I'd ordered the filet mignon, and for a moment, looking at the blood on my plate, I thought I was going to be sick. Joe got up and helped me to the car, and then it all came back to me; sitting there, on the plane home from L.A., staring out my window at a sea of clouds that looked so picturesque, it was nauseating. Like one of those sappy stock photos plastered on the front of religious pamphlets I used to find discarded on the subway, with some infuriating verse of scripture, claiming that you are not alone in this world, when, at that moment, I sure as hell was alone.

Even so, I tried — I tried believing in something, anything. For once, I even tried praying — I mean, I closed my eyes, and I told the truth. I said, I'm alone, and I'm scared, and I don't know what to do, and I'm asking for help. Isn't that what you do — that's the gist of it, right? Okay, then, I'm asking, what do I do? Just tell me what to do . . . No answer, nothing but the sound of jet engines ringing in my ears.

Then the driver changed the station, tuning in one of those ridiculously peppy Latino dance-hall polka numbers, and I thought of Michael and Adela again; the sight of her bare back, and the drapes of her dress, and the look in her eyes, seeing me. You know, whether he's screwing her or not, I don't care. Because she's the closest thing I've ever had to a daughter, and he should know better: they *both* should know better. And they do — they do know better — that's what kills me. They do know: they just don't care.

Then I thought, *No, actually . . . I did the right thing; I made the right choice. In fact, I'm just sorry I can't do it all over again. Because I'd lay back and enjoy it this time.* And for the first time in years, I had half a mind to call and tell Michael what I'd done. Not because he deserved the truth: just to fuck with him, of course. Fair is fair.

So I checked my messages in the car, and there were two messages from Bobbie, and I thought, *Wait, does she know about this? Does she know about the two of them? Would she hide that from me?* I didn't know — I didn't know anything except that I was suddenly furious with her, too, as if she was in on it or, or I don't know what — I was just so furious with everyone, everything. So by the time I walked through my front door, I had to talk to someone, and in my stupor, I dialed Sonja.

What — what can I say? Just once in my life, I wanted to tell her that I needed her: I wanted to say, Mom, I need you. That's it: that's all I want. Let me say I need you — let, just let me say *I need,* period, and your job is done, okay? But then, when she answered, I froze. She kept saying, Hello? Hello? And then I hung up on her. It was all I could do to get up, pop two, three Xanax, and down a glass of bourbon before I crawled into bed and passed out. Deep, black sleep . . . Bliss.

Jordan

OKAY, BUT WHY are guys so fucking retarded? I mean, seriously, Lance pokes his head in my door, before he went out Saturday night — oh, *right,* like he ever checks on me. He goes, Hey, what're you doing? And I'm just like, what's it look like I'm doing, you know? Nothing, I said, staring at the television.

Toph's having a party, he said, wanna come? I was like, *No.* That guy's such a fucking dick, and Lance was just like, He's all right —. To *you,* maybe, I said, and he goes, We don't have to stay long. And I was just like, thanks, but I'd rather stare at the wall, you know. And he goes, Come on, it'll do you good to get out of the house, and I go, Lance, I said no, okay? And he goes, Suit yourself, then, and I was just like, whatever.

I mean, why not just say you're sorry you've been such an asshole to me for like the past three years, you know? I mean, seriously. But then he turned back, and he goes, Hey, Jordan? What? I said, wishing he would just leave me alone, already. Love you. That's what he said — he goes, Love you, in this sheepish voice, and I just looked at him. I didn't want to forgive him for being such a jerk for half my life, but I did. I said, I love you, too, and he closed the door.

Bobbie

WHEN MY PHONE RANG Saturday night, my heart stopped. I checked the number, preparing my apology, but it wasn't Paul; it was Adela. I answered, but she was so hysterical, I couldn't understand her, and I had to keep telling her to slow down. Slow down, baby, I can't understand you, I said. Take a breath, and tell me what's happened.

You're never, you're never going to speak to me again — you're never going to speak to me again, she said, sobbing. I said, Del, what are you talking about? Then she told me. She said she was with Michael. With Michael? I said, Michael *who*, Adela? Michael Petrucci, she said, and I said, *When?* When were you with him? Now, she whined, just now. Now? I said, I don't understand —. I've been seeing Michael, she said, and I said, What do you mean *seeing*? And then I stopped.

I had a terrible feeling, but I asked anyway. Why are you telling me this now? I said, trying to stay calm. Because Joyce saw us, she said. We just ran into her, and —. Joyce saw you together? I said. Yes, she said, starting to cry. I was shocked.

Mom? Mom? she said, but I couldn't answer, I couldn't stop shaking my head. I'm pregnant, she said, and I felt . . . I just sat there, staring at — staring . . . This, I said, this is . . . I know, she said, but let me explain, and I said, *You know?* No, you don't know. If you knew, I said. How could you? I'm sorry, she said, *I'm so sorry.* Adela, I can't — I can't talk about this right now, it's just too much. I'm sorry, I said, but I need some time, and then I told her I'd call her later, when I had a chance to calm down. Soon as we hung up — five minutes later, at most — I called Joyce, but she didn't answer.

I don't know how long I sat there, before I stood and then I had to sit down again. Shock. Then I picked up the phone and dialed Paul — I wanted to tell him how sorry I was for my behavior on

Thursday night, and to ask him to come over. Even just to say the words, I need you — I need my friend . . . But then I hung up.

Lynne

I TRIED TALKING to her Saturday, when I went in to say good night. I knocked on her door, and when she answered, I went in and sat on the side of her bed. She was lying sideways in bed, watching TV. I said, Can I get you anything? No, thanks, she said. Jordan, I'm sorry they had to call Lisa, I said. I'm not, she said, or Dad would've had to pick us up. I know, I said, I just want you to know how sorry I am.

What were you on, anyway? she said, looking completely disinterested. I don't know, I said. What do you mean you don't know? she said. I mean I found some pills, and I took them, and I'm not sure what they were, I said. Oh, that was smart, she said, holding the remote in the air, changing channels, and I waited for her to tell me what a bad mother I was, what a fuckup . . . I thought, *Say it, so I can stop saying it to myself.*

Am I supposed to say something? she said, looking at me for a moment before she returned to the television. No . . . no, I just wanted to talk to you about something —. He didn't call, if that's what you're talking about, she said, shaking her head at me. He hasn't called me. But if you want to tell me it's because he doesn't care about me, I'm not listening — I'm just not listening anymore, she said. *Anymore?* I said — it just slipped past my lips, and I couldn't help laughing — but she just rolled her eyes at me.

Jordan, that wasn't what I wanted to talk to you about, I said. But it was too late; I'd already set her off. You know, she said, it must be *amazing,* living in a world where love means you never screw up. Isn't that what love means to you, Mom? she asked, but she didn't give me a chance to answer. Doesn't matter, she said, I know why he's not calling. Why is that? I said, so relieved the moment had finally come.

She looked at me . . . not glaring, really, but not — just not liking me. She had this look on her face that made it so clear she just doesn't like me, and then she said: Because he doesn't know how, that's why.

It doesn't mean he doesn't care about me, it just means — god, Mom, it just means he doesn't know any better than the way he's behaving . . . Anyhow, I don't care what you think, he's still my friend. I mean, seriously, is everything always so black and white? No, I said. No, Jordan, it's not. Whatever, she said, rolling over, turning her back to me.

Bobbie

I DON'T THINK about Michael, as a rule. Because there's no point — I just get angry, and there's no point. What's done is done. But despite everything, I still remember those moments. I remember the time we were sitting in the living room, polishing off a third bottle of wine, and Michael said, Hey, Joyce? Hey, Joycie, is he awake? he called over his shoulder, flipping through some records.

Oh, he's awake, all right, she said, reemerging with the baby on her hip. Wide awake, she said, and baby wants to party. Like father, like son, Michael said, giving her a randy wink and quietly growling before putting the album on. Well, that answers that question, Joyce said, sitting down beside me on the couch. Which is? he said. Why God gave me two tits, instead of one, she said.

Ohhh, he moaned, *alley-oop!* You see that, Bob? Did you see how I fed her that pass? *Slam dunk,* he said, swooping his arm around and stuffing the air basket. Joyce just looked at me, as if to say, Yeah, Bob. D'ja see how he did that? And now, I'd like to dedicate this next song to my beloved wife, the sugar-and-fork-tongued mother of our son, he said, carefully dropping the needle. Give her a hand, he said, turning back to us and throwing out his arm: Joyce Kessler, ladies and gentleman, Joyce Kessler . . . With that, he bit the right side of his lower lip and scrunched his nose, grooving his head, hunched over, air-guitaring as the bass line started. Joyce stood the baby on his feet, shaking him to the beat: naked, save his fresh diaper, Benjie's rolls of fat jiggled in opposite directions, more like a fleshy cabasa than a tambourine.

Michael had chosen Chicago Transit Authority's cover of the Spencer Davis Group's "I'm a Man," and I started singing to Benjamin, *I'm a man, yes I am, yes I am* . . . Michael shot me a look, surprised I knew the song; Yep, Joyce sighed, reading him perfectly, I've trained her well.

Michael returned to the stereo, turning it up. Come on: *shake it, baby, shake it!* he said, pounding both fists like castanets in the air, dancing, getting down with his family. It was a sight not to be missed, that's for certain. Then Michael said, Seriously, Bob, why don't you call your girls and have them come over? Hey, I said, snapping and pointing my finger at him: watch it. I'll take you out so fast—. Take him, Bobby, *take him!* Joyce jeered, clapping and bouncing on the couch. Ahh . . . just look at this mug, Michael said, picking up his son and kissing Benjamin's cheek, pressing it against his own: What woman could possibly resist?

When I left that night, they were dancing to Jose Feliciano's cover of "California Dreamin'." Michael had finally gotten his big break and he was headed to L.A. for a few months to shoot a film. Despite everything, I still remember those moments, and to this day, I've never seen two people so in love—in their own completely demented sort of way, of course.

Joyce

NO, I'LL TELL YOU what happened, I'll tell you exactly why our marriage failed—I mean, it's no great mystery. Our marriage failed because we were selfish, egotistical assholes. Separately, but equally, yes. And there's no place for that in marriage. Which is why I have no intention of ever marrying again.

That's my bit. And it's a good line, I have to say. But I've never used it, and I never will. Because it's nobody's business but ours, what really happened. I mean, call me old-fashioned, but I still believe in something called privacy.

Lisa

ON MY LAST DAY, or what would prove to be my last day, when I finally got back to the gallery, I blew through the doors, running

317

to drop off my coat. Then I almost jumped out of my skin, finding Joyce, standing on the floor, like she was waiting for me. Lisa, she said, smiling, and it scared me. I'll be right there—just let me throw these things on my desk, I said, and then she said, Take your time—no rush.

The rest of the day, she kept trying to send me home, so we finally had it out. I reminded her that I'd told her three times about the doctor's appointment, and that it was urgent. And then she goes, Yes, well. Fortunately or unfortunately, this is an art gallery, not a women's shelter. And then I just had to laugh—I was just like, that is fucking priceless. I said, Joyce, have you taken a look around? Because that's *exactly* what this place has become, it's a shelter for fucking has-been conceptual-art hags—this place is nothing more than a public urinal! I'm telling you, it was *my* idea: *mine*. That's where she got the idea for Urinals—that's where she got all her artists and her ideas, from *me*. And there I was, still arguing with the people we used to be, cruising up Eighth Avenue, with my feet turned at an angle, making sure my precious feathers didn't touch the cab's mud flaps or whatever they're called.

I was the first person through the door Sunday. The first and only person there, except for the girl at the front desk, with her bright red Clara Bow lips and white Comme des Garçons blouse and platinum hair pulled back in a chignon, playing the part of the chic gallery assistant perfectly, right down to ignoring me completely. I had the whole place to myself, but I was still shaking as I took a seat, petrified that Joyce would walk out at any moment, even though she never works Sundays. I mean, she couldn't have changed that much, could she?

I had to take several deep breaths to stop my hands from shaking as I took a seat on the bench and pulled out his artist's statement: blah, blah, blah. Then I took a look at the titles: *She Wears Ostrich Feathers, I Married a Situationist, Blue Blood in the Morning*. I could hear his voice: *Did you see the show?* And then I looked around the room, making sure it was true. And it was. It was true, damn him. And then I let it out: *Goddamn you, you motherfucker!* I screamed, and the gallery expanded, the cement walls practically quivering, and then, silence. Silence, followed by fear, and then the click-clack of

318

seven-hundred-dollar heels, as the girl at the desk, this year's Auden, tried walking purposefully across the polished cement floor, reassuring herself, *don't be afraid, don't be afraid.* A moment later, she peered into the gallery only to find me sitting there, alone.

Hello, I said, smiling and giving her a little wave. Can I help you? she said, giving me the once-over. You can gauge a great deal by a pair of heels, and she'd gauged she better be polite at the very least — I might actually be Somebody. Smart girl. Yes, actually. Is Joyce available? I said, raising my voice in that haughty singsong I'd learned so long ago, and she said, No, she's not in today. Oh, what a shame. We go way back, I said, smiling. Would you like to leave a message? she said. No, never mind, I said, I'll give her a call later. All right, she said, trying to smile, but only managing to arch her thin brow just slightly. Thanks, anyway, I said. I'm just going to sit here and enjoy the show.

So I sat there, nodding and smirking and nodding, on the verge of tears, laughing my ass off: *You bastard . . . you smug fucking bastard.* Then I stopped nodding and covered my mouth, thinking, *You did it, babe. I always believed in you, I believed in you so much, I hated myself for it at times, you fucking fuckup.* I laughed, as though I'd said it to his face, and for a moment, I felt like the old me again. Where the hell you been, gorgeous? I asked myself, wiping away my tears, then I bent my arm, pressing my knuckles against my mouth, trying to hold on a second longer before I had to let go.

Joyce

HAD THE STRANGEST feeling when I woke Sunday — couldn't place it at first, then it hit me, right between the eyes: sobriety — pow! *Fucking awful,* I thought, covering my head with the pillow. I was supposed to go to the gallery for a few hours, but I couldn't go to work in that state. So when I turned back over, and the clock read one, I finally rolled out of bed and headed to the shower. And I was fine, until I turned and saw myself naked in the mirror. Then I remembered walking into the hotel, seeing Adela, and I thought, *That's — that's who Michael was with when I called to talk to him about our son?*

She knew it, too. Adela sat right next to me at brunch while I told them what Benjamin had done, and she knew the whole time. I held my face in my hands, because I finally understood the look in Adela's eyes at brunch; I heard Michael on the phone, saying my name out loud ... and I thought, *Well, you know what?* Fuck you. *Fuck you all ... I might be a real cunt sometimes, but I don't deserve this — I don't deserve any of this.*

I turned on the water to drown out the sound, not because anyone else could hear me but because *I* could hear me. And I can't stand the sound of my own sobs. I pressed my back to the tile wall and slid down to the floor, and then I cried until I couldn't cry any more. I blew my nose, rinsed the snot down the drain, and hoisted my ass up. *Enough,* I decided, turning off the water. I got out, got dressed, and then I got to work on his room.

I confiscated everything: computer, stereo, speakers, flat-screen, DVD player, portable DVD player, laser printer, scanner, CD player, iPods, PlayStation . . . everything. I hauled everything to the front door, and then I called down to the doorman, Robert.

I said, Hey, Robert. Joyce Kessler. Tell me, how many kids you got now, three? And he said, I'm not sure, myself, Ms. Kessler. I said, Well, you know what? Christmas came early this year. You got a car? Yes, he said, but it's in Queens. Why, you need a ride? And I said, No, but you will — don't worry, I'll take care of it. What time do you get off? Three o'clock, he said, and I said, Perfect. Would you mind stopping by before you leave? No problem, Ms. Kessler, he said. And I said, Oh, Robert — one other thing. Bring the trolley, will you?

Bobbie

SHE SAID, MOM, PLEASE. It's not how it looks —. Are you sleeping with him? I said, turning to look her in the eye, and she didn't answer. Because that's how it looks, I said, and she stood there, staring at the ground. Does he know — does Michael know you're pregnant? Yes, he knows — he knows everything, she said. And what does Michael have to say about this? He said he stands by me, whatever I decide, she said, clenching her jaw. Stands by you? I said, He stands by you? Really, Adela, how stupid . . . how *stupid* could you be? He loves me, she said, and you can't —.

He loves you? Yes, she said, he loves me: Michael loves me. Did he say that, did he say he loves you? Yes, he did, she said. Many times —. I'm sure he did, I said. But just out of curiosity, did he ever say it when you had your clothes on? I shouldn't have said that, but I meant it, I did. What . . . what would you know about love? she said. No, really, what man loves you? What man has ever said he loves you — Paul? Has Paul ever said he loves you? That's none of your business, I said, stepping away from her.

Why? Because the answer is no? she said, looking in my eyes for an answer and finding one. He hasn't, has he? Leave, I said. He doesn't, does he, Mom? she said. Paul doesn't love you, and you can't stand that a man loves me and will stand by me! Michael loves you? I said. Yes, *he loves me,* and you can't stand that, can you?

No, I said. No, Adela, what I can't stand is seeing how naïve you are. *Stand by you?* I said, trying not to laugh. Like he stood by Joyce when she got pregnant, and he was off fucking some girl half his age? I said, and that shut her up. But of course you already knew that, didn't you? Because you know him so well, you already knew he was so busy fucking around, behind Joyce's back, that he didn't even *know* she was pregnant, I said, feeling the advantage swing my way. If he didn't know, she said, obviously stunned, then you can't blame him —. Oh, can't I? I said.

No, you're right, Del: I'm sure Michael will stand by you. That is, until something better comes along — someone younger, prettier — and trust me, someone better will come along, Adela, no matter *how* beautiful you think you are. Speaking from experience, you mean, she said, and I said, Yes, that's right. Speaking from experience, having known the guy twenty years to your, what? What is it, two months now? Three, she said, giving me a curt little smirk that I wanted to slap right off her face. It's been three months, and you've been seeing Paul how long? she said.

Adela, I said, I want you to leave now. Sure, she said, just answer the question, and then I'll be more than happy to clear out of your house —. I said, My *best friend*, Adela . . . Do you know what that means? Do you know how much she's done for us — for *you*? I know, she said. I don't think you do — I don't think you have *any idea* what you've done, I said. Don't speak to me like I'm a twelve-year-old! Then stop acting like one, I said. *Grow up*, Adela! No wonder you've been avoiding Joyce, I said, at least you have some sense of shame —. At least one of us does, she said.

I said, How many other lives do you want to ruin? How dare you, how *dare you* ask me that? she said. Who are you to talk? Are you referring to my work? I said. My job, which you have always been so quick to judge, pays for your expensive clothes and your expensive school and your expensive trips and the rest of your life, and for some reason, you've never had a problem with that, have you? I said, and she glared at me.

I said, Have you made an appointment? Yes, she said, with an obstetrician. You plan on having the baby? I said, shocked. You mean you're having this child and you're going to keep it? Yes, she said, *yes*, Mom. Jesus, have you been listening to anything I've said, anything? Adela . . . Del, I said trying to calm down, you're twenty-three years old —. I'll be twenty-four in two months, she said, and I'll hardly be the first twenty-four-year-old to have a child. No, you won't, I said. And you'll hardly be the first twenty-four-year-old child to have a child —. It's not your choice, she said.

I said, You're twenty-three years old, why *on earth* —. Mom, have you ever been pregnant? Do you even *know* how it feels? she said, but I didn't answer. Jesus, *answer me* for once, do you have any idea how it feels to have a life inside of you? she said, and I wanted — I wanted to say, Yes, sweetheart, yes, I do: I've had you inside of me for twenty years now, I know exactly how it feels. But I couldn't say that. Because that's not what she was asking, even if it were true. No, I said. No, I don't how it feels. She looked at me, exasperated: Then how could you even begin to understand, no matter what I say?

Adela, I told you I wasn't prepared to discuss this —. What, you want me to make an appointment so I can have an hour of your precious time? she said, and that was all I could take. I said, Adela, what do you expect me to say? I expect you to say you love me — that you still love me even if you think I'm making the biggest mistake of my life, and that you'll stand by me, regardless. Because you're still my mother, she said, waiting, pleading with her eyes, but I didn't answer. Really, what is crueler than silence?

Adela

I SAID, I'LL LEAVE when you answer the question. Please, answer the question, Mom: Has Paul ever said he loves you? Do you know how it feels to —. *No,* she said. No, Paul has never said he loves me. And I know exactly how it feels not to hear those words — it's shameful, if you want to know. I feel ashamed. Now, please, she said.

There were tears in her eyes, and she couldn't look at me — but not like before, not out of anger. I've seen my mother cry once in my life, when my grandpa died. I've heard my friends mention seeing their fathers cry once, at most — and I always thought, *Wow, your dad's like my mom.* I wanted her to know how I felt, and she did — she does. I just didn't have any idea that I'd feel even more alone when I found that out.

It was the only time in my life that my mother has ever looked small, but it was only for a moment. And the strange thing is that I didn't feel like a bad daughter, I felt — I felt like a bad parent, a mother, seeing her like that. And it was deafening, my own heart. I wanted to apologize, to say, I'm sorry, Mom. I'm so sorry . . . and I do know how that feels. And for months — for so long now — that's all I've known.

But I didn't say it — I was going to, and then she pulled it together; she gathered it up again, like some dirty sheet bundled quickly in her arms, heading straight for the hamper. Please, she said, and it was gone again. Please, Adela, I can't do this right now, she said. Please, go.

She started to walk away, and I said, You know, Mom, you always said it was the best thing you ever did. Because she'd always said adopting me was the best thing she'd ever done with her life, then she stopped and turned around. Yes, it was, she said, looking at me . . . looking at me like I couldn't have disappointed her more if I'd tried.

And that's why — that's the real reason I didn't tell her until now — it wasn't because of Paul or timing or wanting to see her happy, no. I didn't tell her sooner because I knew she'd never support this decision, and I was afraid. I was afraid because I didn't think I could do it without her support. But I will, if I have to. I know that now.

I mean, she knows more about my body than I ever will, but my mom doesn't know what she's asking because she doesn't have a fucking clue how it feels. So how do I explain that when I found out I was pregnant, for once, I was absolutely certain what I wanted to do, what was right for me. I am being myself, and for the first time in my life, she can't even look at me. So I grabbed my bag and I walked out, biting my tongue so I could make it out the door without breaking down sobbing.

And yes, part of me was furious because I knew she was right — as much as I denied it, she wasn't wrong. I did need him, or at least I needed somebody, and Michael was there. So maybe I *was* using him. And maybe he was using me, too, who knows.

I mean, what, what did I imagine for us. *Us,* I thought. *God, what us?* I would never be able to take him home; he could never be a part of my family, and my friends — I hadn't introduced him to anyone. Did I honestly see myself with a man old enough to be my father? Did I see myself with Michael, period? I thought so; I really did, but why? Because he loves me? Even if it's true, is — is that enough? Really?

I don't think so, no. It sounds nice, but . . . but that's just not how things work. No, it's not enough: love. Suddenly, I wanted nothing to do with him — I wanted him out of my life, gone, goodbye — just go away, will you? He was just some old lech who'd spent the past twenty years fucking women half his age; the whole thing was so pathetic, Mom was right. She was right about everything . . . almost everything.

I knew what it said about me, too: that Michael had seen the worst in me, but I couldn't do the same. And he didn't even know about Joyce, he had no idea, but I did, and I blamed him for it — contradicting everything I'd just said to my mother. But still, how could I ever look at him again? No, I don't love him the way he loves me — I don't love him unconditionally, it's true. But what do you do then?

So I stood there, in the middle of the sidewalk on Fifth and Eleventh, covering my mouth with one hand, horrified, thinking, *Ohmygod, what have I done?* Then I walked back to the curb and I retched. Right in front of the church, too. And when I could stand again, all I could think was, *Too bad. Joyce would've gotten a kick out of that.* It actually made me smile, wiping the tears from my eyes with the palm of my hand, thinking how sorry, how truly sorry I was she'd missed it.

New York Magazine

DISCUSSING THE FUROR *surrounding* The Fourth Type of Sex, *often compared to the oft-referred-to 1999* Sensation *exhibition scandal, Kessler says, "I appreciate the comparison, but the difference is that the work I show is a hell of a lot better than the shit they showed. On the other hand, I invited Rudy Giuliani and his lovely third wife to join us for the opening. Being the patriot he is, I know John (Waters) very much wanted to meet America's Mayor — unfortunately, Rudy had a prior speaking engagement with some corporate execs and his press secretary politely declined."*

For his commission Exploitation, *the Spanish artist Alejandro Parejo had the bathrooms relocated from the interior to the front of the gallery, where he had a two-way mirror façade installed by no less than six renowned architects which I cannot name, and positioned cameras in every corner of the bathrooms. "I admit, I had my doubts about that commission," Kessler says. "The time, the expense, the thought of how few people, especially women, would dare use the toilets that season, knowing they could be seen from the street, not even able to see who was watching them. I thought, well, on the bright side, we won't have to clean the bathrooms for a couple of months, guess we'll save a few dollars there. But, in this case, I'm glad to say that I was dead wrong. You can't imagine the footage we got during those twelve weeks.*

"So, after viewing the tapes, I called Alejandro and had him fly back," she says. "We then had a wall of surveillance screens installed in the front hall, showing every angle of every camera, from floor to ceiling, and everything in between, and played the tapes for the next four months, while we were setting up the next show.

"I mean, we had . . . Christ, we had old ladies with canes, we had mothers with prams, we had cabbies pulling over, eating their lunch on the street, peeking through the front door, just to see what was going on inside. And then, lo and behold, after finishing their sandwich, they came inside to take a look. No, they aren't going to buy anything, and I don't expect them to. I just wanted them to step through our doors, and they did. Fait accompli," she says, looking up at the ceiling with, for a second, a glimmer of possible true emotion.

Or maybe not.

"Look," says Kessler, "I give people what they want, okay. And people want art in their lives, and they want their lives in art. Exploitation? Oh, bullshit. I'm sorry, but that's just totalfuckingbullshit: because you cannot exploit an exhibitionist. And believe me, over the course of twelve weeks, we had thousands, literally thousands of people beating down our doors in the hopes of getting on camera. We're talking a line around the block, all the way to Tenth Avenue, with people waiting to get in and take a piss, shit, and/or fuck in that bathroom.

"We had so many people — Christ, we had crowds showing up on Sunday to see what all the fuss was about, people who didn't know galleries aren't open on Sundays, because they never go to galleries. And because everything else in this city is open on Sunday, why would an art gallery be closed half the weekend, when people are actually able to get out? Well," Kessler continues, crossing her Pilates-toned legs with such force, you'd think she had just tossed a cigarette butt to the floor and ground it out with her gleaming five-inch heel.

"Fortunately," she says, pulling a dark lock of hair behind her two-karat ear, "that first weekend after Fourth Type opened, I was about to sit down to brunch when a friend called me and he said, 'Joyce, there are a hundred people waiting to get in your gallery — you better get down there.' So I ran down and I opened up, and what do you know? People came all day, and they came the following Sunday, and they just kept coming. So I decided to stay open on Sundays.

"Of course that ruffled a few feathers, and my staff threatened to revolt, so I had to do the math for them. Tuesday to Saturday, twelve to six, Sunday, twelve to five: that's thirty-five hours. I said to them, 'You want a thirty-hour workweek, move to fucking France. But this is New

326

York, and in case you missed the welcome sign, it reads, 'Make money or get the fuck out, people.' Look, I'm not going to be yet another New York gallery that does seventy percent of their year at Miami Basel and thirty percent the other fifty-one weeks a year, uh-uh," she says with a cold rigid wag of her index finger. "No: I want that same seventy percent every fucking week of every fucking year: and I'm not apologizing to anyone for that, either." And with that, Kessler sits back in her chair, grinning, as she recrosses her legs and laces her fingers on her lap.

"To answer your question," Kessler says, "where do I get my inspiration? My family, of course—particularly my mother, who's always been an incredible inspiration to me. You know my grandfather was a steelworker who moonlighted on weekends as a janitor in order to support his wife and three sons. He was also a card-carrying member of the Communist Party and instrumental in unionizing Pennsylvania steelworkers. But, that said, I don't believe in bringing art to the masses, I believe in bringing masses to the art. So that's what I intend to do," she says, "one toilet at a time." As she says this, it must be noted, she is digging her Louboutin heels particularly far into the floor. Because she wants to.

Joyce

BOBBIE STOPPED BY after work that night to show me the copy of the magazine she'd just bought at a newsstand. Joyce, she said, slapping me sideways, I can't believe you got the cover of *New York* —. I didn't, Greg did, I said. Which was a smart decision on their part: he's far more photogenic.

Did Sonja see this? she said, flipping through, looking for the article. She called, yes, I said. And what did she say? That all her friends and relatives saw the article and that her phone has been ringing off the hook since five o'clock this afternoon. I'm sure, but has she read it? Bobbie asked, appearing starstruck for the first time in our lives.

No, I said. No, she said she hadn't had a chance yet, but she just wanted me to know she was *very excited* to read it, I said, smiling: but not half as *very excited* as I am, Sonja, believe me. Oh, she's in for a real treat, I said, laughing. Joyce, look, she said, opening to the story and holding it up, showing me a picture of myself: You're famous! *Oh, no* . . . is that the picture they chose? Let me see that, I said, taking it from her. Oh, for fucksake, I told them I could get a real photographer — ugh, I *hate* that picture! I said, but she pushed me away, taking it back, and reading aloud: *Joyce Kessler has a burning question* —. Burning question, my ass: I had a UTI, and I needed to pee, I said, getting up and heading to the kitchen to get a corkscrew.

Yes, Sonja called. Yes, she picked up the phone, but she just couldn't say it — a million people were reading about me and my work, and she still . . . she still can't say it to save her fucking life. And all . . . all I wanted to say was, why? Why can't you ever tell me that I'm smart or pretty or that you believe in me or even just recognize that I've made something of myself without being told by fucking *New York* magazine? Me, fat Joyce Kessler from Scarsdale, New York? Proud: the word was proud. Would it kill you to say it, just once?

Adela

I WALKED BACK to Tompkins, Sunday afternoon, and then I called Joyce. I had to — she didn't answer, so I kept trying. Because if there's one thing Joyce respects it's persistence. So I kept calling her cell, and then I called her at home again, and I started leaving another message: It's Adela. I've been trying to call you, but you don't answer, so I'll just have to talk to your machine. And then she picked up. She didn't say hello, she didn't say anything, but I could hear her.

So I cut to the chase, thinking it might be the last time she ever spoke to me. I'm pregnant, I said. It's not Michael's — it's not his, it was this guy, and . . . he's not in the picture; he doesn't want anything to do with me. And Michael was there — I needed someone, and he was there. And I don't know . . . I don't know what else I want from him now. But I'm keeping the baby. And I'm sorry — I'm *so sorry*, Joyce. I wish I could explain how it happened, but I can't — I fucked up, that's all there is to say. I fucked up, and I'm sorry. And I know . . . I know you won't believe me, but I love you. Silence.

I said, You don't have to speak to me ever again, but at least let me apologize in person. And I'd expected her to rip me a new one at any moment, but she didn't — she didn't say anything. It was so unlike her, too, I almost said, Hello? Are you still there? But I knew she was there, listening. I don't know if she heard a word I said, but she was listening.

Adela? she said, finally. Yes? I said, thinking, *This is it.* Then she said, I don't know if I can forgive you. I know, I said. One other thing, she said. What? I said. I can meet you for coffee Tuesday morning, but I want those earrings back, so bring them with you, she said. She wanted the earrings she gave me as a baby, the diamond earrings she gave me for my eighteenth birthday, standing next to Mom, joking that they must look like a couple of well-dressed dykes, doting over their adopted daughter. She wanted them back. Okay, I said, anything. Christ, I was *kidding,* she said, but I'd already started crying.

Jordan

I FINALLY GOT out of bed, just before dark, and Rusty followed me — he hadn't left my side all weekend. So I took him outside to play ball for a while, and then I got in the swing when my hands got too cold from all his slobber on the ball. I just sat there, and then I heard the screen door shut, but I knew it was Lance. And the thing is, it's like I knew he'd come home to be there for me, even though no one said that was why — no one said anything about it.

Anyhow, he walks over and he goes, What're you doing?, and I just shrugged. We're watching the game, if you wanna watch, he said, and I said, Later, and then I stood up, in the middle of the tire. Okay, he said, walking away, as I stepped back, ready to swing. Then he turned back around, and he goes, Hey, Jord? And I was just like, What? And he goes, Remember Blacky?, and then I just started laughing.

Our first dog was a chocolate Lab, and after Dad put up the swing, we used to try to get Blacky to play chicken with us. We'd never had a dog, so we thought you could teach a dog to do anything. So we thought we'd train him to joust, like the two of us against Blacky, you know. We'd get him to stay about twenty feet away from the swing, then we'd get in position and go: Okay, Blacky, we're going to swing to you, and then you're going run to us, okay? On the count of three . . . So Blacky'd stand ready, waiting for us, then we'd swing toward him and he'd step back, looking at us, like, *What, you think I'm stupid?* We were so bummed, too, because we were going to call him Blacky, the Black Knight.

I hadn't thought about that in a long time. He was smarter than the two of us, Lance said, and I go, Yeah, speak for yourself. And I know he was trying — trying to make up for all the times he wasn't there, trying to say he was sorry, but I was just like, say it. If you're sorry, why don't you just say it?

Come in, he said, nodding at the house, come watch the game. In a minute, I said, stepping back in the tire, waiting for him to leave. Hey, Lance? I said, holding on to the tire, thinking, *God . . . don't you wish we could be kids again?* Then he turned around, but all I said was, I'll be in in a minute, and Lance just shrugged, like, it's up to you. So I waited until he closed the door, then I took two more steps, pulling the chain as far as it could reach before letting go.

Lynne

SUNDAY NIGHT I stood at the kitchen window, debating whether or not to go outside and talk to Jordan, tell her the truth, finally. She was reclining across the tire, her body rocking gently back and forth, into the sky. And then she suddenly looked over, catching me watching her. I waved, instinctively, protecting myself, then I practically slapped my forehead, thinking, *Damn it! I did it again . . . now she thinks I'm hovering, not giving her any space. When, in truth, I'm just realizing what a complete ass I've been. My god, what a mess I've made.* I smiled and turned away, changing my mind. I know what I'm doing is wrong, but I only did it because I love her.

Joyce

WELL, NEEDLESS TO SAY, the kid didn't have much to say at dinner Sunday night. I mean, not a word. Finally I said to him, Look, I'll make you a deal —. We'll talk when I get all the stuff back you stole from me, he snarls, brave enough to look up for a whole split second. I just smiled: No, sweetheart, stealing is when you take something without paying: and I paid. Trust me, I paid in full. Fear not, my child, I said, standing and placing my hand upon his head, all hope is not lost. Remember, even the spy was saved. Be right back, I said, walking to my room and returning with the folder.

So I gave him a choice. I spread out all the catalogues and brochures on the dining table. Plan B, of course, was to get a job. But plan A? Ah, plan A . . . so what'll it be? Señor Swanky or Señor Swankier's? You think you're so funny, he said, and I said, With good reason. Needless to say, he didn't look up from his plate.

Benjamin? I said. I'm listening, he said to his plate. Then here's the deal, I said, and I swear to you — I swear on Poppy's grave I'll keep my end of the bargain, okay? Are you listening? I'm *listening*, he said, mopping his plate with a forkful of mashed potatoes.

The deal is: you strip off all your clothes, step out that door, I said, pointing to the front hall, and you walk around the block — around the *entire* city block — naked as the day I nearly died bringing you into this world, and you can have all your stuff back. He just looked at me, stunned. Wait, I said, wait . . . *plus*, I'll throw in an upgrade. All new equipment, top of the line. Any make, model, brand your wee little heart desires.

Or, you get a job and buy yourself whatever your wee little heart desires on Canal Street. So. What do you say? I said, leaning across the table, offering my hand . . . But of course he couldn't respond because he was beside himself. Debating, deep in thought, thinking it through, step by step, mapping his route, weighing the odds of how many people would see him, what they would say, do. Would someone call the cops on him? Would people honk, shout, laugh? Oh, god. Bribing your delinquent son: fifty grand. Watching his miscreant wheels in motion: priceless.

I just sat there, waiting, watching, eyeing him — you want to fuck with me little man? You're out of your league. Like I said, Benjamin, I swear that I will keep my end of the bargain. The only conditions are noon; you do it at noon, I said. Twelve o'clock, on the dot, on a clear day, and I will need a urine sample just before you streak. Soon as I run it over to Quest Diagnostics, on Twelfth, you're in the clear, free to shop.

That's right, I said. Because sooner or later, if you haven't already, your little mind will arrive at the conclusion that you'll just drop some Ecstasy and run a lap around the block and then, *poof*, you'll wake up at the Apple Store. No, I said, been there, done that, so think again, my little friend.

I'm telling you, my tongue was almost bleeding, imagining the throngs of people on Broadway on a Saturday afternoon . . . Just so happens that we live on Mercer. Which is neither here nor there, except that, in order to walk around the block, the youth would have to brave Houston *and* Broadway. Smack-dab in the middle of SoHo, yes . . . Model Central. Beautiful People Central. Fugly Tourist Central. Yes, he'd have to walk Houston and Broadway, then Prince and Broadway; he would have to pass in front of the Prada store, directly across from Equinox gym. Ah, SoHo . . . at the corner of Tacky and Posh.

Oh, wait — wait, wait, I said, getting up again, and pulling some more literature out of the hutch. Before you say anything, I thought you might want to look at these first, I said, spreading the selection of pamphlets across the table. I have to say, the Bang & Olufsen speakers are simply to die for, I said, sitting down and pulling in my chair. Check it out, I said, opening the brochure, thinking, *That's right: get a good look.*

Look at me, I said, and he looked me in the eye. One time, that's all — that's it. One lap, I said, holding up my index finger. I'll give you seventy-two hours to make up your mind, I said, knowing that for the next three days, he was going to be looking at himself, long and hard and limp, in the full-length mirror. Oh, he's not going to sleep for days, tossing and turning, agonizing; imagining himself actually walking the walk — in pixel. Could he do it? Could he actually do it? Does he have *The Stuff*?

That's right, I thought, looking at him, hiding his eyes. *You think you're man enough, Benjamin? Come on, then — give me your best shot.* Well, I said, standing from the table, about to take my plate to the kitchen, you think about it. You got three days, I repeated, turning on the faucet. Then the offer expires, and you can figure out how to get your stuff back your own damn self. And like I said, anything — anything you want, Benjamin. Because, as I like to tell all my boys, price is no object . . . *but your ass is.*

Nostrils flaring — he got Sonja's tiny nose, too, because he certainly didn't get it from Michael. Oh, I had him — I had him by the balls, all right. You could hear a pin drop on the floor of his sad little psyche. Personally, I've always found humiliation a terrific motivator.

Finally, Benjamin said, I'm going to talk to Dad. We'll see what he says —. Yes, well, I've got some bad news, son: Daddy's doing the babysitter . . . *the hills are alive with the sound of music.* No, what I said was: I've got some bad news, I'm afraid. Which is that I've already spoken to your father, and he supports this decision, one hundred and ten percent. And, if you don't believe me, there's the phone, I said, cocking my chin toward the living room.

Please, call him — you remember where we keep the landline, right? I said. It was a bluff, of course. Then again, I was willing to bet the farm on one of two things: One, he wouldn't dare call Michael because then he would have to tell him about the spy cams himself. And two, even if he did call, Michael would have no choice but to back me up. So really, my bet was covered.

At which point, he lost it. He started screaming at me at the top of his lungs: I hate you! I hate you, you fucking bitch! And then I explained to him, in no uncertain terms, that if he ever said that to me again, I'd kick him out. Then I stood up and I walked over to his chair, where he was now standing, daring me, waiting to see how far he could push me, and I said, Benjamin, if you don't believe me — if you doubt me for a second — remember one thing: Have I ever, *ever* lied to you? Have I ever failed to keep my word? Have I ever once, in your entire life, been even five minutes late to pick you up?

Finally, he broke down sobbing. I stood and watched him for a minute or two, moved by how angry and frustrated and embarrassed, how deeply ashamed he must have felt at that moment. Here, I said, handing him a tissue so he could blow his nose.

I was enraged by the violation — justifiably so. But even that doesn't necessarily make it right. I said, Benjamin, I still love you,

you know? And he nodded. Look at me, I said, and he did as he was told. I love you more than anything in this world, I said, and I forgive you for being so fucking stupid. But aren't you forgetting something?

He looked at me, and then he stared at the ground, drawing a blank. Benjamin? What? he said, raising his voice, not in anger but because he truly didn't know what I was talking about. An apology, I said. I think an apology is the very least you can do, don't you?

Then he had to recover from the shock of not thinking of it at all, never mind not thinking of it first, and then the insult of having it pointed out to him, schooled yet once again by his mother. All this before he could even approach being too proud to debate whether or not to say the words. It was a veritable steeplechase, and he didn't have a leg to stand on. I'm sorry, he said, crying again. I know, I said, patting his back.

But let me tell you something, Benjamin Petrucci: we're having a serious talk Wednesday night. And at this point, I said, frankly, I don't really care *why* you did what you did. Honestly, Ben, I don't care how incredibly and completely fucked up the reason. I just want the truth. You've got three days to think it over, and I want the truth, or we will have a *serious* problem, you and me, I said, flicking my finger back and forth between us. Understand?

Adela

THE MURAL WAS GONE. I wasn't crazy — well, maybe I was crazy, but the mural had been painted over during the weekend. I went back Sunday, around five, and Ixnomy — Nixzmary, I'm sorry — Nixzmary's face was covered by some Community Action mural. Didn't matter, I had her picture in my bag, so I went there to pray anyway. But once I got there, I realized I don't know how to pray. I mean, of course I know you're supposed to bow your head, that that's the proper way. But can't you just stand there and think of someone? Can't you just think of someone and talk to them, like they could hear you and they can understand what you're trying to say, even if *you* don't know what you're trying to say?

So I stood there, in front of a freshly painted mural that read, LOISAIDA, CABLE TV, PHONE, INTERNET, NEIGHBORHOOD, RCN, and I closed my eyes, and I apologized for screwing up her name. I felt terrible about that, I really did, but then I started laughing. It was so inappropriate, I know, but then again, why not? Aren't you allowed to laugh when you pray? So I asked her, I said, What I mean is . . . is there no place for laughter in prayer? Because if that's the case, I can't do it — I'm sorry, but I can't pray if there's no room for laughter.

Anyhow, I'm sorry about that, I said. I looked at her — I looked up, where her face had been, two days ago — and I thought, *You missed so much school, you probably didn't learn pig latin, did you? I don't actually know pig latin, either, but I think it might've been invented around the time my mom was a girl, or around the time they came up with the Name Song. Do you know that one? I can't really do it with your name, but I can do it with Ana's — her name's perfect for the Name Song — Ana, Ana, Bo Bana, Fee, Fi, Fo, Fana, Me, My, Mo, Mana . . . Ana!*

I told her everything I'd done, all the terrible mistakes I'd made. I even told her about Marshall, though she was probably too young to hear. I asked her, How could he do that? How could a guy just watch me cry and feel — nothing? Well, probably like I could watch an orphan on TV, and then check my ass in the mirror, huh? No, I told her everything — about that girl, Michael, Joyce, my mom. I told her about hurting the people I love most in this world, and I asked her to forgive me. And I asked her to believe in me, if she could find it in her heart, because I don't want to be that person anymore.

I don't know how long I stood there, staring at the brick wall, remembering how big she'd been the last time I saw her — she was larger than life, if only for a few weeks. Her smile alone was at least a foot wide, and it humbled me to think how much courage, how much strength she had, just to smile, despite everything she knew. She was more like the woman I want to be than any woman I know. Okay, I said, sighing, that's all — that's it, really. I had to go; Ana was waiting for me because I told her we needed to talk. So I started walking, hoping I'd figure out where to begin by the time I got there.

Jordan

HEY, I SAID, walking into the TV room. Hey, sweetie, come sit down, my dad said, making room. Where's Mom? I said, taking a seat beside my dad on the couch. Oh, she's getting her craft on —. *Dad,* I winced, please don't say that, please don't say getting his or her anything on, okay? God, that drives me crazy. I'm here, Mom said, walking into the room. What are you doing? I said. I was just looking for my pinking shears, she said, laughing at herself. Can you believe it? What did I do with all my scissors?

Mom, you want a beer? Lance said, just to be polite, I'm sure, and then she said, I'd love one, thanks. They're in the fridge, he said, nodding his chin sideways, in the direction of the kitchen. Glad to hear it, she said. Now get me a beer, you ungrateful wretch. Can I sit with you two? she said. Sure, I said, beginning to get up. No, don't get up, Jordan. Just lift your feet, she said, and I did. She sat down, taking my feet in her hands . . . I couldn't remember the last time she rubbed my feet.

It's like everyone's kissing my ass, you know. But I have to say I don't mind it, really. I mean, tomorrow everything goes back to normal, but for a few hours, why not?

Joyce

BENJAMIN WAS HUNCHED over the kitchen counter, reading the *Times* when I walked in the kitchen Monday morning. Good morning, I said, and he muttered, Hey. I'd been cruel, and I owed him an apology this time. Because I wasn't yelling at Benjamin — well, not entirely. It was Michael: I was yelling at Michael. And God help me, there was a part of me that wanted to tell him, too, my own son — to say, *You know what kind of man your father is?* A part of me that wanted to drag him into our failure, our betrayals . . . but I didn't.

I just wish he knew that. I wish he knew how many things I will never say, that there's a line I won't cross — for his sake. I mean, I can't even tell him that, you know. I guess he'll learn that someday, when he has children of his own, maybe. But still, after all these years, what I've finally realized is just how many things we can't share in this life — which has everything and nothing to do with love.

He started folding up the paper, about to hand it to me, and I said, Benjamin, I'm sorry I got so angry with you last night. Look at me, I said, raising his chin and looking him in the eye. I love you, but if you ever do that again, I'm liable to kill you — I mean that. Okay? I said, ruffling his hair. Get movin'.

I had to get out of the house, so I went to the gallery, and soon as I got there, I decided I better call Sonja back and apologize. First thing she says to me, first thing out of her mouth is, No more. *No more*, Joyce, she says. I don't know what's going on, but this has got to stop. And I said, Mom —. So either you tell me what's going on —. Mom, I said. Because I cannot —. Sonja, shut up, okay? Please, I said, will you just shut it for a second, and I'll tell you? And then she stopped.

Listen, I'm sorry I keep calling. And I'm sorry you're upset — that wasn't my intention, I assure you. I've just had the most trying weekend — trust me, I can't even begin to describe the things that have been going on on my end, but never mind. The reason I'm calling is to say that I love you, and — and that's it. I love you, okay. That's all I wanted to say.

Finally, she says, Joyce, what's wrong? I want you to tell me what's wrong. I said, Nothing. Nothing's wrong, Sonja — honest. Nothing's wrong, you're just calling to tell me to hang up the phone so you can call me back and tell me you love me, that's all? she says. And I have to say she was in prime form that morning; it was classic Sonja, all right. What, you think I was born yesterday? she says, and I said, Yesterday? I'm still not convinced you were born in the twentieth century, okay.

So then she goes, *Is, is, is* — she was so outraged, she was stuttering — is this funny to you? Is this some sort of *joke*? she said, and I said, Mom, I swear to you. That is the only reason I was calling, I said. To say you loved me, she says. *Yes*, I said. Well, then why couldn't you just tell me that before, Joyce? And I wanted to tell her because I

didn't know before — I'm sorry, I didn't realize that's why I was calling, but all I said was, I don't know, Mom. I really don't know.

What I realized at that moment was that I was never going to tell
her any of those things about myself, and that she would never know
much more about me than she knew at that moment. But that was
okay for once, because that's just how things work out sometimes.
Which is exactly what my dad would have said, too; he would've said,
I'm sorry, Joycie. I'm sorry things work out this way. And for just a
split second there, I could even hear his voice, and I thought, *Me, too,
Dad. Me, too.*

So there I am, being scolded by my eighty-five-year-old mother,
and the crazy thing is, she sounds so angry and helpless and just so,
so — *human*, I have to bite my tongue to keep from laughing, thinking, *You know, I love you, you old bat, I really do.* And deep down, she
knows it, she knows I love her. But still. If she thinks I'm going to forgive her for that, too, on top of everything else, she's out of her fucking mind, okay. Seriously, don't press your luck, lady.

Adela

I TRIED HER again at noon, but she didn't answer, so I finally called
Michael back. He'd left at least six texts and three voice mails since
I left Sunday morning: Are you all right? Are you still breathing?
Please call me as soon as you can. But I hadn't answered. So I finally
called him back Monday afternoon, and the first thing he said was,
Are you alive? God, where have you been? Adela, I was worried —.
I'm okay, I said, it's only been a day, you know.

Where are you? he said. Are you still at the apartment? No, I said,
I stayed at Ana's last night. I said, Listen —. And he said, Didn't you
get my —. I said, Michael, listen. I'm not returning to the hotel . . . I
need some time, okay? He didn't say anything, but I could hear him.
I just need some time to figure out what I'm doing, I said. I'll stop by
tomorrow, all right? All right, he said, and I felt such a wave of relief — I had no idea it would be so easy, and then he said, So is this it?
And I couldn't answer. I don't know, I said. And it was true. For the
first time in months, I'd told the truth, such as it was.

Lisa

DADDY, SHE SAID, kneeling before him, speaking as calmly as a kindergarten teacher. Listen to me, she said, you're being paranoid. We've talked about this before: no one stole your shirt. It's in the laundry, and you'll just have to wait. That's, that's what you said last time, he whined, with this look of agony, and she took his hand in hers and she said, Yes, I did, Dad — the last time they washed your shirt. Daddy, we go through this every year at this time, remember?

She's so much more patient with him than I could ever be — an hour alone with him and I'd be screaming. But that's Lynne, too. Patient and kind and . . . well, I was about to say always responsible, and I can't say that anymore. But she's got a hell of a record, she really does. I just . . . I just don't understand.

When we got into the car, I said, Why, Lynne — why should I believe you? I mean, it doesn't make any sense! You see him almost every day, as you're always the first to point out. If — if that were true, how . . . how could you stand to look at him? How could you possibly visit him every day, Lynne? *How?* Because, she said, her eyes welling with tears, because he's still my father.

Lynne is a better daughter to him than I am — and it's not fair, no. Whatever she says about him, it's just not fair. So I called her before I went to therapy Monday, but she didn't answer her phone. I had a feeling she wasn't speaking to me — for once she wasn't going to answer — and I can't say I blamed her. I mean, I wasn't sure what I was going to say, really. But I had to try.

Lynne

MONDAY MORNING, DON took Lance to the train station, and I dropped Jordan off at school. I got to work by eight, sat down at my desk, and everything was exactly where I had left it. Everything was in place: files, pens, postcards for preholiday sales offering fifteen percent discounts for one day only . . . My feng shui was mocking me, and all I could think was, *Who is this person? Who is this woman that washed and dried her coffee cup every day at five o'clock, then used*

339

the wet paper towel to wipe down the tops of the pictures frames of her family, tidying her desk one last time, arranging everything just so, before turning the calendar ahead to Monday, as though she would return, unchanged? I don't know you.

But you carry on. Whether you like it or not, you carry on because, more often than not, there's no choice, really. I sighed and turned on my computer because I needed to write an announcement for a chamber mixer, which just seemed so, so — depressing. I don't know why, really, because I do it all the time, but I couldn't make sense of the words. Dear Merchants, please join us for a night of . . . *Of what*, I thought? Please join us for a night of cheap white wine in plastic cups and a few handfuls of Goldfish crackers?

I tried to make sense of it, but I couldn't. I couldn't even bring myself to cut and paste the same wording I'd used on all the other announcements I'd written during the past two years. An hour later, I finally told Tom I wasn't feeling well, and I felt terrible, because I'd been out on Friday, but he said, Lynne, you've got about two weeks of sick leave; take the day off. So I went home and crawled back into bed at ten thirty in the morning. Honestly, I cannot remember the last time I'd slept so much in three days.

I don't know how long I'd been asleep when my phone rang. I checked the number and it was Lisa, so I didn't answer. *No*, I thought, silencing the ringer, *I can't argue with you any more, Lisa, no more fighting.* Then I turned off my phone and closed my eyes, pulling the covers over my shoulder.

Jordan

MONDAY I WALKED into the cafeteria at lunch and grabbed a tray, and then I saw the girls I usually sit with, my so-called friends, right, sitting at the table, just like talking, laughing, whatever. Then I just looked around the room for a second, and I was like, who else could I be friends with here? Who else could I talk to? But there's no one, really. And it's been that way for the past two years, you know, but I just felt sick.

I mean, I felt a thousand times better than I did on Thursday—ohmygod, that was so awful. Every morning, I was just like, *bleh*. But I couldn't take it anymore, just like school, and the halls, and having to smile and say hi every time I see someone I know—I mean, I'm so tired of pretending, you know? And then my heart starting pounding like crazy—I don't know what happened; I think I had a panic attack or something. I mean, my hands started shaking, holding the tray, and I couldn't breathe—seriously, for a second I thought I was going to pass out. So I dropped my tray and I almost ran out the door.

I didn't know where to go, so I went outside to the parking lot, and I thought, *I'll call Lisa—I'll, I'll get on a train—I don't care, just get me the fuck out of here, you know*. So I went outside, and I tried calling Lisa, but I got her voice mail. And I thought about walking to the train station, but I didn't know what to do—all I knew was I just couldn't stay there anymore, so I called Mom.

I called her at work, but they said she'd gone home sick, so then I called her at home, but she didn't answer her phone. And by then, like I couldn't breathe, and I was just like, where are you, Mom? I need you, please, just answer the phone. So then I called our house, but by then I was so angry, I'd started crying, but when she answered, all I could say was, Mom?

And she goes, What's wrong, honey? And I said, Mom . . . I can't, I can't *do this*. I'm sorry, but I—I just can't do this. I mean, I hate this place, I hate everyone here, I look at the clock every fucking second of the day—*please, Mom*. Please don't make me stay. I'll be right there, she said, and then she hung up. I couldn't believe it. I mean, she didn't even argue with me, you know?

Joyce

OF COURSE, AFTER talking to Sonja, I needed a drink—must've had two martinis before they'd even brought our menus, but anyhow. Then Paul says, And you wonder why men don't understand women. And I'm . . . I'm telling you, I practically snorted: no. I said, *No, Paul*, as a matter of fact, I don't—I don't wonder. The fact of the matter is that men don't understand women because men are just plain *stupid*, that's why. Christ, a fucking sea anemone knows more about women than men do.

Seriously, Dr. Phil knows more about women than men do, all right? Which reminds me: I need a drink, I said, looking around, thinking, *Where the hell is our waiter, anyhow?* Joyce, you have one, right in front of you, he said, nodding at my martini glass. Oh. Which reminds me, I said, downing it: I need another drink. And you wonder . . . ?

Look, I'm not calling her, Joyce. I'm not calling to say: Why aren't you talking to me? What have I done, Bobbie, please tell me? he said. And why not? I said. Because I didn't do anything wrong —. I said, You didn't do anything wrong? What are you, four years old? Please, do me a favor and don't act like you were born yesterday, okay? You know that's beside the point. He balked, shaking his head, trying to digest that one.

Then why don't you tell me what's going on, he said. No. Oh, no, I said, smiling, I'll let Bobbie share all the gory details — when you call her and ask her, yourself. Joyce, I said I'm not calling her because she's behaving like a child, and I don't have time —. Paul, I know. I know she is, but it's good for her, I said, and he looked at me. All right, I said, well, it's a first, let's put it that way. Plus you get to gloat, he said. And there's that, too, I said, nodding my head to the side, in agreement.

Joyce, he said, leaning forward, I appreciate that you're best friends, but fact is she's a grown woman, and this is *bullshit.* You know it as well as I know it —. Paul, I'm not getting in the middle, here, okay? Joyce, you asked me out to lunch to discuss it —. At long last, he returns, I said, interrupting Paul as the waiter approached. Another, please? I said, tapping the rim of my martini glass. And make it dirty.

Please, Paul said, correcting my manners for the waiter's benefit. I love it when you beg, I growled, leaning forward, giving him everything but a ruff, before I sat back again. I said, Here's what I can tell you: Bobbie's had a rough weekend, and she needs a friend right now. And beyond that, I don't really care what you did or didn't do or what did or didn't happen — sorry, I just don't fucking care, okay.

Paul, I said. All I know is that she would call you if she could, but she doesn't know how — she just doesn't know how to pick up the phone: you know it, and I know it. So whether or not you understand anything about her, or women in general, that's what I can tell you, okay. If you don't want to help her out, or at least give her a chance to explain herself — if, all things considered, that's just too much to ask of you — I understand. Your choice, and that's all I have to say. *Basta*.

Then again, I said, sighing, reclining deep into my chair, you do owe me one, you know. And you can start by paying for lunch, simply because it's the right thing to do. He looked at me, shaking his head, trying so hard not to grin that he had to bite his lower lip. You're a real piece of work, you know that, Kessler? And I smiled. I just sat there, and I smiled and smiled. Check, please, he said, speaking in the waiter's direction.

Lynne

I LEFT HER ALONE the whole way home. I didn't try to talk about it; I didn't say anything, really. When we got home, we both walked upstairs, and then, when we got to the top of the stairs, I asked her if she'd come lie down with me. She was about to say no, it was so instinctive, I could see the word on her lips before she'd even given it any thought, before changing her mind. I held out my hand, waiting, wrinkling my nose, trying not to scare her off with the welling in my chest.

We peeled off our clothes and crawled into bed, and then I moved my head closer to hers, looking her in the eye, and I said, Jordan, I have a secret. What? she said. Promise not to tell? I said. Yes, what is it? she said, and I said, You have to promise first. I *promise,* she said, and then I told her: I tore up Grandpa's shirt the other night. What shirt? she said, frowning. His Mets shirt, I said, and her eyes popped open as she covered her mouth. *Why?* she gasped. Mom, why would you do that? You know he loves that shirt more than anything —. Yes, I know. *That's* why, I said, trying not to laugh.

She said, *Mom,* that's so *mean!* I *know,* I said, that's why it's our secret, honey. You want to see it? I said, and she looked at me, shocked.

Hold on, I said, and I got out of bed and ran downstairs, retrieving the remains. What do you think? I said, returning to the bedroom, holding it up for her. What is it? she said. It's a Mets rug, I said, I'm turning his shirt into a braided rug — he can put it beside his bed or in his bathroom, I said, starting to laugh. A Mets rug? she said, covering her mouth again.

No? I said. I could still turn it into a hat — a Mets rug hat, I said, twisting it in a knot on top of my head. I mean, really . . . you don't need a T-shirt to still believe, right? Then it really hit her, what I had done. She said, Oh, Mom . . . you tore up Grandpa's Mets shirt? Yes, I said, and she said, Why, Mom? *But why?* Because, I said. Because I was very angry and I wanted to hurt him and I couldn't think of a better way.

How did you do it? she said. With scissors, I said. No, I mean, how did you get it off of him? Oh, I said. I took it off when they had him sedated. I can't believe you did that to him, she scolded me. I know: it's awful, I said. Mom, he *loves* that shirt. Look, I admit that it's awful of me. What more can I say? She said, Wow, Mom, that's . . . that's *really* crazy.

Jordan, promise you won't tell? I said. Mom, he's going to ask, she said. I know, he already has, I said. Promise? Maybe, she said. Maybe what? I said. Maybe, what's in it for me? she said, trying not to smile. Well, what do you want? I said, then she just shrugged, before I crawled back in bed, lying beside her.

I said, Jordan, can I ask you something? All right, she said, tugging on the corner of the pillowcase. Why do you blame me? I said. Why do you blame me for what happened with Dad and Barbara? What did *I* do? I said. Nothing, she said, looking away. I'm serious, Jordan —. I mean it, she said, you didn't do anything. Then why were you so angry with me? I said. Because I had to blame someone, she said. Well, of course, I said, laughing, but why me? Why not Lance, or Rusty, even? I said, joking.

Tears came to her eyes as she smiled, biting the inside of her cheek. Because you'd never leave me, she said, and I thought if I blamed Daddy, he'd have that much more reason to leave us. Jordan, you think your dad would ever leave you, really? He left you, didn't he? she said. I said, Jordan, sweetheart — it's not like that. How do you know? she said, and I thought about it. You're right, I said, I don't know.

But I still wish you'd blamed him, instead of me, I said. Next time, she said, and then she looked at me: Mom? Yes, baby? Did he love her? she said, and I said, I think so, yes. But then he got sick, she said. But then he got sick, I said. So he stayed, she said. So we both stayed, Jordan. What an *asshole*, she said, and I sighed, not knowing what to say. Finally I said, Jordan, I hate to be the one to have to tell you this, but we're all assholes — some more than others of course, but still. Honestly, you live with someone twenty-five years, it happens.

Are you going to stay with him? she said, folding the ends of her pillowcase and looking me in the eye, just inches from my face. We'll see, I said. After you graduate — or after you do whatever it is you need to do — we'll see. We haven't been alone in so long, I don't know, I said. Really, what more could I say? How could I explain to her that I think it was right for us to stay together, but it was still a terrible mistake? That no matter what, there are always consequences, regrets . . . I suppose she'll learn that soon enough.

Mom, would you let me go, honestly? she said. Would you really let me live with Lisa? Yes, I said, on one condition. Oh, here we go, she said, rolling her eyes at me. On the condition that it's what *you* want: not what I want, not what Lisa wants, so long as you promise me it's what you want, you can go, I said. Yeah, but . . . but what would I do? she said, frowning with worry.

Well, I have an idea — I mean, *before* you make up your mind, I said. What? she said. Let's run away, I said. Together — just once — just you and me. Are you *serious*? she said, rolling over, leaning on one elbow. *Yes*, I thought, *you bet I am. Yes, just once, I want to run away — just once, I want to know how it feels to do something so flagrantly irresponsible and live to suffer the consequences — to live.* Yes, I'm serious, I said, putting my hand on her face, giving her my word.

So what do you say? We won't even tell anyone, I said. We'll just leave a note for Dad, telling him we'll be in touch, and we're outta here. But where? she said, trying not to giggle at the thought, but still doubting me. Where would we go? she said. Well, I was thinking Mexico — I've never been to Mexico, can you believe that? I said, and she goes, *Yes*. Watch it, or I just might leave you with the note, I said.

We can't, she said, in a tone halfway between whining and scolding me. Why can't we? I said, Give me one good reason. Because you have work, and I have school, she said, and I said, No, I said a *good* reason. Honestly, there's nothing stopping us. And if we hate it, if we hate sunbathing topless, drinking margaritas —. *Eww*, Mom, she said, wincing. Jordan, I said, if you hate it, we'll come right back. We can leave tomorrow, if you want. She said, Promise you aren't kidding, Mom? You *swear*? And I said, I swear on your mother's grave.

Think about it, and if you're up for it, we'll wait for Dad to leave for work tomorrow, and then we'll pack our bags and run for it. I still don't believe you, she said. Oh, Jordan. Jordan, Jordan, Jordan, I sighed. You know what I wanted to name you? I said. No, what? she said. Morgan — like the Joni Mitchell song "Morning Morgantown," I said, and I started humming. *Mom*, she warned me. It's a beautiful song — come on, I said, singing: *When morning comes to Morgantown, the merchants roll their awnings down* —. Ohmygod, Mom, that's *so* corny, she moaned in mother-mortification. I know, kills me every time, I said, pulling her to me.

I decided to spare her, wrapping my arms around her and humming a few bars instead. Mom . . . ? she said, turning to face me, and I said, Yes, baby?, thinking she was going to beg me to stop humming, enough with the Joni Mitchell. Then she said, I'm sorry, Mom . . . I'm so sorry, she said, crying, shaking in my arms, and I just stroked her hair, letting her cry.

When she stopped and caught her breath, I whispered, Now close your eyes. Close your eyes, I told her, before closing my own. I'll tell her, one day I'll tell her I spoke to him, threatened him — I'll tell her everything, I swear, even if she never speaks to me again. I knew she might very well hate me for the rest of her life for what I'd done, but honestly, I didn't care, because I couldn't remember the last time she let me put my arms around her. And I don't know who I was trying to strike a deal with at that moment, but all I could think was, *Let me have her back for one hour, and we'll deal with the rest later, okay? Just let me remember how she feels in my arms.*

Joyce

WE WENT BLOW FOR BLOW, just like old times — neither of us willing to back down. *How dare you?* I said. How dare you mention my father! Fine, she said, but you don't know what you're talking about because you've never *had* a daughter, she said, and that hurt, it really, really hurt. That's true, I said, I never had a daughter, but I know you don't deserve the one you have right now.

She's in pain, and she's scared, and you have no idea — you don't have a fucking clue how alone she feels right now, because you're all she's got in this world, *you're it . . .* And you should know better than to just leave her hanging like that — like you could take her or leave her. What gives you the right to treat her this way, Bobbie? She didn't answer. I said, My whole life, since the day I first saw you, I wanted to be like you, Bobbie. I wanted to *look* like you and *talk* like you and for people to look at me the way they look at you. But I don't anymore.

I said, You know what's sad? And she said, Just say what you have to say, Joyce. Fine, I said. What's sad is that you've spent your whole life trying to save a mother who's long dead, and you won't even pick up the phone and speak to your daughter, who's alive and well, save for the fact that you aren't there for her when she needs you most. Are you through? she said, and I just had to nod my head. Yes, I'm through, I said, getting up and walking away.

Bobbie

SHE SAID, JESUS, Bobbie, I would think you — you, of all people — would know how short, how precious and, and —. *Precious?* I said. Oh, fuck you, she said. She'd never spoken to me like that before, ever. I didn't mean to insult her, I was just trying to play it off, or, I don't know. It was knee-jerk, and then I realized how condescending it sounded. You know, I'm trying to be here for you, but you aren't even listening to me, she said, brushing a tear from her face.

You don't know what I've been through the past few days, and you still haven't asked me because you've appointed yourself judge and jury — what, like that's going to make anything *better*? I'm sorry, I said, but she wasn't listening. You know, what I was going to say was that I'd think you of all people would know how short and *fragile* — that was the word I was going to use — how truly fragile life is. But you don't, do you?

It was the first time in our lives she'd ever walked away, and she was right. Then again, sitting there, on the bench, I didn't feel angry, and I didn't feel scared — frankly, I didn't know what to feel, so I decided not to try. I had to smile, thinking, *Is this what it's like to be a man?* Because I can see the appeal, I said, realizing I'd spoken out loud, as though Joyce was still sitting beside me, even though, at that moment, I was watching her walk away.

The strange thing was, I'd never seen her look so beautiful. She was wearing this amazing fitted coat and four-inch heels, striding like she'd just walked out some old Dior fashion photograph. I wasn't the only one who noticed, either, and I wanted to call her cell and say, Don't look now, but there's a very young, very hot guy checking you out, eleven o'clock. At which point, Joyce would turn and stare him down, quickly shuffling her best pickup lines like a deck of cards.

I replayed that scene in the restaurant once more; watching Adela stand from the table; looking at my menu; looking up to find Paul watching Adela walk away . . . Sitting there, I honestly couldn't say if he was looking at her for two seconds or two minutes; if it was him, or — or me. For a moment, I caught a glimmer of my own insanity — just a glimmer, but still. My jealousy was so obscenely female; so, so — *wicked,* I thought, realizing what I had done. Then again, nobody ever said Vanity didn't have a pretty face.

As for Adela, I didn't know where to begin, really. But it was the most burning sense of shame I had ever felt, and the one person I could tell was walking out of my life. All I knew is that I couldn't let her go. Even if it meant saying I was sorry. And I was wrong. And she was right. Okay: anything. Then I took out my phone and dialed.

Joyce

IT'S ME, SHE SAID, and I said, Tell me something I didn't know. Well, for starters, she said, did I ever tell you that you have got one *amazing* ass? And I thought I was just having a hot flash, I said, ugh. You guys gotta do something about menopause, Bobbie, because this, I said, switching hands as I peeled out of my coat: this is total *bullshit*. Feels like I'm sweating buckets on the inside — you can't get away from it.

Anyhow, I said, then a horn honked, echoing through the phone, and she said, Joyce, where are you? At the corner of University and Fourth, I said. What are you doing over there? she said. Eating a pretzel, I said, taking a bite. I figured you'd call, so I thought I'd give you a chance to pull your head out of your ass — you know you really took your own sweet time picking up the phone, princess. I'm sorry, she said. Agreed, I said, walk me home? Sure, she said. Be there in a sec, I said, and then we can discuss my amazing ass in graphic detail.

Bobbie

SHE TOLD ME about Benjamin and his job application while I walked her home, and then we started laughing hysterically, working out our choreography for his ambush dinner, Wednesday night. Wait, I said, trying to stand straight: should I snap both fingers *and* kick my foot behind me, like this, I said, demonstrating, shouting: *Olé!* Or is that too much? Joyce furrowed her brow: *Too much*. Who are you talking to, *too much*? Do it again, she said, so I did. Honestly, I nearly pissed my pants — and I wasn't even on drugs.

When we got to her building, I said, Can I ask you an honest question? You tell me, she said, and I rolled my eyes at her. Joyce, do you forgive her, Adela? Do you honestly forgive her? I said, and she winced. I don't know, Bob . . . but I'm gonna try, she said, lifting her brows and shrugging. You know what helps? And I said, What's that?

Tequila, she said, curling her arm and flamenco-snapping her fingers above her head. Wanna come up and do some shots with me? I shook my head . . . she will never change, I swear. Not tonight, I said, I have work to do, and she said, Bob, you've been telling me that for half our lives —. Because I've had work to do for half our lives, I said, and she said, *Come on,* live a little? I had to smile, placing my hand on the side of her face. I'm trying, I said.

Joyce, I'm so sorry, I said. For what? she said. For everything, I said, absolutely everything. Well, it's a start, she said. Do you forgive me? I said, and she said, *Of course.* Come here, she said, hugging me, then pulling back to look at me. How could I not forgive you? You're going to be a grandmother, she said, and I pushed her away, *bitch* . . .

Call her, she said. I promise, I said, I'll call her when I get home. *Hey,* she said, turning back. *Sí?* I said. I love you, she said. God help me, I said. And, she said, and: *When I say I love you you say you better, you better you better you bet!* You better you bet, and I love you, too. How's that? I said. Not bad, doc, she said. But don't give up your day job. All right, then, she sighed: *Mañana, mañana.*

She opened the door, and I knew I had to tell her before Adela did — not that Del would tell her on purpose, but still. I kept waiting for the right moment to explain that it slipped out — in anger, yes. I was so angry, I told Adela about Joyce's abortion, and then I couldn't bring myself to tell Joyce because she'll never forgive me. She'll think I betrayed her, and she's right, I did. Not on purpose, but the end result is the same, isn't it?

What was it she said? People fuck up, and you just have to forgive them. We'll see. *We'll see about that,* I thought, as I walked down the street — literally, walking straight down the middle of the cobblestone street, remembering when this neighborhood used to be a ghost town. Reminded what it was to be an eighteen-year-old girl, arriving in New York City, when everything — your whole life — lay just beyond your fingertips. It was dangerous back then, yes, but such magic, too.

I didn't know where I was going; I just needed to walk. What's funny is that I've always loved this street — I always thought I would live on this street one day, when I grew up. So imagine how bitter the irony that I don't live here, Joyce does, and she's never had any intention of growing up. But no matter how many complaints I have about this place, I still love walking in this city. And I will always love that dreamy blue light, walking through the canyons of SoHo just before nightfall. I'd almost made it to Canal when my phone rang. I reached in my purse and checked the number, then I took a deep breath and answered: Hello?

Acknowledgments

My family, of course: Mitch and Cathy Uttech, and Vanessa Nilsson. Special thanks to Laura Wehrman, James Ellsworth, and Piper Nilsson, as well. Dan Ferrara and Stephen Milioti helped tremendously with their time and attention. Rachel Horowitz, Amy Goldwasser, Peter Arkle, Bentley Wood, Enid Nilsson, Keyin Choi, Catharine Dill, Kate Donovan, Annie Leuenberger, Deanne Koehn, Rebecca Bauer, and Dr. Jo Carney. Also, Drew Souza, Roger Hirsch, and Vincenzo Conigliaro, for all their technical and moral support over the years. Anthony Timpson, Dan Deluca, Daniel Arsand, Violaine Binet, and Nelly Thienpondt. The Montauk gang: Stephen Earnhart, Susan Benarcik, Brian Goblink, and Greg Pierce. Amy Hempel and Rick Moody, always. Marc Fitten, Frederick Barthelme, Jenni Ferrari-Adler and Jofie Ferrari-Adler. Nat Sobel, Emily Russo, and Julie Stevenson. André Bernard, Michelle Blankenship, David Hough, Karla Eoff, Lisa Glover, and Tom Bouman, bless you.

I would like to acknowledge the generous support of the Ucross Foundation and the Edward F. Albee Foundation. For the record, Edward Albee is reported to have said, "*Twat* is spelled with an *A*, not an *O*." I would also like to acknowledge that the mural of Nixzmary Brown was painted by the graffiti artist Chico and actually appeared at the corner of East Sixth Street and Avenue C, Manhattan, from January 29, 2006, to May 10, 2006. It read, IN LOVING MEMORY OF NIXZMARY, R.I.P. One last note: Robert Szot's painting exhibit The Generosity of Women appeared at Bolm Studios, Austin, Texas, from December 11, 2004, to January 8, 2005.

Finally, Adrienne Brodeur has been an incredible editor and a true friend, in no particular order, and I am indebted to her for her tireless work on this book.